Home

www.penguin.co.uk

Home

Amanda Berriman

Doubleday

LONDON · TORONTO · SYDNEY · AUCKLAND · JOHANNESBURG

TRANSWORLD PUBLISHERS

61–63 Uxbridge Road, London W5 5SA
www.penguin.co.uk

Transworld is part of the Penguin Random House group of companies
whose addresses can be found at global.penguinrandomhouse.com

Penguin
Random House
UK

First published in Great Britain in 2018 by Doubleday
an imprint of Transworld Publishers

A CIP catalogue record for this book
is available from the British Library.

ISBNs 9780857525314 (hb)
9780857525321 (tpb)

Typeset in 11/15 pt Electra LH by Jouve (UK), Milton Keynes
Printed and bound in Great Britain by Clays Ltd, Bungay, Suffolk

Penguin Random House is committed to a sustainable
future for our business, our readers and our planet. This book
is made from Forest Stewardship Council® certified paper.

MIX
Paper from
responsible sources
FSC® C018179

1 3 5 7 9 10 8 6 4 2

In memory of Ros and Bill Berriman

'Just because I find myself in this story,
It doesn't mean that everything is written for me.'

'When I Grow Up' from *Matilda the Musical*
by Tim Minchin

1

THERE'S A GAP where the living room curtains don't touch and night-orange has sneaked in and painted everything in the room so it's hardly dark at all. My fayvrit green pen is on the windysill, where I hided it from Toby, and I take it and squeeze ahind the telly to get to the peeling-paper. It's soft and soggy on my fingers and under it there's even more black dots than afore and my pictures of the house with lots of windows and the horse and the apple tree and the swing have slided down the wall a bit. There isn't a pond yet so I join some dots up in a pond shape and add tails to the dots inside the pond so they look like tadpoles.

'Jesika!'

My arm is pulled hard and hard and Mummy is screaming, 'Moles! Moles! Dirty, Jesika, dirty!' and she pulls me fast away from my picture and the telly hits my head and I'm shouting, 'Ow! Ow! Ow!' But Mummy keeps pulling and pulling me and we're at the bathroom sink and the light's on bright and hurty and my eyes are stingy and my head is spiky and hot and she's scrubbing and scrubbing my hands and my fingers with the scrapy-brush that's apposed to be just for cleaning nails and she's being cross about dirty moles and I'm crying and shouting, 'They're not moles, they're *tadpoles*,' but Mummy's not got her listening switched on cos now she's being cross cos I got out of bed afore the clock says seven and I'm trying to tell her about being too wriggly to stay in bed but I can't make the words proply and Mummy says, 'I'm too tired for this, Jesika. I'm just too *tired*,' and her words are spiky.

Mummy stops scrubbing and she tugs at the towel and there's a snapping noise and the towel hanger-up bounces on the floor and Mummy bashes her hand on the sink and shouts, 'I HATE this bloody flat!'

It's quiet in the space after Mummy's shout.

I say, 'What's a flat?'

Mummy scrunches up her face and her eyes and says, 'Flat, house, just another word for this dump we live in,' and her voice is all fast and cross, and then she's coughing and coughing and leaning over the sink and her face is going red and I reach up on tiptoes and rub her back cos that's what Mummy does when Toby's coughing.

After ages, Mummy stops coughing and she makes her breathing go slow and then she wraps my hands up in the towel and puts them atween her hands and she's squeezing gently and wiggling each finger through the towel.

She says, 'Sorry for shouting, poppet. I didn't mean to. I just don't want you getting poorly too.'

She rubs my head where the telly banged it and gives it a kiss and then holds my hand and we walk back out of the bathroom and she's pointing to my secret corner and she says, 'No more playing with dirty moles, OK?'

I say, 'But Mummy, they're not moles . . .' but then Toby's crying and coughing in the bedroom and Mummy has to run and give him cuddles and rub his back and it's *not fair*.

Mummy puts my shoes on tight with tuggy fingers cos she's still cross about the moles and she's cross cos Toby coughed and coughed til he sicked up his breakfast milk all over his clean clothes and the bag for the washing machine shop is more heavier. We're going to the doctors after the washing machine shop so

Mummy can tell the doctor that Toby needs medicine to make his chesty fecshun better.

On the landing, Mummy fights the front door shut and I'm doing my job holding Toby's buggy cos the brake doesn't always work and all the door fighting is making Mummy cough like Toby and it remembers me about her coughing in the bathroom and I go and rub Mummy's back again and I say, 'Have you got a chesty fecshun too, Mummy?'

Mummy says, 'Both hands on the buggy, Jesika!' and her voice is snappy like a crocodile so I grab the buggy again but it hasn't rolled away cos the landing is flat and not hilly. I don't really know why Mummy says I've got to hold it.

Next-Door Lady huff-puffs up the stairs and I say, 'Hello,' cos I'm allowed to say hello to people when Mummy's with me and it's a friendly thing to do. But Next-Door Lady walks straight past us, not even looking or smiling, which is actually rude and not friendly, and I'm still thinking this when she opens her door and I forget to not breathe and the eggy-yucky smell comes out and right into my mouth and up my nose afore I can stop it.

Mummy finishes fighting the door and we bump and bang down the stairs and round and down more stairs and we're almost at the bottom and Mummy remembers me to be quiet past the door at the top of the last stairs cos the other day a nasty man opened it and said scary words. But he's not there today and then we're down at the bottom and Mummy's bags have got all tangled on the buggy cos of all the bumping so we have to stop next to the Smelly-Stairs so Mummy can make them not tangled.

The Smelly-Stairs go down to the door that's never open. Mummy says it's dirty and dangerous but I always look cos sometimes there's people down there and maybe they're trying to open the door and if they get it open, I want to see what's ahind it.

There's nobody down there today but while Mummy gets cross

with the bags I spot something interesting on one of the steps. It looks like a jection, not like the one in my doctor bag for Baby Annabelle, but a proper jection like the one the real doctor scratched my arm with so I don't get nasty germs.

Oh! That's something useful!

'Look,' I say. 'There's a jection for Toby to make his chesty fecshun go away,' but Mummy's still fighting the bags. I know I'm not apposed to go down the Smelly-Stairs but Toby's coughing and crying and the jection will make him all better and Mummy will be really pleased, won't she?

I hold my breath to make the smells go small and I press a hand against the wall to keep my feet safe and I hold my belly with my other hand cos it's doing scary jumps inside cos it's dark at the bottom and I don't want a monster to jump out and scare me. But I do want Toby to be not-poorly. I step down and down, *one-two-three-four-five . . .*

'Jesika! Get back up here right now!'

Mummy is squeezing my hand tight and tight and pulling me up the Smelly-Stairs so my feet almost fly and her voice is all shouty. 'What do you think you're doing? You hold the buggy and you don't let go! That's the rule!'

I point down the stairs. 'I was getting the jection to make Toby not poorly,' and Mummy looks and I think there really must be monsters down there cos when she looks down the stairs her eyes go scary-wide and she's pressing her hand to her mouth and she's so scared that we have to hurry out the big outside door and bump down the steps into all the rush and busy-ness and then run away fast and fast and Mummy's so scared that she forgets about the washing machine shop and then she forgets about the doctors and she even forgets to say scuse me to all the busy people on the pavement and some of them make cross faces as we push past them and I want to stop and explain that Mummy's not actually rude, she's just running away from the monsters, but I have to hold tight to the buggy and make my legs go fast and fast so Mummy doesn't leave me ahind.

Mummy presses the doorbell on a white door that's got a number 1 and a 3 and a 2 on it in gold metal letters. I say, 'I know this house! We've come to this house afore, haven't we, Mummy?'

Mummy presses the bell again and pushes her ear against the door and then she says, 'Doorbell's not working,' and she knocks on the door loud and loud.

I say, 'This is where we pay the man for our house,' but Mummy's too busy listening to see if her knocking has worked to hear me.

The door opens and it's not the man, it's a lady I don't know and she's got huge golden rings in her ears like a pirate. She must have just got out of bed cos she's got her dressing gown on and not proper clothes.

The lady says, 'Yes?'

Mummy says, 'I'm sorry for bothering you, but can I speak to Darren?'

The lady says, 'At this time of the morning?' She shakes her head and it makes the giant rings wiggle about. She says, 'Try again later,' and she steps back in and pushes the door shut but Mummy puts her hand out to stop it closing and she says, 'Please! Could I leave a message for him, then? It's very important.'

The lady opens the door again and huffs out a breath, like she's cross.

Mummy says, 'Please can you tell him that Tina Petrowski called round? I rent one of his flats on Ashbury Road, the ones just up from the laundrette?'

The lady looks like she's smelling something really bad. I look around to see what it is. There's a great big red bin on the edge of the road. The lid's not shut proply cos it's stuffed full up of bags. I bet it smells like farts and Toby's dirty nappies.

Mummy's saying my name. I turn back round but she's not talking to me, she's still talking to the lady. She says '. . . dirty needle! I told him about the problem with those stairs the last time he came round for the rent.'

The lady says, 'Don't let your little girl go down there, then. You can't blame Darren if you can't control your kids.'

Mummy's eyes and mouth go wide and wide and she takes a step back and she's looking at the ground and then her eyes go so scary and her head snaps up and I know she's going to use her cross voice now.

She says, 'You tell him that it needs to be cleaned up and the lock on the main door needs fixing or I'll have no choice but to phone the police and let them know what those stairs are used for!'

Mummy bumps Toby's buggy away from the door fast and Toby starts coughing and crying and she grabs my hand and my arm pulls at my shoulder and my whole body tugs forward and then we're running again, fast and fast, away from the lady's door and back up the big, long hill to where the shops and our house is and my legs are getting worn out and hurty and I say, 'Mummy, my legs are hurting.' But Mummy keeps going fast and fast and I say, 'Muuummmyyyy, you're going too fast.' And then, right outside the park gate, Mummy stops and I bump against all the dirty washing bags but Mummy doesn't see cos she's pressing her hand to her chest and her face is all wrinkled up like something's really sore and I say, 'Mummy, what's wrong?'

Mummy doesn't say anything, just breathes and breathes and wrinkles her face up even more so her eyes go wrinkly-shut and now she's leaning her head right down on the buggy and she's still pressing her chest and I don't know what's wrong and I tug at her arm and say, 'Mummy?' And I think her speaking has stopped working cos she won't answer and I say:

'*Mummy?*'

'MUMMY?'

'*MUMMY?*'

Mummy looks up and her face is flat again and she blows out a breath and she says, 'I shouldn't have walked so fast up that hill.'

I say, 'We weren't walking, Mummy, we were running, and now my legs are worn out!'

Mummy strokes my hair and says, 'Oh, poppet, I'm sorry, I didn't realize I was making you run. Come on, let's have a rest.'

She pulls the buggy over to the bench next to the park gate and we sit down and Mummy says, 'We've got time to sit for a few minutes before the next battle.'

I say, 'What's a battle?'

Mummy says, 'Like a fight.'

I say, 'But you're not allowed to do fighting. Hitting and kicking is naughty.'

Mummy smiles and says, 'Not that kind of fight. I mean a fight with words, when you have to use strong words to get something done that's not being done properly.'

Toby starts coughing again and Mummy unclips him from the buggy and lifts him out and sits him on her knee so she can rub his back.

I wonder what words are strong? Maybe 'giant' cos giants are strong. And 'elephant' cos elephants can pull over whole trees just with their trunks. And tipper trucks like the one in our veekles book cos they can carry huge big rocks. And rocks are strong too cos you can't break them even if you jump up and down on them.

Mummy puts Toby back into his buggy and she's trying to do his straps up but he's pushing his belly against them and shouting,

'Out! Out! Out!' cos I think he wants to stay on Mummy's knee and I say, 'I know lots of strong words, Mummy.'

Mummy says, 'Do you?' And then she says, 'Ha! Got it!' cos she's managed to do the straps up and Toby's still shouting and she leans over and kisses his head and says, 'It's just until we get to the doctors, Toby, and then you can get out again.' But I don't think Toby wants to sit in his buggy even for a minute cos he doesn't stop shouting.

Mummy says, 'Come on, Jesika, let's get going.'

I say, 'Is it time for the battle?'

Mummy smiles and says, 'Hopefully it won't have to be a battle. But we'll see. Hand on the buggy. Off we go.'

I hold onto the buggy and we walk along the pavement and I'm thinking up more strong words like 'metal' and 'tractor' and 'bear' and 'lamppost' and 'space rocket' cos they're all strong things, and if it is a battle and Mummy can't remember all her strong words, I can tell her some of mine.

2

WE GET TO the doctors and Mummy presses buttons on the machine inside the door but something's not working so we go and see the man ahind the desk and Mummy tells him Toby's name and the man says, 'I'm sorry but you've missed your appointment.'

Mummy says, 'But we're only a few minutes late!'

The man shakes his head and says, 'Your appointment was twenty minutes ago. I'm sorry but we can't hold appointments for more than ten minutes.'

Mummy says, 'But that's ridiculous! You can't just cancel my appointment! We never get seen on time anyway!'

The man taps a piece of paper on the wall next to him with his pen and he says, 'We're trialling a zero-tolerance policy to improve on waiting times and to cut down on the number of missed appointments each month.'

Toby presses himself against his buggy straps and shouts, 'Out! Out!' and the shouting makes him cough and cough.

I say, 'Mummy, Toby's coughing,' but Mummy's still talking to the man and the man says, 'How long has he had the cough?' and Mummy says, 'About two weeks,' and I know that's for *ages*.

The man says, 'OK, I can re-book the appointment for the morning. I've got appointments at . . .'

Mummy says, 'And what do I do in the meantime? I really need him checked over today.'

Toby's still coughing and his face is red like a tomato. I try to reach round Toby's back to rub his cough away but he pushes my hand away and he shouts, 'Out!' and then coughs some more and I don't know why he won't let me rub his cough better.

The man says, 'Have you tried putting him in the shower twice a day, for the steam?'

I say, 'What's a shower, Mummy?'

Mummy says, 'It's a . . .' She shakes her head fast. 'We haven't got one.' She turns back to the man and says, 'We've only got a bath and that's if the hot water's working.'

I say, 'And it's got a leaky crack in it.'

Toby shouts, 'Out! Out! Out!' and Mummy bends down and undoes Toby's straps and lifts him out and bounces him and rubs his back and at last Toby stops coughing. Mummy's magic rub is the best.

The man says, 'Also, keep your house well ventilated, especially the room he sleeps in.'

I say, 'What does ventilated mean?'

Mummy says, 'It means we have to open our windows . . .'

I make my eyes wide at the man and I say, 'We're not ever *never* allowed to open our windows or even touch them!'

Mummy frowns and blows out a breath and says, 'Just the broken one in the living room, Jesika. And I do open the windows when I can.'

I didn't know Mummy opened our windows. *I've* never seen them open. I say, 'When do you open the windows, Mummy?'

Now Mummy is coughing and she puts Toby on his feet and Toby stretches his arms to Mummy and says, 'Up!' and Mummy says, 'Jesika, take Toby to play with the Lego, will you?' But Toby stretches his hands right up and grabs at Mummy's leg and shouts, 'Up! Up!' so Mummy picks him back up and bounces him and rubs his back.

The man says, 'And get him out in the fresh air as much as

possible. Avoid anywhere that's damp and don't smoke in the same room.'

Mummy's lips are pressed together tight so I can't actually see them. I press my lips tight too and touch my finger to my mouth to see if I've also hided my lips away and I can't feel them at all but I can feel my teeth through my skin.

Mummy says, 'We live in a smoke-free home. I don't smoke.'

I giggle and say, 'That's silly! Mummies don't smoke. Only fires make smoke.'

Mummy wrinkles up her forehead at me. But that's right, isn't it? Smoke doesn't come out of *people*! I look at Mummy and then I look at the man but they're not laughing. I think Mummy's too busy pushing Toby's hand away from her dangly earring and now Toby's giggling cos he thinks Mummy's playing a game with him.

Mummy says, 'I really want someone to check him over today.'

The man says, 'I'm sorry, but there are no routine appointments left for today. Obviously, if you become worried or your son becomes distressed, you can phone up for an emergency appointment at any time.'

Mummy says, 'I am worried, *right now*! And he is distressed, *right now*!'

Toby claps his hands and reaches for Mummy's earring and he's still giggling and I say, 'What does distressed mean, Mummy?'

Mummy spins round and her eyes are scary-wide. 'Jesika, will you just go and play with the toys. NOW!'

I step backwards away from Mummy's scary, shouty face and my back bumps against Toby's buggy and it falls over backwards and lands on the washing bags. Mummy shouts, 'Oh, for God's SAKE!' And she's pushing past me and picking up the buggy and fighting with the bags with the hand that's not holding Toby and Toby's head is dangling right down and now he's crying, not giggling, and my eyes are stingy and I say, 'Sorry, Mummy, sorry!'

Mummy turns the buggy round so the handles are against the wall and she crouches down, still holding Toby, but he's the right way up now, and she wobbles and has to put her hand out onto Toby's buggy cos she almost falls over and she says, 'Just go and play with the Lego, please. That would really help me.'

I do want to help Mummy so I walk over to the Lego table. There's a girl already sitting on my fayvrit green chair. I sit on the blue chair. I don't want to play Lego. I want to cuddle with Mummy.

The girl on the green chair holds out a red brick and says, 'Here you go,' and a lady next to her says, 'That's so kind, Leila. Are you trying to cheer the little girl up?' The girl called Leila nods and smiles and she puts the red brick down in front of me and then she gives me a blue one and a green one and a black one and a yellow one and it's making a big pile so I stick them together but I don't know what I'm making. I don't want to make a princess tower or a rocket. Leila gives me another brick. Oh! It's got eyes on it! Now I know what to do! I build lots of bricks up tall and tall and put the brick with the eyes right on top and it's not a princess tower or a rocket, it's a giraffe!

I shout to Mummy, 'Look, Mummy, I made a giraffe!' but she doesn't look. She's talking to a lady ahind the table now. I don't know where the man's gone.

Leila's Mummy says, 'That's a very nice giraffe.'

I say, 'I'm not saying it to you,' and I hide my face and turn away from her and I pretend my giraffe is walking next to a lake, cos there's a bit in the middle of the Lego table where all the bricks are that's just like a lake. I tell my giraffe he has to watch out for the crocodiles that are hiding in the lake cos they're mean and snappy today.

Giraffe says he's hungry so I pick out lots of bricks and I make a yellow banana tree and a red strawberry tree and a blue water tree, so he can have a drink, and a green leaf tree. Giraffe walks atween all the trees and nibbles each one but he likes the green one best of all cos giraffes like eating leaves. He eats up all the leaves and I have to make him another green tree cos he's so hungry.

'Jesika, come on, we have to go!'

I look over and Mummy's waving her hand at me to tell me to hurry up and come to where she is but I have to finish up making the green leaf tree or Giraffe will be hungry. Giraffe says his green leaves are delicious.

'Jesika! Now!'

Mummy's right next to me and she grabs my hand and pulls hard and Giraffe falls onto the floor and breaks into a million-thousand pieces and I shout, 'Mummy, Giraffe! Giraffe's all broken!' But Mummy's pulling and pulling and now we're at Toby's buggy and Toby is crying and pushing himself against his buggy straps and Mummy's rushing us through the door to out-side and I'm crying and trying to go back cos I have to fix Giraffe and it's *not fair*.

'ENOUGH, Jesika!'

Mummy's voice is loud in my ears and her face is like a scary monster pushed up close to mine. I stop crying and stop pulling Mummy's hand. I didn't know Mummy could make her face like a monster. I don't like it.

Mummy covers her face with her hands and when she takes them away again the monster's not there any more. She stands up and blows out a breath and says, 'Hand on the buggy, Jesika.' And I hold the buggy and we're whizzing and whizzing all the way up the busy street. I hope someone else fixes poor Giraffe.

Mummy bends down and pulls all the clothes out of the washing machine into a big basket and squeezes past Shiny-Head Man, who's putting his clothes into another washing machine, and Not-Smiley Lady, who's pulling all her clothes back out, and Mummy

takes the basket over to one of the drying machines and pushes all
the clothes into it and I say, 'Why did you forget my colouring
book and my pens, Mummy?'

Mummy slams the drying machine door, BANG, like Nandini
the Boss Lady showed her to, and she puts the pennies into the
penny hole and pushes them in and the drying machine whooshes
round and she says, 'Jesika, if you ask me that one more time, I'm
going to scream. I just forgot, OK?'

Shiny-Head Man says, 'Don't you be giving your mum a hard
time,' and his face is frowny like he's cross and his shiny head goes
all wrinkly but then he smiles and winks his eye to me so I don't
think he's actually cross and maybe he might play a game with
me cos he does that sometimes.

I whisper to Mummy, 'Can I play with Shiny-Head Man?'
cept then he opens the door and walks outside and stands next to
Nandini.

Mummy says, 'He's called Leon, remember? Why don't you
play peekaboo with Toby again,' and she pulls more clothes out of
the other washing machine into the basket.

I say, 'I'm hungry.'

Mummy says, 'No, you're not. You're bored.'

I say, 'I'm *hungry*. Can I have another banana?'

Mummy says, 'No, I only brought one banana each. We'll
have some lunch when we get home.'

I say, 'Did you forget to bring more food too?'

Mummy stands up fast and says, 'Jesika, go and play with
Toby,' and she takes the basket over to another dryer.

I run round to where Toby is in his buggy and I laugh. 'I can't
play with Toby. He's asleep!'

Mummy drops the basket at the dryer and rushes round to
where I am and she says, 'No, Toby! Don't sleep now! I need you
to sleep later, not now!' And she crouches down and she's stroking

his cheek and tapping his chest and waving his hands up and down for him saying, 'Wake up, Toby! Wakey-wakey!' But Toby's not even moving his eyelids and Mummy always says that she knows when he's proply asleep cos he doesn't move his eyelids.

I say, 'I think he's really, really asleep!' Mummy wipes one of her hands down her face and blows out a big breath and says, 'Yep. Perfect.'

Perfect is good and I smile and say, 'Yes, that's *perfect.*'

Mummy goes back to the dryer but Not-Smiley Lady is putting her clothes into it and Mummy says, 'Excuse me, but I'm using that dryer,' and Not-Smiley Lady says, 'Doesn't look like it, pet.'

Mummy says, 'I left my basket right there. I was just coming back to put the washing in.'

Not-Smiley Lady lifts her shoulders up and down and slams the door, BANG!

Mummy says, 'I really need that dryer.'

Not-Smiley Lady puts her pennies in the penny hole and says, 'Not my problem, pet.' And then she walks outside and stands with Nandini and Leon.

Mummy picks up her basket and brings it back over to Toby's buggy and starts putting all the wet clothes into the big washing bag.

I say, 'What are you doing, Mummy?'

Mummy presses her lips tight and then says, 'We've got to get home and get some lunch and get you to preschool. We haven't got time to wait for another dryer.'

I say, 'You should've told the lady about Nandini's taking turns rule.'

Mummy says, 'Too many battles today, Jesika.'

I say, 'What battles?' and then I hear *jingle-jingle-jingle* ahind me and it sounds like lots of teeny-tiny Tinkerbells but I know it's really Nandini and she's come back in and she's trying to creep up and say, 'BOO!' but she can't trick me cos I can hear all her jingly bracelets that go all up her arms and she can't ever never stop them making noises, only if she stands like a statue. I wait and wait til she's really very near and then I jump off the bench and whizz round and shout, 'BOO!' afore Nandini can say it and she jumps back with her hands pressed tight against her chest and her mouth wide-wide-open like she's proply scared and I laugh and laugh and so does Nandini.

Nandini says, 'Anything to report, Boss?'

I say, 'Mummy got to the drying machine afore that lady outside but she wouldn't let Mummy put her clothes in,' and Mummy says, 'Jesika, it's not really . . .' and Nandini says, 'Oh, she did, did she?' and I say, 'Yes, and now Mummy has to come back and dry all those wet clothes later cos we've got to go home and get lunch afore I'm late for preschool and Mummy only brought us one banana each, and I'm *really* hungry,' and Mummy shakes her head quick and says, 'Jesika, you're not hungry, you're bored and I'm sure Nandini doesn't—'

But Mummy stops talking and she's staring at Nandini cos Nandini has lifted the bag of wet things off the back of Toby's buggy and she says, 'Is this the wet stuff?' And Mummy's mouth is open but she's not saying anything so I say, 'Yes,' and Nandini says, 'Come on, then, I've got a machine out the back we can pop it in.' And she walks through to the back with the bag of wet things to the machines that only Nandini is allowed to use, though sometimes she lets Emma use them too when Emma's helping cos the shop is Nandini's and Emma's.

Mummy doesn't move, cept to push both her hands through her hair and then press them against her face. She says, 'I wish you hadn't told her that, Jesika. I wasn't going to make a fuss, and now . . .'

Nandini pops her head back round the corner and she's taken

off her zippy top so I can see her black T-shirt with the white scribbles all over it and she says, 'Come on, then! Don't be shy. And bring Sleeping Beauty with you, too.' She waves her hand and goes away again.

I look all around and say, 'Where's Sleeping Beauty?' and then I laugh and I say, 'Oh, she means *Toby* cos he's fast asleep.' But Mummy's not laughing at Nandini's joke. Her face is frowny like there's something wrong.

Mummy pushes Toby, still asleep in his buggy. Nandini waves us past the washing machines and the drying machines and right through and right through til we're in a little room where there's another drying machine and a table and chairs and two doors and a sink and a cooker and wooden cupboards on the floor and on the wall, and one that reaches all the way from the floor up to the ceiling. I didn't know that washing machine shops had kitchens!

Our bag of wet things is on the floor next to the drying machine and Nandini is pulling it all out of the bag and pushing it into the machine and this machine doesn't have a pennies hole, Nandini just shuts the door and twists a big button and presses another button and it swooshes, round and round.

Mummy says, 'You really didn't have to . . .' and Nandini says, 'Nonsense.' She stands up and pushes her hand into her hair and all the stripes get mixed up.

I say, 'Your hair, Nandini!'

Nandini shakes her hair and all the stripes go back to the right places and she says, 'Better?' and I say, 'Now it looks like a bumble-bee again,' and Nandini laughs and pulls two chairs out at the table. 'Sit yourself down, both of you,' and she says, 'I've got bread and butter and stuff. Why not save yourself the trip home?' She opens up a cupboard and stands on a little step and stretches up high and her scribbly T-shirt stretches up too so I can see her belly button and there's something sparkly right in the middle of it but her T-shirt goes back down and I can't see and Nandini is holding a packet of bread and it remembers me that she said bread and butter afore.

I say, 'Are we having some bread and butter? I'm really hungry.'

Mummy says, 'Jesika, you're not . . .'

Nandini says, 'Tina, let me do this for you.' Then she smiles at me and says, 'Do you like jam sandwiches?' and she's holding a jar of jam and my eyes go wide and wide and I'm smiling so big cos I've never had jam on a sandwich afore, only jam on toast, and I look at Mummy and say, 'Can I, Mummy? Please?' Mummy's resting her head on one of her hands and I think she's saying no cos she's shaking her head and then she says, Yeah, why not? and I don't know if that means yes or no and I say, 'Please?' and Mummy says, 'Yes, Jesika. Yes.'

I dance about and say, 'Yeah, yeah, yeah!' and Nandini laughs and all her bracelets jingle.

Mummy and Nandini are drinking hot tea and I'm munching on my jam sandwich and swinging my legs and the sandwich is yummy.

I say, 'You never make jam sandwiches, Mummy.'

Mummy says, 'You never ask for them.'

I say, 'I want jam sandwiches every day.'

Mummy laughs and Nandini laughs and says, 'Not every day, Boss.'

I say, 'Why not?'

Nandini says, 'Not good for these,' and she taps her teeth with her fingernail and it makes a clicky sound.

Mummy says, 'You can't spoil a child with love but you can rot their teeth with sugar.'

I say, 'What does that mean, Mummy?' and Mummy's face goes sad and she says, 'Just something your Bab-bab used to say,' and now I know why Mummy's face is sad cos we can't ever never see Bab-bab again and that's always sad. Mummy blows out a breath and rubs her hands over her face and Nandini says, 'You need some time off. Some time to yourself.'

Mummy says, 'I can't . . .' and she shakes her head.

Nandini says, 'Isn't there someone who can help? Family? Friends? What about their . . .' Nandini nods her head to the side and her eyebrows jump up and down and I giggle cos it looks funny.

Mummy doesn't laugh. She says, 'Not interested. And I don't have the energy to keep chasing him.'

Nandini says, 'Sorry, I don't mean to be nosy.'

Mummy says, 'It's OK. I seem to have a knack for losing people.' And she presses her lips together tight and lifts her shoulders up and down fast.

I say, 'Who did you lose, Mummy?'

The door at the back bangs open and cold air whooshes in and blows some pieces of paper onto the floor and Toby's eyes go wide-open-awake, staring right at me, then he closes them and goes back to sleep afore Mummy and Nandini have even noticed he waked up and that's cos Mummy and Nandini are picking up all the pieces of paper on the floor. And there's someone else helping too but I can't see who it is cos Mummy's head is in the way and then the person stands up and it's Emma and she stares at me and I look away cos I don't like Emma staring cos she's a not-smiley person and sometimes she has a bitey voice.

Nandini says, 'Sorted?'

Emma says, 'Loose screw.'

Nandini says, 'Kettle's just boiled if you want a brew,' and Emma says something but it doesn't sound like proper words. She goes to the kettle and she takes a mug out of the cupboard and she didn't even have to stand on the step or stretch like Nandini cos Emma's big like a giant. She's the most biggest person of everybody. And her hair's big too. It sticks out all over her head like Mr Messy on the wall at preschool.

Mummy pushes her chair back and says, 'We better get going . . .'

Nandini says, 'Don't be daft. You've got ages yet. Finish your tea. Jesika, would you like another sandwich?' and I'm about to say, 'Yes, please!' but then Toby starts coughing and his eyes fling open and then he's coughing and coughing and coughing and Emma turns round and says, 'That sounds nasty.'

Nandini says, 'Can you believe the practice cancelled her appointment, just because she was a few minutes late? Some ridiculous new policy. And she's not well herself.'

Emma's face is frowny and then she says lots of things to Mummy about breathing and sleeping and eating and lots of words I don't know and Mummy just says yes or no afore Emma says something else and then Emma says, 'I'll have a listen to his chest.'

Emma goes ahind me and I look round and she's opened a door and I can see a bit of a sofa and some stairs going up and she says, 'Bring him through here. It's quieter.' And she's gone.

Mummy says, 'Oh . . .' and Nandini says, 'Go on, let her put your mind at rest.'

Mummy stands up and pushes Toby through the door and the door closes and then it's just me and Nandini.

Nandini says, 'Right. Another jam sandwich, Jesika?'

I eat up the jam sandwich I've already got and then I eat up the one that Nandini makes and then she makes me *another* one and then says she has to do a quick job for Mummy and she goes away to the front of the shop and I sit and eat and eat and I finish the jam sandwich and my belly feels all full up and I love jam sandwiches and I want to have jam sandwiches every day!

Nandini comes back and she's carrying Mummy's other

washing bag and I say, 'If you were my Mummy, I could have jam sandwiches every day!'

'I'm just the wicked witch who says no all the time!'

Nandini's head turns quick and her hand rushes up to her mouth and she says, 'Oh, Tina, she didn't mean it like that!' and I look ahind me and Mummy and Toby and Emma are back in the room and Mummy's lips are pressed tight and tight like she's so cross but I don't know what she's cross about.

PING!

I say, 'What was that?' and I look all around and Nandini says, 'That's your washing all dry.'

Mummy goes to the machine and opens the door and pulls the clothes out and pushes them into the bag on the floor. Nandini crouches down next to her and she's rubbing her back even though Mummy's not coughing. She's saying something quiet in Mummy's ear and Mummy says, 'I know. I know. I'm just being silly.' Then the bag is full and Mummy stands up and hangs it on Toby's buggy. My belly goes hard and hurty.

Mummy's crying.

Emma hands Mummy a tissue and Mummy wipes her eyes and her nose and I say, 'Mummy, what's happened? Have you hurt yourself?' and Nandini says, 'Don't worry, Boss, your Mum's just having a moment.'

Mummy sniffs and smiles all wobbly and says, 'I'm fine, Jesika. Nothing's happened.' And I think it can't be nothing cos people cry when something happens, not when nothing happens.

Mummy smiles again and it's not wobbly this time and she says, 'Come on, poppet, we need to get you to preschool. We'll be late if we don't hurry.' She picks up my coat off Toby's buggy and holds it out so I can put my arms into it and she says, 'Chin up,' and zips my coat right to the top and then she says, 'What do you say to Nandini?'

I say, 'Thank you for the jam sandwiches, Nandini,' and Nandini says, 'You're very welcome, Boss.'

Nandini picks up another bag from the floor and hangs it on the other side of Toby's buggy and says, 'Here's the washing that was in the other dryer.'

Mummy says, 'Oh! I forgot all about that. I'm sorry!'

Nandini puts her hand on Mummy's shoulder and says, 'Tina, it's not a problem. You don't have to do this alone. We can help. Just ask, OK?'

Mummy's smile wobbles again and she says, 'OK.'

Mummy zips her own coat up and Emma grabs Toby's buggy and says, 'I'll give you a hand with that. I've got to get going too,' and she kisses Nandini and pushes Toby back through the shop.

On the busy-rushy street, the wind zooms all round us and it's bitey and cold and everyone rushing past is bending over like the wind is pushing them along. I can feel the wind pushing me too but I stick my feet hard on the pavement and the wind pushes and pushes me but I'm more stronger than the wind.

Mummy takes the buggy from Emma and says, 'Thanks, Emma, I really appreciate the reassurance.'

Emma lifts her shoulders up and down and one side of her mouth is smiling and the other side isn't smiling. She says, 'Tell the docs what you told me. They should give you some antibiotics for it.' She shivers and stamps her feet and pulls her furry hood up and her Mr Messy hair peeks out the sides and blows around her face and then she squeezes Mummy's shoulder and says, 'And get them to check you out too,' then she walks away and crosses the road quick, not even looking at the green man, and Mummy says only grown-ups are allowed to do that, and Emma gets to the other side and I see her looking at us and I smile and wave and she smiles and waves too and then there's a noisy blue lorry next to me and Mummy and Toby and I can't see Emma now.

Mummy says, 'Time to dash, Jesika. We're going to be late!' And we walk fast and fast away from Emma and I think maybe she's not a scary person after all. Maybe she was just pretending to be scary.

3

THE INSIDE DOOR to preschool is locked so Mummy has to ring the bell and we wait and wait and wait and then I see Stella coming to open the door and I think she looks cross but when she opens the door she's all smiley at me and she says, 'Hello, Jesika! We didn't think you were coming today!' and her voice is squeaky-happy. Then she says to Mummy, 'You're very late this afternoon, Tina,' and she's speaking in her grown-up voice now cos Stella can switch her squeaky-happy voice on and off.

Mummy says, 'Sorry, it's been one of those days.'

Stella does some more talking and Mummy's still holding my hand and she's squeezing and squeezing tight and tight and I say, 'Ow! Mummy you're squeezing my hand too tight!' And Mummy lets go and says, 'Take your coat off and hang it up, Jesika,' and I unzip my coat all by myself, cos that's more easy than zipping it up, and then I stop and stare cos I've just seen something actually really *special*.

Stella's spiky fingers have proper tiny rainbows on them and there's a sparkly jewel stuck under each one! I tug Mummy's hand and whisper to her, 'Guess what, Mummy! Stella's got rainbows on her fingers!' But Mummy doesn't look like she thinks it's special.

Stella says, 'It's for Rainbow Week,' and she flutters her fingers in the air and then shows me one nail proply close and points another nail to all the colours and I know red and yellow and orange and green and blue but I didn't know there were colours called violent and indy go. Stella stands up and then she's looking at me and her face says that something's wrong and she says, 'Oh dear, did you forget it was Red day? Green day isn't until Wednesday. Everyone's in red today.'

I peep past her to the preschool room and I can see lots of red jumpers and skirts and trousers and T-shirts and Stella's face is all creased and sad cos I'm wearing my fayvrit green skirt and green jumper that's got stripes so I think that means I can't go to pre-school today cos I'm not wearing red like everyone else and now my eyes are stingy and I really want to go and play with the toys and it's all Mummy's fault cos she forgotted to tell me I was apposed to wear red today and my foot is stamping and I say, 'It's all *your* fault, Mummy. You didn't tell me it was Red day. You should have told me!'

Mummy says, 'Oh, for goodness' sake,' all spiky in my ear and she tugs my coat off all cross and hangs it on my peg.

Stella says, 'Jesika, I'm sure your Mummy didn't forget on purpose.'

I say, 'Mummy's forgotted everything today. She even forgotted our lunch and Nandini gave me jam sandwiches instead.'

Mummy says, 'Well, sorry, Jesika, for not being a perfect Mummy who remembers everything and gives you jam sandwiches every day. Maybe you should go right back to the laundrette and ask Nandini to be your Mummy!'

I stare and stare at Mummy and I say, 'I don't want Nandini to be my Mummy.'

But Mummy doesn't say anything cos she's putting her hands far, far into one of the clean washing bags on the back of Toby's buggy and she pulls out a red zippy top and I hope it's the one with the strawberry on it cos I like that one best but I can't see cos she tucks it under her arm and then she says, 'Arms up,' and she pulls the green jumper over my head and puts it on the back of Toby's buggy and then crouches down and holds out the red zippy top so I can push my arms in and I'm looking down to see if it's the strawberry top and she zips me up fast and fast.

OW! HOT-STINGY-OW! OW! OW!

My hand flies through the air and then Mummy is squeezing it tight and tight and her eyes are zapping me and she says, 'You *do not* hit me, young lady!' And I didn't know I was going to hit Mummy but now I'm crying and my chin is stinging and stinging cos Mummy forgotted to say, 'Chin up,' when she zipped me up and I'm trying to tell Mummy that my chin is stinging and I didn't mean to hit her but I can't stop crying and my foot is stamping and stamping and then Stella is holding my hand and pulling me away from Mummy and I haven't said I'm sorry to Mummy yet but Stella keeps pulling and she says, 'Leave her with us. She'll calm down as soon as she can't see you. Three thirty for pick up, remember. Don't worry, she'll be fine,' and she whooshes me away from Mummy and Toby afore I can kiss Mummy better or even kiss her and Toby for goodbye, and now I'm crying more and more.

Stella stops me just inside the playroom and she kneels down and everyone's noisy-busy all around and Stella says, 'You need to calm down before you go and play, Jesika. Take some big breaths, Jesika. Big Breaths.' And she's using her grown-up-important voice cos she wants me to listen to her and I know Big Breaths and I do them and do them and it stops me crying but it doesn't stop the hurty pain in my belly and I want Mummy to cuddle it better but Mummy's gone away and Mummy says I have to go to Nandini and tell her to be my Mummy now and . . .

Stella's pulling me into the playroom and she's telling me all about the toys I can play with and I *know* all about the toys cos I play with them every day but I don't want to play with them today and I don't want to go into the playroom, I want Mummy to come back.

26

Stella pulls my hand again and she says, 'You must want to play with something, Jesika. What about the sand? You loved the sand last week,' and her voice is squeaky-happy but her eyes are zapping like Mummy's so maybe she's cross that I tried to hit Mummy too and I think if she is cross, why is her voice not cross? How can you do cross eyes and a squeaky-happy voice at the same time? And she's smiling and zapping and zapping and smiling and I don't *like* it and I can feel my heart thumping and thumping and I pull back hard but Stella holds my hand tight and she's pulling and pulling and I want my Mummy, I want my Mummy . . .

hand-stuck-let-go-let-go-not-Mummy-scared-LET-GO-BITE! Oh!

I'm pulling and pulling at the door and I can't see Mummy through the window and Stella's crouched right next to me and her eyebrows are right up at her hair and she's grabbing my arm and her spiky fingers are pinching and her eyes are scary-bad and her face isn't smiling any more and my belly's twisting like I'm on a roundabout that's whizzing too, too fast and my face is hot and I'm pushing and pulling away from Stella cos I have to find Mummy and Stella turns her head ahind her and she says, 'She *bit* me!' and then my feet lift right off the ground and I'm wrapped up tight and squashed, warm and soft, and I can't see but I know it's Kali cos it smells like Kali and it feels like Kali and it's her bubbly-soft voice in my ears. I stop pushing and pulling and my belly stops twisting and I just cry and cry and Kali says, 'It's OK,' lots and lots of times.

When I stop crying, Kali lifts me off her knee and puts me back on my feet and holds my hands soft and soft and she says, 'OK?' and we're in the Safe Corner where the Feelings Dollies are and then she lets go of my hands and I know she wants me to choose a dolly but I can't cos my brain is whizzing all jumbled up and my belly's whirling around again and Kali holds my hands again and says, 'Smile. Take a deep breath. And Relax.' And she says it again, and again, and again, and does the breathing with me.

After a long-a-long time she says, 'I think lots of things upset you all at once, didn't they?' And Kali's voice wraps me up warm and soft and the whirling in my belly stops. She picks up three dollies and puts them on the squashy cushions in a line and she says, 'Sad or Scared or Angry?' And she says their names again and all the whizzing in my brain slows down and I pick up Scared and Angry and put them back in their pockets and I pick up Sad and cuddle her to me. Kali nods and says, 'Can you tell me why you're feeling sad?'

I think about not wearing red and being cross with Mummy and Mummy being cross with me and changing my top and the zip biting my chin and me almost hitting Mummy and not saying sorry proply and Stella taking me away afore I could say it or even kiss Mummy better and not saying goodbye to Mummy or Toby and Stella pulling me and I think I hurted Stella and Stella hurted my arm when she pinched and Mummy's so cross that she wants me to go and ask Nandini to be my Mummy instead and I don't want a different Mummy and I say, 'I want my Mummy!' and my lips are wobbly and my belly hurts and hurts and Kali holds my hand soft and soft again and smiles and tells me Mummy will be back afore I know it and I say, 'No, she won't!' and Kali says, 'Of course she will, Jesika. Why wouldn't she?' And I say, 'Cos she was cross and she said I have to ask Nandini to be my Mummy,' and I'm crying again and Kali does the breathing words with me and I breathe and breathe and breathe.

When I'm not crying any more, Kali says, 'Have you ever done something you didn't mean to when you were feeling cross?' And I think about biting Stella and I nod my head and Kali says, 'Well, your Mummy was feeling cross too and she said something she didn't mean too. And I promise you, she'll be back for you at home-time. I promise.'

I say, 'I have to say sorry to her for hitting.' Kali nods and says, 'Yes, and you also need to say something to Stella too, don't you?' My belly goes tight and tight and I look at Kali but her face isn't cross and she says, 'You felt sad when your Mummy left and you wanted Stella to let go of you so you could run after her and so you bit Stella because she wouldn't let go. You may not bite. You can say, "Stop it!" or "Let go!" but you may not bite. Biting hurts people and you hurt Stella.' And she gets me to hold my hand up like a STOP sign and I have to try saying, 'Stop it!' and 'Let go!' and then Kali says, 'Well done, Jesika. You try that next time someone's doing something you don't like.'

Kali takes my hand and we walk over to where Stella is and she's doing silly dancing with Amber, Lucia and Katy, swooshing floaty scarves about and it looks very fun. Stella sees us and dances over breathing fast and fast and her cheeks are all pink and she crouches down next to me and her face and her eyes are both happy this time. Kali smiles at me and says, 'Go on, Jesika,' and I say, 'I'm sorry I hurted you, Stella.' And Stella says, 'Thank you, Jesika.' And I think it's Stella's turn now cos she hurted me too and I think she also didn't mean it but you still have to say you're sorry, but Stella doesn't say anything. She's dancing again with the scarves. Maybe grown-ups don't have to say sorry. But that's not right cos Mummy always says sorry when she does something she didn't mean to.

Kali squeezes my shoulder and says, 'Well done, Jesika. Now, what do you want to do this afternoon?' But then she has to dash away cos Azim's knocked over one of the painting stands and there's paint and water everywhere.

I watch the floaty scarf dancing and I wait for Stella to ask if I want to dance with the floaty scarves too but she doesn't look at me at all and I think maybe I'm not allowed to dance with the floaty scarves cos I hurted her, so I go and sit in the house cos no one else is in there and I don't think I actually want to talk to any-one else and I think maybe I'll just sit and sit til it's home-time.

The door on the house slams and I jump round from tucking baby in the cot and I see a girl squeeze herself small and small under the table and she's not wearing red and I know this girl. She's the girl that came to preschool with her Mummy the other day and her Mummy stayed with her all the time til it was time to go home again, but I don't know what her name is.

She stares at me with scary-wide eyes.

I say, 'You're not wearing red.'

Her lip wobbles and I think she must be scared and sad at the same time, and it remembers me that I felt scary-sad not wearing red too so I say, 'My skirt's not red,' and I twirl right round so she can see it's green all over. I crouch down so I can see her proply and say, 'You came with your Mummy afore, didn't you?'

She keeps staring at me.

I say, 'What's your name?'

She's still staring and not saying anything. Maybe my voice didn't go in her ears cos there's a lot-a-lot of busy noise and maybe that's going in her ears instead. I crawl a bit closer and say, 'My name's Jesika.'

She keeps staring. Maybe she doesn't know what I said cos not everyone knows my name and sometimes people put the wrong letters in it and Mummy has to tell them the right letters.

I say, 'My Daddy picked my name from Poland. That's where Bab-bab used to live a long-a-long time ago afore Daddy was a baby and now Daddy lives there all the time.'

She turns right away from me so I can't see her face, like Toby does when he's hiding. Maybe she's playing hide and seek!

I say, 'Are you playing hide and seek?'

She doesn't say anything.

I say, 'Can I play too?' cos I love playing hide and seek with Mummy and Toby.

The girl unhides her face and stares at me again and then she says, 'Do you have sweeties?'

I say, 'No.'

She says, 'You have to have sweeties.'

I say, 'Why?'

The girl's face is frowny and she says, 'Cos you hide and then you get found and then you be a special-good-girl and then you get sweeties. That's what you do. So you can't play if you've not got sweeties.'

Now I'm frowning and I say, 'I didn't know that. I don't have any sweeties.'

The girl stares at me.

I say, 'We could just play hiding and not have sweeties. That's what I do with my Mummy and Toby.'

The girl says, 'I don't want to,' and she hides her face again.

I tap her shoulder and I say, 'Do you want to play babies with me instead?'

She doesn't speak and she curls up tight and tight. I think she doesn't want to talk to anyone now.

I go back to the cot and finish tucking baby in and I start singing Mummy's bedtime song cept I forget some of the words and then I hear Tamanna singing, 'Snack-time! Snack-time!' And then she's there, stretching tall as tall like a giraffe over the top of the house walls and tickling the top of my head and she says, 'Time to go and wash your hands, Jesika.' I don't think she's noticed the girl under the table but afore I can say anything, she's danced over to the other side of the room singing, 'Snack-time! Snack-time!' for the other boys and girls. I tell the girl that we need to go but she's still hiding her face and then Stella's there telling me to hurry up and I point to the girl under the table but Stella's already gone afore she sees and I say, 'Come on, it's time to go for snack,' but the girl still isn't listening, so I go to wash my hands.

I want to sit on Kali's table at snack-time today but we have to always sit on the same table with the same grown-up and my grown-up is Stella, not Kali. I sit down with Amber and Lucia and Lewis and Azim and Toby (Big Toby not *my* Toby – he's too little for preschool) but Stella doesn't sit down too like she usually does. She's with Kali and Tamanna and Lauren and they're all looking like something's wrong and I hear Lauren say, 'She must be here somewhere.' And Tamanna says, 'I'll check the toilets again,' and then rushes off and Kali goes to look in the Safe Place and Lauren goes to look in the book corner and Stella says, 'Where *is* she?' but she doesn't seem to be looking cos she just stands there.

I look and look around the room and I'm wondering who it is they've lost cos everyone's sitting at their proper places at the tables and the only empty chairs are the grown-up chairs and then the answer shoots into my head and I run over to Stella and tug her sleeve but Stella just tells me to go and sit back at my table so I say, 'I know where she is,' but Stella tells me to go and sit down again so I run to the house corner and open the door and she's still there squeezed right under the table cept now she's lying down on the cushion that's apposed to be on the play bed and she's got the blanket that I tucked baby in and it's covering her all up, cept her face, and she's sucking her thumb and she's got her eyes closed and I think she might actually be asleep which is very strange cos preschool's not a sleeping place, it's a playing place. I reach out a hand to touch her shoulder and wake her up and tell her she's missing snack-time when I feel a hand on *my* shoulder and I turn and Kali's there with her finger on her lips and she doesn't say anything but shows me with her hands that she wants me to come out so I do and then she says, 'We'll leave Paige to sleep, she must be very tired,' and her voice is quiet as quiet so she doesn't wake Paige up.

I say, 'Why is she so tired?'

Kali says, 'Well, she's had a very busy time moving house and starting at a new preschool and making new friends and it's all a bit scary.'

I say, 'Does scary make you tired?'

Kali smiles and says, 'Yes, sometimes.' Then she says, 'We'll leave her to rest for now. You go and get your snack,' and I skip back to my snack table and I'm smiling and smiling cos now I know the girl under the table is called Paige and that means when she wakes up I can ask her to be my friend.

Everyone's saying well done for finding Paige and I sit down at my snack table and even sitting down I feel all floaty like I'm a butterfly or a sparkly fairy or . . . or . . .

Stella says, 'What's that on your forehead, Jesika?' and she pushes my hair out of my face and she presses her thumb on my forehead.

OW!

Stella says all smiley and squeaky-happy, 'Goodness, that's quite a bump there. How did you get that?'

I press the sore bit with my own fingers, not as hard as Stella, and I think and think and I don't remember bumping my head at preschool and I say, 'I've forgotten,' and she says, 'Did you do it this morning, before preschool?' And I think about all the rushing about we did afore preschool but I didn't fall over and bump myself then so I say, 'I don't know,' and Stella says, 'Maybe you bumped it in your house?' And that remembers me that my house is called lots of different names and I say, 'Do you know you can call my house a flat and a dump?'

Stella frowns and says, 'I don't think you call your house a dump, Jesika. A dump is a dirty, smelly place where you put rubbish.'

I say, 'Mummy says our house is dirty and smelly and it's noisy too and everything always keeps being broken but not toys or the telty cos they always work.' And I'm thinking about the telly and I touch the sore bit on my head again and then the answer shoots into my brain and I say, 'I hitted my head on the telly!'

Stella says, 'Oh? How did you do that?'

I think I better not tell Stella about my secret pictures on the wall cos you get in trouble for drawing on the walls at preschool and Stella might not know that in my house my pictures are hided away under the peeling paper so no one can see them so I just tell her about Mummy getting cross and pulling me hard and hard so the telly hitted me and made a bump on my head. I think Stella will be pleased that I remembered how the bump happened but Stella doesn't look pleased. She just says, 'Hmmm,' and then she helps Amber to fill her cup up with more milk and she doesn't talk to me again for the whole of snack-time. Then at the very end of snack-time, when it's time to go and play again, she says, 'Jesika, stay there a second, will you?' All the other children go off and play and I sit at the snack table and wait and then Stella and Lauren are sitting at the snack table too.

Stella says, 'Tell me all about how you hit your head on the telly again,' and I laugh and say, 'I didn't hit the telly. The telly hitted me!' and Lauren smiles and then hides her smile ahind her hand and Stella says, 'OK, well, tell me how the telly hit you.' And I say, 'I told you already,' and Stella says, 'I know, but Lauren wants to listen this time.' And I tell Stella and Lauren how Mummy pulled me hard and hard and the telly hitted me and made a bump and I don't think Lauren does want to listen cos she's not looking at me, she's just writing on a piece of paper.

Stella says, 'Has your Mummy ever hurt you before when she's been cross, Jesika?' I think about another time Mummy hurted me and I can only think of one time and I say, 'The other day, she trapped my fingers in the bedroom door but she wasn't cross that day.'

Stella says, 'Why did she trap your fingers?'

I say, 'Cos she shutted the door and my fingers were in the way.'

Stella says, 'Hmmm,' and then she says, 'Your chin looks sore too. Do you remember hurting it?' and I think Stella is very silly not to remember the zip cos she was there so I giggle and say, 'That was afore with you!'

Stella frowns and Lauren says, 'Stella hurt your chin?'

I say, 'No, Mummy did it cos she zipped my red top up fast and fast and she forgotted to say, "Chin up," and it bit my chin and it really hurt and I cried and Stella took me away.'

Lauren looks up and puts her pen down and Stella does zapping eyes at her and Lauren says, 'Stella, I don't think we need to . . .' and Stella says, 'We write *everything* down. If it turns out to be nothing, all we've wasted is a bit of time and paper but I'm not going to sit back and be responsible for another Baby P.'

Lauren picks up her pen again and I say, 'What's a baby pea?' but Stella says, 'Off you go and play now, Jesika,' so I don't think she listened and when I try to ask her again, she's busy talking to Lauren quiet as quiet and not looking at me so I walk away.

Maybe a baby pea is like a pea afore it's growed big enough to eat. One time, Ade showed me a green vegetable that was long and bendy like a smile and he said it was what peas growed in. I said he was being silly but then he pressed his thumbs into the middle and it ripped open and there were four huge peas inside, two for me and two for Toby. They were yummy and Ade said they're really easy to grow but Mummy said we can't grow things til we have a garden and we can't have a garden til she wins the Lottery and that won't happen til a pig flies past our window and that'll only happen if a witch or a wizard comes along and puts a spell on one.

Tamanna dances past me and she's about to start a music train and I love the music train cos you choose an instrument and then stand ahind Tamanna in a long train and then you have to follow Tamanna where she goes in and out and round and round and you have to sing and play at the same time and we always end up getting tangled up giggling somewhere in the end, usually on the floor!

I run after Tamanna and get to her instrument basket first and I pick out two shakers and Tamanna says, 'You've got one for each hand – one and one makes two,' and then there's lots of children picking out instruments and Tamanna says, 'What colour is our train today?'

I shout, 'GREEN! GREEN! GREEN!' and I'm the loudest shouting and Tamanna laughs and says, 'Green it is,' and then Stella walks past and says, 'Shouldn't it be red, seeing as it's Red day today?' And Amber shouts, 'Yeah! RED! RED! RED!' And then everyone's shouting, 'RED! RED! RED!' cept me cos I don't want it to be red, I want it to be green and I make my face cross and frowny and then Tamanna says, 'We'll do red next time,' and she actually winks at me and starts singing, 'Chuff-chuff-chuff goes the little green train,' and I smile my biggest smile and shake my shakers extra loud and sing all the words as shouty as I can and we all follow Tamanna all around the room singing and shaking and then, cos it's not raining, Tamanna takes the train right outside to outdoor play but the wind is bitey so she makes the singing go very fast and that means the train has to go faster and we all dash and dash back inside and we have a squash and a squeeze in the door and the whole train collapses on the floor and everyone's giggling and I knew we'd end up on the floor!

Tamanna says, 'Now we'll do a red train,' and I don't mind cos we've done my fayvrit green train and I join on the back of the train ready to sing and then I see Paige and she's waked up now and she's watching the train and she's holding Kali's hand and Kali says, 'Do you want to join the train, Paige?' and Paige shakes her head and hides her face ahind Kali's arm. I think maybe it's cos everyone's got shakers and the instrument basket is empty so there's no shakers for Paige and you can't join the train if you don't have a shaker.

I look at my two shakers, one for each hand, and I have a clever think cos I remember that I'm going to be friends with Paige and friends are kind and helpful and I run over to Paige and say, 'You can have one of my shakers, Paige,' cos my hands don't actually both need a shaker and they don't mind sharing just one. I hold the other one out to Paige and she takes it but she's not smiling and she's still holding Kali's hand so maybe she doesn't want the shaker, or maybe she doesn't want to be friends, cos sometimes when you ask someone to be friends, they say, 'I don't want to be your friend.' Amber and Lucia always say that to me. Sometimes they tell the other children to say it too and they all run away and only Big Toby plays with me.

Kali says, 'That's very kind and helpful, Jesika,' and right then Tamanna's train comes past us and Kali says, 'Paige, why don't you go with Jesika and she can show you what to do?' But Paige shakes her head again and Tamanna's train is going past and past and I shake my shaker to show Paige and she shakes hers so it makes a tiny mouse sound and she even smiles a tiny mouse smile but then she's hiding ahind Kali's arm again and I'm about to miss the train and I run to catch up the back of the train and I don't miss it and I'm shaking and singing and running in and out all the places Tamanna takes us on the train.

We go past Paige and Kali two times and Paige is shaking her shaker more and more and her smile is getting bigger and bigger, so the next time we go past I shout, 'STATION!' which means the train has to stop to let passengers on and Tamanna stops the train and shouts, 'ALL ABOARD!' and I hold out my hand to Paige and say, 'Come on, Paige, it's very fun!' and Paige actually lets go of Kali's hand and she holds my hand and then Tamanna's train goes again and this time we're a blue train and everyone's singing, 'Chuff-chuff-chuff goes the little blue train . . .' and I think maybe Paige wants to be my friend after all.

4

IT'S STICKER TIME and that means it's almost home-time and Kali gives Paige a smiley sunshine sticker and she says, 'This is for being brave and joining in on your very first day.' And Paige is smiling and smiling and I'm smiling and smiling too and then Kali says my name and I look and she's waving me to come up. I'm getting a sticker too!

I stand up and Stella scrunches up her face and bends her head right next to Kali's ear like she's telling a secret and she says, 'For *biting?*' and her voice is bitey just like what she's saying and I think, Kali's not giving me a sticker, she's going to tell all the other boys and girls about the naughty thing I did to Stella and everyone will be cross at me. I want to sit down again but I can't make my legs move and my belly feels funny, like it's all filled up with freezing water.

Then Kali holds out her hand and says, 'Come on, Jesika, you've got a sticker too,' and she's smiling and smiling and now my legs are moving again and she holds my hand and presses a sticker on my zippy top and says, 'This is for being helpful to Paige on her first day without her Mummy. You made her feel welcome and you cheered her up when she was feeling scared. You have been a very kind and thoughtful friend today.' And everyone is smiling right at me and clapping their hands, cept Stella cos she's turned away to tidy up the jigsaw table.

Everyone else keeps clapping and clapping til I'm sat down next to Paige and Paige pushes her hand through my arm and holds on tight and now my belly's all filled up with warm and it's filling up all of me and it feels nice and it feels like the Best Day Ever.

Kali opens the door and all the grown-ups come in.

Where's Mummy?

My heart's thumping hard and hard.

There's so many legs in my way, and I look all the way up the legs to the faces high, high up but none of them is Mummy, and then some of the legs move apart and there, in the middle, is Mummy's face bending down and her arms are stretched out and she's smiling and smiling and I jump up and my feet fly.

'MUMMY!'

And we're hugging and squeezing and my face is squashed right into Mummy's belly and I say, 'You came back,' right into Mummy's belly and she squeezes me tight and tight.

We go into the peg room and it's busy and squashy and it's hard to move cos there's so many tall legs like trees, but they're moving trees not standing still trees and they're all moving and squashing and squeezing and pushing me one way and then another. When we get to my peg, I say to Mummy, 'I got a sticker!' and I bend my chin down far and far so I can see the sparkly star and show it to Mummy and Mummy says, 'Brilliant! What did you get that for?' But I don't get to tell her cos Stella says, 'Tina, may I have a quick word?' And Mummy looks at me quick and my face is hot and hot and I know what Stella is going to say and Mummy is going to be so so cross with me and she won't let me keep my sparkly star.

Mummy says, 'Put your coat on, Jesika, and wait with Toby. I'll be right back.' And she walks over to the playroom door where Stella is and Stella's face is not a happy face and she's bending her head down to Mummy's ear and talking but I can't hear cos there's so much busy going-home noise in the peg room but I know she's saying, 'Jesika *bit* me. Jesika *bit* me. Jesika *bit* me.'

'Are you Jesika?'

I look up and it's a man I don't know and his hair is brown and his eyes are blue as blue and he's smiling and smiling and his cheeks look like they're made of playdough and someone's stuck a finger in each side of his mouth just where his smile stops, like a hole but not all the way through his skin. I nod and he says, 'Paige says she's had a lovely time playing with you today.'

And then I see Paige hiding ahind the man's back and she peeps out a tiny bit round his arm so I can see one eye and a little bit of her smile and I smile and wave at her and she disappears back ahind the man's arm again.

I say, 'Are you Paige's Daddy?'

He shakes his head and says, 'No, I'm her Uncle.'

I don't know what an Uncle is but afore I can ask him he points to where Mummy and Stella are still standing talking and he says, 'Is that your Mummy over there?'

I nod again. It feels like a big bird is flapping about inside my belly. Mummy's face is tight and cross.

The man says, 'I think I know your Mummy,' and then he says, 'Can I help you put your coat on?' and I look at my hands and I'm holding my coat and I say, 'I can put my coat on all by myself!' The man laughs and I think it's cos he doesn't believe me so I push my arms into my coat and then I have to make the zip go together at the bottom and it's tricky fiddly but I know I can do it if I really try and I try and I try and – YES! – the zip starts moving up and I pull it up and up and remember to lift my chin out of the way and when it's right at the top I say, 'See?' And the man laughs again and says, 'Well, you are a grown-up girl, aren't you?'

There's a hand on my shoulder and I look up and it's Mummy and she's pulling me away from the man and her face is cross probly cos Stella told her about the biting and she says, 'Time to go, Jesika.'

The man says, 'Hi, I'm Ryan, Paige's Uncle. Don't I know you?'
Mummy shakes her head fast and says, 'No, no, I don't think so.'

Ryan lifts his shoulders up and down and smiles and says,
'Well, it was Paige's first day by herself today and your Jesika
looked after her,' and that remembers me that I didn't tell Mummy
why I got the sticker and I say, 'I got a sticker, Mummy!' And
Mummy's smiling now and she says, 'Ah, so it wasn't all bad,' and
her hand that was on my shoulder is now stroking my hair. I don't
think Mummy would stroke my hair if she's still cross with me.

I say, 'Yes, and I didn't get it for biting Stella.' Mummy stops stroking and stops smiling and I say, 'Are you cross with me, Mummy?'

Mummy stops looking cross and she crouches down and holds
both my hands and says, 'I'm not cross with *you*, Jesika. We'll talk
about it later, OK?'

I don't get to ask who Mummy is cross with cos then Ryan says,
'My sister and Paige moved back here last month.' And then he
says something so quiet that I can't hear it even opening my ears
right open but I think it's something bad cos Mummy's face goes
sad and I say, 'What is it, Mummy?' and Mummy strokes my hair
again and looks at me with sad eyes and says, 'I'll tell you later,
poppet,' and Ryan says, 'Yeah, so I've been helping where I can
with childcare so Lorna can get back on her feet and I persuaded
her that preschool would be a good idea so Paige can make some
new friends,' and then he smiles right at me and says, 'And it looks
like she's made one already!'

Mummy smiles and then she gets my bag from my peg and
she pushes it under Toby's buggy and then Ryan says, 'Look, do
you want to do something together now? Like a play in the park,
or come back to Lorna's for a brew while the kids play? Lorna gets
home from work in an hour and you could meet her . . .'

Inside my head, my voice is shouting YES!YES!YES! and
I'm looking up at Mummy and smiling and smiling but then

Mummy's hand is hard on my shoulder again and her sad eyes are gone and her face is all scrunchy and I know she's going to say, 'No,' and it's not fair and she says, 'I'm really sorry but I've got to take Toby to the doctor now. Maybe another day?'

My foot stamps and I say, 'I don't want to go to the doctors again. I want to play with Paige!' but Mummy's rushing me over to Toby's buggy and rushing out of the preschool door and rushing down the street and I say, 'But why . . . ?' and Mummy says, 'Not now, Jesika,' and her voice is rushy just like our feet and we rush and rush and rush.

We get all the way to the green man crossing and there's running feet ahind us and I turn round and it's the man and Paige is bouncing on his back and I tug Mummy's hand and she turns round and says, 'Oh!' and the man is puffing out his breaths fast and fast and he says, 'Tina Green! It is you, isn't it?'

Mummy says, 'Petrowski. My name's Petrowski now.'

The man says, 'Look at you, all married and grown up!'

Mummy says, 'Was married. Not sure about the grown up,' and her mouth makes a tiny smile.

The man says, 'You don't remember me, do you? Ryan. Ryan Selwood.'

Mummy says, 'I remember you.'

The man smiles big and big and says, 'Wait until I tell Lorna! There's me thinking she could really do with a friend to talk to and I bump into her best mate from school! Look, have you got a pen?'

Mummy frowns and then she puts her hand into her bag and pulls out a pen and the man pats his coat with his hands and says, 'And something to write on?' and Mummy puts her hand in her bag again and pulls out a piece of paper with squiggles on it and she folds it over to hide the squiggles and gives it to him and he writes something and gives the pen and the piece of paper back to

Mummy and says, 'This is my number. I know you're busy today but Lorna would love to meet up with you again. I know she would.'

Mummy frowns more and says, 'I don't know. We haven't spoken in years.'

The man says, 'We all need friends, Tina. Think about it. See you soon,' and then he turns and walks away. Paige twists round on his back and waves her hand at me and I wave back at her and when I look back at Mummy she's still frowning.

We cross the road and keep on walking to the busy-rushy road and when we've walked a long-a-long way on the busy-rushy road we walk right past the doctors and I say, 'Mummy, we've walked past the doctors!' and Mummy says, 'We're not going to the doctors. We're going to the shops and then we're going home.'

I say, 'But you said to the man that we had to go to the doctors.' Something plops on my head and it's shivery-cold and wet.

Mummy says, 'I went to the doctors while you were at pre-school and it was a waste of time and now I want to go home.'

I say, 'But that's why we couldn't play with Paige cos you said we had to go to the doctors.' There's another PLOP and it's right on the end of my nose!

Mummy says, 'I just want to go home, Jesika. Toby's not well and I'm not well and today's not the day for going and playing with friends.'

I say, 'I *never* get to go and play at someone else's house. It's *not fair*!' And I stamp my foot and Mummy says, 'Jesika,' and then she stops and blows out a breath and she doesn't say anything else and now there's raindrops PLOP! PLOP! PLOP! all around us, big and fast, and Mummy says, 'Rain. Fantastic.'

I say, 'Rain's not fantastic, Mummy,' but Mummy's too busy fixing Toby's rain cover on his buggy so I don't think she hears me. She helps me put my hood up and she says, 'Come on, I want to go to Ade's on the way home and we'll get very wet unless we go quickly.'

Oh! We're going to Ade's on the way home! I skip along the street shouting, 'Yeah, yeah, yeah!' cos I love going to Ade's shop. It's like a rainbow inside cos all his fruit and vegetables are all different colours and sometimes he gives me and Toby something we've never had afore like mango and blueberries and star fruit that's actually like a real star when you cut it open.

Mummy grabs my arm and pulls it and says, 'Watch where you're going, Jesika!' and then Mummy says, 'So sorry,' to a lady that's walking on the pavement and the lady smiles and says, 'It's OK,' and then she's gone and I don't know why Mummy had to say sorry.

Mummy says, 'Hand on the buggy, Jesika,' and I try to keep skipping but it's hard cos my leg keeps bumping Toby's buggy.

The rain on Toby's rain cover is going SPLAT! SPLAT! SPLAT! and the raindrops are having races down to the bottom and I'm watching a raindrop that's sliding very faster than all the others and . . .

OW! OW! OW!

Mummy says, 'For goodness' *sake*, Jesika, will you just walk in a straight line and then I won't run you over with the buggy!'

My foot stings and my eyes sting and my cheeks sting and Mummy has to stop and check my foot's OK. She puts a magic kiss on her hand and touches it on my foot and then she stands up again and says, 'Hold the buggy and walk *forwards*, Jesika, and look where you're going this time,' and it's not fair cos I *was* holding the buggy and I *was* walking forwards and I *was* looking where I was going, cept when I was watching the raindrops racing.

We walk a bit more and my feet squelch in my shoes and we go under the big roof that sticks out of the big food shop and it's not raining on our heads now, it's raining on the roof and it sounds like a giant stomping his feet and there's lots of people standing and listening and we have to squeeze past. I want to stop and listen too but Mummy keeps pushing the buggy and my feet have to keep walking past the red heart shop and back into the rain.

I tip my head back and stick my tongue out and the rain is tap-tap-tapping my tongue and making it all wet and it's not tickly and not hurty but sort of—

'Jesika!'

Mummy's face is cross and I don't know why cos I'm holding the buggy and I'm walking forwards. Mummy says, 'It's raining, Jesika, can we go a bit faster, please?' I make my feet go quick and Mummy says, 'That's better,' and we get to a really puddly bit and we're zig-zagging around all the puddles like a fast car race and I'm looking at the puddles and the raindrops are making big splashes in them.

Oh! That one's got a swirly rainbow in it!

I let go of the buggy and say, 'Mummy, Mummy, look! Look at this!' But Mummy doesn't stop and I run to catch up and pull on Mummy's sleeve and say, 'Stop, Mummy! Look at this!' And she says, 'Jesika, come on, it's *raining*!' but I know a rainbow puddle is something so special and Mummy needs to see it and I run back to the puddle and crouch down and point and say, 'Look, it's a rainbow puddle!' And then Mummy's crouched next to me and I say, 'It's a pretty rainbow puddle, isn't it?' and Mummy says, 'Yes, it's very pretty.' And I look at Mummy and I giggle cos there's a big drip of water hanging off the end of Mummy's nose and I tap Mummy's nose to make it fall off and I giggle again and Mummy says, 'Oh, that's so funny, Jesika,' and she's trying to look cross but her laughing face keeps pushing the cross away and I giggle again.

We walk back to where Mummy left Toby in his buggy and Mummy says, 'Hand on the buggy,' and we walk along the street again and I say, 'How did the rainbow get into the puddle?' and Mummy says, 'It looks like someone spilled some oil or petrol on the ground,' and I say, 'What's oilorpetrol?' and Mummy says, 'It's what people put into their cars to make them work,' and I say, 'Why did someone spill it in the puddle?' and Mummy says, 'It was probably an accident,' and I say, 'Or maybe it's cos it's Rainbow Week at preschool,' and Mummy laughs and says, 'Maybe,' and I say, 'Is oilor-petrol made of rainbows?' and Mummy says, 'No, it makes rainbows when light from the sun bounces off it, or something like that.'

I say, 'The light from the sun bounces? Like a ball?' Mummy laughs again and says, 'That's a question for another day. Come on, it's *raining*!' And she shakes her head and raindrops fly off her head cos her hair is really, really, really, really wet! It's sticking all over her face and the raindrops are sliding down her nose and her cheeks and even her eyelashes have drips on them.

I say, 'Mummy, you should have put on the coat that's got a hood,' and Mummy says, 'The zip's broken. I had to wear this one.' And just then we're walking past the shop that has clothes and coats and shoes in the window and the coats have all got hoods and I point to the window and say, 'I've got an idea, Mummy, why don't we go in here afore Ade's shop and get you a new coat that's got a hood?' But Mummy says, 'You need pennies to buy coats and I've not got enough pennies at the moment,' and then she says, 'It's just a bit of rain, Jesika, I don't mind getting wet.' But then we get to Ade's shop and she says, 'Out of the rain, at last,' so I think she does mind really.

Ade's shop is busy with people putting different fruits and vegetables into their baskets. One of the ladies that helps in the shop is putting more apples out and she sees me and smiles and waves but Ade doesn't see us straight away cos there's a man giving him pennies at the paying table and I'm waiting and waiting for him to turn and see us and then he does and he shouts, 'Hey, Jesika!' and he comes over to us slow and slow and he's using both his sticks today so it must be a hurty day and not a day for doing jumping high fives cos he can't let go of his sticks so I fist bump him instead like he showed me last time and then Toby says, 'Me, me!' and Mummy pushes the buggy right up to Ade and he leans his stick right near to Toby so Toby can do a fist bump too cept Toby always forgets to make a fist and he does a high five on Ade's fist instead and Ade bends his head right back and laughs loud and loud and his hair bounces up and down like springs and now I'm laughing but not Mummy and Toby cos they're coughing and coughing.

Ade says, 'Did you get to the doc's with that?'

Mummy's still coughing but she nods and then lifts her shoulders up and down and makes a scrunchy face and when she's finished coughing she says, 'Nothing to worry about at the moment. Just more sleepless nights and grumpy days.'

Ade makes a sad face and says, 'Not much fun,' and I say, 'What's not much fun?' but now Mummy's talking to Ade about the family bargain bag and Ade says, 'Yep, got one all ready for you.'

We follow Ade across the shop atween all the people to Ade's paying table and Ade leans his sticks against the wall and leans his bottom on his high-up stool and he points to a bag on the floor and says, 'You'll have to help yourself. I can't do bending today.'

Mummy lifts the bag up and pushes it under the buggy and Ade says, 'I put in your usual, plus a couple of peppers and some satsumas that need using today or tomorrow, and *someone*' – he nods his head at the Apple Lady – 'over-ordered the broccoli, so you got one of them, too.'

The Apple Lady says, 'Are you still trying to blame me for that one?' And she makes a 'tut' sound that's cross but she's also smiling so I don't think she's actually cross.

Mummy's face isn't cross but it is frowny and Ade holds his hand up and he says, 'Please, it's wasted food if you don't take it and I can't stand wasted food. Plus you need that vitamin C.'

I say, 'What's that?'

Ade says, 'Vitamin C? It's a magic warrior right inside your fruit and veg and it fights colds and coughs.'

My eyes go wide and wide cos I didn't know that magic warriors could live inside food and I look at Mummy to check if she knows about the magic warriors and she's got a tiny smile even though her face is still a bit frowny and I say, 'Are there really magic warriors in fruit and vegetables?'

Mummy smiles even bigger and says, 'Yes, there are, so that's why you have to eat all your fruit and veg up,' and she gives Ade some pennies for the bag and I say, 'Well, you and Toby better eat this whole bag up and then the warriors can fight your coughs and make them go away.'

Ade gives Mummy some pennies back cos she must have given him too many and I say, 'Ade, have you put any surprises in the bag?'

Mummy says, 'Jesika!' and I don't think she wanted me to ask that but Ade laughs loud and loud and his hair bounces again and he says, 'No surprises today, but I think you might have one behind your ear.'

I lift my hand up and touch ahind my ear but there's nothing there.

Ade says, 'No, not that one.' And he reaches ahind my other ear and, *oh!* He's pulled out a big, red strawberry! That's *magic*! He twists off the green leaves and passes it to me and I say, 'Thank you!' and then Toby says, 'Me, me!' and Ade grabs one of his sticks and leans on it and reaches ahind Toby's ear and he pulls out another strawberry and he twists off the green leaves and passes it to Toby and I don't know how he did that! I put the whole strawberry in my mouth and bite it and my mouth is sweet and juicy and lovely and some of the juice squeezes out of my lips and tickles down my chin and I lick it off and it's the most yummy taste in the whole of the world.

Mummy says, 'Thanks, Ade,' and Ade says, 'I've got something for you too,' and I think he's going to magic a strawberry from ahind Mummy's ear but he reaches under the paying table and it's a book and he says, 'It's the one I was telling you about on Friday. I've finished it now – and I didn't see that ending coming!' and his eyes go wide and he makes a whistle with his mouth.

Mummy says, 'I can get it from the library.'

Ade pushes the book at Mummy and says, 'Go on. You can give it back after. But read it quick so I can talk to you about the ending!'

The Apple Lady comes over to the paying table with a man who's got a basket full up with fruit and veg and she says, 'Please take it and read it because then he'll stop talking to me about it.'

Ade says, 'Cheeky!' and he makes his face cross but it's just like the Apple Lady's pretend cross face and his cross mouth keeps trying to smile and Mummy and the Apple Lady are both smiling so they don't think he's cross either. Grown-ups do a lot of pretending to be cross when they're not really. Why don't they just be cross or not be cross?

Outside Ade's shop it's not raining any more but everything is dripping. I count all the drips I can see on the shop windows and the bus stop and the car mirrors and the metal poles and the doorways and the buggies and the bikes and the traffic lights, but then I run out of numbers and then we're crossing the road and almost back home and we get to the steps that go up to the big outside door and there's two men standing at the bottom and they're shouting scary-horrible words and one of them is jabbing his finger at the other one's chest and that must really *hurt*.

'Don't *look*, Jesika!' Mummy's voice hisses like a snake. She pushes the buggy round the men and says, 'Up the steps, quick, and wait at the top,' and she pushes me forward and then she turns round so she can pull Toby's buggy up the steps.

I run up the steps and I'm not apposed to look at the men but I do cos they're still shouting and I think they can't be friends with each other cos you're not apposed to shout at your friends or hurt them.

Mummy gets to the top and she pushes her bottom against the big outside door and it pushes open and then we're inside and the big outside door bangs shut and all the shouting noise and the busy-rushy street noise goes more quiet.

Mummy goes backwards up the stairs, pulling Toby's buggy, and I go forwards cos only grown-ups are allowed to go backwards on stairs and Mummy is huffing and puffing and it's a shame Shiny-Head Man's not here today cos sometimes he helps Mummy carry Toby's buggy up the stairs if he's going up to his house at the same time as us and that's a nice thing to do and I'm thinking about those two men being horrible outside and I say, 'We've got nice friends, haven't we, Mummy?'

Mummy stops pulling and looks at me and she says, 'Do we?' And I say, 'Yes, our friends are really nice and helpful and they don't shout at us or hurt us.'

Mummy starts pulling the buggy up again and she says, 'Who do you think our friends are?' I skip up the steps and I say, 'What's the man who's got the shiny head called?' and Mummy says, 'Leon?' and I say, 'Yes, Leon and Kali and Ade and Nandini and . . .' I stop and I think about Emma being smiley and winky today and I say, 'Is Emma our friend too?'

Mummy's at the top of the steps and she pushes Toby's buggy round the corner to the flat bit and she crouches down and says, 'Jesika, these people aren't really our friends, you know.'

I say, 'Why not?'

Mummy shakes her head and says, 'They're just . . . very kind people who like to help others.'

Mummy stands up and pushes Toby round to the next stairs and then she pulls Toby up, bump, bump, bump.

I say, 'But they're not our friends?' and I'm sad cos I want Leon and Kali and Ade and Nandini and Emma (when she's smiling) to be my friends.

Mummy stops at the top of the stairs again and she's huffing and puffing and she does some slow breathing and then she says, 'Friends are people who you meet up with and spend lots of time talking or playing with. They do nice things for you because they like you and they want to, not because they feel sorry for you. You can trust them to help you if you have a problem, anytime, anywhere. You can't trust someone just because they give you a sticker or a jam sandwich or magic a strawberry out of your ear. Do you understand?'

I don't understand. Mummy pushes Toby round to the last stairs. I think and think about who my real friends are who I talk and play with all the time. Mummy bumps Toby up the last stairs, bump, bump, bump. I talk and play with Mummy and Toby all the time. And I play with lots of different children at preschool, cept when they don't want to play, so maybe they're not my friends cos they don't play with me all of the time. I did play with Paige a lot today. Maybe she's my friend now. But not Daddy or Bab-bab cos I don't talk to them or play with them any more. Is that right?

Mummy says, 'Jesika, keep up, please.' I run and catch up and I say, 'So, you and Toby are my friends? And is Paige my friend too? Have I got' – I hold up my fingers – 'one, two, three friends?'

Mummy pulls Toby up the last step and she pushes the buggy round to our front door and she says, 'Well, me and Toby are your family, really.'

Mummy fights the door open and I say, 'So we're not friends?'

Mummy pushes her shoulder against the door and gives it a big bump and it bangs open and she says, 'Well, yes, we are. Family means the most special kind of friends. But the friends you mean are the friends that you don't live with.'

We all go in and I say, 'So, Paige is a friend I don't live with and you and Toby are special friends I do live with?'

Mummy says, 'Yes,' and she fights the door shut again and I think about Bab-bab and Daddy cos they're in our family too but they don't live with us and I don't talk or play with them any more and I say, 'What sort of friends is Bab-bab and Daddy?'

But Mummy says, 'Coat and shoes off, Jesika,' so I don't think she heard me and she unclips Toby from his buggy and takes off his coat and shoes and he runs over to the box of bricks and tips them all over the floor and me and Mummy say, 'Oh, Toby!' at the same time cos Toby's always doing this.

Mummy hangs all our drippy coats on the chairs at the big table and then she goes into the bathroom and she comes out and she's rubbing a towel into her hair and she sits down on the sofa and she's looking at me and her face is sad and she blows out a breath and it makes her lips wobble and I think her eyes are stingy cos she keeps blinking them fast and fast.

I say, 'What's wrong, Mummy?'

Mummy shakes her head fast and pulls her phone out of her trouser pocket and then a piece of paper out of her other pocket.

I say, 'What's that, Mummy?'

Mummy says, 'It's the phone number that Ryan, Paige's Uncle, gave me.' And she holds the phone in one hand and the piece of paper in the other hand and she's biting her lip.

I say, 'Why are you just holding it?'

Mummy blows out another breath and her lips aren't so wobbly this time and she says, 'I think I'm going to send him a message. He's right: we do all need friends. You need friends. I'm going to send him a message,' and she taps her phone lots of times quick and quick with her finger.

5

NOISES ARE ACTUALLY *waves.* Not waves that you can see at the beach, *invibisle* waves that go from the noise into your ear. That's what Nina and the New Rons says on CBeebies.

Mummy shouts, 'Ten minutes until tea-time!' from the kitchen and I switch CBeebies off cos Nina's finished and it's Grandpa's Shrinking Cap now and I don't like that.

The thump-da-thump-da-thump music is louder when the telly is off. I press my ear to the floor cos that's where the music is and now the music is loud and the carpet tickles my ear when the music goes thump. I think about why the music is making the carpet tickle my ear and I think music is noise so it must be going to my ear in the invibisle waves and maybe invibisle waves are tickly.

I skip to the kitchen and I say, 'Mummy, do you know why the thumpy music makes the carpet tickle my ear?'

Mummy's face goes frowny and she says, 'Jesika, have you been listening through the floor again?'

I forgotted I'm not allowed to do that.

Mummy says, 'That's someone else's private house and it's rude to listen into other people's houses.'

It's funny thinking our floor is also a ceiling. Mummy keeps saying we have to be careful not to bang about on it too much cos it'll be very noisy below but that's just silly cos it's already noisy below.

Mummy keeps stirring with one hand and the other one is

holding Toby against her side and she's jiggling with the music cos that means Toby won't cry but he's still coughing lots.

I say, 'What's for tea? Is it pasta? Pasta's my *fayvrit*!'

Mummy nods her head and jiggles at the same time and her earring swings and jiggles too, but not the other one cos she's taken it out and put it on the worktop probly cos Toby's been grabbing it again and she says, 'Pasta-peppers-carrots, onions-and-peas, mix in the tomatoes, and grate a bit of cheese,' and it's like she's speaking a song to go with the thump-da-thump music.

I say, 'Why can't I?'

Mummy stops jiggling Toby and he starts crying.

'Why can't you what?'

'Listen on the floor.'

Toby cries and cries and Mummy jiggles and stirs and she says, 'Because you might be listening to things I don't want you to hear.'

I say, 'What things?'

Mummy says, 'Just . . .' then she huffs out a breath, 'Do as you're told, Jesika, *please*.' And then she jiggles and stirs but I don't think she's doing it proply this time cos Toby won't stop crying.

I go and pick up Baby Annabelle and jiggle her about and she keeps crying too so I lay her down and rock her in my arms and she goes to sleep straight away, not like Toby who has to be picked up and rocked and put down and picked up and rocked and put down til Mummy gets tired arms and a tired voice. Sometimes I'm asleep afore Toby and I'm a big girl and he's only a baby.

Mummy walks into the living room with two bowls and puts them on the table and Toby is running all wobbly ahind her and he pats his high chair with his hands and says, 'Up, up!' and Mummy lifts him into his chair and I climb on my grown-up girl's chair with the cushion so I can reach the table.

I look in my bowl and I say, 'Mummy, you are silly, you

forgotted the melty cheese on top!' I laugh but Mummy doesn't laugh. She sits next to Toby and wipes her hands down her face and she says, 'We don't have any cheese.'

I say, 'But you said "grate a bit of cheese",' and Mummy puts some pasta on Toby's spoon and holds it out to him cos he's learning how to use a spoon but he still needs help and Mummy's making her what-do-you-mean face and I say, 'You *did*! When you did the pasta song, you said "grate a bit of cheese".'

Toby pushes Mummy's hand away that's holding the spoon and Mummy holds it up to his mouth but he turns his head away and she says, 'Come on, Toby, just a little bit. You'll feel much better,' and I say, 'You *did*, Mummy!' And Mummy says, 'Yes, I did say that, didn't I, but then I looked in the fridge and there wasn't any cheese.'

I say, 'Did you forget to buy it from the shops?'

Mummy shakes her head and tries to push the spoon up to Toby's mouth again and says, 'No, I didn't forget, I didn't realize we'd run out,' and I say, 'Can we go and get some now?' Mummy huffs a breath out and says, 'We're not going now, Jesika. It's teatime.' She pushes the spoon at Toby's mouth again.

I don't *like* my pasta without melty cheese. I push my bowl away and say, 'I don't want it,' and I stare at Mummy hard and make my face cross.

Mummy says, 'Fine. Go hungry, then,' and she's not actually looking at me cos she's still trying to get Toby to open his mouth and I say, 'Toby won't eat it cos it's not got melty cheese.'

Now Mummy's looking at me hard and cross and she says, 'Well, maybe he *would* eat it if he sees his big sister eat it. Come on, Jesika, I need your help with this.'

But I don't *want* my pasta without melty cheese so I fold my arms and screw my mouth up like Toby's and make my face even more cross. Toby laughs at my face and then he's coughing and crying and then he sneezes and coughs at the same time and a big, green bogie shoots right out of his nose and right onto Mummy's hand and it's so funny that I forget my cross face and laugh and laugh and laugh.

BANG!

'JUST EAT YOUR BLOODY PASTA!'

eyes-open-scary-wide-heart-thumping-burning-hot-hot-HOT—

'YOU'RE ALWAYS SHOUTING! I *HATE* YOU!'

Mummy's mouth is open and Toby's mouth is open and all I can hear in my ears is THUMP-THUMP-THUMP-THUMP but it's not the music through the floor it's my heart and it's going to burst right out of my head.

Mummy pushes her chair back not carefully at all and it goes BANG! on the floor and she shouts, 'Find yourself a new Mummy who doesn't shout, then!' And her eyes are wet and her mouth is a funny shape and then she runs into the kitchen where I can't see her but I can hear her coughing and coughing.

I don't want to find a new Mummy.

Toby's looking at me and I don't think he wants to find a new Mummy either cos his lips are wobbling just like mine and then me and Toby are crying and crying cept now Toby's coughing too and I think it must be hard to cough and cry at the same time cos Toby's breathing hard like when I run up the stairs fast like a cheetah and his face is going red like a tomato and then Mummy runs back through and her face is red too and her cheeks are all wet and she pulls Toby out of his high chair and she takes him into the bathroom and pushes the door shut and then it's just me sitting at the table.

Toby doesn't have to find a new Mummy.

Just me cos I shouted.

Maybe they're going to hide in the bathroom til I've gone and found one.

I can hear Toby coughing and Mummy coughing and now there's also the splashy-wooshy-water sound which means it's bathtime but that's strange cos we haven't finished tea and we haven't done playing so why is Mummy doing bathtime now? I run to the bathroom door and I bang my hands on it and I shout, 'I DON'T WANT TO FIND A NEW MUMMY!'

The door opens and Mummy's standing right there and she says, 'What's all the shouting about? And why are you banging on the door? Why don't you just open it?'

I run forwards and wrap my arms tight and tight around Mummy's legs and I need to tell her that I don't want to find a new Mummy but I can't stop crying.

Mummy says, 'Oh, for goodness' sake, Jesika!' and she pulls me into the bathroom and closes the door again. Toby's standing up against the bath with no clothes on and he's bouncing his bottom up and down and saying, 'In, in, in, in!' so Mummy lifts him into the bath and then she kneels down and puts her arms around me in a great big cuddle and I cuddle her tight and tight and tight and all my crying stops. I don't ever *never* want to let go, but then Mummy says I can get in the bath too so I take off all my clothes and get into the bath, and when I sit down the water goes up the sides of the bath and gets too near the leaky crack and I shout, 'Leaky crack, Mummy!' and Mummy pulls the plug out so the water goes back down a little bit.

All the room is smoky and I say, 'Mummy, you forgotted to put the buzzy fan on to suck out the smoke,' cos we always, always have the buzzy fan on even though it makes a horrid noise cos there isn't a window in the bathroom and Mummy says it's not good to leave the smoke in the room.

Mummy smiles again and says, 'It's steam, Jesika, not smoke, and it's good for Toby's chest, and good for mine too. Look, we've both stopped coughing.'

We stay in the bath a long-a-long time cos Mummy says she wants Toby to breathe in lots and lots of steam afore he goes to bed to help him go to sleep and we do lots of splashing and laughing and Mummy says she wishes she could put all the laughing into a bottle and then when she's feeling sad she can open the bottle and all the laughing would fill up the room.

After, Mummy sits on the sofa with Toby on her knee so she can give him his bedtime milk and that remembers me that I'm very hungry and I go and sit at the table and I eat up all my pasta fast and fast even afore Toby's finished his milk and it's YUMMY.

When Toby's in bed, it's my turn to cuddle with Mummy and I run over to the books and pick one of my fayvrit Tilly books and Mummy's fairy-tale book and take them to Mummy on the sofa. Her head is flopped right back and her eyes are closed and I giggle and say, 'Wake up, Mummy, it's not bedtime, it's story time!' and I drop the two books on Mummy's knee and jump up on the sofa next to her and cuddle into her side.

Mummy opens her eyes and yawns and yawns and puts her arm around me and I cuddle Mummy tight and tight, and Mummy says, 'I don't always shout, do I?'

I say, 'You do shout quite a lot.'

Mummy's lips are pressed tight and tight like she's about to be cross and my belly squeezes. I don't want Mummy to be cross again. She might remember about sending me away to look for a new Mummy. I say, 'But only a little bit.'

Mummy opens her mouth and it's all wobbly and she presses it tight shut again and now my heart's thumping hard and I squeeze my thumb and my finger together and I say, 'Only a teeny-tiny bit.'

Mummy laughs and coughs and says, 'I'll try harder not to shout, OK?' Then she says quiet as quiet, 'It was Bab-bab's birthday today.'

I say, 'Do you still have birthdays after you die?'

Mummy says, 'I suppose you do if the people in your family think about you on your birthday.'

I say, 'I'm thinking about Bab-bab now so that means she's having her birthday,' and I smile and smile and Mummy smiles too and then I say, 'And if I think about Daddy on his birthday, he can have his birthday too.'

Mummy stops smiling and she says, 'Yes, he can have his birthday too.'

I say, 'Or maybe he might come back for his birthday cos he's not dead like Bab-bab, is he? He might come back for a surprise.'

Mummy says, 'Poppet, I don't think . . .' She stops and strokes her hand down my hair. 'I don't know what your Daddy will do, but can we talk about it another day? Is that OK?' I say, 'That's OK,' cos Mummy gets cross when she talks about Daddy and I don't want Mummy to be cross.

Mummy says, 'There's something else we do need to talk about,' and her voice is saying listen-to-me-Jesika and I look at Mummy's face and it's saying listen-to-me as well and Mummy says, 'Well, two things, actually.'

She stops and waits and I say, 'What is it, Mummy?'

Mummy sits up a bit and holds both my hands and says, 'OK, first. Did you tell Stella that I pushed you against the TV this morning?'

I don't know what Mummy means and I wrinkle up my nose and then Mummy touches her fingers gentle on my head and it hurts and I remember about drawing tadpoles and Mummy being cross and I say, 'You didn't push me, you pulled me and the telly hitted me.'

Mummy blows out a breath and says, 'Did you tell Stella that?'

I say, 'I told her the telly hitted me cos you pulled me too hard.'

Mummy blows out another breath and says, 'Jesika, you know

I didn't mean the telly to hit your head? I only meant to pull you out of the way. It was an accident.'

I say, 'I know. Can we do stories now?'

Mummy says, 'Wait a minute, there's something else. Why did you bite Stella? That's not really something you can do by accident.'

My face goes hot and hot and I don't want to look at Mummy cos she's going to be so so cross with me and shouty and I don't want her to be shouty again and—

'Jesika.'

Mummy's fingers are under my chin and she's lifting my face up so I have to look at her and I don't want to look at her and Mummy says, 'Jesika, look at me,' and then, 'Jesika, why did you bite her?'

I know I bited Stella, and I know Kali told me about not biting, but I don't know why I bited. I say, 'I've forgotted.'

Mummy says, 'Stella told me you were trying to run out of pre-school? She said she was trying to stop you?'

I did try to run out of preschool. I was running to Mummy cos the zip bited my chin and I hitted Mummy and Mummy was going away and not coming back cos I didn't say sorry and Stella wouldn't let me go back and she pulled and pulled and . . . *Oh!*

I say, 'Stella hurted me and she didn't even say sorry!'

Mummy says, 'She *hurt* you?'

I say, 'She was holding me and squeezing.' I squeeze my arm with my hand to show Mummy what I mean. 'And it hurted and she wouldn't let go.'

Mummy says, 'So you bit her?'

I say, 'No, I bit her and then she hurted me. And Kali said I had to say sorry but Stella didn't even have to say sorry!'

Mummy says, 'But why did you bite her?'

My skin feels hot and spiky all over and I can't stop wriggling and I say, 'I've *forgotted*! It was an *accident*!'

Mummy puts her hands on my shoulders and strokes them

60

down my arms and the wriggly inside me goes away and she says, 'OK, it's just . . . sometimes it's OK to bite and I want to know if this was one of the OK times.'

I say, 'But Kali said I shouldn't ever never bite and I have to do my big STOP IT voice next time.'

Mummy says, 'Yes, Kali's right. You always use your big voice first. But if that doesn't work and you feel trapped and scared and in danger, biting is OK. Do you understand?'

I say, 'But it's not OK to bite and kick and hit someone for other times cos that's naughty.'

Mummy nods and says, 'Exactly.' Then she says, 'But I think Stella made you feel trapped. Because you were trying to run out and she wouldn't let go.'

I remember Stella not letting go.

Mummy says, 'Can you remember why you were trying to run out?'

I'm thinking again about the zip biting and hitting Mummy and Mummy going away all cross and never coming back.

I press my face into Mummy's side and I breathe her smell and she strokes my hair.

Mummy says, 'Tell me, Jesika.'

My belly hurts.

I can't tell Mummy. I don't want Mummy to remember about sending me to find a new Mummy. I don't want a new Mummy. I want my Mummy.

Mummy says, 'Jesika, you can tell me anything. I won't be cross.'

I shake my head side to side and Mummy's soft jumper tickles my nose.

Mummy strokes my hair some more and then she says, 'OK. We'll leave it for tonight. You need a good night's sleep. Come on.' And she moves me away, puts the books on the floor and stands up, holding her hands out to me.

I look at the books and I say, 'What about stories?'

Mummy says, 'Not tonight, Jesika. It's sleep you need, not stories.'

My lips wobble and my eyes sting and they go blink, blink, blink, blink and I say, 'But Mummy, you said . . .'

Mummy says, 'I know, Jesika, but it's been a very long day and it's already past your bedtime.'

I say, 'But Mummy . . .'

Mummy squeezes her fingers on her nose and closes her eyes and says, 'You need to go to bed.' She opens her eyes. 'I need you to go to bed.'

I think she might be remembering.

I don't want to find a new Mummy.

I stand up and hold Mummy's hand and we creep into the dark bedroom.

6

I'M APPOSED TO be asleep. There's a stripe of night-orange on the wall and it's moving side to side and my eyes are moving side to side following it. Why is it moving? I twist my head round and look at the window and the curtain is moving side to side too. Maybe the curtain is pushing the night-orange side to side when it moves. But I don't know why the curtain's moving.

The rain on the window goes SPLAT! SPLAT! SPLAT! and I can hear the cars and the buses and the lorries whizzing past outside with a swish-ROAR-swish and there's people shouting and banging doors and the thump-da-thump-da-thump music is below and above and other places too and all at different times.

I curl up under my covers to get warm and tickle my finger round and round on the inside of my hand and I whisper the moon words that Mummy says at bedtime, cept I keep getting them muddled. Mummy didn't say them tonight. Tonight she said, 'Night-night, sleep tight, and don't let the bed bugs bite.' That's Daddy's bedtime words. He always did tickly nips, pretending his fingers were the bed bugs, and sometimes Mummy would get cross cos Daddy was making me too giggly for bed, but he's not done it for a long-a-long time cos he went away and stopped being my Daddy.

Bab-bab went away too. She didn't mean to, it was cos her heart stopped working.

If Mummy goes far away too, it'll just be me and Toby, cept Mummy will take Toby with her, so it'll just be me, and then I'll have to find a new Mummy.

Now there's new music and it's nearer than all the thumpy music. It's floaty and shivery and it's coming from the living room. I push back the covers and my feet reach down to the floor and the carpet is scratchy on my toes and the air is shivery-cold and I know night-orange means stay-in-bed-time but the music is telling me to come and listen.

I put my dressing gown on and creep over to the bedroom door and kneel down on the carpet and push Mummy's dressing gown to the side so I can peep through the jaggy hole in the wood. The light from the living room is hurty-bright on my eyes and I shut them tight but I keep my ears open and the music fills them up and it tells me to lift my arms up above my head and pretend I'm a ballerina.

Now Mummy's singing with the lady in the music and I open my eyes a teeny-tiny crack and I can see a shape in the living room moving about. I open my eyes a little bit more and a little bit more and the shape is Mummy and she's turning and swaying all slow in the space atween the sofa and the eating table just like a beautiful ballerina, and her hair is twirling and floating, and she's singing, not like the singing she does with me and Toby when we all end up giggling but beautiful, shivery, whispery singing. I didn't know my Mummy could be so beautiful.

BANG! BANG! BANG!

Mummy stops dancing and stops singing. She's looking at the door but she's not opening it. Why isn't she opening it?

BANG! BANG! BANG! BANG!

A voice is shouting and then the letterhole flaps and snaps and then stays open and the voice is loud in the letterhole shouting, 'Open the door, Tina! I've not got all fucking night!'

I can't hear the shivery music now. Mummy moves fast round the sofa to the door and she's not a floaty ballerina any more cos she bumps into everything on her way past and she's coughing and coughing and then she's fighting the door open and the door makes a CRACK! when she opens it and ahind me Toby cries but just one cry, not lots and lots, and that means he might still be sleeping.

I crawl over the scratchy carpet and peep through the stripy bars of his cot. He's lying on his back and his eyes are shut and he's got his arms right up above his head and his hands are tight like fighting fists and I think maybe he's having a dream about fighting a dragon or a tiger or a monster. It's good he's not actually awake cos he doesn't like going back to sleep again.

I crawl back to the hole in the door and peep through again and Mummy's giving something to a man. I know that man! Mummy says he's the Money Man cos he's always asking for more and more money so me and Mummy and Toby can keep living here. Money's the same thing as pennies cept it's maked out of paper. Sometimes the Money Man comes here so Mummy can give him the paper and sometimes we have to walk all the way to the house where the Pirate Lady was today.

The man says, 'Is that it?' and his big, hairy eyebrows squash right together.

Mummy is saying something but I can't see her face and I can't hear the words. The man's face goes even meaner. He pushes it right up to Mummy's face and says, 'You think you've got a fucking choice?'

Then his face changes. He smiles and steps forward and puts one of his arms right round Mummy and he's stroking it up and down her back like Mummy does to me and Toby when we're crying. He's whispering something right in Mummy's ear. I think he's whispering, 'Sorry,' for having a mean face afore.

Mummy's twisting her face away.

Oh.

Oh!

He's squeezing Mummy's chin in one hand and pulling all Mummy's hair in his other hand. He's hurting Mummy! Mummy needs to do her Big Voice and shout, 'STOP IT!'

Mummy isn't shouting.

Why isn't she shouting?

She cries, 'Sorry! I'm sorry!'

Why is Mummy saying sorry? The Money Man has to say sorry, not Mummy.

The Money Man still hasn't let go. He's twisting and pulling and Mummy says, 'Ow! Ow!'

Stop hurting Mummy!

I stand up quick. I have to tell him to stop. Mummy's crying!

But what if he pulls my hair too?

My heart is thumping and thumping.

I'm scared.

'Oi! Stop it! Leave her alone!'

I drop back onto my knees and press my eye up to the hole. It's Next-Door Lady!

The Money Man lets go of Mummy and turns to Next-Door Lady, standing just inside our door. He walks right up to her and says something I can't hear but it must be something funny cos Next-Door Lady laughs with her mouth open wide and her laugh is like a witch's cackle. I didn't notice that afore. I don't think she brushes her teeth very good cos she's only got four or five or six teeth and they're all brown and yellow and black and there's lots of holes where her other teeth are apposed to be.

Next-Door Lady walks backwards out of our house and she's still laughing and the Money Man follows her out of the door pointing his finger like he's telling her where to go and I can't see them now but I hear the Money Man shouting and Next-Door Lady laughs and laughs and laughs.

BANG! BANG!

Oh! Mummy's slammed the door shut and she only had to bang it two times. She only does that when she's angry. She turns away from the door but I can't see if her face is angry cos she's hided it ahind her hands and she slides her back all the way down the door til her bottom bumps on the ground. She doesn't look angry.

The letterhole flaps open and Mummy drops her head down to the floor and curls up on her side. The Money Man shouts, 'I'm a generous man, Tina. You've got two days to decide how you want to pay me. Sweet dreams, darlin'.' The letterhole snaps shut.

Mummy stays curled up on the floor. Her shoulders are shaking.

She's not angry – she's crying!

I pull open the bedroom door and I run and run as fast as a cheetah and throw myself onto Mummy and hug her tight and tight and tight.

Mummy sits up and hugs me too and does lots of big breaths and wipes and wipes her face with her sleeve and then she says, 'You're supposed to be asleep!'

I say, 'I love you, Mummy.'

Mummy says, 'Was it the door banging that woke you up?'

Will Mummy be cross if I tell her I was awake all the time?

Afore I can decide, Toby coughs and coughs and then he's crying and coughing and crying and this time he's actually awake and Mummy's head drops down and she says, 'Not Toby, too,' and then we have to hurry into the bedroom and Mummy tells me to take my dressing gown off and she tucks me into the warm covers and kisses my cheek and she says, 'See if you can get back to sleep before Toby,' then she lifts Toby out of the cot and she holds him next to the window and she rocks him and pats his back and says, 'Shhh, shhh, shhh,' and Toby stops crying and Mummy's *shhh* gets quiet and quiet and she leans over the cot to put Toby back in.

BANG!

A door slams somewhere and there's people shouting and the thump-da-thump-da-thump music stops and then starts again, different and more loud. Toby's arm flings out of Mummy's cuddle and he starts coughing and crying again and Mummy has to start all over again with the rocking and the shhh-ing and she sings my fayvrit song about the beautiful tree and the green grass and that always helps me go to sleep and she sings, '. . . and on that twig, there was a nest, the most beauuuutiful nest you ever did see . . .' and I'm apposed to be asleep but I can't make myself go sleepy. I keep seeing a picture of the Money Man inside my eyes when I close them and he's pulling Mummy's hair and squeezing her chin and she's not telling him to stop.

7

EYES OPEN.

Dark.

Dark *and* quiet.

Not the quiet like when I jam my fingers in my ears and quiet-noise leaks past them so I can still hear the busy-ness and the veekles and the door-slamming and the yelling and the thump-da-thump-da-thump music. This is Real Quiet. This is Magic-*Amazing* Quiet.

I roll over and lift my head to look over Mummy's hilly bump. The clock says five – it's not Getting-Up Time unless it says seven. How much counting does it take to get from five to seven? I count one-two-three-four-five-six-seven, but the clock doesn't change. Maybe if I count to a-hundred-a-thousand-a-hundred-a-hundred, *then* it'll be seven.

I need a wee.

I push back the covers and put my feet on the floor and, ugh! It's not scratchy like it should be. It's soft and soggy and cold. I roll back onto the bed and push at Mummy's hilly bump and I say, 'Mummy, Mummy, the rainy-hater's leaked again.'

Mummy groans and coughs two times and moves a bit and says, 'Jesika, it's not morning. Back to sleep.'

I say, 'But Mummy . . .'

'Back to sleep, Jesika. Please.' Mummy's eyes aren't open cos they're not shining. I don't think Mummy's actually awake. I shake her shoulder and say, 'But Mummy!'

Mummy's head lifts up and her eyes flick open and her hand shoots out and grabs my shoulder tight.

'SHHH! Do *not* wake Toby!' Her voice hisses like a snake and then she coughs and coughs and she pushes her face into her pillow and coughs and coughs some more and then Toby coughs and coughs again and then he cries and Mummy rolls over and flops onto her back and says, 'Fan-bloody-tastic.'

I make my voice whispery-quiet and say, 'But Mummy, the chewy-gum's gone hard again and the rainy-hater's leaked all over the floor and the carpet's all soggy and it's maked my feet wet and I need a wee.'

After we've got up and got dressed and had toast and milk and Mummy's fixed the rainy-hater with more chewy-gum, I help Toby build tall towers with the bricks, but he keeps knocking them down afore I'm finished so I go and play with Baby Annabelle instead. I change her clothes and tuck her into the pram and we go for a long walk through the jungle. There's lots of trees in the jungle and monkeys and snakes and rabbits and tigers. Oh! There's a tiger! Quick, hide!

Mummy says, 'Jesika, that was my foot!'

I peep out from under the table. Mummy is leaning down and she's holding a piece of toast and she points it at the sofa and she says, 'Go and play over there, please.'

I say, 'But I'm hiding from the tiger.'

Mummy says, 'And you can hide over there. Let me finish my breakfast, poppet. I won't be long.'

But Mummy is long cos after she's finished eating she still sits at the table and she puts her head down on her arms and she sits there for a long-a-long time and I can't find anywhere to hide from the tiger and it's not fair.

Beep-beep. Beep-beep.

I say, 'What was that?' and Mummy's head comes up fast and she yawns and rubs her eyes and pulls her phone out of her pocket and she looks at it and she says, 'Someone's sent me a text,' and now she's smiling and she's pressing buttons on her phone and then the phone beeps again and her smile is a bit bigger.

I say, 'What's a text?'

Mummy says, 'It's a message on my phone.'

I say, 'Who's the message from?' But Mummy doesn't answer me cos she's too busy smiling and pressing buttons on her phone and her phone beeps and beeps and beeps. She's getting a lot of messages. Then she stands up quick, pushing her chair back and says, 'Time to get going.'

I say, 'Where are we going?'

Mummy says, 'We're going on a bus!'

I say, 'On a bus? You mean like the buses that whizz down the busy street? The buses that have an upstairs and a downstairs? A bus like that?'

Mummy smiles and nods her head and I say, 'Yeah, yeah, yeah!'

Mummy says, 'We do go on buses sometimes, Jesika. It's not that exciting.'

I say, 'It is! It is! We're going on a bus!' and I dance around the living room til Mummy gets cross cos she says she's told me five times to put my shoes on. I don't think she did cos I didn't even hear her.

When we're all ready and we're outside the door, Mummy fights the door shut and I hold Toby's buggy. Next-Door Lady puffs up the stairs and I say, 'Hello,' but she just pushes past and doesn't say anything and I open my mouth to ask Mummy why she never says hello but then Next-Door Lady is about to open her door and today I remember about the eggy-yucky smell and I take a big deep breath and hold my nose. But she doesn't open her door, she turns right round and comes back to Mummy, just as Mummy does one last bang with the door and gets it closed proply, and Next-Door Lady says, 'Leon'll fix that if you ask him.'

Mummy's mouth opens and closes and opens again but she doesn't say anything and then Next-Door Lady says, 'A good man, Leon. Does it cost price, and *he* won't ask for any extra favours. A good man.' She points above her head and says, 'Next floor. You go ask him,' and then turns round and walks back to her door saying, 'A good man. A good man,' quiet as quiet and then she opens her door and the eggy-yucky smell is all in my nose and my mouth cos I was so surprised that Next-Door Lady speaked to us that I forgotted to not breathe.

The door bangs shut and the smell gets smaller again. I say, 'What was she telling you about Leon, Mummy?'

Mummy makes a noise like a hiccup and says, 'She said I should ask Leon to fix the door.'

I say, 'I didn't know Leon did fixing.'

Mummy says, 'Nandini said I should ask him about the broken window too but . . .' She scrunches up her face and shakes her head quick and says, 'I've already given Darren money towards fixing it. I can't afford to pay twice.' She puts her hands on her hips and stares at Next-Door Lady's door and shakes her head again and I say, 'Is Darren the Money Man?' but then Toby shouts, 'Out! Out! Out!' and pushes himself against his straps and we have to bump quick as quick down all the stairs cos now he's crying and shouting and making so much noise and we have to rush out into the busy street afore someone comes out of one of the doors and shouts scary words at us.

We have to stand in a line at the bus stop and I'm jumping up and down cos I'm so excited we're going on a bus.

Mummy says, 'Stand still, Jesika, it's too busy for jumping

around,' but I can't stop wriggling cos I can't wait to go upstairs on the bus.

After ages of waiting, the bus comes and everyone's squashing and Mummy tells me to go in front of her so she can lift Toby's buggy on and I step on and it's so squashy with legs, I can't see where the stairs are and I'm pushing my head past all the legs to have a better look.

'I SAID YOU CAN'T COME ON WITH THAT!'

The Driver Lady looks very cross.

Mummy says, 'But it says you take buggies. On the front. It's got the buggy and wheelchair sticker.'

The Driver Lady points at all the people squashed on the bus and says, 'When there's space, Madam. You'll have to wait for the next bus.'

Mummy says, 'Will there be space on the next one?'

The Driver Lady looks out of her front window and says, 'I have no idea, Madam,' and she waves her hand at the door.

'Excuse me!'

There's a man squeezing past people to the front of the bus and I know this man! He's the man that took Paige home, but not her Daddy, her . . . something else.

He says, 'There's room in the buggy space, if everyone squashes up a little.'

I say, 'Mummy, what's that man called?'

But when I look at Mummy, she's not looking at me, she's looking at the man and she's smiling at him.

The man walks up the bus and he says, 'SQUASH UP. COME ON EVERYONE, MOVE UP A BIT,' and Mummy says, 'Follow Ryan, Jesika,' and that's what he's called. Ryan. I remember that now!

I follow Ryan and Mummy comes after with Toby in the buggy and people are squeezing up against the sides and then the whole bus shakes and starts moving and people are falling towards me and I'm falling backwards cept there's a push on my back and a pull on my arm and I'm standing on my feet again. A lady next to me huffs and says, 'She could have waited just another minute.'

It's hard to walk on the bus now cos when it drives on the road it's all wobbly but there's lots of helpful hands holding me and smiley faces and voices that say, 'There you go,' and 'Almost there,' and 'Careful, lovey.'

Ryan is the last person to hold his hand out for me and he pulls me over to a seat and then Mummy is standing next to me with the buggy and everyone is smiling cept Toby who pushes against his straps and shouts, 'Out! Out! Out!' Then the bus does a great big bounce and Toby's eyes go so wide and he stops shouting.

The bus bumps and bounces along the road and I look at all the houses and shops bumping up and down out of the window. I didn't know buses were so bumpy. Bumpy like a kangaroo, but loud and roary like a lion. A kangaroolion!

I say, 'Mummy, this bus is actually a kangaroolion,' but the bus is roaring and Mummy doesn't hear me and she keeps talking to Ryan and Ryan's talking too and I can't hear what they're talking about cos the kangaroolion bus is too bouncy and roary. Then the bus stops and more people get on and off and I can hear Ryan talking and he says, 'So what made you move away from there? Sounds like you had a nice place.'

Mummy lifts her shoulders up and down and says, 'The bed-room tax. Magda died, and we suddenly had a spare room.'

Ryan says, 'But couldn't they move you to a smaller flat?'

Mummy says, 'There weren't any to move to. I didn't have Alex's wages, my benefits didn't cover it and I couldn't work to earn more because Magda had been my childcare. Then Toby was born so it was impossible anyway. I was completely stuck.'

I say, 'Toby was born in the bath when I was sleeping, wasn't he, Mummy?'

Ryan's eyebrows shoot up to his hair and he says, 'Wow, was he?'

Mummy makes a funny cross face at me and says, 'Thanks for sharing that, Jesika,' but I don't think she's actually cross cos when Ryan laughs Mummy laughs too.

Ryan says, 'But Alex, he pays maintenance, doesn't he? Did that not help?'

Mummy says, 'He should, but he doesn't. And how do you chase someone living in Poland? He ignores my texts and I can't afford to keep phoning him. And does he really care? He left me with a toddler and a baby on the way, he completely blanked us at Magda's funeral . . .' Mummy presses her hand on her mouth.

Ryan says, 'I'm so sorry.' Then he says, 'So how did you get out of it?'

Mummy rubs her forehead and says, 'I looked all round for a private rent and the only one I could afford was here. Seemed like the right decision at the time, because I grew up here and I know the area, and I thought I could cope with the flat being a bit of a dump, but . . .'

The bus roars and bounces forwards and my belly jumps up and down inside me and I can't hear what Mummy and Ryan are saying now cos it's too noisy again.

The bus stops and starts lots and lots of times and after a long-a-long time Mummy says, 'Our stop next,' and the bus stops and it's much easier getting off the bus cos it's not squashy like when we got on. Mummy tells me to walk with Ryan to the front of the bus and she pushes Toby out ahind us.

We walk past the stairs that go up to the top and we forgotted all about going upstairs and I say, 'We didn't go upstairs! Can I go and look? I want to see what it looks like!'

Mummy says, 'Not now, Jesika, we have to get off the bus.

We'll go upstairs another time. Maybe one day when Toby's not in the buggy any more.'

I say, 'But that'll take ages!' and my foot stamps hard and hard, cos Toby's only a baby and he has to do a lot of growing afore he's not in the buggy.

Mummy says, 'Jesika, come on, you need to move.'

I say, 'I *want* to go up*stairs*!' My foot stamps again.

Ryan says, 'Hey, Jesika, have you seen the golden postbox?' He waves me towards him with his hand and points out of the door of the bus.

My foot stamps again and I say, 'That's *silly*,' cos postboxes are red, not golden.

Ryan says, 'Come on, I'll show you,' and I follow him and step down onto the pavement and Ryan points over to the side and says, 'There. See?'

Oh! It really is golden! I run over to it and stroke it with my fingers and it's smooth and cold and I can see teeny-tiny sparkles all over it and I say, 'Why is it golden?'

Ryan says, 'It means someone who lives near here won a gold medal for a race.'

I say, 'Wow!' cos gold medals are special, and I say, 'Was it an egg and spoon race?' cos I like the egg and spoon race and I was the only person not to drop my plastic egg when we did our races at preschool afore the big holidays.

Nobody answers and I look round and Ryan and Mummy are talking again and Ryan says, 'You know where you're going?'

Mummy says, 'Yes, thanks.'

Ryan says, 'And you know what you're going to say?'

Mummy says, 'I think so.'

Ryan says, 'And you'll text me after? Let me know when you're ready to head back? I should be less than an hour.'

Mummy says, 'OK.'

I say, 'Where are we going?'

Ryan says, 'You're going to find out if you can get a new house!'

I make my eyes and my mouth go wide and wide and I say, 'A new house?'

Mummy frowns and says, 'Ryan, I wasn't . . .' and Ryan says, 'Oh, sorry, maybe I shouldn't have said that,' and now Mummy smiles and she says, 'It's fine, don't worry. I'll let you know how we get on.'

Ryan waves his hand and walks away and I say, 'Where's Ryan going?'

Mummy says, 'He's going to give blood.'

I say, 'Give blood?'

Mummy says, 'He's having some blood taken out of his body and given to someone who's poorly and needs new blood to make them better.'

I say, 'How do they take his blood out?'

Mummy says, 'You can ask him all about it later. Come on, we have to get going.'

Mummy turns Toby's buggy round and I say, 'Are we really getting a new house?'

Mummy says, 'We're going to talk to someone about it, but we might not get one.'

The place we have to go to talk to someone about a new house is a huge, giant*nor*mous tower and it's got a special door to go in that you walk into and you push it round and round and sometimes people come right back out to the front again and I want to go in the round-and-round door and I bet Toby wants to as well cept Toby's buggy won't fit and he's asleep, so a man has to open a normal door next to the round-and-round door.

I say, 'Please can I go in the round-and-round door? Please? Please?'

Mummy's smiling and smiling and she says, 'Go on quickly, then.'

So Mummy pushes Toby through the side door and I go in the round-and-round door and it's easy to push and I keep going round and round and round, inside and outside and inside and outside, and I'm giggling and giggling cos every time I come past inside, Mummy pretends she's trying to grab me but I go past too quickly and her laugh zooms away and near and away and near.

Then Mummy does grab me and she pulls me hard and it hurts and Mummy's not laughing now.

The man who opened the normal door isn't smiling or laughing. He says, 'I've just told your Mum – it's not a toy, young lady.'

Mummy's cross. She tugs my hurty arm and says, 'Come on, Jesika,' but I pull my arm back and say, 'Ow! You're hurting me!'

Mummy lets go and says, 'It's time to go. Now.'

I don't want to go. I want to play the round-and-round game again. It's not fair.

Mummy says, 'I'm going now, Jesika,' and then she turns round, and she's pushing Toby's buggy so so fast, I think she's actually leaving me ahind!

I shout, 'Wait, Mummy! Wait! Come back!' But Mummy keeps walking fast away from me and I run and run even more fast til I'm right next to Toby's buggy and I hold onto it cos then Mummy can't walk away without me.

We get to a shiny metal door and Mummy pokes a button next to it, hard like the Driver Lady on the bus, and she's just staring at the doors and not saying anything. I think she's still cross that I went round and round in the door too many times.

The metal doors slide open and it's a lift like the one we used to have in the place we lived afore with Daddy and Bab-bab. We step inside and Mummy pokes another button and the doors slide shut.

I say, 'I wish we had a lift in our house now, like where we used to live.'

Mummy's head turns fast and then my belly goes WHOOSH! and I hold it tight and I say, 'Oooh! I've left my belly ahind!' and Mummy crouches down and she smiles so big and she says, 'You used to say that every time we went in the lift, do you remember?'

I think about the place we used to live and there's lots of pictures in my head, whizzing past so fast, and then I see one that I like a lot and I say, 'I watched the trains with Bab-bab from high up in the air.'

Mummy puts her hand on my cheek and she says, 'Yes, you did.'

I say, 'But then Bab-bab's heart stopped working and we had to go and live in our new house cos you didn't have enough pennies to pay for Bab-bab's bedroom.'

Mummy says, 'Yes, yes, we did. That's right.' And then she's squeezing me tight and tight til there's a bump under my feet and the doors open and it's time to get out of the lift.

We walk into a huge room and Mummy says it's a waiting room and it has windows that touch the ceiling and the floor and lots of shiny, red chairs and people sitting on them and waiting and being noisy and at the front there's people sitting at tables.

Mummy pulls a piece of paper out of a machine and we go and sit down. I sit on the chair next to Mummy. It's very hard and my bottom keeps sliding down. I put Baby Annabelle on the chair next to me and her bottom slides down too and she falls onto the floor and the carpet is all swirly like a whirlpool. I lean over on my belly and grab Baby Annabelle out of the whirlpool just afore she gets sucked under but now a shark's leaping out of the water and snapping his sharp teeth. SNAP! SNAP! But it's OK cos I'm holding Baby Annabelle and she's safe, cept now my bottom's sliding down again. Oh no! Watch out, Baby Annabelle, the shark's trying to get us again! Hold on tight . . .

'Jesika, sit on the chair properly!'

Mummy looks cross. And then she doesn't look cross and she says, 'It's boring waiting, isn't it?'

I say, 'When will it be our turn?'

Mummy says, 'Soon.'

I say, 'When is it soon?'

Mummy says, 'I don't know, Jesika. Not too long, I hope.'

A man and a lady get up and walk to the tables at the front.

I say, 'Is it their turn?'

Mummy says, 'Yes.'

I say, 'Is it our turn next?'

Mummy says, 'Jesika . . .' and then she coughs and coughs and I rub her back and when she's finished coughing she says, 'Soon. It'll be our turn soon.'

It's our turn when a number machine on the wall beeps and shows the number on Mummy's paper and flashes an arrow on and off and on and off so we know which table to go to. At the table, there's a lady sitting on the other side and she's got a computer and lots of bits of paper and pens in a tub and next to the table on the floor there's a little tree in a pot. I didn't know you could grow trees in a pot inside. Trees usually grow outside.

The lady says, 'I hope you've not been waiting too long,' and I say, 'We've been waiting for ages and there's not even any toys to play with.'

Mummy says, 'Jesika!' and I think she's going to be cross but the lady laughs and says, 'I keep saying we should have toys but Management think they'll be more trouble than they're worth. What do they know, eh? Now, how can I help you today?'

Mummy starts telling the lady all about our dump flat and the broken things but I've just spotted something more interesting. I slide off my chair and crouch down next to the little tree cos there's a teeny-tiny spider swinging down on a long, long spider-string all the way from the leaf at the top and I think it's trying to reach the floor. I don't know if the spider can make enough string to get all the way to the floor cos the tree is bigger than my head and the spider's only tiny and what if he runs out of spider-string afore he gets to the bottom? Then he'll be stuck just swinging about. I hold my hand out and the spider lands on my hand and it starts running all over my hand and it's so tiny and I can't even feel it tickling. I put my hand right next to the floor so it can run onto the floor but it keeps running the wrong way and—

'I just want somewhere SAFE!'

My body and my hand jumps and the spider's gone. I can't see it anywhere and I think it must be hurt falling out of my hand but then I see it running fast and fast under the table.

The House Lady says, 'I understand, but you have to meet specific criteria . . .'

I sit back on the chair and I want to hold Mummy's hand but she's got them both curled up tight in fists on her lap.

Mummy says, 'I'm a single mum with two children under five, my youngest keeps getting ill because of the conditions we're living in, and that's before I list all the dangers in the flat. I can't afford anywhere better, not with the benefit cap. And how come they don't put a cap on rent too? How is that fair? I mean, how much more desperate does it need to be?'

The House Lady looks sad. She says, 'You've got a roof over your head. I know it doesn't seem it, but according to the criteria, that makes you a lot less desperate than some. You've got a roof.'

Mummy hisses like a snake and then she says, 'And a cracked bath, and faulty hot water, and damp, and mould all over the walls,' and I say, 'They're not moles, Mummy, they're *tadpoles*,' but Mummy keeps talking and now her voice is squeaky like a mouse. 'And a man who shouts and swears at my children and dirty needles in the stairwell and a landlord who demands extra money for repairs he never makes, who threatens to make up reasons to have us evicted, who says he'll let me off the extra money if I . . . I . . .' Mummy puts her hand to her mouth and she's pressing hard and she breathes and breathes and then takes her hand away and she says, 'And Toby's chest infection just won't go away,' and her words are wobbly and she says, 'And a guy I know said there were empty flats where he is and I should ask about them, and I just thought . . . I thought we'd qualify.'

A tiny drop of water slides out of Mummy's eye and down her cheek and then another one races down straight after.

Mummy's crying cos she doesn't want my tadpoles on the wall.

I shouldn't have drawed on the wall.

I push through her arms and climb onto her knee and put my arms around her neck and squeeze extra very tight and say, 'I love you, Mummy,' and Mummy squeezes me hard and I say, 'I'm sorry I drawed on the wall,' and Mummy does a little hiccup and squeezes even harder and kisses me one, two, three, four on my head and that's Bab-bab's secret code that she teached us that means, 'I love you too.'

I stay on Mummy's knee cuddling with my ear pressed into Mummy hard so I can hear her heart beating. The House Lady gives Mummy lots of pieces of paper and says lots of words and each time Mummy does a squeaky, 'Yes,' or a squeaky, 'OK,' and then Mummy lifts me off her knee and it's time to go and the House Lady's shaking her head and she's got pretty earrings that hang down from her ears almost to her shoulders and they jingle and sparkle like treasure.

Mummy stands up and the House Lady says, 'Mrs Petrowski, I can't stress enough, inform yourself, and put your complaints in writing to us now. It'll be investigated. In fact, put everything in writing from now on, and get receipts for everything you pay him. And keep a record of any harassment. He can't evict you without the right paperwork, and if he tries to, contact us immediately.'

She closes her eyes for a second and blows out a breath, just like Mummy does, and then she says, 'I'm sorry I can't be of more help today.'

Mummy dips her head down and says a squeaky, 'Thank you,' and she pulls Toby's buggy round fast and it almost tips over and Mummy pulls it back and the wheels bang back down on the floor. Toby's eyes open wide and his mouth opens wide and Mummy says, 'Come on, Jesika,' and her voice is spiky and Toby yells, 'Out! Out! Out!' and pushes at his straps and then he's coughing and coughing and I think Mummy needs to stop and rub his back but she's not stopping, she's walking fast and fast so I have to run and she doesn't stop til we get back to the lift doors.

In the lift, Mummy gives me a banana and gives Toby his bottle. Toby shouts, 'No!' and throws it on the ground and then she gives him a banana but it breaks in his hand and he throws the banana on the ground too and then cries, 'More nana, more nana,' but there isn't any more banana cos I've already eaten mine all up. Mummy says, 'Well, at least no one else is in the lift,' and she leans against the wall and closes her eyes and Toby cries all the way down to the ground.

He's still crying when we get to the bus stop. Mummy gets her phone out of her pocket and she tap-tap-taps on it and then puts it away and sits down on the seat and I cuddle into her side and kiss her hand one, two, three for, 'I love you.' She starts shaking and shaking and she's covering her face up and I think she's laughing so I kiss her again, one, two, three, and then I see water leaking atween her fingers and she's not laughing, she's crying again.

I say, 'What's wrong, Mummy? Mummy? What's wrong?'

Mummy shakes her head. I look at the grown-ups at the bus stop cos I think Mummy might need help from a grown-up, but no one looks at me or Mummy or Toby crying and crying in his buggy, and all the busy people on the pavement just keep walking past and the cars and the buses and the lorries whizz by and nobody stops. Why does nobody stop? Why does nobody stop and ask Mummy what's hurting?

I say, 'Mummy, you can ask a grown-up to help you.'

Mummy does big noisy swallowing and then she says, 'There's no one to help, Jesika. I'm on my own and no one can do anything for us and I don't know how much more I can take.' She flings her hand out at Toby in his buggy and says, 'I can't even stop Toby crying,' and then she cries and cries some more.

I crouch down at Toby's buggy and try to give him a cuddle but he pushes me away and cries even more louder and he doesn't want to be tickled either so I cuddle Mummy instead, and after ages she's not crying any more, just sniffing, and then a man does stop, and it's Ryan and he's huffing and puffing and he says, 'Tina? I just got your text. No good then?'

Mummy takes her hands away from her face and pulls a tissue out of her pocket and wipes her eyes and her nose and looks at her knees and lifts her shoulders up and down and says, 'They can't help. We're not priority enough.'

Ryan says, 'Really?' and he reaches over and puts his hand on Mummy's shoulder and his arm is heavy on my shoulders and I wriggle forwards so his arm falls off me and Ryan looks at me and he's smiling and he says, 'Come to Lorna's. She's not working 'til later. Paige and Jesika can play and you can have a bit of a break and catch up with an old friend.'

Play with Paige? Did he say play with Paige? I make my eyes wide and my mouth wide and look at Mummy and I say, 'Can we, Mummy? Please, Mummy?'

Mummy waves a hand at Toby still crying in his buggy and says, 'I don't think it's a good idea today. And Jesika needs to have her lunch before preschool.'

I say, 'But I want to play with Paige!'

Ryan says, 'Come to Lorna's. It won't be any trouble to do lunch for everyone.'

Mummy says, 'No, I can't . . . I don't . . .'

Ryan holds up his hand and says, 'You can. Come to Lorna's.'

Mummy says, 'I can't put Lorna to that trouble. We've not seen each other in years!'

Ryan says, 'It's no trouble at all. She's so chuffed to find you again and she really wants to see you.'

I say, 'Please, Mummy, please!'

Mummy looks at me and I squeeze my hands together tight and tight, and Mummy looks at Ryan and looks at Toby still crying and wipes her hands down her face and blows out a breath and says, 'Are you sure she won't mind us just turning up?'

Ryan says, 'Of course not!'

Mummy says, 'Maybe a change of scene is a good idea.'

Ryan says, 'Absolutely.'

I say, 'Are we going? Are we going to Paige's?'

Mummy smiles and says, 'Yes. Yes, OK.'

I jump up and down and say, 'Yeah, yeah, yeah,' and Ryan smiles his biggest ever smile at me so I can see all his teeth, white and shiny.

8

PAIGE'S BIG OUTSIDE door is green! I say, 'Green's my *fayvrit* colour!' and Ryan laughs and says, 'That's funny because green is *my* favourite colour, too!'

Mummy doesn't laugh. We walk up the path to Paige's door and she says, 'Are you sure this is OK?'

Ryan says, 'Don't worry, it's fine.' He stops at the door but he doesn't push it open, he presses a button next to it.

I say, 'Why don't you push the door open?'

Ryan laughs again and says, 'I have to wait for Lorna to open it.'

I say, 'That's not how our big outside door works.'

The green door opens and there's a lady and I think she must be real-life Rapunzel cos her hair is twisted together all the way down her front to her trousers.

Then I see Paige, right there, peeping out from ahind Rapunzel's legs and I'm so excited and I smile with all my teeth, like Ryan, and I say, 'Hi, Paige! I didn't know Rapunzel lived at your house!'

Toby shouts, 'Out! Out! Out!'

Then everyone's laughing and talking at the same time and Rapunzel and Mummy are hugging and then Mummy lifts Toby out of his buggy and Rapunzel steps to one side and says, 'Come in, come in,' and we all go inside and Mummy and Rapunzel are talking about how long it is since they saw each other and I say to

Mummy, 'Do you know Rapunzel?' and everyone laughs again and Mummy says, 'This is Lorna, Paige's Mummy, and yes, we went to the same school,' and Lorna says, 'Best friends at school!' and they're both smiling and smiling and I am silly that I thought Paige's Mummy was actually Rapunzel cos princesses don't live in houses, they live in castles and palaces and giant*normous* towers.

It's like a garden inside Paige's. Everything smells of pretty flowers and there's red flower pictures all over the walls and there's a table at the bottom of the stairs that's got lots of different flowers in pots. It doesn't look at all like the stairs inside our big outside door.

Mummy says, 'Shoes off, Jesika,' and she bends down to take her own shoes off, and Ryan's taking his shoes off and I don't understand cos I can see two doors downstairs and I can see one door at the top of the stairs and there's maybe more doors upstairs too, and I don't know which one goes into Paige's house but you don't usually take shoes off til you're inside the house.

Lorna says, 'Do you want some help, Jesika?' and she's looking at me and smiling and I whisper in Mummy's ear, 'Don't we have to go inside Paige's house first?'

Mummy says, 'We're in Paige's house now, poppet. This is all Paige and Lorna's house,' and then she stands up and says to Lorna, 'We live in a flat, and another one before that. I think this might be the first time she's seen the inside of a house.'

I say, 'Cept in books. I've seen lots of houses in books, like Tilly's yellow house.'

Lorna says, 'Oh, Paige likes the Tilly books too, don't you, Paige?'

Paige peeps out at me and I say, 'I want to see all round your house, Paige.'

Mummy says, 'Shoes off first, Jesika.'

When my coat and shoes are off, I'm so excited and I grab

Paige's hand and pull her and say, 'Let's go and look at all the rooms in your house!'

But Paige pulls her hand back and hides ahind Lorna again and Lorna says, 'Go on, Paige,' and Ryan says, 'Come on, I'll come with you,' and Paige says, 'NO!' and then she says, 'I want Mummy to come with me,' and her voice is quiet now and I think only I hear it cos Toby's shouting cos Mummy won't let him pick the flowers out of the pot and Lorna's showing Mummy where she can take Toby to play with some toys so he doesn't pick the flowers and Ryan's asking Paige to go with him and she's holding tight as tight to Lorna's leg and it's all so noisy right now.

'PAIGE! Will you let go of my leg!'

Lorna looks cross and everybody stops making noise, even Toby, and afore anyone can make more noises I say, 'Lorna, Paige wants you to come with us.'

I think Lorna's going to shout again but then she blows out a breath, just like Mummy does, and she smiles and says, 'Come on, then! Ryan, sort Tina and Toby out in the front room. Sorry, Tina, I'll be back in a minute.'

Lorna and Paige go up the stairs first, holding hands, and I follow. At the top there's four doors and she opens all of them so I can see. One's the bathroom, so now I know where to go if I need it, and one is Lorna's bedroom, but she says that's not for playing in, and one door she can't hardly even open cos there's boxes and boxes piled up and that one's not for playing in too, and the last one is Paige's bedroom and it's a proper princess room! The walls are princess pink and the carpet too and she's got a proper princess bed with a princess curtain, and a special princess mirror-table with pink princess lights all round it. I'm going to tell Mummy that I want a princess bedroom just like this when we get a new house, cept I want mine to be green.

I say, 'Your princess bedroom is so pretty, Paige!'

Paige smiles so big and I've never seen her smile that big and she lets go of Lorna's hand and she says, 'I've even got lots and lots of princess dresses!' She runs over to her princess mirror and pulls out a pink box and inside are dresses and dresses and dresses!

Paige says, 'Do you want to play princesses?'

I say, 'Yes, yes, yes!'

Paige picks up a pink dress and I'm looking if there's a green one, and there is!

I say, 'I'm going to be Princess Jesika!'

Paige says, 'No, you have to be Princess Tiana cos that's Princess Tiana's dress and I've got Princess Roarer's dress so I'm being Princess Roarer.'

I say, 'OK, I'm Princess Tiana.'

I take off my trousers and pull the dress on and I say, 'Have you got a sword? Princess Tiana needs a sword so she can fight the baddy pirates.'

Paige's dress is all muddled and tangled and she's trying to make it go the right way out and she says, 'Princess Tiana doesn't fight pirates. Only boys do fighting.'

Paige steps into her dress but she trips on the end and bumps onto her bottom and giggles. I try to help Paige get back up again cept then I bump onto the floor and then we're both lying on our backs giggling.

I say, 'Girls can do fighting too if they're good-girl pirates fighting baddy pirates.'

Paige sits up and says, 'You don't get girl pirates,' and I sit up and say, 'You do!'

Paige says, 'Don't!'

I say, 'Do!'

'Don't!'

'Do!'

'What's all the bumping and banging, girls?'

I look to the door and it's Ryan. Lorna must have sneaked away when I wasn't watching.

Ryan says, 'Ah, two princesses getting ready for the ball,' and he bends down to fix the back of Paige's dress together but she rolls away and says, 'No!'

Ryan says, 'OK, I'll help Princess Jesika get ready,' and he holds his hand out to me and I take it and he lifts me up onto my feet and fixes the back of my dress, then he picks up two tiaras from the floor and says, 'Tiaras?'

I say, 'Yes, please!'

He holds one out to Paige and she makes a frowny face and then takes the tiara from Ryan and throws it on the floor.

Ryan makes a silly frowny face back and I giggle and he puts the other tiara on my head and moves me in front of the mirror-table so I can see myself all dressed up like a princess and he says, 'Isn't Jesika a beautiful princess, Paige? She knows how to behave like a princess too,' and he reaches round my neck and collects up all my hair into a ponytail and then lets it go and strokes it down my back and his fingers are tickly and now I have to wriggle and jump away and I say, 'Tickly!'

Ryan says, 'Ah, well that's because I'm THE TICKLE MON-STER!' and he roars like a monster and leaps towards me and tickles and tickles so I can hardly breathe cos there's too many giggles bursting out of my mouth and then I manage to wriggle away again and he leaps towards Paige but she moves so fast and she slithers under her bed like a snake and Ryan can't follow her cos he's too big so he chases me again but I run like a cheetah and then I slither under the bed too.

Ryan says, 'Where have my two princesses gone? Where could they be?'

Paige grabs my hand and squeezes tight and I push my other hand on my mouth to stop my giggles popping out. Ryan's feet thump around the bedroom and my heart is thump-thump-thumping too and my nose is tickling and I'm screwing my eyes up tight like I'm scared, but I'm not really scared, just pretend scared. All Ryan's looking is making more giggles inside me and they keep just popping out and Paige is squeezing me tight as tight . . .

'OW! Paige, you're hurting me!'

Now Ryan is kneeling down and looking under the bed and he shouts, 'Found you, Princess Jesika!' and I crawl out from under the bed and I'm still giggling and then he shouts, 'And found you too, Princess Paige!' and Paige crawls out too.

Ryan says, 'Who wants to play again?'

I shout, 'Me! Me! Me!' and Ryan says it's my turn to do the finding cos he found me first and he says, 'Do you know how to count, Jesika?' and I say, 'I know lots of numbers all the way to a-hundred-thousand-a-hundred.'

Ryan says, 'Hmmm. I think I'll give you something to help,' and he pulls his phone out of his pocket and presses some buttons and then puts the phone on the mirror-table and he says, 'Wait until my phone beeps, then you can find us. Do not come until the phone beeps, OK? Because that would be cheating.' His face is frowny, but not silly frowny, and he says, 'What do you have to wait for?'

I say, 'Til the phone beeps.'

Ryan says, 'Good.' Then he smiles again and says, 'And don't forget to shout that you're coming to get us! Do you know what to say?'

I shout, 'COMING READY OR NOT!'

Ryan smiles even more big and says, 'Perfect,' and then he's holding Paige's hand and pulling her out of the room and he's pulling the door closed but just afore it closes I hear him say, 'Let's hide downstairs, Paige.' The door clicks shut and I hug my arms around myself and giggle cos now I know where to go and find them when Ryan's phone beeps.

I sit on Paige's bed and wait and wait and then I'm wondering what it's like to lie on Paige's bed inside the princess curtains and I push them to one side and crawl inside and lie down. Paige's covers are super soft and so snuggly. I pretend I really am a proper princess like Rapunzel trapped at the top of the tower cos it's so quiet, just like the top of a tower would be.

I'm lying on Paige's bed and then all the colours in Paige's room change, like someone has turned a light on. I sit up and push the curtains to the side and look out and it's not the light in the room, it's light from the sun outside and it's coming into Paige's room much more bright than afore and now Paige's room is filled with tiny, sparkly dots in the air, like fairies. I climb off Paige's bed and the fairies are floating in the air all around me and there's so many of them. I don't think I could even count up that far!

Oh! I'm apposed to be counting for hide and seek! I forgotted all about that! I count as quickly as I can, 'One-two-three-four-five-six-eight-nine-ten-leven-sixteen-eighteen-tenty!' and then run to the door and open it and stand at the top of the stairs and I can feel the giggles bubbling in my belly again cos I know they've hided downstairs and I'm going to really surprise them when I find them.

I creep down the stairs and I can hear all the quiet house-creaking noises and ticking and humming and I can hear Toby's voice and then Mummy's and I know which door they're ahind cos I saw Ryan showing them the room and I think maybe Ryan and Paige are hided in there too. I jump off the bottom stair and tiptoe to the door and it's not proply closed and I listen and listen for Paige and Ryan's voices but I can only hear Mummy talking and she says, 'We were trying to keep it together for Jesika, but getting pregnant again, I think it was too much. His heart was somewhere else. In Poland.'

Mummy laughs, short and spiky, and I know who she's talking about. She's talking about Daddy cos Daddy had to take his heart to Poland, but I don't know why. Maybe his heart got broken and he took it to get it fixed and he'll come back when it's all better. Maybe Bab-bab should have took her heart to Poland too and then her heart wouldn't have stopped working. She said that her heart was broken lots and lots after Daddy went away so why didn't she take it somewhere else to fix it like Daddy did?

There's a bump above my head and I look up and it remembers me that ceilings can also be floors like in our house and the bump might be something bumping on the floor, but there's nobody upstairs now so I don't know what bumped but it remembers me that I have to find Paige and Ryan. I put my hand on the door and Lorna says, 'But he keeps in touch with the children? Helps out? Sends money?'

Mummy says, 'Everything's been . . . difficult since Magda died,' and then nobody speaks and I know Magda is Bab-bab's real name and I push the door open a teeny-tiny bit so I can peek and I can see Mummy sitting on the yellow squashy sofa and Lorna is rubbing Mummy's arm like it's poorly and Mummy says, 'We last spoke when Toby was newborn and it didn't go well. Now he doesn't even answer texts and I'm . . . I'm afraid of letting him know how bad things are in case he decides he can do it better. Is that stupid?'

Lorna says, 'I moved back here after David died because I felt like my mother-in-law was waiting for me to fail so she could swoop in and do it better, all perfect and calm. So, no, I don't think you're stupid.'

Mummy's head nods down and back up and then she's looking straight at me and she says, 'Oh, Jesika!' and my heart thumps cos

I have to see Paige and Ryan afore they see me so I jump into the room and shout, 'Found you!' and I look all around, but I can't see Paige or Ryan anywhere. Mummy smiles and says, 'So you have! Are you having fun?'

I say, 'I'm looking for Paige and Ryan.'

I look ahind the squashy yellow sofas and ahind the door. Toby's got toys out all over the floor and there's a big telly in the corner but you can't squeeze ahind it like in our house and there's nowhere else they could be hiding.

Lorna says, 'Paige is always playing hide and seek with Ryan.'

I say, 'But where are they?'

Lorna says, 'Have you tried under the table in the kitchen?'

I say, 'Where's the kitchen?'

Lorna points out of the door and says, 'Right next to this room.'

I run out and creep up to the next door and I press my ear against it to hear Ryan or Paige but it's all quiet and I think they are very good at not making any sounds at all. I open the door and take a big breath to shout.

My shout whispers out of my mouth into the empty kitchen – no one is hiding under the table or ahind the door. I go back to the other room and I say, 'They're not there!'

Lorna says, 'They must be hiding upstairs, then.'

I say, 'But I heard Ryan tell Paige to hide downstairs.'

Lorna laughs and says, 'That's Ryan tricking you, I think.'

Or maybe Ryan changed his mind?

I say, 'I'll go and check upstairs.'

Mummy and Lorna wave bye-bye and I run out of the door. Lorna calls after me, 'And if you find them hiding in my bedroom again, tell that cheeky Uncle Ryan that *he*'s not allowed to play in there either!'

I creep back up the stairs and peek in the bathroom but there's no one there so I tiptoe into Paige's room cos maybe they sneaked back in there when I was downstairs but there's no one there either. I look in the room with the boxes but there's so many boxes, I don't think there's space for people too. There's only Lorna's room left. We're not allowed to play in Lorna's room but Lorna said I might find cheeky Uncle Ryan in there and she was laughing so it must be OK to just peep, cos I have to find them, don't I?

I push the bedroom door open quiet and slow and . . .

BEEPITYBEEP-BEEPITYBEEP-BEEPITYBEEP!

Ryan's phone in Paige's bedroom! I was apposed to wait for that! It keeps beeping and beeping loud and loud and Ryan and Paige will hear the noise and see me first and then they'll win so I push the door open all the way quick and quick and shout, 'FOUND YOU!'

Paige is on the other side of Lorna's bed and she's holding her dress right up so I can see her belly button. Ryan's pulling her pants up but he's looking at me and I think his face looks scary but then he smiles big and says, 'You didn't shout you were coming, Jesika!'

I say, 'You tricked me! And Lorna says you're cheeky cos you're not allowed to play in here as well.'

Ryan's smile gets more big til I can see all his shiny teeth then he puts his hand up to his mouth like he's telling me a secret and says, 'We had to come in here so we could change Paige's pants. She had a little accident.'

I say, 'I have accidents sometimes. Mummy says I have to go as soon as I need to go and not wait for ages.'

Paige is still holding up her dress and her pants are pink with butterflies flying all over them and I love butterflies and I say, 'I like your butterfly pants, Paige. They're pretty.'

Paige drops her dress and Ryan says, 'Do you have pretty pants on today, Jesika?'

I can't remember what pants I have on today so I pull my Princess Tiana dress up and have a look and they're yellow pants with nothing on and I say, 'Just yellow pants. But I've got other ones with flowers all over them and they're pretty like butterflies. But I've not got them on today.'

Ryan says, 'Ah, well, never mind. Maybe you can wear your pretty pants next time.'

I say to Paige, 'Come on, we have to play princesses now.'

I go back to Paige's bedroom and I hear Ryan's feet thumping back down the stairs but Paige isn't coming to play. I walk back to the door and Paige is standing outside her bedroom not moving, and her whole body and even her face looks like a statue. I hold her hand and pull her and say, 'Come on, Paige,' but she pulls back and she doesn't move and she says, 'I want my sweeties,' and I remember that Paige said you're apposed to have sweeties when you play hide and seek and maybe Ryan's gone to get them but then Paige's face goes mean and cross and she says, 'You're not allowed in my bedroom,' and she pushes me hard so I fall on my bottom and she runs into her bedroom and pushes the door shut, BANG! and I'm crying and crying and I can't stop and Mummy rushes up to me and she's holding me and she says, 'What hurts, Jesika, what hurts?'

But I can't make my crying stop and then Lorna's there too and she goes into Paige's bedroom and Mummy keeps cuddling me til my crying does stop and then Lorna comes out of Paige's bedroom and she kneels on the floor and she says, 'Paige won't talk to me. Did she hurt you, Jesika?'

I say, 'She pushed me and I fell over.'

Lorna closes and opens her eyes and her face is sad and she says, 'I'm sorry, Jesika. She's . . .' Lorna stops talking.

Mummy puts a hand on Lorna's arm and says, 'It's OK. Honestly. Jesika's not hurt.'

I say, 'I hurt my bottom!'

Mummy says, 'You'll be fine, Jesika. She's fine, Lorna. Please don't worry.'

Lorna says, 'I know it's just – this is what I was saying before. This move was supposed to be a fresh start, with Ryan nearby to help, but we seem to be going backwards again.'

I look at Lorna sitting on the floor and she's not going forwards or backwards and I screw up my nose and I say, 'Going backwards?'

Mummy says, 'Come on, Jesika, let's go and check that Toby's not causing chaos for Ryan,' and she stands up and lifts me onto my feet and we go downstairs.

I play with Toby in the room with the squashy yellow sofas and after a long time Lorna and Paige come in and Paige says, 'Sorry,' and then plays with a doll all by herself and doesn't talk to me at all.

She doesn't talk to me in the kitchen when we have lunch either, and when Lorna tells her to stop being rude she makes a growly face and a growly noise like a bear and Lorna has to take her out of the kitchen to tell her off for being naughty. Why isn't she being nice like afore?

After lunch, we have to take the princess costumes off cos it's time to get ready to go to preschool and we're all by the big out-side door putting on shoes and coats and Paige says, 'Are you taking me today, Mummy?'

Lorna says, 'No, petal, Mummy's got to go to work. Uncle Ryan's dropping you off, but I'll be picking you up.'

Paige wraps her arms around Lorna's leg and says, 'I want *you* to take me.'

Lorna says, 'I have to go to work, Paige. You'll have fun at pre-school,' and Paige is stamping and crying but Lorna tells Ryan to lock the door and rushes out of the house.

We all go out the door then and Ryan has to hold on tight to

Paige while he locks the door cos she's pulling at Ryan's arm and crying and Toby's shouting cos he doesn't want to go back into the buggy. Then Ryan whispers into Paige's ear and she stops crying and stops pulling and stands still and Mummy gives Toby his fay-vrit zebra toy and he stops shouting and wriggling and everything is quiet.

We get all the way to the end of Paige's long, long road and Toby shouts, 'Seb! Where Seb?' And Toby's dropped Zebra but not here cos he's not on the ground and Mummy says, 'We'll have to go back and look, Jesika,' and then, 'We're going to be late, *again*.'

Ryan says, 'Jesika can carry on with us, if you want?'

Mummy looks back down the road and back to us and her face is frowny and she says, 'I'm sure he can't have dropped him that far back,' and then she says, 'OK, I'll be as quick as I can and I'll catch up. OK, Jesika?'

Paige growls at me and I think Ryan will tell her to stop being naughty but Ryan just laughs and says, 'Come on, tiger, let's get you girls to preschool.'

Mummy kisses my head and says, 'I'll catch up in a minute, poppet. You go on with your new friend.' And she smiles and smiles and then rushes back down the long, long road and I don't want her to go and I don't want to walk on with Ryan and Paige, cos Mummy's wrong that Paige is my new friend. I don't think Paige wants to be my friend at all.

9

WE'RE ON THE road that preschool's on and Mummy's still not catched us up and I keep turning my head and looking ahind me and I can't even see her. Why can't I see her?

I say, 'Where's my Mummy, Ryan?'

Paige growls at me.

Ryan says, 'She's just catching up, Jesika.'

He stops at the green man and presses the button and we wait and on the other side of the road a bit further down I can see Amber walking with her Daddy and near to preschool I can see Lucia's Mummy holding the car door open so she can climb out but I can't see my Mummy anywhere. She might be lost.

The green man beeps and we walk across the road and I say, 'Does she know which way to go?' Cos I didn't know which way to walk to preschool from Paige's house.

Ryan says, 'She knows which way to go. She'll be here in a minute, Jesika, don't worry.'

Paige growls at me again. I don't like it when she does that. What if Mummy's not here in a minute? My belly feels funny, like someone's spinning me around on a roundabout, and I press my hand right into the squashy bit where my belly button is but it doesn't make the spinning go away.

We get all the way to the preschool door and I don't want to go in cos I still can't see Mummy and Ryan pulls my hand and tells me to come and take my coat off and hang it on my peg. But if I go inside, I won't see if Mummy's coming and I want to see and I pull my hand away from Ryan and stand outside the door and look and look and look and . . .

THERE SHE IS!

I shout, 'Mummy! Mummy!' and she's walking fast and fast down the road and I wave and wave and she sees me and she waves and I'm laughing and laughing and I say, 'Mummy's coming! Mummy's coming!'

Ryan says, 'See? I told you she would catch up. Let's surprise her now by getting your coat off and hung up before she gets here.'

I follow Ryan into the peg room and I'm still laughing and I'm taking my coat off quick to surprise Mummy and hanging it on my peg with the picture of the wibbly-wobbly jelly, jelly-j-for-Jesika and . . .

'Goodness, Jesika, you're one of the first today!'

I know it's Stella even afore I turn round to see cos she's the only one who makes her voice squeaky like a mouse, and when I turn round Kali is there too.

I say, 'I walked with Ryan and Paige today!'

Kali smiles and says, 'Did you?'

Stella says, 'And you're wearing the right rainbow colour today!'

I look down at my brown trousers and my yellow cardigan and I say, 'Is it yellow or brown today?'

Stella laughs and says, 'There's no brown in the rainbow, Jesika. It's yellow and orange today. You can be either or both.'

I don't think I'm both. I unzip my cardigan and I've got a white T-shirt with a yellow sunshine on and I say, 'I don't have any orange but I've got more yellow on my T-shirt and I've also got yellow pants,' cos I remember when I showed them to Paige and Ryan at Paige's house.

Stella laughs again and says, 'We don't need to know about

your pants, Jesika,' and then she says, 'Jesika's mum didn't inform us that someone else would be dropping her off. We'll need her consent if you're picking her up too,' and her voice isn't squeaky now and I look round and it's Ryan she's speaking to.

Ryan says, 'I'm not dropping Jesika off, we just walked ahead. Tina's behind us,' and Tina is my Mummy's proper name and I say, 'My Mummy's coming,' and at the same time I say it, Mummy comes puffing through the door with Toby in the buggy fast and fast and . . .

CRASH!

The buggy bashes against the door. Everyone in the peg room looks at Mummy and she laughs and says, 'Ooops!' and Toby says, 'Ooops!' and I laugh and the other grown-ups laugh too, like Kali and Ryan and Amber's Mummy cept not Stella. She's not smiling and she walks to the other side of the peg room shaking her head like she's saying, 'No.' Who is she saying it to? There's no one over there.

The peg room is getting squashy and Kali says we have to move through to the playroom if we're ready but I'm not ready cos I'm cuddling Mummy.

Mummy says, 'Go on, then, Jesika. Paige has already gone in.'

I cuddle tight.

Mummy says, 'What's up, poppet?'

I whisper in Mummy's ear, 'Paige kept growling at me. I didn't like it.'

Mummy strokes the hair away from my face and says, 'When we get home today, I'll explain to you why she's a bit growly, but for now will you try very hard to be her friend?'

I say, 'How do I be her friend if she keeps growling?'

Mummy kisses my forehead and says, 'Just keep being kind and helpful. She needs people to be kind and helpful, and you're so good at that.'

I smile and say, 'I am good at being kind and helpful.'

I kiss Mummy goodbye, and I blow a kiss at Toby cos he's asleep now, and I run into the playroom to find Paige so I can start being kind and helpful, but I can't see her anywhere. I run round the whole room looking for her and there's Amber and Lucia and Azim and Big Toby and all the other children too but Paige is nowhere anywhere.

Then I have a very clever think cos I remember Paige hided from everyone yesterday and I remember where she hided and I bet that's where she's hided now. I creep over to the house and I open the door quiet and I sneak in and there she is hided under the table just where I thinked she'd be! She's curled up with her face turned away from me and she can't see that I've found her so I pat her back and whisper, 'Found you, Paige!' cos I don't want to give her a fright. She turns her face to me and growls.

I'm thinking what to do next, cos Mummy said I should be helpful and kind, then Kali pushes her head through the door and asks me to come and help her sort out some jigsaws that have got all messed up. She says, 'Paige will come and play when she's ready.'

But Paige isn't ready for a long time. I sort the jigsaws and I do cutting and sticking and I play pirates outside with Azim and Lewis and I don't see Paige at all til snack-time and then she sits down next to me. I say, 'Hi, Paige,' and Paige scrunches up her face like she's going to growl again cept Big Toby comes rushing over and he says, 'That's my chair, Paige, I was there first,' and he tries to push her off the chair.

Paige holds onto the table and she says, 'Get *off*, stop *pushing* me,' but her voice is so quiet and I don't think Big Toby can hear cos he's still pushing her and saying, 'That's *my* chair, I was there *first*,' but he's not telling the truth cos he wasn't there first, Paige was, and Paige is trying to tell him but he's not listening. My face is hot and my heart is thumping and I stand up and look straight into Big Toby's eyes and I say, 'Don't do that to my friend!'

Big Toby says, 'But I was there *first*!'

I say, 'Paige was there first and she's my friend and you're not sitting in her chair so stop pushing her.'

Big Toby stamps his feet and his lips are wobbly and his eyes are going wet and I think he's going to cry, then Stella is there with the drinks and the snacks and she's putting them in the middle of the table and she tells Big Toby to sit down atween Lewis and Azim and he forgets about being cross cos the snack is crumpets and everyone always likes crumpets.

I turn to Paige and I say, 'Do you like crumpets, Paige?'

Paige looks at me and I think she's going to growl again, then suddenly she squeezes her arms tight around my neck and whispers in my ear, 'I love you, Jesika,' and I'm so surprised I don't say anything and Paige squeezes and squeezes til Stella tells her it's time to let go and eat up her snack, and when she lets go, Stella says, 'I'm not sure Jesika wanted that cuddle, Paige.'

I say, 'I did! Me and Paige are best friends, aren't we, Paige?' and Paige smiles big and I smile big right back and then we're both giggling and we can't stop, not even to eat our crumpets, so we have to eat and giggle at the same time which is a bit messy and Stella gets cross.

After snack-time, I say, 'What do you want to play, Paige?'

Paige says, 'I don't want to play, I want to hide.'

I say, 'Can I hide too?' and Paige stares at me and she's not smiling and I have a good idea and I say, 'I can show you a different place that nobody knows about!' and now Paige is smiling cos she likes this idea.

We run outside holding hands and whizz round to the back of the climbing frame and I show her how to climb over the wooden bar and squeeze into the hidey-hole under the slide. There's just enough space for both of us to kneel down with our knees touching. Above us, other children are thumping and banging and shouting and I say, 'They don't even know we're here,' and I press my hand to my mouth so I don't giggle loud cos then the other children might find us.

Paige squeezes her arms round my neck and she says, 'This hidey-hole is just for us and not for anyone else,' and her breath tickles my ear.

We sit quiet and then Paige says, 'You're so special,' and then she pushes her hand atween my legs.

I push her hand away and say, 'What?'

Paige says, 'It's how you be special,' and then she stands up and she says, 'I'll show you how to do it,' and she pulls my hand so I have to stand up too and my head is touching the top of the hidey-hole and I can feel the thump, thump, thump of feet above me, like they're running right on top of my head. Paige pulls my hand again so I have to step closer and her other hand pulls her trousers and her pants down a little bit and she pulls my hand forwards and then she tries to push my hand down into her trousers and pants and she's squashing my hand and I don't like it.

'Jesika, what are you doing?'

Paige drops my hand and there's Tamanna crouching under the slide and peeping into the secret hidey-hole. She looks like she's just eaten something that tastes horrible, like lemons or mushrooms, and she says, 'Paige, pull your pants and trousers back up, sweetpea,' and then she says we're not allowed in the hidey-hole and she helps us both climb out and when we're back out on the play area, she says, 'Remember, pants are private, girls,' and I want to ask her what she means but Tamanna runs away afore she can tell me cos Amber's shouting for help at the top of the slide.

Big Toby rushes up and he's dressed up in a sparkly pink

princess dress and a pirate eye-patch and he's waving a pirate sword at us and he shouts, 'You're not allowed under the slide. I saw you and I told the teacher. Ha ha ha!'

I look at Paige and I know exactly what she's going to do and at the same time we both look at Big Toby and we do a giant*nor*mous tiger-fierce ROAR! in Big Toby's face and he runs away. Then me and Paige run inside into the house and no one else is in there and I slam the door and Paige says, 'We're not letting anyone else inside our house today,' and we play at putting baby to bed and having some tea and when Amber and Lucia try to come in, me and Paige ROAR! and they run away again.

Kali's head appears at the window and she says, 'Have you heard? There're two tigers hiding in this house! You better be careful, girls!'

Me and Paige giggle and then we ROAR! at Kali but she doesn't run away. She says, 'Oh, I'm so glad it's just you two. I was very worried that you might get eaten up.'

Me and Paige are still giggling and then Kali says, 'I think Amber and Lucia would like to play in the house now I've checked there are no real tigers and it would be lovely if you two could share your game with them.'

I say, 'OK,' and Kali opens the door and Amber and Lucia come into the house. Paige throws down her teacup and runs straight out and I stand up to follow her but Kali says, 'Actually, Jesika, could you stay here and show Amber and Lucia your game? I've got something to do with Paige for a few minutes.'

Kali closes the door and Amber goes to the bed and picks up the baby even though he's still sleeping and Lucia sits down at the table and messes up all the plates and cups. I don't want to play with Amber and Lucia. I want to play with Paige cos she's my best friend.

10

THE PEG ROOM is noisy and full of wet, drippy people and I can't see Mummy or Toby, just lots of legs, and shoes that make wet, muddy marks on the floor. I'm holding Paige's hand and she can't see her Mummy too. Then I hear, 'Jesika! Over here!' and I look and look and some of the legs move and now I can see Mummy and she's standing next to Lorna and they're both waving and they've already lifted our coats and bags off our pegs. I say, 'Come on, Paige, let's ask if we can play at your house again.'

We go forward but Stella squeezes my shoulder spiky-tight, pulling me back and Paige too and she says, 'Hold on, Jesika, Paige, I want to speak to your Mummies.' And she says, 'A quick word, Tina, please,' and her voice is loud and everyone stops and looks and Stella says, 'A quick word with you, too, Paige's Mum.'

Lorna squeezes through all the legs but Mummy has to wait for some people to leave cos there's no room for her to squeeze Toby's buggy through.

Stella says, 'You two wait here,' and she steps back through the door to the playroom with Lorna. Stella talks quiet and Lorna's face is frowny and Stella gives her a piece of paper and Lorna looks at it and laughs and says, 'It's curiosity, isn't it?' and Stella says something else so quiet I can't hear and then Lorna laughs again and says, 'I'm sure you do, and that's good, and I'll have the chat with Paige but I'm not worried.' She folds the piece of paper up and pushes it into her coat pocket.

Something bumps against the back of my foot and I turn round and it's Mummy pushing Toby's buggy and she says, 'Sorry, poppet,' and then Lorna and Stella have come back and Stella says, 'Tina?' and she waves her into the playroom and Lorna says, 'Leave Toby with me, if it's easier,' and Mummy leaves Toby and follows Stella in and Lorna says, 'Let's get coats on while your Mummy's having her chat, Jesika.'

I say, 'What are they saying?'

Lorna snorts like a pig and says, 'Something and nothing.'

I don't know what that means, but when I ask, Lorna just says, 'Come on, coats on.'

I've just got my coat zipped right up and Mummy comes rushing out of the room and her mouth is small and her eyes are zapping.

Lorna says, 'Don't worry about it, Tina.'

Mummy says, 'Can we just get out of here first?' so we all go rushing outside and it's raining hard and the rain is bouncing off my hood and Toby's rain cover and the pavement and we have to run fast and fast along the road and we don't stop til we get to a bus shelter and Mummy says, 'In here, Jesika,' and there's no one waiting in the shelter and I say, 'Are we getting a bus again?' but Mummy says, 'No, we're just getting out of the rain for a minute,' and she's coughing and coughing and I say, 'And it's so you can have a rest too, isn't it?' but Mummy's too busy coughing to answer me and then she's too busy pulling back the rain cover and giving Toby his milk to drink cos he's coughing too.

Lorna and Paige squash up next to us and we're all dripping rain and it's making lots of tiny rivers on the floor of the shelter and on the roof the rain is stomping and it's like we're in the climbing frame hidey-hole again and lots of children are running around above us, cept I don't think anyone could climb on top of the bus shelter cos it's so high up and there's no ladder.

Lorna puts a hand on Mummy's shoulder and says, 'Don't worry about it, honestly.'

Mummy coughs and then says, 'But where did she get the idea?'

Lorna says, 'It's just normal curiosity, nothing else.'

I say, 'What are you saying, Mummy?'

Lorna pulls the folded paper out of her pocket and unfolds it and says, 'Did she give you one of these?'

Mummy pulls the same piece of paper out from her pocket and unfolds it and it's got a picture of a washing line with lots of pants pegged onto it and she says, 'Snap.'

I say, 'What's that, Mummy?'

Lorna says, 'It's dealing with grief I need help with, not this. This isn't exactly rocket science, is it?' She screws the piece of paper up, steps out of the shelter and throws it in the rubbish bin.

Mummy's still holding hers and I say, 'Can I see it, Mummy? What is it?'

Mummy says, 'Later, Jesika,' and she folds it up and puts it back in her pocket.

The rain gets even more noisy and then nobody can even speak cos even shouting isn't loud enough. Paige pushes up against me like she's cuddling and holds my hand. I think she maybe doesn't like the noisy rain.

Suddenly, the noise stops.

I say, 'Somebody's switched the rain off!'

Mummy and Lorna laugh and then Mummy and Lorna are both talking at the same time about getting home quick afore the rain starts again.

Paige says, 'But I want to play with Jesika!'

Lorna says to Mummy, 'You'd be very welcome,' and I say,

'Yeah! Yeah! Yeah!' but Mummy says, 'Oh, Toby!' and I look and he's sicked up all his milk down his front and now we can't do playing cos we have to go straight home so Mummy can clean him up and Lorna says, 'Maybe tomorrow?' and I say, 'They could come to our house to play,' and Mummy says, 'No. No, I don't think that's a good idea,' and I say, 'Why not?' and Mummy says, 'Our flat isn't . . .' and Lorna says, 'Tomorrow's fine, at the park or at ours, depending on the weather,' and then she's telling Paige it's time to go and Paige is crying cos she wants to play with me and I want to play with her too but now Toby's coughed and sicked up even more milk and now we really have to go home cos Mummy's got a lot of cleaning up to do. Lorna and Paige walk away and Paige keeps turning her head to look back at me and I shout, 'I'll play with you tomorrow, Paige!' and I wave and wave til I can't see Paige and Lorna any more.

Mummy's still wiping and wiping Toby's clothes and she's used lots and lots of wipes. She gives me the packet and says, 'Put these under the buggy, poppet,' and she throws all the smelly, dirty wipes in the bin.

There's not much space under the buggy cos there's all Mummy's shopping and Toby's bag and my bag and there's a little bag that's made of paper and it's got red stripes and there's something poking out of it and . . . oh, it's a gingerbread man! We maked them at preschool one time and Tamanna read the gingerbread man story and at snack-time I pretended I was the fox biting off the gingerbread man's head and it was yummy! I say, 'Mummy, why is there a gingerbread man under the buggy?' and I pull the paper bag out and look inside proply and it's a giantnormous gingerbread man and he's got tiny black eyes and a red nose and a red mouth and three green sweetie buttons on his front.

Mummy laughs and says, 'Trust you to spot that!'

I say, 'Who's it for?' and I really, really want Mummy to say it's for me cos gingerbread men are my fayvrit and then she says it *is* for me and I'm dancing and dancing with the gingerbread man in the paper bag and Mummy takes it off me and puts it back under the buggy cos she says I might break it and that would be a shame and she says I have to wait til after tea-time to eat it and that's *ages* but Mummy says if we walk home quickly, it won't be long at all afore it's tea-time.

I make my legs walk fast and fast up the long hill to our house and I'm looking in all the shop windows cos I don't know where Mummy got the gingerbread man and when we've gone past lots of shops and I've not seen any gingerbread men at all I say, 'Which shop did you get it from, Mummy?' Mummy says, 'Actually, Ryan bought it for you, so don't forget to say thank you to him when we see him next.'

I say, 'Ryan bought me the gingerbread man?'

Mummy nods and smiles and says, 'He took me and Toby to a cafe while you were at preschool and before we left he said he must get something for you, so he picked out the gingerbread man with the green buttons because you like green. Wasn't that thoughtful of him?'

I say, 'I do like green. It's my fayvrit!' and then I say, 'Have I ever been to a cafe?'

Mummy says, 'No . . . I don't know . . . Maybe a long time ago with Bab-bab?'

I say, 'What do you do at a cafe?'

'You eat and drink and chat.'

'What did you have to eat and drink?'

'A coffee and a slice of cake.'

'And what did you chat about?'

Mummy laughs. 'All sorts of things! I used to know Lorna and Ryan a long time ago, so mostly we were remembering things from when we were at school and talking about what we've been doing in the years since then.'

I say, 'So are Lorna and Ryan our friends?'

Mummy makes a funny shape with her mouth, all squashed up, and then she says, 'We were friends a long time ago, so, yes, I suppose we are still friends, but we have to get to know each other all over again.'

I say, 'That's easy. We can go and play lots and lots at Paige's house cos you said that's what friends do.'

Mummy says, 'Yes, I did say that, and it sounds like a lovely idea.'

I say, 'Yeah, yeah, yeah!' and I let go of the buggy cos I can see our big front door and I'm allowed to run up the steps by myself and wait for Mummy and I get there fast as fast and I shout, 'Hurry up, Mummy!' cos I really want to taste my gingerbread man.

It's bedtime but Toby won't go to sleep cos the boiler that makes hot water for magic-steamy baths isn't working. There's a pilot inside the boiler but the pilot's gone away and even when Mummy whispered, 'Please, please, please,' the pilot didn't come back again. Mummy did try just putting Toby in his cot but he cried and cried and coughed and coughed and now he's snuggled up atween me and Mummy on the sofa and we're all wrapped up in the duvet cos the rainy-haters are cold cos it's the boiler's job to make them hot too.

Mummy closes the rabbit book that Toby likes and I say, 'Tilly next!' but Mummy doesn't pick up the Tilly book, she's got a piece of paper in her hand and it's the one with all the different coloured pants on it that Lorna throwed in the bin. Mummy looks at me and strokes her thumb round and round on my shoulder and she says, 'Jesika, do you remember when the banging door woke you up last night?'

I say, 'I didn't wake up last night.' I pick up the pants picture and I say, 'Some of these pants are for boys and some are for girls, aren't they, Mummy?'

Mummy takes the picture back and says, 'Remember? When you got out of bed and came through and gave me a cuddle because I was upset?'

I remember cuddling Mummy but I didn't wake up cos I wasn't actually asleep, I was watching Mummy dancing and then there was that man and he . . . oh!

I say, 'That man pulled your hair and hurted you. That was naughty.' And I remember that Mummy didn't tell him to stop. Only Next-Door Lady did.

Mummy reaches over and holds my hand and squeezes it tight and she says, 'Did you see him . . . I mean . . . is that all you saw him doing?'

I say, 'Next-Door Lady told him to stop and he talked to her and then she laughed and you banged the door shut and he shouted through the letterhole and he went away.'

Mummy says, 'And that's all you saw?'

I say, 'Yes, but Mummy, why didn't you tell him to stop?'

Mummy squeezes my hand again and says, 'I should have, you're right.' She presses her lips tight.

I say, 'You have to use your Big Voice next time, Mummy, cos then he'll know he's being naughty and you don't like it.'

Mummy nods and nods but she doesn't say yes cos her lips are still tight together, and then she presses her hand to her mouth and turns her head away so I can't see her face at all.

I pick up the pants picture again. There's a red pair with stars on and I like them. Maybe I can have some pants with stars on. That remembers me about Paige's butterfly pants and I say, 'Mummy, can I have some butterfly pants like Paige's?'

Mummy says, 'We need to talk about Paige's pants. That's why I've got this,' and she takes the pants picture back again.

I say, 'But Paige's pants aren't on there. They've got butterflies on them and that's the ones I want.'

Mummy says, 'No, I mean, we need to talk about the underwear rule, about private pants.'

I say, 'Private pants?' and I giggle cos 'private pants' sounds funny.

Mummy says, 'Yes, private pants,' and her eyes are telling me not to laugh and to listen and she says, 'Private means that it's yours and only yours and it's not for anyone else to see or touch. So, private pants is to help you remember that your pants and everything under your pants is not for anyone else to see or touch. Do you know what I mean when I say everything under your pants?'

I say, 'My bottom!' and then I giggle again cos bottoms are funny too and then I look at Toby and I say, 'Bum-bum! Bum-bum!' cos Toby always laughs when I say it but he doesn't laugh tonight. He's not even proply looking at me. He looks sad.

Mummy says, 'Do you understand, Jesika?' but I'm looking at Toby and I say, 'Why is Toby sad?'

Mummy says, 'He's still feeling a bit poorly, that's all,' and she leans down and kisses the top of his head. Then she says, 'Jesika, private pants means your pants and everything under your pants is just for you and no one else. Do you understand that?'

I think for a bit and then I say, 'But you and Toby always see my pants and my bottom!'

Mummy's face is frowny and she says, 'Yes, we do. But only when you're getting dressed or on the toilet or in the bath and that's OK because we live in the same house as you. But you always wipe your own bottom and dry your own bottom because those bits are private, just for you.'

I giggle cos Mummy said bottom lots of times and I say, 'My private bottom!'

Mummy says, 'Exactly.' And then she says, 'So, today at preschool, Stella says you were touching Paige under her pants and it's not OK to do that because that's Paige's private pants and it's just for her.'

I say, 'But Paige did it. It wasn't me.'

Mummy says, 'Paige touched *you*?'

I say, 'No, Paige maked me touch *her*,' cos she did. She grabbed my hand and pushed it down into her pants and I didn't even want to do that and that remembers me that I didn't say stop, just like Mummy didn't, and I say, 'I should have used my Big Voice.'

Mummy says, 'Jesika, Paige can't *make* you touch her. Only you decide where your hands go.'

Toby coughs and coughs and then cries and Mummy picks him up and lays him against her front and rubs his back.

I say, 'But she did, Mummy. She maked my hand go there.'

Mummy says, 'Jesika, I don't think . . .' and then Toby coughs and coughs and sicks milk all down Mummy's front and Mummy says, 'Oh, Toby, not again!' and then she says, 'Just tell Paige next time that pants are private, OK?'

I say, 'PANTS ARE PRIVATE!' in my Big Voice and Mummy says, 'Yes, just like that,' and then Toby is sick again and we all have to get up quick so the sicky milk doesn't go on the duvet and Mummy says, 'Jesika, go and jump into bed. I'll come through in a minute,' and she rushes Toby into the bathroom to get all cleaned up.

I look at the duvet on the floor and I think Mummy is so silly sometimes cos I can't go to bed with nothing to cover me up. I try to pull the duvet along the floor to the bedroom but it's heavy and draggy and it keeps getting stuck on things like the sofa and the table and the bedroom door and it's so shivery-cold so I lay down on the duvet and try to roll myself up like a sausage, but it's a bit of a tangly sausage. I flop back on the floor and pull the duvet on top of me. The thump-da-thump-da-thump music tickles my cheek.

Mummy comes back out of the bathroom with Toby and he's only got his nappy on and he's crying and crying, probly cos he's shivery-cold too, and Mummy says, 'Jesika! Go to bed! Why are you messing with the duvet?'

I say, 'It won't go back on the bed.'

Mummy says, 'Oh, for goodness' sake!' and she puts Toby down on the floor and pulls the duvet off me and it's cold, cold, cold! She carries it into the bedroom and I jump up to chase after her and then fall over Toby cos he's crawled right in front of me and he cries and cries and Mummy rushes back out of the bedroom and she says, 'Careful, Jesika!' but it wasn't my fault! She picks Toby up again and she's bouncing him up and down and she says, 'Into bed, Jesika,' and I go into the bedroom and get into bed and wriggle under the duvet but then I remember that Mummy didn't read me my Tilly book and I say, 'You didn't read my story!'

Mummy says, 'I can't tonight, poppet, not when Toby's like this.'

But that's not fair cos Mummy read Toby's book but she didn't read mine and I say, 'I want my story!' and now Toby and me are both crying and Mummy needs to put Toby down cos it's my turn to have a cuddle but Mummy says, 'Don't start, Jesika!' and she's not putting Toby down and she's not cuddling me and she says, 'We'll read your story tomorrow, I promise. Now, please help me and go to sleep so I can sort Toby out.'

She bends over and kisses my head and Toby's hand bashes my head and I say, 'Ow! Toby hitted me!' and Mummy says, 'Oh, Jesika, he hardly touched you. Go to sleep, poppet. Sweet dreams.'

She goes out of the bedroom and shuts the door and it's not fair. He did hit me and it hurted. Outside someone is shouting and it's angry shouting and I think maybe the person who is shouting didn't get to read their story too or maybe they also got bashed on their head. Then there's more angry shouting and more and louder and I don't like it. It's scary. I want Mummy.

I get out of bed and open the bedroom door. Mummy spins round and says, 'Bed, Jesika, *please*. I'll come and see you in a minute.'

I go back into the bedroom and Mummy pulls the door shut again but I don't go back to bed cos there's still people shouting outside. I kneel down at the door and peep through the hole and I can see Mummy walking up and down and rubbing Toby's back and whispering words in his ear and she walks one way and the other way again and again and after a long-a-long time Toby stops crying. That's good. Now Mummy will come and put him in bed and I can have a cuddle.

Cept Mummy doesn't come back to the bedroom. She walks over to the sofa, with Toby still cuddled on her front, and she sits down and I can only see the top of her head now. What is she doing? Why isn't she coming to cuddle me? I wait and wait for a long-a-long time but Mummy stays on the sofa not even moving and I can't sit still on the floor cos my shoulders and my back and my front and all over me won't stop shivering.

I creep back into bed and pull the covers over my head to hide from the shouting. It's not so cold under the covers. I curl up small, like a caterpillar in a cocoon. My breath is warm on my hands. I close my eyes cos that's what caterpillars do while they wait to change into butterflies, but I'm not going to sleep. I'm going to stay awake til Mummy comes to cuddle me.

11

EYES OPEN.

Hurty light.

Hurty light and noisy.

Squeeze eyes shut.

Is it morning? Listen.

Zooming cars, thump-da-thump music, shouting, talking . . .

Not Mummy talking.

Eyes open again. Hurty bright!

Rub eyes, rub, rub. Rub again. Not so hurty.

The bedroom door's open and light. That's where light is.

Things moving – big and dark.

Monsters?

Mummy!

I roll over for a cuddle with Mummy, but she's not there.

Sit up. Look.

Mummy's not in bed.

Toby's not in his cot.

'I didn't know what else to do!' Mummy's voice!

Mummy!

I push back the covers and slide off the bed and walk to the bedroom door, still rubbing the hurty out of my eyes. Mummy is standing next to the sofa and a big, green man is standing next to her and he has his hand on her shoulder.

He's hurting her!

He's hurting my Mummy! Stop him, Mummy! Use your Big Voice!

Mummy doesn't. She twists her face away and the Green Man is still holding her shoulder. I remember Next-Door Lady shouted. Next-Door Lady shouted loud. I run and I run and I shout, 'STOP IT! YOU LEAVE MY MUMMY ALONE!' and I bash into the Green Man's leg and he steps backwards away from Mummy and in the gap atween I see another person and it's a lady and she's all green too and she's kneeling down in front of the sofa and Toby's lying on it and she's . . . SHE'S HURTING TOBY!

'Jesika! Stop!'

My feet lift up and I'm wrapped up in Mummy's cuddle and she's pressing my face into her chest so I can't see anything and I fight and fight cos the Green Lady's hurting Toby. She's holding something on his mouth so he can't breathe and—

Mummy sits down with me on her knee and I'm twisting to see Toby but Mummy puts her hand on my cheek so I can't see and says, 'Jesika! Stop!' and her voice is scary and her eyes are wet. My belly whooshes fast like I'm on a roundabout.

Mummy says, 'Toby's very poorly. He has to go to hospital and these people are helping.'

I look at the Green Man and he's bending over the Green Lady and she's saying something to him quiet and spiky and I say, 'Are they ambulance people?'

Mummy says, 'Yes, they are.'

The Green Man stands up and says, 'Time to go. Are there things you need to bring for your daughter?'

Mummy stands up, putting me back on my feet, and she pushes her hands into her hair and looks all round the room and she says, 'I don't know, I don't know, I can't think,' and her face is scary and my belly whooshes round and round.

The Green Man says, 'Something warm to go over her pyjamas. It's cold out,' and I say, 'My dressing gown!' and I run into the bedroom and pull it from the hook and put it on and run back to the living room and Mummy's already holding my slippers and she gives them to me and the Green Man says, 'And a change of clothes,' and Mummy picks up my preschool bag that always has extra clothes in it and then she grabs her handbag and the Green Man says, 'All set?' and Mummy says, 'I think so.' Her face is still scary and I say, 'What are we doing, Mummy?' and my voice is all shaky and that's cos my whole body is all shaky and that's cos it's shivery-cold. Mummy doesn't say what we're doing and she doesn't cuddle me and she doesn't say it's OK and I'm scared. Then the Green Man looks straight at me and he winks and my belly whooshes slow and stops, cos winking is happy and smiley and good. Mummy holds my hand and squeezes it tight.

The Green Lady is lifting Toby and the Green Man is helping her and they're moving slow and slow. I try to peek at Toby's face but I can't see it proply cos the Green Lady is big like a giant and all I can see are Toby's legs dangling over her arms and his legs are bare cos he doesn't have his babygrow on. He'll get cold out-side, won't he? Then the Green Lady and the Green Man go out of our door and me and Mummy follow and we're outside the door and Mummy has to bang the door five times afore it shuts and she says, 'Come *on*, come *on*!' and it makes her cough and cough and the Green Man and the Green Lady carrying Toby have disappeared down the stairs and me and Mummy have to hurry to catch up but there's a horrid eggy-yucky smell and I know what it is and I look over to Next-Door Lady's door and she's star-ing right at me and then Mummy says, 'Hurry *up*, Jesika,' and Next-Door Lady shuts her door fast and Mummy picks me up and she zooms me down the stairs and it's like flying.

Outside there's a light whizzing about and it's blue and hurty in my eyes and it's a real-life ambulance flashing its lights but not making the siren sound. The back doors are open and I think Toby and the Green Man and the Green Lady must be inside cos I can't see them but we're stuck on the steps cos there's some big boys in our way and they're shouting noisy things and laughing and pushing each other and bumping against the ambulance and I can smell yummy food and it remembers me that we've not had breakfast and I look at Mummy and say, 'Do hopsipals do breakfast?'

Mummy doesn't say. She holds my hand tight and tight and more tight and she's staring past me and then the Green Lady is there and she's saying shouty things and making the big boys go away and then she says, 'Come on, lovies,' and her voice is soft, not shouty, and she takes us to the back of the ambulance and I've never been inside an ambulance in my whole life and it's a big step up so Mummy has to lift me and, oh, strange things! Machines and cupboards and wires and things and I don't know what any of them are cept the seats and the bed. Toby! He's on the bed on the Green Man's knee and then the Green Man stands and now Mummy's on the bed and Toby's on her knee and the Green Lady is bending over him and what is that on his face? It's like a pot, pressed onto his nose and his mouth, and it's like a window pot cos I can still see his mouth and his nose, but it's not a glass window cos it's not shiny like glass, and it's got a metal thing stuck to it that Mummy has to hold with the hand that isn't holding Toby and I don't know what any of it is but I think it might be making Toby sleepy cos he keeps opening and shutting his eyes slow as slow and . . .

Oh! The Green Man has lifted me right up and now I'm on the seat next to the bed and he pulls a strap tight on my chest and my belly. I can't see Toby! Toby? I twist and twist and the Green Man pushes his hand on my shoulder but not hard and he says, 'Sit back while I get your seatbelt on, Jesika.' I sit back and he says,

'Your little brother's doing just fine. We'll soon get him properly looked at.'

I say, 'What's that on his face?'

The Green Man stands up and says, 'It's a special breathing mask that helps your little brother to breathe more easily.' He turns to the Green Lady and says, 'All set?' and she nods and the Green Man goes away somewhere I can't see and the Green Lady sits back on another chair and pulls her strap on and then the ambulance is moving and I say, 'Where's the Green Man gone?' The Green Lady laughs and says, 'You mean Max? He's driving the ambulance!'

The ambulance zooms fast and fast, siren on then siren off then siren on and the Green Lady says that's cos you're not allowed the siren on at night-time cept when there's something in your way cos it's very noisy and night-time is apposed to be quiet and Mummy does a strange laugh that's not a happy laugh and says, 'It's never quiet where we live,' and we keep zooming with sirens on-off-on-off for a long-a-long time til my head and my eyes feel so so heavy . . .

I'm standing in the garden outside Tilly's yellow house and I'm knocking on the red door, cept when I knock it turns green and it's not Tilly at the door, it's Paige and Lorna and they tell me to come in and we go into the kitchen and Paige keeps biting my shoulder and she won't stop . . .

Eyes open.

The Green Man is shaking my shoulder and smiling at me and he says, 'Hello, Jesika, we're here now.' Everything's still and quiet. The Green Lady opens the back door and there's cold and noise and lights. The Green Man helps me to take my straps off but something's got stuck and he says, 'Blasted thing needs fixing. I keep telling them,' and the Green Lady is holding Toby and Mummy is off the bed and she's got her handbag and my preschool bag and she climbs down out of the ambulance. Where's Mummy gone? Where is she? The Green Lady climbs down too with Toby in her arms and now they've disappeared too! Where are they? I try to twist and look around the Green Man but he's too big. Come back, Mummy! The Green Man says, 'Don't worry, Jesika, we're right behind them.' And then the strap pops off and the Green Man says, 'At last!' and he pulls the strap off and stands up and I run for the door and I shout, 'Wait for me, Mummy!' and then I stop cos right out of the back door is another ambulance and there's a Green Lady driving it and it's Emma and she's staring right at me. I say, 'I didn't know . . .' Then my feet fly right off the floor and the Green Man is carrying me and he jumps out of the back of the ambulance and he walks fast and fast and I'm bumping up and down and I look ahind to see Emma again but I can't see her any more.

We get to magic doors like the ones on all the shops that slide away when you stand in front of them and I think the Green Man is going to crash right into them but they open just in time and there's a room that stretches a long-a-long way in front of us. I say, 'Ugh, smelly!' cos it smells like toilets and lemons and there's doors and doors and doors and I can't see Mummy or the Green Lady. Are they ahind one of the doors? How do we know which door to choose?

I say, 'Which door is it?' and the Green Man says, 'Just up here,' so maybe he knows which door even though they all look the same as each other and there's so many!

I count the doors that whizz past and the Green Man's feet go squeak, squeak, squeak on the shiny floor and I say, 'You need to buy a new pair of shoes.'

He laughs and says, 'Why's that?' So I tell him about his squeaky feet and I say, 'And that means your shoes must be broken.'

The Green Man laughs even more loud which is strange cos I'm not telling a joke. He really does need to fix his shoes.

We stop going so fast and get to a door and the Green Man turns round and pushes it open with his back and we're in a big, noisy room with people rushing and I look and look but I can't see Mummy or Toby anywhere. I can see people lying on beds and there's a man right next to us and he's got bleeding on his head and there's people calling things out and beeping noises and someone's crying and the floor is sparkly like those pebbles in the touching boxes at preschool and there's blue and yellow swirly curtains all around us that swish about when we walk past them.

Then I spot something a bit different and I say, 'I know where Mummy and Toby are!' and I don't have time to say why cos the Green Man has made giant steps right up to the teddy bear curtains and there's Mummy right aside them and I knew she'd take Toby here cos Toby likes teddy bears and teddy bears aren't for grown-ups, they're for children, and now we're there I can see pictures all over the walls and they're just for children too. There's a big oshun with turtles and rainbow fish and an octopus and above that a jungle with tigers and lions and elephants – and there's even parrots flying across the ceiling!

Mummy's talking to a Blue Lady and I can't see Toby and I say to the Green Man, 'Put me down, put me down!' and he does and I run to Mummy and fling my arms around her legs and squeeze and squeeze and she picks me up and holds me so very tight and I still can't see Toby but I can see machines and wires and a writing board like preschool that a man is scribbling squiggles on, and there's other people and they're all different colours and some don't have a colour and there's the Green Lady and she's talking and everyone's standing around something but I can't see what it is but I think it must be Toby cos they're saying Toby's name. I wriggle til Mummy puts me down. The Blue Lady is still talking to her and I squeeze through all the people and it's a bed they're all standing round and now I can see Toby and he looks all cold cos he only has his nappy on and a man is sticking a huge metal stick into the back of his hand and it looks so hurty but Toby can't tell him to stop cos he's still got the breathing pot on his face so I shout, 'Stop it! You're hurting Toby!'

A lady turns and looks down at me and she shouts, 'Get the child out of here NOW!' And she looks so cross and I jump backwards from her shouty voice and I bump on my bottom on the floor and then Mummy folds her arms around me and lifts me up and the Blue Lady puts her arm around Mummy and we're walking away from the teddy bear curtains and she's saying things and Mummy's saying things but I don't know what they're saying cos I'm looking back at the teddy bear curtains and I can see Toby in a gap atween all the people and he's just lying there and people are putting hands on him and there's wires and machines and the breathing pot and he's not crying and he should be crying cos that's what Toby does when something's wrong and there's got to be something wrong cos we came in an ambulance and all these people are putting things on him, so why is Toby not crying?

Mummy puts me down and squeezes my hands in atween hers and that makes me look at her and her eyes are all wet and she says, 'I need you to be a very brave girl, Jesika. Can you do that for me?'

Mummy tells me I'm brave when I hurt myself and I don't cry. Am I going to get hurt now? Does she want me to not cry? I try to look over her shoulder to where Toby is but I can't see him. I need Mummy to lift me up again and I try to hold out my arms but Mummy squeezes my hands more tight and I say, 'Hold me up, Mummy,' but Mummy shakes her head and says, 'Listen to me, darling,' and she lets go of my hands and puts both her hands on my cheeks and she says, 'Are you listening?'

I nod my head.

Mummy says, 'A lady is going to take you into a waiting room and look after you, just for a little while so I can talk to the doctors about Toby.'

I don't want to go with anyone else. I shake my head and I reach out to Mummy but she's still holding my cheeks with her hands and she's stroking her thumbs round and round and she says, 'I need you to be brave, remember?'

The Blue Lady steps forwards and she says, 'Jesika, this is Paulina, and it'll be her job to keep you safe while your Mummy is looking after your little brother.'

I look and there's a new lady and she's all violent like the violent on Stella's rainbow nails and Mummy says, 'Toby needs me and I need you to go with Paulina. I promise I'll come and see you very soon.'

Mummy lets go of my cheeks and I push myself right into Mummy's chest and wrap my arms tight as tight so she can't make me go but she gently undoes my arms and moves me backwards and she says, 'I won't be long, I promise,' and she stands up and the Violent Lady is holding out her hand to me and Mummy's lips are pressed tight and she nods and she whispers, 'Go on, poppet,' and then the Blue Lady takes her back over to where Toby is and the Violent Lady's hand feels warm and crinkly around mine.

She says, 'I'll show you some toys, OK?' and she doesn't try to pull me, she waits and she smiles and I look back at Mummy and Mummy's not looking cos she's talking to the cross lady that shouted.

I go back through the noisy-rushy room holding the Violent Lady's hand and out into the long, stretchy room, and when the door thuds shut it's so so quiet. Then the noise goes loud again cos the door opens and it's the Green Man and he crouches down in front of me and says, 'I almost forgot to give you this, Jesika. It's specially for you for being such a brave girl,' and he gives me a teddy in a plastic bag and the teddy is wearing green just like the Green Man and I say, 'He's just like you,' and the Green Man says, 'He's a special Para-Ted. I don't give him out to anyone, you know, just the really brave boys and girls.'

I want to tell him that green's my fayvrit colour and I want to say thank you very much and I want to ask the Green Man what he's called and I want to ask him if he can stay with me too cos I know he's kind and nice but my mouth is stuck and there's a hurty-pain right at the back where my food goes and afore I can make my mouth work, he's standing up and he squeezes my shoulder and says, 'You keep being brave for your Mummy and your brother, little lady,' and then he's walking back through the noisy door and the door shuts all the noise away again. Now it's just me and Para-Ted and the Violent Lady.

The Violent Lady goes to another door and opens it and we go in and it's a room that smells like the hopsipal but it's just got chairs and a squashy sofa going around a little table and there's purple leaves and blue circles on the walls and no beds or machines or wires. The Violent Lady shuts the door but I don't want the door shut cos now I can't see the door where Mummy and Toby are and when it's time to go home they might not see me and they might go home without me and—

'Jesika? That's your name?'

The Violent Lady sits on the squashy sofa and she pats the space next to her and I sit down and she says my name again, 'Jesika?' and my name sounds funny in her voice like a bee buzzing and I nod and she nods and says, 'Jesika,' again and she says, 'Nice to meet you, Jesika. I am Paulina,' and I'm looking at her mouth when she speaks and my belly feels warm and it makes me smile and Paulina smiles too and her smile makes wiggly lines all round her mouth and her eyes.

I say, 'You say my name like a buzzy bee.'

Paulina laughs and says, 'A buzzy bee!' and then she says, 'My voice sounds different?'

I say, 'Your voice is nice.'

Paulina smiles and says, 'I come from a different country called Poland and—'

I say, 'I know Poland! My Daddy went to live there!'

Paulina's eyebrows jump up and back down and she says, 'Oh, really?'

I say, 'He went away and he's not coming back. Do you think that's where Mummy and Toby might go too?'

Paulina shakes her head and says, 'Your Mummy and Toby are right here, kochanie, they're not going anywhere.' She smiles but I can't smile too cos my belly hurts. Paulina pats her hands on her knees and she says, 'I know a good idea. My little granddaughter is just the same age as you and she loves colouring in. I will see if there's any colouring books in the cupboard here.'

Paulina slides onto the floor and opens the cupboard and she pulls out a pile of books and there's a Tilly book right on the top and it's the one that I wanted Mummy to read at bedtime last night that she didn't read to me cos she sent me to bed without reading stories and she didn't come back and cuddle me and I want Mummy now but she's not here and what if she never—

Paulina picks me up and I'm sitting on her knee and she says, 'You're OK, kochanie, it'll be OK,' and I want to tell her the scary thing but my mouth just says, 'Oh, oh, oh, oh,' and I can't stop it, not even to breathe, and Paulina talks in my ear but it's not words I know and then she sings and my eyes feel sleepy and it's easy to snuggle into Paulina cos she's warm and squashy and soft and she keeps singing and it's a song with strange sounds and I know it and I shut my eyes and I can smell baking, and I can see a room and it's got pink daisies all wobbly in a line and I'm cuddled up on a chair that rocks forwards and back and forwards and back and Bab-bab says the rocking chair rocks away your bad dreams.

'Bab-bab, look at me! Bab-bab! Bab-bab, look at me, look at me!'

I'm giggling and giggling cos Bab-bab is sitting on the

sunshiney balcony and I'm running out and in and out and in, and Bab-bab is laughing and trying to catch me when I go out but I'm quick as a cheetah and she can't catch me.

The out is hot and bright and it feels rough and bumpy on my feet and the in is cool and dark and my feet tickle on the soft carpet. Every time I jump from the hot, rough balcony to the cool, soft carpet I think my feet have forgotted what carpet is cos it feels new and different every time.

On my next out, I forget to be a cheetah and Bab-bab catches me and cuddles me and tickles and tickles and does raspberry kisses on my neck and then she stops and lets go and shouts, 'Train!'

I jump up quick and Bab-bab holds me up at the balcony and we watch from high high up and see a long train like a red snake going over the vie-duck and Bab-bab is holding me and she's pushing me up a bit more so I can see all the cars and the buses and the people down below and they are all so tiny like I could pick them up in my hand. Bab-bab points to all of them and says all the words for car and bus and lorry and train but they are different words and they buzz in my ear and I try to say them and my tongue feels funny in my mouth and Bab-bab laughs and I giggle and Bab-bab says, 'Mummy will be home from work soon,' and I wriggle down and run back into the darkness.

I'm curled up warm and soft and Mummy says, 'Poor Jesika.'

Bab-bab says, 'She's been sleeping for most of the time.' And then, 'She called out in her sleep a few times for "Bab-bab".'

Mummy says, 'She misses her Bab-bab a lot. It's amazing how much she remembers. She was so little,' and then she says something else but I can't hear proply and Bab-bab says, 'I tried teaching my little granddaughter to say "Babcia" but even now she's older she says I'm not her Babcia, I'm her Bab-bab, so I think it's stuck.'

Bab-bab means me. She told me the other word lots and lots but it was too hard. Bab-bab is easy.

Bab-bab says, 'And how is your little Toby doing?'

No, that's not right. I try to open my eyes. Toby's not here yet. Toby doesn't come til after Bab-bab has gone. I need to open my eyes and ask Bab-bab how she knows about Toby. I need to open my eyes but my eyes are stuck shut.

Bab-bab says, 'Try not to worry. He's in safe hands now.'

Mummy coughs and coughs, and coughs and coughs some more, and her coughing won't stop and I have to open my eyes so I can rub Mummy's back but my eyes are still stuck.

Mummy stops coughing. There's a swish and a thud and then rushing feet and a door opens and closes and it's quiet and warm and soft and then there's noise and feet and people talking.

Mummy shouts, 'Magda! Magda! Talk to me! Oh God, oh God, oh God,' and she runs and picks up her phone and Bab-bab is on the floor and her face is a funny colour and Mummy shouts, 'Jesika, go into your bedroom now!' but I can't make my legs work and Mummy shouts, 'Ambulance! I need an ambulance!'

The ambulance drives right into the living room and the lights flash blue and the daisies on the wall are blue, not pink, and the Green Man puts Bab-bab on a bed with wheels and the ambulance drives off without waiting so the Green Man has to bump Bab-bab all the way down the stairs and I blink three times at Bab-bab for 'I love you' but her eyes are closed so she can't blink at me and she doesn't wave either and then she's gone and it's just Mummy and me in the room and the daisies are pink again and Mummy is crying and crying and she's bending over and holding onto her big baby belly and I'm crying and crying too and when I look again, Mummy's not there and it's just me.

12

IWANTMUMMYIwantMummyIwantMummyIwantMummyIwant
MummyIwantMummyIwantMummyIwantMummyIwantMummy
IwantMummyIwantMummyIwantMummy . . .

'Jesika?'

IwantMummyIwantMummyIwantMummyIwantMummyIwant
MummyIwantMummy . . .

'Jesika?'

IwantMummyIwantMummyIwantMummy . . .

A warm hand on my cheek, stroking.

Mummy?

Eyes open.

Not Mummy.

It's the Violent Lady. She's called . . . ?

What's she called?

Will she be cross if I can't remember?

She's kneeling on the floor in front of me on big squashy knees.

I'm lying comfy on soft cushions but my heart . . . thumping fast and fast.

Bab-bab went in the ambulance.

BAB-BAB WENT IN THE AMBULANCE.

I sit up quick.

The chairs are untidy and different, not where they are apposed to be round the little table, but the purple leaves and the blue circles are still in the same places on the walls and I can smell toilets and lemons so I think it's the same room as afore, still in the hopsipal, just someone's messed it up.

Mummy disappeared too.

The Violent Lady squeezes my hand and she has kind eyes but my heart still thumps, BANGBANGBANG! The lady says, 'I am Paulina, remember? I'm looking after you in the hospital.' She pulls something tight round my shoulders, covering my hands. It tickles. I look down and I'm all covered in red and it's soft, like the blanket I tuck Baby Annabelle into. Baby Annabelle's not here. Bab-bab's not here. Mummy's not here.

I say, 'Where's Mummy? I want Mummy.'

Mummy cried and cried cos Bab-bab went in the ambulance.

Paulina squeezes both my knees and she says, 'Your Mummy came to see you but she felt poorly so the doctors are looking after her. Try not to worry, kochanie. I am looking after you right now and I won't go anywhere.'

My heart thumps and thumps and my belly hurts.

I say, 'Bab-bab is poorly, not Mummy. The ambulance drived into the room and took her away and Mummy cried.' But that's not right cos ambulances can't drive inside houses. But Mummy did cry and she cried so much that it made Toby come out when I was sleeping.

Paulina says, 'I think you had a bad dream, kochanie,' and her eyes look sad at me.

My belly hurts and hurts and I say, 'I want my Mummy.' My lips wobble like jelly and I can't make the words sound right. I say, 'I want my Mummy,' again, but I can't stop my lips wobbling and now I'm crying and Paulina leans forward and holds me tight and whispers, 'Shhh, shhh,' in my ear and she whispers other words I don't know but I think they are magic words cos they make my belly feel warm and it stops hurting and then it's easy to stop crying.

Paulina gets up from kneeling and there's a strange pop-pop-pop-pop sound and Paulina laughs and says, 'There go my poor knees again.' Then she bends over and picks something up and sits down next to me on the squashy sofa. 'Here,' she says, 'I've found your special Para-Ted.' I push my hand through the gap in the blanket and take him and hold him tight and push my nose right into him and he smells strange. I say, 'I wish Mummy had bringed Baby Annabelle.'

Paulina says, 'You have a baby sister, too?' and her eyebrows shoot right up into her hair again.

I say, 'No-oo! Baby Annabelle is my dolly. Bab-bab maked her for me and she maked me lots of clothes for her too and I always cuddle Baby Annabelle when I go to bed so I'm not scared of the dark and the noises.'

Paulina says, 'I think Para-Teds are very good at helping little children feel not scared. Do you think your Para-Ted could help you until you can cuddle your Baby Annabelle again?'

I hug Para-Ted tight and he is soft and warm, even if he doesn't smell right.

I nod my head and his ears tickle my cheek, like he wants me to smile, and I do smile and Paulina smiles too. Then she picks up a pen and a piece of paper from the little table and says, 'Jesika, we're trying to find out if there's someone who can look after you tonight while your Mummy and your brother are in hospital. Is there anyone else in your family?' And then, 'Do you know the word "family"?'

I know family is who lives in your house with you and I say, 'There's only Mummy and Toby and me in our house.'

Paulina says, 'What about family that don't live in your house with you? You said your Daddy lives in Poland. Are you sure about that? Are you sure he doesn't live near you?'

I say, 'Daddy lives in a different land. A far, far away place. He made Mummy cry a lot and he made her be angry and one day she throwed one of Bab-bab's plates really hard on the floor and broke it and Bab-bab didn't even get cross with her cos she said it was Daddy's fault for making Mummy be angry.'

Paulina says, 'And your Mummy said Bab-bab is your Daddy's Mummy?'

I don't know what Paulina means. I say, 'Bab-bab is just Bab-bab. But she's not alive now. Her heart stopped working and then we had to move to a different house cos Mummy didn't have enough pennies. Mummy says someone else lives there now and we live in a different house and it's not so high up and it's a dump and Mummy gets cross cos it's noisy and smelly and dirty. I liked living in Bab-bab's house cos I got to see the trains going past.'

Paulina blinks and blinks again and suddenly I can see Bab-bab right in front of me and she blinks three times for our secret 'I love you' code and then she's gone again and I want her to come back cos I didn't blink 'I love you' back to her, but she doesn't come back and I can't even think her face inside my head now.

Paulina says, 'OK, do you have any other Grandmas, Grandads, Aunties, Uncles?'

I know 'Uncle' and I say, 'Like Uncle Ryan?'

Paulina writes squiggles on her pad of paper and says, 'Uncle Ryan? Does he live near you?'

I say, 'I don't know where he lives. I saw him on the bus and he took me round to Paige's house to play and then he took me and Paige to preschool and Mummy was taking me too but she was being very slow with Toby so I walked up ahead with Uncle Ryan and Paige.' Paulina writes more squiggles on her paper and then she says, 'So does Uncle Ryan look after you sometimes?'

BRRRING! BRRRING!

Eyes wide, heart thumping.

BRRRING! BRRRING!

What is it? What's that noise? I look all around me.

Paulina says, 'It's the telephone. Wait here, Jesika,' and she goes to the door and there's a phone stuck on the wall and Paulina lifts up the talking bit and she says 'Hello?' and then 'Yes, yes, yes . . .' and then she looks over to me and smiles and then she turns away from me and talks and talks but I don't know what she's saying cos she's made her voice quiet and quiet.

The red blanket on my shoulders slips down. I try to pull it tighter round me but it won't stay on my shoulders. I put Para-Ted on my knee and hold both the edges of the blanket and pull the blanket round and it slides soft across my shoulders, but when I let go to pick Para-Ted up again, it slides back down. I try again and the same thing happens so I try it again and this time I hold on with one hand and then pick up Para-Ted with my other hand but that's hard too and I drop him on the floor and then the blanket slides right off when I try to reach down to get him back. It's too hard!

Then Paulina's kneeling there in front of me and I didn't even see her put the phone talker back and she picks up Para-Ted and hands him to me and then pulls the blanket around my shoulders proply so it doesn't fall back down this time.

I say, 'Who were you talking to on the phone?'

Paulina sits on the sofa next to me again and says, 'It was a lady called Dolphin.'

I think that's a very strange name for a lady, but afore I can say that, Paulina says, 'She's in charge of finding someone to look after you while your Mum is in hospital.'

Paulina pulls the blanket even more tight round my shoulders and it's warm and snuggly and I have a good idea and I say, 'You can look after me cos you're really good at doing it.'

Paulina smiles and says, 'Ah, kochanie, I would love to look after you, but I can't because you need a proper bed to sleep in and soon I will be needed again to help look after the poorly children staying here in hospital.'

I don't want Paulina to look after the poorly children. I want her to stay here.

But Toby's a poorly child.

I say, 'Will you look after Toby?'

Paulina smiles and says, 'I hope so. I will wait and see if he's been sent to sleep in my ward.'

I say, 'I think you should look after Toby cos you make things not scary and he might be scared in the hopsipal.' I hug Para-Ted tight and tight.

Paulina blinks her eyes lots of times and cuddles me tight and says something in my ear that is soft and buzzy and tickly and then she lets me go and pats her knees and says, 'Dolphin said she will be here soon. What would you like to do while we wait? We can read stories or do some colouring or get the building bricks out?'

I choose stories cos I like being snuggled under the red blanket next to Paulina and I like Paulina's buzzy voice that tickles my ear and makes me feel warm.

Paulina is reading a funny story about pirates and there's a swishing noise and I look round. A lady has walked into the room and she's also carrying a book but it's not got any pictures or words on it, it's just brown. Her head turns from me to Paulina and then to me and to Paulina again and she says, 'Hey, Paulina, long time, no see. How's it going?'

Paulina smiles big and says, 'It's lovely to see you. Is it good being back?'

The lady walks over and sits on the table right in front of the sofa and she says, 'First week and already feel like I've never been away, but at least I'm busy.' Maybe she doesn't know that tables are not for sitting on, they're for putting things on, like cups of tea and colouring books and Mummy's phone and Toby's bricks.

Paulina reaches out and puts her hand on the lady's shoulder and it looks like they're saying something to each other just with their eyes but I don't know what it is and then the lady looks at me and says, 'And you must be Jesika?' and she says, 'My name is Delphine.'

Paulina says, 'This is the lady I told you about who's finding someone to look after you, Jesika.'

I wrinkle up my nose and I say, 'But you said her name is "Dolphin".'

Paulina and the lady who's not called Dolphin laugh and Paulina says, 'It must be my accent,' and the lady says, 'Dolphin would be an epic name! But I don't think I look much like a dolphin, do you?'

I look carefully at her thin body and her stretchy neck and her pointy nose and her dark eyes and her head that never stays still and she's right and I say, 'No, I don't think you look like a dolphin at all, I think you look like a meerkat.'

She laughs even more. That's cos meerkats are very funny animals. Then she says, 'Let's start again.' And she holds out her hand and says, 'My name is Delphine. Pleased to meet you, Jesika,' and I push my hand out of the red blanket and hold Delphine's hand and she shakes it up and down and it's a bit silly.

Delphine opens up her brown book and it's not actually a book with pages. It's just got lots of pieces of paper inside. Paulina picks up the piece of paper that she was writing on and hands it to Delphine and says, 'I'm afraid I didn't find out anything useful.'

Delphine takes the paper and puts it in the brown book and waves her hand in the air and says, 'No worries, it's all sorted, for tonight at least.' And then she turns to me and says, 'Jesika, I think Paulina has already explained to you that your Mummy needs to stay in hospital tonight?'

There's a quiet space after she speaks. I think she wants me to say something and I say, 'I want to go home with Mummy,' and that's not what I meaned to say cos I know Mummy's staying in hopsipal today but the words just popped out of my mouth afore I could stop them.

Delphine says, 'I'm sure you do, darling, and we want you to go home with your Mummy as soon as possible too, but for now, we need to find you a safe place to stay until your Mummy is feeling better.'

Delphine sorts through the pieces of paper and she turns one round for me to see and there's a picture of a lady and a man smiling and Delphine says, 'This is Jane and Duncan. They're foster carers, which means they look after children, like you, who need a safe place to stay while they aren't able to stay with their grown-ups.' She lifts the piece of paper up and pushes it towards me like she wants me to hold it, but my hands are holding tight to Para-Ted.

Paulina takes the paper and puts it on her knee so I can still see the lady called Jane and the man called Duncan and I look at Jane and then Duncan and then Jane again and they're looking straight back at me and I'm not really sure why Delphine is showing me pictures of this lady and this man.

Delphine says, 'Is that OK, Jesika?'

I look at Delphine. I don't know what she is asking me. She's nodding her head so I think she wants me to nod mine and so I do.

Delphine says, 'Now, Jane and Duncan live a little way away from here and because they normally look after older children – they're looking after you as a special favour – they don't keep any spare car seats, so I've arranged to drive you over there myself. OK?'

Delphine nods her head again when she asks but I don't nod back this time. I look at Paulina and I look at the picture of the lady called Jane and the man called Duncan and I say, 'I want to go home with Mummy,' and the words just pop out of my mouth again like last time cept this time my lips are wobbling and Paulina puts her arm around my shoulders and squeezes me tight and says, 'Shhh, shhh,' lots and lots of times.

Delphine gets off the table and kneels down in front of me and says, 'You must be feeling very scared, Jesika, but I *promise* you that Jane and Duncan are lovely people and they will look after you very carefully, and first thing tomorrow I will contact the hospital and find out how your Mummy's doing and, before you know it, I'm sure you'll be back at home with her.'

I look at Paulina and her eyes are sparkly and she's smiling and nodding her head and she kisses me right on top of my head and whispers buzzy words in my ear and it fills me up all warm and then she says, 'Be brave, kochanie. You're safe with Delphine and you'll be safe with Jane and Duncan and soon you'll be back home safe with your Mummy. OK?' And she nods her head again.

I want to be safe with Paulina til I can go home with Mummy but I remember that Paulina is going to look after Toby so I nod my head too and Paulina lifts me onto my feet and she unwraps the red blanket and she says, 'Would you like to carry Para-Ted or shall I put him in your bag?'

I squeeze Para-Ted tight to my chest. Paulina picks up my bag and gives it to Delphine and then she kneels down and wraps me up in a warm, squeezy cuddle and she whispers, 'Your Mummy will be so proud of you, Jesika,' and then I'm holding Delphine's hand and we're walking down the long, long room back to the magic sliding doors.

Just afore we get there, I look ahind me and Paulina is standing by the door of the room and she smiles and waves and blows me a kiss and then we're outside in the shivery-cold dark and we're walking, walking, walking past cars and cars and cars til we get to one that beeps. Delphine opens the door in the back and she lifts me onto a car seat and pulls my straps over me and clicks it in and pulls it tight and then she gets in the front and the engine roars and the car moves and we're out on a road and orange lights are sliding down and down and down on me.

I want Mummy.

13

IT'S HOTHOTHOT, LIKE T-shirt and shorts hot, cept I've got a big, squashy coat on and a hat and gloves and a scarf tight around my neck and I'm wet and sticky all over and too too hot. My feet SLAP, SLAP, SLAP on the pavement cos I'm running but I don't know where I'm running to. Maybe it's the swings cos I think this is the right way to go there, cept the street looks different, like someone's picked up all the shops and put them back down in the wrong places and some are bigger and some are smaller and some aren't even the right colour.

I keep running and running and there's more and more and more shops and I don't know when I'm going to get to the swings. I need to have a rest but I can't make my legs stop, they just keep running and running.

'Jesika, stop!'

I can't stop. I look ahind me but my legs keep running. Far, far, a long way ahind me is Mummy and she's pushing Toby in his buggy and he's leaning over holding out his hands to me and Mummy shouts, 'Jesika, STOP!'

But I can't stop and I can't turn round and run back to Mummy, my legs just keep running far and far and far away and Mummy keeps shouting, 'Jesika, Jesika, JESIKA!'

*

Eyes open.

'Jesika?'

Where am I?

'Hi, Jesika.'

I'm not running now. I'm lying in a small, soft bed all by myself and the walls are yellow and the curtains are yellow and there's swirly patterns on the curtains and they touch right down to the floor and it must be sunny on the other side cos the curtains are shining with light and I can hear birds singing like when we go to the park and I can smell a yummy baker-shop smell.

'Just a bad dream, Jesika, but it's gone away now.'

My belly squeezes hard. I turn my head away from the window and there's a man sitting near the bottom of the bed. I know his face and his eyes and his glasses that are like Daddy's. He stands up and comes and kneels on the floor next to me and he lifts a hand like he's going to stroke my head like Daddy used to cept he stops and puts his hand away again.

He says, 'Do you remember me, Jesika?'

I remember his face and his voice but I don't remember why I'm in this room that I don't know. Where's Mummy?

The man pushes his glasses against his nose. My Daddy does that too. Am I at my Daddy's house far, far away? Did Mummy bring me to see Daddy?

I say, 'Daddy?'

The man shakes his head and says, 'Duncan.'

I say, 'What's Duncan?'

The man says, 'No, Duncan is what I'm called. It's my name. I'm Duncan. Do you remember? Me and my wife, Jane, are looking after you for a day or two until your Mummy is better.'

My belly squeezes even more hard. What's wrong with Mummy? My belly squeezes and pushes, getting more and more big inside me, and it's hurting and hurting. Am I still dreaming the bad dream?

He says, 'Do you remember? Delphine brought you here from the hospital in the night.'

The hopsipal?

. . . flashy blue lights . . . shivery-cold . . . Toby on a bed . . . blue circles and purple leaves . . . a lady with crinkly eyes and a buzzy voice . . .

The hopsipal! We went in an ambulance cos Toby wasn't breathing proply. I went with Paulina and Mummy said she'd come and find me, but she didn't. Did she get lost?

Duncan says, 'Jesika, do you remember? Do you remember Delphine?'

. . . a dark, shivery car . . . orange lights sliding down and down and down . . . on a pavement, pink light in the sky . . . holding a scratchy hand . . . a red door . . . and falling, falling . . .

Did Mummy come with me to the red door? She doesn't have scratchy hands.

Duncan says, 'You were barely awake when you got here so I carried you upstairs and I put you straight into bed, right here.'

My hurty belly fills up all my insides and it's a really BIG hurty that squeezes and squashes all my breathing. I need to wake up and tell Mummy it's a bad dream and Mummy will cuddle me and the hurty pain will go away. I have to tell Mummy RIGHT NOW afore I stop breathing like Toby.

I sit up quick as quick and push the bed covers off and cold smacks my legs. I look down and my pyjama bottoms are all wet and sticking to my legs and it feels real cold and real wet and not like a dream at all.

Duncan says, 'Oh dear, not to worry. Let's get you out of those wet things. I've got your clothes right here in your bag.' He reaches over to something and then he's holding up my preschool bag and unzipping it and pulling out my yellow top with the red and orange butterfly and my purple trousers and my green zippy top and my pants and socks. How did all that get here? Did Mummy bring it?

Duncan stands up and bends over me and, oh! He's lifted me right out of the bed and now I'm standing on the carpet and it's so fluffy and my toes sink right into it. Duncan picks up my clothes and holds out his hand to hold and says, 'Let's go to the bathroom,' and I think maybe that's where Mummy is and I take his hand and we walk out of the bedroom into a big space with doors and stairs that go down and it's like the upstairs at Paige's house but there's more doors.

We walk to one of the doors and Duncan opens it and inside it's a giant*nor*mous bathroom that's shiny white all round the walls and there's sparkly blue bits that look like oshun waves and there's a bath and a toilet and *two* sinks next to each other with a huge mirror above them and next to that there's a cupboard that has glass walls all the way from the floor to the ceiling and there's nothing in it cept some metal thing stuck on the wall.

Mummy's not here.

I say, 'Where's Mummy?'

Duncan kneels down in front of me and says, 'Your Mummy and your little brother are both staying at the hospital so the doctors can look after them and help them get better. You're staying here for a day or two with me and Jane until your Mummy feels better and can come and get you.'

The Big Hurty squeezes and squashes inside me. Mummy's not here.

Duncan puts his hand on my shoulder and says, 'Try not to worry. As soon as your Mummy feels better, she'll come and get you.'

But Mummy doesn't know the way. Mummy didn't bring me

here. The other lady bringed me here. Mummy doesn't know where this house is.

Duncan says, 'Come on, let's get you sorted. Do you want me to take your bottoms off, or can you do it yourself?'

I say, 'I can do it myself,' and I start to pull them down and it feels cold on my nudey bottom and then I remember Mummy saying at bedtime about private pants and I stop and pull my bottoms back up again cos Duncan doesn't live in my house.

He says, 'Do you want me to help you?'

I say, 'No.'

He says, 'OK, you take them off, then.'

I say, 'No.'

He says, 'OK. Right. Well, I think you'll have to take them off if you're going to get dressed.'

I need to tell him about private pants but all the words that Mummy said are tricky and they're all mixed up in my head and I can't make them come out of my mouth. I need Mummy to come and tell him.

I say, 'No,' cos that's easy to say.

Duncan pushes his glasses against his nose again and he looks over his shoulder out of the bathroom door and he looks at me and I don't think he knows what to do. I don't think he knows that he has to go away and then I can take my bottoms off and get dressed myself.

I say, 'You need to go away.'

Duncan says, 'Right, OK. Wait right there,' and he stands up and walks out of the bathroom and I hear him outside the room calling, 'Jane?' and then, 'Jane?'

I take off my bottoms and my skin feels all sticky. I have to wipe off the sticky cos that's what Mummy tells me to do when I have a wet bed. I can't see any sponges but there's a blue cloth hanging on the edge of the bath, just like the cloths that we have in our bathroom for wiping our faces, so I make it wet under the bath tap and squeeze it and wipe myself all over the sticky bits and then I look around and there's a blue towel hanging on a metal bar next to the sinks and I pull it off the bar and dry myself and it's so so fluffy.

'Jesika?'

I turn round and Duncan's coming back through the door and my bottom's all nudey and I have to use my Big Voice now cos he's not listening to me so I shout, 'GO AWAY!' and I run to shut the bathroom door but he's come too far in and there's a lady with him and she's got a frowny face and Duncan says, 'It's OK, Jesika, this is Jane, and she's going to help you and I'm going to go away, OK?' and he goes out and shuts the door and it clicks and then it's just me and the lady called Jane. But Jane doesn't live in my house either. I need Mummy. Only Mummy is allowed to help me.

I say, 'You're not my Mummy. You have to go away.'

Jane sits on the edge of the bath and she presses her hands atween her legs and she's still frowning but she's smiling a bit too and she says, 'No, I'm not your Mummy, but it's my job, and Duncan's, to help you and look after you until your Mummy feels better.'

Then Jane stands up and she says, 'So, let's get you dressed, OK?' and she picks up my pants and she holds them out to me to step into but I have to put them on myself, cos of private pants, and I need Jane to go away but she's not going away so I pull my pants out of Jane's hands and I say, 'No!' and I run to the bathroom door and try to push the handle down to open it but it's too hard to push and I can't make it open and Jane's coming to get me and she's not going to let me go out . . .

let-me-out-door-handle-stuck-let-me-out-want-Mummy-scared-LET-ME-OUT-BITE!

The door's open and my feet run and run and I don't know which way to go and then I'm back in the yellow bedroom and I can hear someone coming to get me. It must be Jane, cos I bited her. I didn't even know I was going to do it. Jane must be so cross.

I have to hide!

I can't hide in the bed cos all the covers have been taken off but there's a space under the bed so I get on my belly and Para-Ted's on the floor next to my bag so I grab him and I squeeze and squash right into the corner and it's dark and I squash my face into Para-Ted and he smells nice and I keep breathing and breathing and breathing his smell and I can see Paulina in my head and it remembers me about her magic words but I can't hear them and all my whole body hurts and hurts and I curl up tight and close my eyes and pretend I'm playing hide and seek with Toby and Mummy and if I squeeze my eyes tight and tight Toby or Mummy will creep up ahind me and tickle me and shout, 'Found You!'

It's not Mummy that finds me. It's Jane and she's reaching under the bed to me and she must be so so cross. She says, 'You must be cold and uncomfortable under there, Jesika. Why don't you come out and I'll help you get dressed.'

I'm not cold. It's warm under here. I'm lying on a fluffy carpet that's snuggly like a teddy bear and not scratchy and hard like the carpet in my house. And I think Jane still has to be cross with me for biting and I don't want her to be cross. I wriggle right away from Jane's hand and turn to the wall and press my nose into Para-Ted and breathe and breathe his smell.

It's quiet, like the day I waked up afore it was morning, but even more quiet cos I can't even hear veekles outside or Mummy and Toby breathing or the building making clicks and clanks and moans. This building isn't saying anything and all I can hear is my own breath going in and out of my mouth.

Then I hear, 'I don't think I can do this, Duncan,' and it's

Jane's voice and it's not right under the bed now, it's more far away.

I roll back over and I can see two lots of feet standing near the bed. One has blue socks on and the other has black socks with pictures of birds. What is it Jane can't do?

Duncan says, 'Shhh!' The birdie feet move away where I can't see them and then the blue ones move away too. I wriggle away from the wall til I can see them again, standing next to the open door.

Jane says, 'High-school kids only. We agreed,' and her voice is whispery and spiky.

Duncan whispers, 'We also said we'd never say "no". I couldn't say "no".'

The feet turn and they're pointing towards each other, almost touching.

Jane whispers, 'I *know*. I *know*. And she must be so scared. But . . .'

The feet shuffle forwards even more close and there's more whispers and I don't know who's whispering now but I think it must be Jane telling Duncan all about me biting. The Big Hurty pushes and squeezes inside me. I think they are whispering that the lady has to come back and take me away and I have to live somewhere else and it might be so so far away that Mummy will never ever find me.

I roll back to the wall and curl up small and press Para-Ted into my face and breathe . . .

Breathe . . .

Breathe . . .

14

IT'S TRICKY-HARD STAYING curled up small. My knees keep slipping down and something keeps tickling on my nose. Maybe it's a spider. I like spiders cos they're clever at spinning webs and so gentle cos they spin their webs with teeny-tiny sticky string that's nearly invibisle and they never even break it, only people do. But can spiders see in the dark? If they can't, the spider might not know I'm here and it might crawl into my mouth or up my nose. Ugh! I don't want a spider to do that!

I press my lips tight and pinch my nose cept now it's even harder to curl up small cos I've got one hand on Para-Ted and one hand on my nose and no hands holding my knees tight. If I was the hungry caterpillar, it would be easy-peasy cos I could just make a cocoon all round me and then everything in my body would stay curled up tight and nothing would tickle my nose and no spiders would crawl anywhere they're not apposed to.

There's a creaking noise above my head. What was that? My heart thumps hard. I roll away from the wall. Oh! Someone's sitting on the bed cos I can see two legs dangling down and two feet on the floor and it's the birdie feet. I shuffle closer to look. All the birdies are the same: blue and yellow and pretty. There must be a-hundred-a-thousand birds. I try counting them but they keep jumping about and not staying still so I point my finger at them and count, 'One, two, three, four, five, seven,' but then my finger points too far and pokes the sock and the foot jumps away from me and then the legs move and they are kneeling down. There's nowhere to hide! Is it Jane or Duncan? They will be so cross I poked and so cross cos I bited Jane. A face appears sideways and upside down under the bed and it's Duncan but he doesn't look cross. He's smiling and he says, 'You missed out six.'

I don't know what he means.

His face disappears and his hand is pointing to the birdies on his socks and he says, 'One, two, three, four, five, *six*, seven.' His face appears again and he's still smiling. Maybe he's not cross.

He says, 'Do you like birds?'

I nod and the carpet tickles my cheek.

Duncan says, 'Liam likes birds too. He's another boy that we look after. He knows all the names of the birds. Maybe he'll tell you some of them when he gets home from school.'

I know bird names too. I know robin and blackbird but I don't know what the ones on Duncan's socks are called. Is Liam a little boy like me? Maybe his Mummy is poorly in hopsipal too.

Duncan says, 'If you come out from under the bed and get dressed, I can show you the bird table. We always see lots of birds on there.'

I didn't know birds had tables like people. I want to see that. But I'm still nudey apart from my pyjama top and I can't get dressed til Duncan goes away.

I say, 'No.'

Duncan says, 'Hmm.' Then he says, 'How about this? I'll go outside the bedroom and close my eyes and count and you see how fast you can put all your clothes on. I bet you can't do it before I get to twenty!'

I say, 'I can!'

Duncan smiles big and he says, 'OK, then!' and his face disappears and the birdie feet walk over to the door and I hear the door open and close and then I hear Duncan counting, 'One, two, three . . .'

I wriggle out from under the bed and there's a pile of my clothes on the floor.

Duncan says, '. . . six, seven . . .' Quick! I pull on my pants and my trousers and my socks and Duncan says, '. . . ten, eleven, twelve . . .' and I pull my pyjama top off and put on my T-shirt but I don't put my zippy top on cos I'm too hot, and Duncan says, '. . . seventeen, eighteen . . .' and I run to the bedroom door and pull it open and shout, 'I did it!' and I'm smiling and laughing cos Duncan looks so surprised.

I say, 'Can I see the bird table now? Is it in one of these rooms?'

Duncan laughs and says, 'No, we don't keep the bird table indoors. That would be very messy!' and he laughs again and he says, 'Come on, this way,' and he walks to the top of the stairs and then stops and waits for me and then he says, 'Now, if you put one hand on the banister and give me your other hand,' and he waits til I'm holding the banister and his hand and then he steps off the top step backwards and says, 'And just take one step at a time, slowly, slowly, that's it,' and we walk down the stairs with Duncan stepping backwards afore me and watching my feet and going so slow and I think it's cos maybe these stairs are slippy or dangerous and that's why we have to be careful cos I don't usually go down stairs like this, I just go down them by myself.

At the bottom is a big room with lots of doors. All the doors are brown and wooden cept for one that's big and red and it's got a window right above it that looks like the top of a shining sun. Duncan and Jane have a lot of doors! Even more than Paige! Or maybe these doors are other people's houses like in my house . . . but I don't think so cos they don't have numbers on them like in my house, and there's no thump-da-thump-da-thump music or shouting or banging or eggy-yucky smell.

I say, 'Where's Jane?'

Duncan points back up the stairs and says, 'She's working in the office.'

I say, 'What's the office?'

Duncan says, 'It's a room upstairs where we both do our work.'

Lorna goes to a different place to work and so did Mummy when we lived with Bab-bab.

I say, 'Don't you have to work in a different place?'

Duncan says, 'Some people do. We're lucky that we've found a job we can do at home so we can be here to look after the children who come and stay with us.'

He bends over and picks up a washing basket like the ones that Nandini has in her washing machine shop. Aren't they apposed to stay at the washing machine shop so other people can use them? I don't know why Duncan's got one in his house, but it's got lots of things in it and I can see the covers that were on my bed. Maybe he's got the basket at his house so he can carry the bed covers to the shop. Maybe he doesn't have a big washing bag like Mummy's.

He says, 'This way,' and we walk down the side of the stairs past two of the brown wooden doors and then at the end of the room Duncan opens another brown wooden door and it smells just like the bread shop that we walk past to get to preschool. My belly growls loud like a bear and Duncan looks ahind to me and says, 'Someone's hungry!' just like Mummy does and now the Big Hurty is squeezing and squashing again and I don't feel hungry cos my belly hurts too much.

Duncan puts the basket down and walks back to me and crouches down and says, 'This is all a bit strange for you, isn't it?'

My eyes sting and I blink and blink.

Duncan says, 'How about some breakfast? Some bread and jam? And then you can eat it while you watch for birds on the bird table. How about that?'

I love bread and jam. It's yummy. Nandini gave me bread and jam at the washing machine shop. And I really do want to see the bird table. I nod and I blink and blink and wipe my sleeve over my eyes and I say, 'Yes, please,' but my voice doesn't speak, it just whispers.

Duncan says, 'Come on, then,' and he holds my hand and we walk into the room and, oh! It's a giant*nor*mous kitchen and it's shiny in black and red, even the floor and the walls and the cupboards, and there's chairs with really long legs like giraffes. I let go of Duncan's hand and walk right up to a red shiny cupboard that stretches far, far up above my head and I can see my face in the cupboard like a mirror cept this is a red mirror and all my face and my eyes and my mouth shine red and not my normal colours.

Duncan slides the washing basket along the floor with his foot and opens one of the red shiny cupboard doors and he picks up all the covers in the basket and pushes them inside the door. Why is he putting them there? Why isn't he taking them to the washing machine shop? Then he stands up and I can see into the cupboard and it's not a cupboard, it's a black shiny washing machine! And when Duncan's put in the washing powder and pressed the buttons the machine starts swooshing, and he pushes the cupboard door shut and the swooshing gets smaller. I go over and press my ear to the door and it swooshes louder and tickles my ear, like the tickly carpet at home. Maybe Mummy doesn't know that you can have washing machines right inside your house. When she comes to get me, I'm going to tell her that we can get one, and maybe we can get one that's green and we could get green shiny cupboards too so I can see what my face looks like all green.

WHIZWHIRRRR!

I jump back from the washing machine cupboard, eyes scary-wide.

WHIZWHIRRRR!

What is it?

The noise is where Duncan is. He's moving something along on the worktop but I can't see what it is.

WHIZWHIRRRR!

I go to look and Duncan turns round and sees me looking. He points to a red, shiny machine on the worktop and says, 'It's a bread slicer.' And he shows me a round metal circle with jaggy spikes like shark's teeth and he presses a button and, WHIZ-WHIRRRR!, the round metal bit spins round fast and fast so I can't see the jaggy shark's teeth any more. He switches the noise off again and I can see the jaggy shark's teeth again and he says, 'It slices up the bread.' And next to him there's a board and there's lots of slices of bread on it, all leaning over each other like they're trying to push each other down. That's strange that Duncan has to slice his bread up himself. Our bread is already cut up when Mummy buys it at the shop.

When Duncan's finished spreading the butter and the jam, he puts the bread on a plate and he puts the spread and the jam back in the fridge but he doesn't shut the fridge, he looks and looks inside and he says, 'Now, what do four-year-olds drink?'

I say, 'Milk at breakfast, juice at lunch and water at tea-time.'

Duncan looks at me like someone gave him a big surprise and he says, 'OK, milk it is, then.' He pours out the milk into a glass and I stand on the metal bit at the bottom of a giraffe chair and try to wriggle onto the seat. It's tricky and it makes me huff and puff and I keep slipping back down and then, oh! I whizz up in the air and my feet bump onto the floor and it was Duncan lifting me right off and he says, 'No, no, no, that's a bit high for you, Jesika,' and he picks up my milk and my bread and he says, 'Better through here,' and he walks over to some funny black curtains that have been cut in lots and lots of straight lines from the top to the bottom and I think he's going to walk straight into them but he stops and puts the bread and the milk on a worktop near the curtains and then pulls on a long string and the curtains slide open and ahind them are two glass doors and through the glass doors is a glass room and it's full of GREEN!

Duncan opens the doors and we walk through and I can't stop looking at all the green. There's green leaves and green chairs and a green sofa and a table made of sticks with a green cloth on top and even green outside in a park on the other side of the glass walls.

Duncan puts the tray on top of the green cloth and points to the green sofa and says, 'How about you sit right here, and then you can watch for birds while you're eating.'

I sit where Duncan says and he sits next to me and I can see right outside at the grass and the trees and the flowers in the park and there's a teeny-tiny house that's just a roof but no sides and it's on a pole that stretches up, up, up and there's a brown bird sitting under the roof peck, peck, pecking. Oh! He must be pecking at food! I know where the bird table is now. And it must be teeny-tiny cos the house is so so small.

There's a far away bang and a thump-thump-thump-thump-thump and afore I can say, 'What's that?' Duncan jumps up from the sofa and rushes into the kitchen and he's saying, 'Liam? Liam, is that you?' and his voice goes small and small and then I can't hear it and everything is so quiet.

I eat some more of my bread and jam and now there's two blue and yellow birds in the bird house. They peck-peck-peck and then one flies away and then the other flies away and then one comes back, peck-peck-peck, and the other comes back, peck-peck-peck, and it's like the song we do at preschool when we have to hide our hands ahind our backs, cept those birds were sitting on a wall and not a bird house stuck on a big pole.

I can hear voices again. Small and then more big and more big. I look ahind me at the glass-room door but there's no one there. Is it Duncan? I stand up and walk to the door and look into the kitchen . . .

CRASH!

The kitchen door bounces against the wall and a big boy rushes through it and runs straight at me and I think he's going to knock right into me and I can't make my legs move out of the way but just afore he bangs into me he stops. His face is scary and his eyes are mean and he says, 'Who are you?'

Duncan hurries into the kitchen ahind him and says, 'Liam . . .'

The big boy says, 'Move it.'

Duncan says, 'Liam . . .'

But the big boy's not listening and he pushes past me and he opens the glass door into the park and runs outside and a bird in the bird house flies off quick as quick. I look where the big boy's gone but I can't see. Duncan walks over to the glass door and pulls it shut and goes and sits down on the green sofa and he pats it to tell me to come and sit down too and I do and he says, 'That was Liam. He just needs calming-down time, that's all. Maybe by the time you've finished your bread and milk, he'll be ready to meet you properly.'

I don't want to meet him. He's scary and mean.

There's footsteps in the kitchen and I look round and Jane comes into the kitchen and she looks at me quick, not smiling, and looks at Duncan, still not smiling, and says, 'They didn't even know he'd left. Again. Is he . . . ?' She nods her head sideways at the glass door into the park. Duncan nods and Jane nods her head sideways the other way where me and Duncan are sitting and she says, 'And what about . . . ?'

Duncan nods again and says, 'Fine, fine . . .'

Jane says, 'Right. Good. I'll talk to him when he comes back in.' And she walks back out of the kitchen. I think she doesn't want to talk to me cos she's still cross about the biting.

Liam stays outside for a long-a-long time and I'm finished my bread and milk, and the extra bread and milk that Duncan gave me next, when Liam comes back in and falls lying down on the chair in the glass room.

Duncan says, 'Ready to talk?'

Liam turns his face into the chair and says, 'No.'

Duncan says, 'How about a proper hello for Jesika?'

Liam turns his head and stares at me and says, 'Hello,' in a grumpy voice and then turns his head back into the chair. I don't think Liam's a nice boy.

Jane comes into the glass room and she bends down and says something in Duncan's ear so quiet I can't hear it and Duncan gets up and says, 'Back in a minute.' He touches Liam on the shoulder as he walks past him and he says, 'Jesika likes birds too, Liam, but she doesn't know all the names. You could help her.' And he walks into the kitchen and I turn my head and I can see him and Jane standing close together and talking.

Liam rolls over on the chair and stares at me again and he says, 'So what you doing here, Jesika? Is your Mum a big fat waste of space too?'

My heart thumps and thumps and the Big Hurty squeezes and squashes all my breathing. I don't like Liam and I don't want him talking about Mummy. I wish Mummy was here. I wish Toby was here too cos he's more nice than Liam and he doesn't not ever talk to me mean.

Duncan comes back into the glass room and sits down next to me and says, 'Jane's just spoken to Delphine. Do you remember her? She's the lady who brought you here from the hospital.'

He looks at me but doesn't say anything else. Mummy's coming to get me? Mummy's coming to get me! I smile and smile and say, 'Mummy!'

But Duncan's not smiling. He says, 'Delphine says your

156

Mummy and Toby are getting better but they have to stay in hospital a bit longer.'

My smile goes away. 'Why do they have to stay?'

Duncan says, 'They've got something called pneumonia and the doctors at the hospital have to give them some medicine to help them get better.'

I don't know what new moania is but I know that getting medicine is quick cos Mummy just sucks it up into a plastic tube and squeezes it into my mouth and I swallow it and then it goes inside me and I feel better.

I say, 'Will Mummy come and get me afore bedtime?'

Duncan shakes his head and says, 'Your Mummy has to stay in hospital tonight, so you'll sleep here and then Delphine will let us know tomorrow what's happening.'

I don't know why Mummy has to stay in hopsipal. I don't want to sleep here tonight. I want to sleep in my own bed with Mummy and Toby aside us in his cot.

Duncan says, 'Jesika, does that all make sense to you?'

My eyes sting and I blink and blink.

Duncan says, 'Is there anything else you want to ask me?'

Liam makes a noise and I look at him and he makes a mean face at me.

Duncan says, 'Jesika?'

I want to see Mummy. I say, 'Can I go and see Mummy?'

Duncan says, 'Not today because your Mummy is sleeping a lot. Delphine will let us know when it's OK to visit. OK?'

It's not OK. I want to see Mummy now.

Duncan says, 'Your Mummy and Toby are being well looked after. Try not to worry, OK?'

The Big Hurty squeezes and squashes.

Liam says, 'Yeah, try not to worry, Jesika. Life's a fucking fairytale.'

I don't want Liam to talk to me.

Duncan leans forward and says, 'Liam, if you can't find something positive to say, just leave it, OK?'

My heart thumps and thumps.

Liam says, 'Something positive? Let me have a think.'

Duncan says, 'No. I think you should go to your room right now.'

Liam looks straight at me and his face is scary and he says, 'Your Mum's not coming back for you because—'

'LIAM!' Duncan jumps off the sofa.

Liam jumps up too and runs for the door into the park and he shouts, '. . . Mums are big, fat, pathetic liars!'

I'm not sitting on the sofa now. I'm running and running and I don't know where, but when my legs stop I'm up at the top of the stairs and I'm looking at all the doors and I can't remember where the yellow room is and I open a door and it's the blue bathroom and I can hear someone coming quick up the stairs and I run fast to the next door and open it and it's the yellow bedroom and I run so fast inside and slide under the bed and roll over to the wall and curl up tight against it and I can hear my breathing so loud in my ears and my whole body thumps and thumps and it hurts so much.

Mummy *is* coming back to get me.

She's coming to get me when she's not poorly. She won't make me find a new Mummy cos I'll be helpful and good and I'll never shout at her ever, ever, ever again and I'll always eat all my pasta even with no cheese. She's coming to get me soon. She is.

15

DUNCAN IS SITTING on the bed again. I know it's him cos I can see
the birds on his socks. I think he's waiting for me to come out
from under the bed but I'm not coming out. I'm staying here til
Mummy comes to get me.

There's a swish and now there's more socks and these are Jane's
blue socks and she says, 'I'm popping to the shop to get those bits
we need. I'll take Liam with me.'

Duncan says, 'Has he said anything yet?'

Jane says, 'Just that he was provoked, but he won't say how.
School rang back and want a meeting tomorrow morning. They
want to suspend him for the rest of the week.'

I can hear whispering.

Duncan says, 'Yeah, good point. I'll try that.'

Duncan's feet move and his legs bend down and he's going to
look under the bed so I roll quick over onto the other side and
squash up against the wall. It feels smooth and hard on my nose.

Duncan says, 'I'm going to do some work, Jesika. I'm only just
outside the door if you need me.'

Everything goes quiet.

Cept for the birds. They sing a lot outside Duncan and Jane's
house. I don't hear birds singing outside the windows in my
house. Maybe it's cos birds can't fly that high cos our house is so
high up above the road. Or maybe the birds are like Mummy and

don't like all the noisy music and shouting and cars and doors banging. Maybe that scares them away. I want to see the birds singing outside the window here. I roll over and look at the carpet. I can't see any socks. I roll a bit further. There's no one in the room. I come right out and stand up and I can see a tree outside the window. I bet that's where the birds are. I creep on tiptoes cos I don't want to scare the birds away.

Oh! There's something hiding on the floor ahind one of the curtains. I pull it back and there's a real, actual pirate's treasure chest!

I stroke the wood with my hand and it feels smooth, cept when my hand bumps over the metal bits that go all the way round. I wonder what's inside it? Maybe real pirate treasure! I push the lid up as hard as I can but it doesn't move at all. Maybe you need more muscles to open it. Or maybe it's locked, cos it does have a hole for a key. The hole is big enough to fit my pointing finger but not my thumb so I think it only needs a little key, but where is the key?

Maybe Duncan or Jane has it? Maybe Duncan or Jane is a pirate! Maybe they sailed on a huge pirate ship on the oshun and found treasure and brought it back home and hided it in this bedroom ahind the long curtains so other pirates couldn't find it.

I want to be a pirate when I grow up cos then I can go on a ship on the oshun and find treasure and go to magical faraway lands with volcanoes and colourful birds and icebergs and things like that. Those places are in one of my story books and Mummy says it's all true and they are real places you can actually go to.

There's more noises outside now, not just birds singing but also shouting and laughing noises, like lots of children, like at preschool. Maybe it's children playing in the park. I stand up and look out of the window but the tree isn't in a park, it's growing right out of the pavement on a road with cars parked on it and all along the road are lots and lots of trees all growing out of the pavement in front of houses that stretch far, far away and I think these trees are where all the singing birds are hiding cos I can hear the birds but I can't see them.

I can see children running and skipping atween the trees and there's Mummies and Daddies pushing buggies and holding hands with each other. Maybe these are children going to preschool like I do, cept I don't go til after lunchtime and I've not had lunch yet. Does Duncan know the way to my preschool? I don't know the way from this house but if he takes me to my house I can show him where to go cos that's easy. I need to tell him that.

I run over to the bedroom door and open it and Duncan's sitting on the floor right outside with his back against the wall and his legs stretched right out and he's got a computer on his legs and a big smile on his face.

He says, 'Hello, Jesika.'

I say, 'When is it time for preschool?'

Duncan pushes down the top of his computer and puts it on the floor aside him and he says, 'You don't need to worry about preschool, Jesika.'

I say, 'Do you know the way?'

Duncan says, 'No, but I know it's on the other side of the city, so Delphine's said not to worry as it's only for a few days.'

I don't know what Duncan means. I say, 'I have to be there straight after lunch and if you're late Stella shuts the door and you have to ring the doorbell.'

Duncan says, 'It's OK, Jesika. You don't need to be there today, or tomorrow. Your Mummy will take you back to preschool when she's better.'

I stare at Duncan. I don't think he understands my words. I say, 'But I want to go to preschool.'

Duncan rubs the back of his neck and makes a wrinkly mouth

and says, 'Let's think of something else that you'd like to do instead. It's a nice day today. We could go to the park. How about that?'

I say, 'I want to go to preschool. I want to play with Paige.'

Duncan stands up and holds out his hand and says, 'How about we get some lunch sorted. Jane and Liam won't be long and we can all have lunch together. Good idea?'

I don't like Liam, but lunch is a good idea cos I can't go to preschool til I've had some lunch. I hold Duncan's hand and he helps me walk down the stairs slow as a snail just like afore, but I don't know why we have to go slow now cos when I runned up the stairs afore they weren't slippy at all.

Jane and Liam come into the kitchen when me and Duncan have just finished making pizzas, like we did at preschool one day cept this time I even got to make the pizza base flat with a huge rolling pin. I'm watching the pizzas through the glass door on the oven and the cheese is bubbling and then Duncan opens the door and lifts one of the pizzas out and it smells so yummy and Liam sniffs and sniffs and says, 'Wicked, pizza!'

Jane says, 'Liam . . . ?'

Liam says, 'Oh, yeah,' and he turns to me and says, 'I'm sorry about what I said, Jesika,' and his face isn't mean now cos he's smiling but I remember his mean face and it wasn't nice.

He pulls out one of the giraffe chairs and sits on it but Duncan says, 'We'll sit in the conservatory, Liam. These chairs are too high for Jesika.'

Liam laughs and says, 'But these chairs are well good. Here, Jesika, I'll show you,' and steps towards me and I'm whizzing up in the air cos he's lifted me and now I'm high, high up on one of the giraffe chairs and it's a long way from the ground and Duncan drops the big cutting knife with a crash and he's rushing over and Liam grabs my shoulders and makes a scary face and pushes me

162

backwards, and I'm going to fall! And then he grabs me back again and laughs and says, 'Saved you!'

Jane says, 'Liam!' and then Duncan's there lifting me up and whizzing me back down to the ground and he says, 'She's only little, Liam, remember.'

Liam's not smiling now and he says, 'It's just a game.' And then he says, 'Kyla loves it,' quiet as quiet. He looks like he's going to cry. I don't know who Kyla is but I don't like his game.

We eat in the green room and I watch lots of birds fly in and out of the bird house. They're having their lunch too. A robin flies in and peck-peck-pecks and then a brown bird flies onto the top of the house but he flies away again cos the robin flies out and scares him.

Duncan says, 'Liam, how about you tell Jesika what the different birds are. She likes birds too. What's that one on the table now?'

Liam says, 'Everyone knows *that* one,' and laughs but it's not a nice laugh and he looks at me like I'm so silly for not knowing robins but I do know them and I say, 'I *do* know robins.'

Liam waves a hand at me and says, 'See?' and he smiles at me but I don't want him to smile at me. I watch the birds again instead so I don't have to smile back.

The robin's gone. It's one of the pretty blue and yellow birds. I don't know what they are but I'm not saying cos Liam will laugh again.

Duncan says, 'Ah, there's the bird that's on my socks. A great tit, isn't it, Liam?'

Liam says, 'A *blue* tit. Y'know, cos it's *blue*.'

Duncan laughs and winks at me and says, 'So which one's the great tit?'

Liam says, 'Yellow breast, black and white head.'

Duncan nods and winks at me again. Why does he keep doing that?

There's two yellow-blue tits pecking at food again and, oh! That naughty robin! He's just chased both of them away and he's eating even more food. I think that's why he has a big round belly, cos he eats his food and the food for all the other birds too.

Liam leans forward and says, 'Did you see what the robin just did?'

I nod.

Liam says, 'That's the boss robin. There's another smaller one that visits sometimes but if the boss robin's around he gets chased away, and when the boss robin's hungry, none of the other birds get to eat. I even saw this boss robin chasing off a squirrel last week.'

My eyes go wide and I say, 'A *squirrel*!' Cos squirrels are big and robins are tiny and I don't know why a squirrel would be scared of a robin.

Liam says, 'Yeah, there's a feeder hanging off a tree over there,' he waves his hand at the park outside, 'and the squirrel was trying to reach it and the boss robin just flew right at the squirrel and the squirrel ran away.'

I say, 'Can I see the feeder? Where is it?'

Liam gets up and walks to the outside door and points and says, 'On that tree, there.' But I can't see so I get up too and Liam opens the door and I look out the door and I can see the bird feeder hanging off the tree and it has nuts in it like the feeders at preschool *and* I can see a giant*nor*mous trampoline!

I say, 'There's a trampoline in the park!'

Liam says, 'In the park?'

I stretch my neck to look further round the corner of the park but I can't see past the trampoline and I say, 'Is there a playground too with swings and a slide and a roundabout?'

Liam says, 'That's not a park, that's the garden.'

I look at Duncan and Jane and I say, 'You've got a *garden*! Can I go on the trampoline?'

Liam does his not-nice laugh and says, '*Everybody*'s got a garden.'

But I don't have a garden. Not at my house. Mummy says the park is like our garden but we have to walk and walk afore we can go and play there.

Jane says, 'Liam . . .' so so quiet and Liam falls back down onto his chair and says, '*What?*' Then he says, 'Hey, Jesika, have you ever been on a trampoline as big as that one? It's awesome! You can have a go after lunch. Can't she, Duncan? I can help her.'

I've only been on the little trampoline at preschool and it's got a bar that you have to put both your hands on when you're bouncing and you're not allowed to let go and I really, really want to try the big trampoline in Duncan and Jane's garden.

Duncan says, 'Ah no, sorry, Liam, but Jesika's too little for that trampoline. She might hurt herself.'

Liam turns away and says, 'Kyla never did,' so so quiet and then he looks at Jane and says loud, 'She'll be fine, won't she, Jane?'

I really want a go.

But Jane says, 'No, Liam, I'd rather go with Duncan's judgement on this.'

Liam's face goes mean and he says, 'Duncan knows nothing!'

And that's very rude but Duncan doesn't tell him off. He says we have to finish eating cos he's taking us to the actual park instead and everyone's talking and talking and then they forget about the trampoline, but not me cos I really, really want a go.

Duncan helps me to get ready to go outside in the big room with all the doors where the stairs go up and it's so exciting cos I've got a new coat and new shoes cos Mummy forgotted to put them in my bag when we went to the hopsipal and my new coat is pink and I've never had a pink coat afore and my new shoes are pink and I've never had pink shoes afore too!

I'm ready and Duncan's ready and Liam's ready but Jane's not ready but then we go out the door anyway and Jane says, 'Have a good time. See you later,' and bangs the door ahind us.

Duncan tells me to hold his hand and Liam goes on the other side on his scooter and he says, 'Why isn't Jane coming?'

Duncan says, 'Jane's got some work to catch up on.'

Liam says, 'But it's Wednesday. You always work on Wednesdays.'

Duncan says, 'We're having a swap around for a few days.'

Liam says, 'Why?'

Duncan says, 'For a bit of variety.'

Liam doesn't say anything else. I look up at Duncan and he looks down at me and smiles. Is Jane still angry that I bited her? Is that why she's not coming too? She hasn't got cross with me yet and neither has Duncan. Maybe they've forgotted to do it.

At the park, Liam goes away where I can't see him and Duncan says he's riding his scooter on ramps and I want to see what Liam's doing but we can't go there cos it's for big boys only and I have to stay in the little girls' and boys' playing area and it's all baby toys that Toby can play with and Duncan won't even let me do it myself cos he says he has to help me so I don't fall and get hurt. He should see the pirate ship at my playground. That's really big and Mummy lets me play all over it without any help at all!

After for ages I say, 'Can we go to preschool now?' cos it's after lunchtime and we've been to the park and I think if we don't go soon we'll be so late.

Duncan frowns and says, 'We can't take you to preschool, Jesika, it's too far away.'

And I remember he said this afore. I say, 'But I want to play with Paige.'

Duncan says, 'Paige is your friend?'

I nod my head.

Duncan crouches down and puts his hand on my shoulder and he says, 'You must be missing everyone so much.'

My eyes sting and I blink and blink and I think he's going to say something else but he just squeezes my shoulder and then Liam's there and he says he wants to go home and I say, 'I want to go back too,' and Duncan says, 'Well, that was a short visit,' but it wasn't, it was so so long.

Liam is grumpy and mean all the way home, and when we get back, he stomps upstairs and a door goes BANG! and Jane comes to the top of the stairs and says, 'What's up with Liam?' and Duncan says, 'Not sure, but he didn't want to stay long at the park. Leave him for now, we can talk to him in a bit.'

Liam doesn't come out of his room all the rest of the day, not when me and Duncan play games, not when it's telly-time and I'm watching the funny pirate programme on CBeebies and not even when it's time for tea and we go into a new room that I've not seen that's got a big glass table and squashy white chairs that I have to kneel up on to reach my plate. Duncan wants Liam to sit with us but Jane tells Duncan he'll come down when he's hungry.

After tea, Duncan says, 'What time do you go to bed, Jesika?'

I say, 'After the CBeebies bedtime story.'

So Duncan checks the telly but CBeebies has already gone to bed so we hurry upstairs to the yellow bedroom and all the covers are back on the bed and Para-Ted is tucked into the covers and my pyjamas are folded on top and there's a nappy next to my pyjamas, like the ones that Toby wears but more big, and I pick it up and I say, 'Why is this nappy in here?'

Duncan says, 'It's not a nappy, it's big-girl pull-ups, so you don't get a wet bed.'

I hold it out to Duncan and say, 'I don't wear this. I have a big wee afore bed.'

Duncan doesn't take it from me and he says, 'How about you wear it just while you're staying here? That's better than waking up in a wet bed, isn't it?'

I don't do wet beds. Only when I've forgotted to have a wee. I don't want to wear a nappy. Duncan walks over to close the curtains and I hide the nappy under my pillow.

I take off my T-shirt and Duncan comes back over and he's watching me and I say, 'You have to go,' cos I think he's forgotted about private pants again.

Duncan says, 'Ah, yes, OK. Shout if you need help,' and he walks out of the bedroom.

I take all my clothes off and I put my pyjamas on. They smell funny, not like my pyjamas. I go out of the bedroom and Duncan's waiting for me and I say, 'Where are my pyjamas?'

Duncan laughs and says, 'You're wearing them!'

I look down and they look like my pyjamas but then I sniff the sleeve. I say, 'These aren't mine.' I sniff the sleeve again. 'They smell like a different person.'

Duncan laughs and says, 'Well, we had to wash them, didn't we!'

I don't remember washing them. I think someone's mixed my pyjamas up with another little girl who lives somewhere else. I tell Duncan but he just says, 'Never mind,' and then he says, 'Let's brush your teeth now.'

I say, 'My toothbrush is at home.'

Duncan says, 'That's OK, Jane bought you a new one,' and he takes me into the bathroom and shows me my new toothbrush and it's *so exciting* cos it's a green crocodile toothbrush and the crocodile head actually covers up the brush and you have to snap it open like the crocodile is opening up its mouth and pull the toothbrush out and that's magicAMAZING! Jane even got me toothpaste that's only for children to use and I've never had that afore.

Duncan stands ahind me at the sink and picks up the toothpaste and he takes the toothbrush from me and he squeezes on lots and lots.

I say, 'Too much! You just scrape it on, that's what the dentist says.'

Duncan makes his mouth squashy and says, 'A scrape doesn't sound enough. We'll just do it this way while you're here.' He kneels down in front of me instead of standing ahind me like Mummy does, and he forgets to say, 'Open wide,' he just pushes the toothbrush into my mouth and brushes slow and gentle, not like Mummy who brushes fast and hard and bangs the brush against my teeth and inside my cheeks.

Footsteps thump, thump, thump and the door opens and Liam slides along the floor on his socks and says, 'I've eaten my tea. Can I watch that film now? Jane says it's your decision cos she's never seen it.'

Duncan says, 'Yes, it's fine, but after I've got Jesika in bed we need a chat about what happened in the park, OK?'

Liam picks up the crocodile head from my toothbrush and says, 'Cool, a crocodile head!'

Then he makes it snap, snap, snap at my face and I don't like it but I can't say, 'Stop it!' cos Duncan's still brushing my teeth and my mouth is full up with toothpaste foam cos Duncan put too much toothpaste on the brush. I try to twist my head away but Duncan puts his hand on my chin and says, 'Keep your head still, Jesika. I don't want to hurt you,' and Liam laughs and makes the crocodile head come nearer and I twist my face again but Duncan holds my chin so I can't move it and he says, 'Put it down, Liam,' but Liam keeps putting the crocodile in my face, snap, snap, snap!

stop-it-stop-it-go-away-KICK!

'Ow!'

Duncan stops brushing my teeth and I spit the foam into the sink and Liam's holding his leg where I kicked him and making a mean face at me and Duncan's going to be cross cos I kicked.

But Duncan isn't cross. He says, 'Liam, off you go and watch your film. Jesika, have a wee and then come and get into bed,' and Duncan and Liam go away.

In the yellow bedroom, Duncan is sitting on the bed and he's holding two story books and I've not seen them afore. He pulls the covers back so I can get into bed and then he reads one of the books and it's about animals on a farm all making different noises but Duncan's not good at reading stories cos he doesn't show me the pictures proply and he doesn't do the different voices like Mummy and Toby's not snuggled with me laughing at the funny bits and my heart is banging hard and my eyes sting and I'm so so tired.

Duncan finishes the book and says, 'That was fun,' and he puts it down and picks the other book up and says, 'Let's see what this one is about.' But I don't want Duncan to read the story. I want Mummy to read it and I want Toby to cuddle and I want to be in my own house.

I cuddle Para-Ted tight and roll over to the wall and squeeze my eyes shut and I pretend I can feel Mummy, leaning heavy and warm on my back, and I pretend I can hear Toby breathing slow and quiet in his cot and I pretend I can hear the thump-da-thump-da-thump music under the floor and the swish-ROAR-swish cars outside the window and then I feel something pat-pat-patting on my shoulder and Duncan whispers, 'Night-night, Jesika, sleep well,' and I hear the door of the yellow bedroom swish and click and Mummy and Toby and the music and the cars all go away and it's just me in the yellow bedroom going to sleep all by myself.

It's morning and a yellow-blue tit is singing on the windysill. I push my covers off and creep out of bed to get a little bit closer so I can see it singing but when I get nearer it grows bigger and bigger and grows lots of fur til it's not a blue tit any more, it's a squirrel. It jumps off the windysill and disappears. I open the window and look down and the squirrel is in Duncan and Jane's garden bouncing on the trampoline but now there's also a swing and a roundabout and a slide in the garden and there's lots of children playing. I want to play too! I run to the bedroom door and now I'm in the kitchen. Liam's in the kitchen making lots and lots of bread and jam and he sees me and he stops and picks me up and says, 'Up you go,' and he stretches me up and up and up and up onto the tallest ever giraffe chair and it's so wobbly at the top and I can't see Liam and I'm so high up and I want to get down and I'm shouting and crying, 'Get me down, get me down, get me down!'

A gentle hand strokes my hair. A soft voice says, 'Shhh, Jesika, shhh, it's just a bad dream. Just a bad dream. Back to sleep now. Back to sleep. Shhh.' The hand keeps stroking soft and soft and the voice says, 'Shhh, shhhh, shh . . .' and the scary inside me gets small and small and I think, 'Mummy?' but I can't make my mouth speak and I can't make my eyes open and it feels like I'm sinking into a warm, snuggly blanket. Then the voice starts singing, 'Lullaby and goodnight, in the sky stars are bright . . .' and that's one of Mummy's songs so it must be Mummy and she's come to take me home . . .

I can hear birds singing. Lots and lots. Twenty or a hundred or a-thousand-a-hundred. I remember a bird singing that was actually a squirrel. No, that was a dream. Mummy! Eyes open. I'm in the yellow bedroom and the sun is shining through the curtains. Mummy came and sang me a song last night in my bad dream. Is she still here? Is it time to go home?

I pull back the covers and jump out of bed and I take my pyjamas off and put my clothes on and put all my things inside my bag and Para-Ted too and then I have to run quick as quick for a wee cos I'm really bursting.

When I come back, Duncan's in the bedroom and he says, 'Wow, you got dressed fast this morning, Jesika!'

I say, 'That's cos I'm ready to go home with Mummy.'

Duncan says, 'Oh, I don't know if that's happening quite yet.'

I say, 'Where is Mummy? Is she downstairs?' and I'm smiling and smiling cos I can't wait to see her.

Duncan's face goes squashy and he says, 'Your Mummy's still in hospital, Jesika. We'll phone after breakfast to see how things are.'

I say, 'But she was here last night when I had a bad dream and she sang me a song.'

Duncan's face looks all sad and he says, 'Oh, darling, that wasn't your Mummy, that was Jane.'

My foot stamps and stamps again. It wasn't Jane. It was *Mummy*. Jane's cross with me cos of the biting and she doesn't talk to me and she doesn't sing me songs. It was *Mummy*. I run out of the bedroom and I shout, 'Mummy! Mummy!' and I go quick down the stairs but Duncan stops me in the middle and he says, 'Steady, Jesika! Hold my hand,' and we have to do the rest of the stairs slow like a snail. But at the bottom, I pull my hand away and I run into the telly room and I run into the table room and I run into the kitchen and then the glass room and only Liam's there. Mummy's not there. And I sit down on the green sofa and I'm crying and crying cos Mummy's gone away again and forgotted to take me with her.

Someone sits next to me and I push my hands out and turn away and then Liam says right in my ear quiet, 'I miss my Mum too, and Kyla.'

I stop crying and I look at him and I say, 'Who's Kyla?'

Liam says, 'She's my sister. She's six.'

I say, 'Where is she?'

Liam lifts his shoulders up and down and says, 'Somewhere else.' Then he smiles and says, 'You know what she loves doing?'

I shake my head and Liam says, 'Bouncing on the trampoline.' Then he bends his head down and puts his mouth against my ear and it tickles and he says, 'Do you want a go?'

I do want a go and I smile and smile but Liam puts his finger to his lips and says, 'Shh, don't let Duncan know. It's a secret, OK? We'll pretend we're going to play football in the garden.'

I blink and blink and wipe my eyes and then Duncan's there with bread and jam for breakfast and a big glass full up of milk, and when Liam asks if we can play in the garden, Duncan says only after I've had my breakfast so I eat and drink so so fast.

Liam helps me put my coat and shoes on and I keep giggling and Liam keeps saying, 'Shh! It's a secret, remember!' and then Liam picks up the football and we go out into the garden and the sun is warm on my face but the wind is bitey and spiky on my cheeks and fingers. I can see Duncan watching out of the window so Liam says we have to kick the ball a few times til he stops watching and it takes for ages and then Liam says, 'Quick, now!'

We run over to the trampoline and there's a net all the way round that stretches up and up and I can't see how you get in but then, afore I can ask Liam, I see a zip and he's trying to pull it up and he pulls and then blows on his fingers and pulls a bit more and blows on his fingers and then suddenly the zip whizzes up all the way and Liam's holding the net back, making a gap for me to get through, but when I try to get in, the trampoline is too high for me so Liam has to lift me up and I wriggle through the gap in the net and on my belly and I stand up and . . . wooo! It's so funny trying to walk! My legs are all wibbly-wobbly and I fall over and my bottom bounces and I giggle and get up and try again and then Liam's inside the net too and he holds out his hands and says, 'Here, hold on,' and I do and he pulls me up and then we're bouncing and bouncing holding hands . . .

Bounce! Bounce! Bounce! Bounce! Bounce! Bounce! Wheee!

. . . this is the funnest fun ever! After lots of bouncing, Liam shows me how he can bounce onto his bottom and bounce right back onto his feet again. I try it but I can't get back up. Then Liam holds my hands and says, 'Try again,' and I do and Liam lifts me right back up and it feels like flying!

Duncan comes rushing out of the glass-room door. Me and Liam stop bouncing and stand still in the middle of the trampoline. Liam says quiet, 'Oops. In trouble now.'

But Duncan doesn't tell him off. His face is all squashed up and he says, 'Jesika, I'm sorry to spoil your fun but Delphine just phoned. We're going to the hospital now to see your Mummy.'

16

GOINGTOSEEMummygoingtoseeMummygoingtoseeMummygoing
toseeMummy-Mummy-Mummy-Mummy-Mummy-Mummy-
Mummy-Mummy-Mummy-Mummy-Mummy . . .

I lean right forward so Duncan can hear me and I say, 'Are we there yet?'

Duncan says, 'A bit further,' and then, 'Sit back in your seat, Jesika.'

I sit back and look out of the window. When we left Duncan and Jane's house, everything went past slow: houses and trees and people and cars and traffic lights and lorries and more traffic lights and buses. But now we're on a HUGE road with so many veekles and bridges and everything is whizzing past fast and it's making my belly feel swirly like when I swing too fast on the swings or zoom around and around on the roundabout.

I look up at the sky. Even the clouds are whizzing by, big and fluffy like pillows. Witches' pillows. That's in a song that Mummy tells me sometimes. That cloud over there looks like a castle with tall towers. Maybe it's the giant's castle that Jack finds cos it's too big for people to live in, but there isn't a beanstalk. It looks so bouncy, like a proper bouncy castle. I bet it feels bouncy too. I bet if you could get up to the clouds and walk on them, it would be like walking on the bouncy trampoline. But I don't know how you get up there, cos beanstalks aren't really real, they're just in a story. I'm going to ask Mummy how you go up to the clouds. I bet Toby would like it too.

Toby!

I say, 'Can I go and see Toby at the hopsipal too?'

Duncan doesn't say. Maybe he didn't hear me. The engine and the road make a lot of noise.

I press my hand against the window and it feels cold and smooth and tickly all at the same time. I pull it off and there's a picture of my hand on the window. Not a proper picture, just the shape of my hand and my fingers and then it disappears. I press my hand again and then pull it off and there's my hand picture again and . . . now it's disappeared again. Is it magic?

I say, 'Are we nearly there?'

Duncan says, 'Not long now.'

Para-Ted is on the seat next to me, poking his head out of my bag. Duncan wasn't going to bring my bag but Jane said we had to just in case. I said, 'Just in case of what?' but they were too busy going round the house and finding all my things and putting them into the bag to tell me. I heard Duncan say something about Mummy wanting to see something so I think it's cos Mummy might want to see the new pants and socks that Jane buyed at the shop cos I didn't have enough clean ones. The socks are stripy and the pants have princesses on them.

We're not on the big, busy road now. We're going slow past buildings and traffic lights and people again. I pick up Para-Ted and I say to him, 'Are we nearly there yet?'

Para-Ted looks out the window and says, 'Hmm. I think it might be another ten-thousand-hundred seconds afore we get there,' and Para-Ted must be right cos he's an ambulance teddy bear so he knows where all the hopsipals are in the whole of the land.

I blow out a big breath like Mummy does and I say, 'That'll take *for ages.*'

Para-Ted says, 'You just have to be patient, Jesika.'

I don't want to be patient. I want to be there now with Mummy and Toby doing cuddles and kisses and when I cuddle Mummy I'm not never letting go and, oh! It's gone dark in the car. I look out the window and the car is driving inside a building and there's lots and lots of other cars all parked. It must be a parking building. I didn't know there were parking buildings! Duncan turns the steering wheel a lot and the car moves slowly into a space atween two cars and then everything is very quiet and everything in the car isn't jiggling about any more and Duncan turns his head round and smiles big and says, 'We're here now!'

Duncan opens his door only a tiny bit and squeezes out of the car and I say, 'Where are we?'

Duncan laughs and says, 'At the hospital, of course!'

Now my car door is open a little bit and Duncan leans in and unclips my straps and he says, 'Out you come.' I'm still holding Para-Ted and I hug him tight to me as Duncan helps me to climb out of the car and then we're standing in the big room that's filled with cars and doesn't have any windows and I say, 'I don't think this is the hopsipal.'

Duncan says, 'You'll see in a minute.'

I walk away from the car and there's a roar like a lion and Duncan grabs my hand and tugs me back and the roar was a car driving fast right next to me and now there's a smell and my nose stings and Duncan says, 'Hold my hand, Jesika. We have to be very careful in car parks.'

We walk along a red path all the way to a door and then we go down stairs that smell like the toilets at preschool, but there's not any toilets here. We go through another door and we're standing outside and there's a very big building in front of us and lots of other buildings aside it and around us and there's roads and people and traffic and Duncan says, 'Now, which way?' And he's looking and looking and then he points and says, 'Ah, I think that's the entrance over there,' but I think Duncan's wrong cos that's not the place that the ambulance took me and Mummy and Toby and I say, 'This isn't the hopsipal me and Mummy and Toby went to.'

Duncan says, 'Yes it is, Jesika. Don't worry, you'll see.'

We walk over the road and up to some big glass doors and they're magic ones that open when you stand in front of them just like the ones at the hopsipal that me and Mummy and Toby went to but it's not the same doors cos we walk into a busy place that's not the long room with doors. Duncan stops and looks at a piece of paper in his hand and a big picture on the wall with lots of squares and colours and words and he says, 'Along that way, I think.' But I think Duncan's wrong. We're in a big space here that's filled with tables and chairs and people and curling steam coming out of cups and plates with cake and sandwiches and yummy smells everywhere. Mummy and Toby's hopsipal didn't smell yummy. I don't think this is even a hopsipal. I think this is an eating shop like the one next to Ade's rainbow shop.

Then Duncan says, 'Aha, I've figured it out. It's this way, Jesika,' and he tugs my hand and we walk away from the busy place with all the chairs and tables and people and we walk along a very long room that stretches and stretches for a long-a-long time. Sometimes there's doors we have to push open and go through but on the other side the long room just keeps going and it's like it's going all the way to the other side of the world. I don't know when we're ever going to stop.

After for ages, Duncan does stop, and he says, 'This way now,' and we turn through a door and there's another long room but this one's not quite so long and we get to the next door so quick and we go through and there's noise and people and busy-ness and beds and swishy curtains and afore we're allowed to go anywhere, Delphine's standing right in front of us and she tells me we have to wash our hands with special soap and she helps me take off my coat and she holds Para-Ted for me and she squirts something cold and slimy onto my hands and tells me to rub and rub and rub and the cold, slimy stuff is magic cos it just disappears and my hands are dry again. I don't even need to wash my hands under water. Then I'm hugging Para-Ted tight and Delphine's standing right in front of us and she's saying something to Duncan but I don't hear it cos I hear something else that's made my heart thump loud as loud and I listen and listen cos I'm not sure I heard it right . . .

'Jesika.'

It's Mummy. It's *Mummy*! Mummy! I look all around me for where Mummy's voice is coming from but I can't see Mummy anywhere and then Delphine taps me on the shoulder and points to where there's a lady on a bed who's sort of lying and sitting at the same time and she's smiling and waving and . . . IT'S MUMMY! *MUMMYMUMMYMUMMYMUMMY!*

I crash into the bed and my head squashes on Mummy's belly and my arms try to cuddle and squeeze as tight as tight and I think that Mummy didn't really look like Mummy when I saw her from far away. She's not wearing Mummy's clothes and she doesn't really smell like Mummy when I breathe in big breaths and her cuddle isn't squeezy and squashy like my Mummy but then she says, 'I've missed you so, so much,' and I know it really is Mummy.

I want to say, 'I missed you too,' but my words get stuck and only crying comes out my mouth. Mummy strokes my hair soft and says, 'Shhhh, shhh. I'm right here. It's OK.' And she says it again and again til my crying goes away.

Mummy's fingers tickle the back of my neck and it's shivery down my back.

I say, 'I didn't like sleeping in a different place to you.'

Mummy says, 'I didn't like it either.'

I say, 'What do you do in hopsipal? Do you have to stay in your bed *all day*?'

Mummy says, 'Yes, pretty much.'

I say, 'That must be boring!'

Mummy smiles and says, 'I've been too tired to be bored. And I've had visitors!'

I say, 'Who?'

Mummy says, 'Nandini came first because . . .' She stops and breathes and breathes and then she says, 'Did you know Emma saw you coming out of the ambulance?'

I forgotted about that! I say, 'I saw Emma too! She was in another ambulance. Is she a Green Lady like the one that drived our ambulance?'

Mummy says, 'Yes, she's a paramedic.' She stops again and breathes and breathes. 'Emma told Nandini and Nandini came to visit and she brought me books and a fruit basket from Ade and chocolates from Leon.' She breathes and breathes again.

I say, 'That's so kind, isn't it, Mummy?'

Mummy says, 'Yes, it is. It's very kind.' She strokes my hair and smiles and says, 'We have very kind friends, don't we?'

I frown and say, 'No, Mummy, you said they're kind people but they're not our friends.'

Mummy smiles and says, 'I think I might have got that wrong. They've all been more than just kind. Nandini stayed with me for ages yesterday and we had such a lovely chat. She didn't even go when visiting time finished. The nurse got quite cross with us!'

I say, 'So Nandini and Emma and Ade and Leon are our friends now?'

Mummy nods and smiles and I smile and smile too cos I like Nandini and Emma and Ade and Leon being our friends.

Mummy says, 'And Ryan visited too, and he even visited Toby for me.'

Toby! I look all around for Toby's cot but it's not there and I say, 'Where does Toby sleep?'

Mummy says, 'He's in a different room.' She breathes and breathes. 'With the other poorly children.'

I say, 'Where is his room? Can we go there? I want to see him.'

Mummy presses her lips tight and shakes her head. She says, 'Not today, poppet.'

I say, 'Why not? Why can't I see him? I want to see him.' My foot stamps and my eyes sting and I want to say it's not fair but my voice hurts and I can't make it speak.

Then Delphine's there right next to me and Duncan's there too and Delphine says, 'Your little brother needs lots of rest, Jesika. He's doing really well but it's best to let him do lots of sleeping for now and then he'll get home to you all a lot quicker.'

I frown at Delphine but I do want Toby to get better quick. Mummy pats the bed and says, 'Climb up here, Jesika, so I can cuddle you properly,' so I climb up and I curl up against Mummy's side and she puts her arm around me and it's the best cuddle ever.

Delphine says, 'Tina, this is Duncan.'

Duncan holds out his hand like he's going to shake it with Mummy but Mummy's cuddling me so he waves his hand instead and says, 'Hi, Tina, it's nice to meet you.'

Mummy says, 'What about . . . didn't you say . . . ?'

Delphine says, 'Jane? Yes, I'm afraid she couldn't come with Duncan. They're also fostering a boy, Liam, at the moment and they have a meeting at his school today that couldn't be rearranged.'

Delphine and Duncan sit down on chairs. I turn my head so I can tell Mummy all about Liam and the bird table and the trampoline but then a man walks over to the bed and he's holding a white cup and I know this man. It's Ryan! I say, 'Have you come to visit Mummy, Ryan?'

Ryan sits down on a chair on the other side of the bed from Delphine and Duncan and his face isn't smiley and he sips from his cup and he says, 'And to check you're being looked after properly, Jesika.'

Mummy's arm squeezes tight on my shoulders and she says, 'Ryan . . .'

Delphine says, 'And that's what this meeting is for. To reassure you, Tina, that Jesika is safe and well looked after while you're in hospital. Duncan's here to answer any questions you have.'

Mummy's arm lets go a bit. Ryan is frowning at Duncan and then he says, 'Where's the other foster carer?' He looks at Mummy. 'Didn't you say she was with a couple, Tina?'

Mummy says, 'Yes, she is. Jane's . . . the other . . . she's not . . .' and then Mummy stops and breathes and breathes and she says, 'Sorry . . . I'm so tired.'

Duncan looks at Ryan and says, 'My wife, Jane, wasn't able to join us as she's at a meeting for our other foster child.' Then he looks at Tina and says, 'She says you can phone her any time you need to if you want to ask her anything or just speak to her. I'm going to leave our number with you today.'

Ryan's still frowning. He says, 'Who's this other child?'

I say, 'He's called Liam and he likes birds and sometimes he's scary and sometimes he's fun and he showed me how to bounce on my bottom on the trampoline.'

Duncan says, 'I did tell him that I thought Jesika was a little too young for the trampoline but . . .'

Ryan says, 'How old is he?'

I say, 'He's a big, big boy,' and at the same time, Duncan says, 'He's thirteen.'

Ryan says, 'So you're looking after a four-year-old and a

thirteen-year-old? How does that work? Is that the best environ-ment for Jesika?'

Mummy says, 'Ryan, I'm sure . . .' and then she stops and I twist my head and look at her and her eyes are closed and then they open again and she says quiet, 'They're foster carers. It's what they do.'

Ryan says, 'I'm just making sure we ask the right questions.'

I cuddle into Mummy and even though Mummy doesn't smell right, my head fits just right and I close my eyes and pretend I'm cuddling up with Mummy on our sofa at home. I can hear everyone's voices talking around me and other noises: squeaks and clicks and beeps and swishes and voices far, far away talking and talking and talking . . .

'Lorna thinks it would be great for Paige and for Jesika.'

I open my eyes and sit up and say, 'What would be great for Paige and me?'

Ryan smiles and says, 'If you came to stay with Lorna and Paige until your Mummy is better. That would be fun, wouldn't it?'

Mummy says, 'Ryan . . .' and I look at her and her face is frowny and she's biting on her lip.

I say, 'But Duncan and Jane are looking after me.'

Delphine says, 'Of course, it's up to you, Tina, but we do need to think about what will be least unsettling for Jesika.'

Ryan says, 'No offence, but by the sounds of it, they're also coping with a challenging thirteen-year-old.'

Duncan says, 'I wouldn't call him challenging . . .'

Ryan turns to Mummy and says, 'Tina, Jesika would have Lorna, she'd have Paige, she could go to preschool. I'd obviously help whenever Lorna's working. It makes sense.'

Is Ryan saying I'm going to stay with Paige now? Mummy breathes and breathes and her face is still frowny and she shakes her head. She says, 'Ryan, you know I appreciate it but Lorna's already dealing with a lot.'

Ryan says, 'And this would be a great distraction for Paige and for Lorna. She said this morning how great it is to be back in touch with you and how you're the first person in a long time who she'd completely trust with Paige. Aside from me, obviously.' He laughs and Mummy smiles a tiny smile.

Delphine holds her hands up so I can see the insides and she says, 'Ultimately, Tina, it's your decision,' and I didn't notice afore but the insides of Delphine's hands are a different colour from the rest of her skin, just like Kali's. Not like mine though. I turn my hands both ways up and it's the same colour on both sides. Why do some people have two colours on their hands?

I turn to ask Mummy but her head is right back on her pillow and her eyes are closed. I think she's still feeling poorly. I snuggle in tight and whisper, 'I love you, Mummy,' right in her ear and that makes her eyes open again and she says, 'Can I talk it over with Jesika, please?'

Delphine and Duncan stand up and Duncan says, 'Of course, of course,' and Delphine says, 'We'll be outside.' Then Mummy looks at Ryan and he's still sitting and she says, 'Give me five minutes, Ryan,' and Ryan stands up too and says, 'Of course, yes.' And then he's gone too and it's just me and Mummy.

I say, 'When can I go and see Toby?'

'When he's better, poppet.'

'But I want to see him now.'

'I do, too.'

I twist and look at Mummy's face. 'Can't you just go and see him when you want to?'

Mummy says, 'I'm not allowed to,' she presses her lips tight and breathes and breathes, 'until I'm all better.' Then she reaches over the top of my head and she's holding her phone and she says, 'But look what Ryan did for us,' and she slides and taps her thumb on the phone and there's a picture moving on it and I don't see what it is straight away and then I hear a voice and it says, 'Hey, Toby, give us a wave,' and it's Toby moving about on the picture! He's sitting up in a great big cot, much more big than the one at our house, and he's got lots and lots of toys all round him and he's just wearing a nappy and the voice says, 'Are you going to wave, Toby?' but Toby doesn't wave. He holds up one of his toys and it's blue but I don't know what it is cos the picture's so small and then he says, 'MummaMummaMumma,' and the voice says, 'Are you saying, "Mummy"? She's coming very soon,' and then Toby says 'MummaMummaMumma' again and then the picture stops.

I say, 'Has it broken?'

Mummy says, 'No, that's it. It's finished.'

I say, 'Can I see it again?' So Mummy puts it back to the start and I watch it all over again and it's almost as good as seeing Toby for real, cept I can't give him a cuddle.

When it finishes another time, Mummy says, 'Jesika, do you mind staying with Duncan and Jane another night or two?'

I say, 'I want to stay with you.'

Mummy says, 'I know that, but until I'm better . . . are they . . . do you feel OK staying there? Do you like it?'

I say, 'Well, I don't really like it when Liam makes scary faces and Duncan doesn't let me do things that you let me do and Jane is cross with me but I like the birds and the trampoline and they have a room that's just for watching telly and the telly is stuck to the wall and it's this big!' And I put my arms as wide as I can stretch them out cos that always makes Mummy laugh.

Mummy doesn't laugh. She says, 'Why is Jane cross with you?'

I say, 'Oh,' cos I forgotted that Mummy didn't know and now she's going to be cross with me too.

Mummy says, 'Jesika, can you tell me?' and her voice isn't a cross one and I look up and her eyes aren't cross eyes either.

I whisper, 'Cos I bited her.'

185

Mummy says, 'Why did you bite her, poppet?'

I think about the day I bited Jane and I remember biting but I don't remember what happened first. I say, 'I've forgotted.'

Mummy's head lies back on her pillow and she closes her eyes and then opens them and she says, 'OK, so if you don't stay with Duncan and Jane . . .' She stops and breathes and breathes. 'Nandini and Emma offered, and now Lorna has too. I don't know.' She frowns.

I say, 'What did Nandini and Emma say?'

Mummy says, 'They said they would look after you if I needed it.'

I say, 'At Lorna's house?'

Mummy smiles and says, 'No, either Nandini and Emma look after you at their house, or Lorna looks after you at her house with Paige.'

I say, 'Oh.' And I'm thinking about this and I like Nandini but I don't really know what Nandini and Emma's house is like cept there's a lot of washing machines in it. I know what Paige's house is like and it's got lots and lots of toys.

I say, 'Do Nandini and Emma have toys at their house?'

Mummy says, 'Oh, I don't really know.'

I say, 'I want to stay with Paige.'

Mummy says, 'Do you like it at their house?'

I say, 'Yes! Paige has lots of toys and we play good games.'

Mummy says, 'Would you like to sleep there? Until I'm better?'

I think about Paige's house and all her toys and her dressing-up costumes and her princess bedroom and I say, 'Will I sleep in Paige's princess bedroom with Paige?'

Mummy says, 'Yes, I think so.'

'And you'll come and get me and take me home when you're better?'

'Of course!'

I'm so excited cos I've never sleeped in a princess bedroom afore and I say, 'Can I sleep in Paige's bedroom, please, Mummy?'

Mummy smiles a little smile and says, 'Is that where you want to stay until I'm better?'

I smile and smile and say, 'Yes, yes, yes!'

Mummy says, 'Are you sure? That's definitely what you want to do?'

I say, 'YES! YES! YES!'

Mummy taps her thumbs on her phone lots of times and then her head falls back on her pillow again and she breathes and breathes and says, 'OK, decision made,' and her voice is only a whisper.

Delphine and Duncan and Ryan all come back after that and everyone's talking and Ryan puts his thumbs up at me, but I'm not sure why, and then there's more talking but Mummy looks like she just wants to go to sleep cos she keeps closing her eyes and breathing slow and slow and then Delphine stands up and says, 'I'm so sorry but I have to dash to another meeting now,' and she touches my shoulder and says, 'Whenever I see dolphins or meer-kats, I'm going to remember you, Jesika,' and she smiles and waves and she's gone.

Next Duncan stands up and he says, 'It really was lovely having you to stay, Jesika.' He gives my bag to Ryan and he says, 'That's all her things. Luckily, Jane told me to bring it just in case, because we weren't sure what was happening.'

I say, 'Just in case you want to see my new socks and pants, Mummy.'

Mummy says, 'That's nice, Jesika,' but I don't think she really heard me proply and her eyes are still closed.

Duncan says, 'I'll tell Jane and Liam bye-bye for you, Jesika,' and he waves and he's gone too. Does he mean I won't see Jane and Liam again? I liked bouncing on the trampoline with Liam.

Now it's just me and Mummy and Ryan. Mummy's lying back

on her pillows again and she's very quiet and still like she's asleep but she's not asleep cos one of her hands is stroking my hair.

Ryan says, 'We should probably go too and then I can get Jesika back to Lorna's in time for lunch and she can go to preschool this afternoon with Paige.'

I say, 'I can go to preschool?' cos I've not been to preschool for ages and Duncan didn't let me go to preschool and it's so exciting to go again.

Mummy smiles and opens her eyes and says, 'Good idea,' and then she says, 'Ryan, thank you. You and Lorna . . .'

Ryan says, 'Don't mention it.'

He bends down and picks up my bag and my new coat and Para-Ted and I slide off the bed and I'm looking at Mummy and she's got her eyes closed and I think she might be asleep this time and I say, 'Can Mummy take me to preschool?'

Mummy opens her eyes and reaches out for my hand and says, 'Not today, darling, I've got to stay in hospital a bit longer. Ryan or Lorna will take you and then you'll go home to Lorna's house after with Paige. OK?'

I want to go to preschool with Paige and I want to play at Paige's house and I want to sleep in Paige's princess bedroom but I don't want to leave Mummy here in hopsipal. I think and I think and I say, 'I'm going to stay here with you, Mummy. I can go to Paige's house another day.'

Mummy squeezes my hand and says, 'It's OK to leave me, Jesika.' She breathes and breathes and presses her lips tight.

Ryan says, 'Tina, she'll be fine. Lorna will look after her like she's her own.' And he smiles at me and says, 'It'll be like having another Mummy for a day or two!'

I don't want another Mummy. I want my Mummy. What if Mummy thinks that Lorna has to be my Mummy all the time?

My eyes feel stingy and Mummy looks all fuzzy and I blink

and blink and blink til I can see her proply again and Mummy squeezes my hand, but only once, not one, two, three for 'I love you', and then she lets go and I say, 'Mummy?' and Ryan crouches down next to me and he holds my other hand atween both his hands and they're soft and gentle.

He says, 'Your Mummy needs to rest and sleep if she's going to get better quickly, so we need to let her do that.' And I look at Mummy and her eyes are closed like she's sleeping and Ryan says, 'And Paige will be so excited to see you, especially when we tell her you're coming for a sleepover!' And he says the last bit in a really excited voice and it remembers me that I am excited about preschool and sleeping at Paige's house but I feel sad too cos I want Mummy to be there and I want Toby to be there.

I say, 'Mummy, can I see Toby's video one more time?' and Mummy's eyes stay closed but her hand strokes my hair and my face and she says, 'Mmm,' and Ryan says, 'The video's on my phone too, so you can watch it all the way back to Lorna's house if you want.'

I say, 'Can I? Can I watch it lots and lots and lots?'

Ryan laughs and says, 'As many times as you want. Give your Mum a kiss and then let's leave her to rest.'

I lean over Mummy and cuddle her tight and kiss her belly and Mummy's hand strokes my hair and she opens her eyes a tiny bit and moves her lips and her voice whispers but I don't know what she's saying and the Big Hurty is squashing and squeezing and Ryan holds my hand and I have to start walking cos he's pulling me along and Mummy lifts her hand like a wave and so I wave too and we're almost at the door and I say, 'Para-Ted! I want Para-Ted!' and if I run back to get him I can have one more cuddle with Mummy, but Ryan is already holding him and he gives him to me and I hold Para-Ted tight and my eyes are stingy and I blink and blink and I try to look for Mummy one more time but Ryan's pulled me through the door and the door swishes shut.

17

IT'S A LONG-A-LONG way on the bumpy bus. It remembers me of
the day when Toby was on the bumpy bus and all the bouncing
maked him stop shouting and fall asleep. I wish I was allowed to
see Toby at the hopsipal.

Toby's video!

I forgotted all about that!

I say, 'Ryan, you said I could watch Toby's video all the way to
Lorna's house!'

Ryan says, 'So I did,' and he gets his phone out and he lets me
hold it and I get to watch the video again and again and again til
Ryan leans forward and presses the bell and says, 'Time to get off,
Jesika.'

We get off the bus and I'm really surprised cos we're at the bus
stop outside the park gates and I say, 'This isn't the stop for going
to Paige's house.'

Ryan says, 'It's too late to go there now,' and he holds my hand
and turns away from the park and starts walking towards the
shops and he says, 'We'll get some chips from the chip shop,
yeah? And then we'll eat them in the park and then I'll take you
straight to preschool.'

My eyes go wide and I say, 'Chips! Mummy doesn't let us have
chips cos they're bad for your heart.'

Ryan says, 'They're a bit naughty, but OK if you don't have

them too often. And they're so tasty,' and he licks his lips and makes a big slurping noise and I giggle and start skipping cos I always think the chip shop smells yummy and I've always wanted to eat chips from that shop.

After Ryan's given pennies to the chip man, we walk back to the park and sit on a bench just inside the gate and Ryan opens up the paper that's wrapped all round the chips and lots of steam flies out of the wrapping. He holds the chips out to me and they smell delicious and I take one but I drop it straight away cos it's hot, hot, hot! Ryan blows on them and folds up some of the paper and waves it over the top of the chips to cool them up and then he picks one out and he bites it in the middle and says it's OK to eat now and he holds it out to me and I try to take it but he pulls it away and he says, 'Bite it,' and I bite it from his fingers and my teeth crunch into the middle that's all soft and hot and fluffy and so so yummy.

Ryan smiles big and says, 'Not too hot?'

I shake my head and Ryan bites another chip in the middle and tells me to open my mouth so he can put the other bit in my mouth and he says, 'Taste good?'

I nod and nod my head cos I can't say yes cos my mouth's all full up with chips.

Ryan says, 'We don't need to tell your Mum about this. It can be our secret,' and he winks and wiggles his eyebrows and that remembers me about Liam and the trampoline secret.

I swallow the chips in my mouth and they go warm into my belly and I say, 'Now I've got two secrets.'

Ryan's eyebrows jump up and down. 'Do you?'

I say, 'Me and Liam had a secret about the trampoline. Do you know they've got a really huge, giant*normous* trampoline, as big as THIS,' and I stretch my arms as wide as they can go.

Ryan laughs and says, 'Wow, that is big!'

I say, 'Duncan said I was too little to go on it but Liam let me go on it as a secret, cept it's not a secret now cos Duncan finded it out.'

Ryan pretends he's cross and puts his hands on his sides but he's also laughing and he says, 'You didn't tell your secret, did you? You're not supposed to tell your secrets!'

I giggle and say, 'I didn't tell! It's cos Duncan saw me bouncing. He came out into the garden cos we had to come to the hopsipal to see Mummy.'

Ryan's nodding and he says, 'Well, that's OK then. I was worried there that you might tell everybody about our chips secret.'

I shake my head and swing my legs and say, 'No, no, no, no, I'll not tell *anyone* about the chips secret.'

Ryan laughs and says, 'Good girl,' and he strokes his hand down my hair.

Ryan said we had lots of time to eat chips but I think he's wrong cos when we get to the preschool road there's lots of Mummies and Daddies already coming out of the door and walking away from preschool and I start tugging Ryan's hand and walking faster cos I don't want Stella to shut the door on us cos then she gets cross about being late, but Ryan is heavy and hard to pull along, like an elephant, and it takes for ages to get to the preschool door.

The door isn't shut but there's only two people left in the peg room when we get inside and it's Stella and Lorna and when they see us they both talk at the same time and Stella's got a sad face and Lorna's got a happy face and all their words jumble together and it sounds like they said, 'Oh, Jesika, how are poor Paige's difficult coming,' but that doesn't make sense at all and I'm not sure if it's something I should be sad or happy about so I don't be either, I just stop my ears listening and go and take my coat off and hang it on my peg.

Now Stella and Lorna and Ryan are all talking at the same

time and there's happy faces and sad faces and they keep changing and I hear someone say, 'Tina,' and that's my Mummy but it's too hard to listen so I say, 'Can I go in now?' cos I want to see Paige.

Stella says, 'Of course, Jesika, in you go,' and her voice is happy-squeaky and she pushes the door open and then she says, 'Poor thing, she's very subdued,' and her voice is sad and slow. How can you be happy and sad at the same time?

Lorna calls out, 'I'll see you at—' and the door shuts and everything is noisy and busy and Azim rushes past chasing Katy with a sword and I have to squeeze right up against the wall so I don't get bashed and I'm looking and looking for Paige and I can't see her, I can just see blue and blue and blue . . . oh! It's Blue day! I look down at my clothes and I'm wearing my new pink shoes and my purple trousers and my green zippy top. I pull the zip down to look at my T-shirt and it's the yellow one that's got the red and orange butterfly on it. I haven't got any blue at all. Stella will be sad.

'Hi, Jesika! It's lovely to see you back in today.'

I whirl round with a great big smile on my face cos I know that voice and I'm right, it's Kali and I'm really very pleased to see Kali, then I remember that I'm not wearing blue and I stop smiling and I say, 'I forgotted it was Blue day today.'

Kali says, 'But you've come as a whole rainbow instead, how lovely!' And she points to all my clothes and says all the rainbow colours, cept blue, and she's right – I've got all the colours of the rainbow cept blue!

Kali crouches right down next to me and then she wobbles a bit and her hand shoots out and grabs hold of the edge of the house window and the house wobbles a bit too and Kali says, 'I hear you've had quite a time since you were here on Tuesday. I hope your Mummy and little Toby feel better soon.'

I say, 'I had to sleep in Duncan and Jane's house.'

Kali says, 'That must have felt a bit strange.'

My belly whooshes and then the Big Hurty pain is pressing again and I press it tight and try to push it away cos I don't want it here.

Kali says, 'Do you want to tell me about it in the Safe Place?'

I press more hard and shake my head and I look and I look all round the room and I say, 'Is Paige here? I want to play with Paige.'

Kali nods and smiles and says, 'She really missed you yesterday.' She turns and points and says, 'Look, she's over there doing a puzzle. Go on, she'll be so pleased to see you.'

I run all the way over to Paige and I think she'll smile and smile when she sees it's me and she'll be so surprised. I'm almost there and I go slow so I'm creeping like a tiger and I creep right up beside her and tap her shoulder and shout, 'Boo!'

She looks round at me but she doesn't smile and she doesn't look pleased, she just stares at me and blinks her eyes and then turns away and picks another piece of puzzle up and pushes it into the right hole.

I sit on the chair next to her and say, 'Did you miss me, Paige?'

Paige turns herself even further away from me so I can only see the back of her head. I don't know why she can't hear me. Maybe if I tell her about the ambulance then she'll hear me cos that's something really exciting and people always listen to exciting things.

I stand up and skip to the chair on the other side of Paige and sit down and say, 'Paige, guess what? I went in an ambulance in the middle of the night!'

Paige looks at me and then looks away and puts another piece of puzzle in the right place.

I say, 'Toby was really poorly and me and Mummy had to go

with him in the ambulance and it went fast like this,' and I zoom my hand through the air and I say, 'Whoosh!'

Paige looks at me again and she says, 'Did the ambulance do its flashing lights and nee-naw?'

I say, 'Only the flashy lights cos it was the middle of the night and the siren could've waked everybody up.'

Paige says, 'Oh,' and then she picks up another piece of puzzle and tries putting it in the right place but she's got it the wrong way round so I say, 'You have to turn it round,' and she turns it round and round and round and then gets it just right so it falls into the space and I say, 'That's it! Well done, Paige.'

Paige smiles and says, 'What's it like at the hospital?'

I say, 'It's a bit smelly,' and I hold my nose and say, 'Like wees and poos,' and me and Paige giggle and then I say, 'Lots of people had to help Toby and then I had to go in a different room with a lady called . . . I've forgotted her name . . . I keep forgetting her name! But she looked after me in a different room and then Mummy was apposed to come and get me but she got poorly too and now Mummy and Toby have to stay in hopsipal til they get better and I'm going to stay at your house now.'

Paige says, 'I know, my Mummy told me. Is your Mummy and Toby going to die?'

I say, 'I think they did almost die but now they're getting better and they're coming home soon.' But my heart thumps hard and the Big Hurty squeezes my breathing. I know what die is. It means you go away and never come back again, not like Daddy who might come back and see me if he gets on a plane, but like Bab-bab when her heart stopped working and we stopped seeing her ever again and she can't never come back to see us now, not even if I do wishes.

Paige says, 'My Daddy went to hospital and he died.'

I say, 'Did his heart stop working?'

Paige says, 'No, he did a lot of bleeding in his head. You only die if you do lots of bleeding.'

I say, 'Or if your heart stops working.'

Paige wrinkles her nose at me and lifts her shoulders up and down like she's saying, 'I don't know.'

But I do know cos that's what happened to Bab-bab. Then I think about Toby and the special breathing mask and I say, 'I think you also die if you can't do breathing and no one gives you a breathing mask.'

Paige says, 'No, I think if you can't do breathing you just go to sleep.'

I say, 'Yeah, and then when you wake up you start breathing again. I think that's what Toby did.'

Azim and Katy come zooming past like racing cars and bump our table and some of Paige's puzzle pieces jump off the table and onto the floor and right under the table. I shout, 'Oi!' but Azim and Katy have zoomed right out of the door to the outside area. Paige looks at the pieces on the floor and she looks sad.

I say, 'I'll help you,' and I get off my chair and crawl under the table to get the puzzle pieces and Paige crawls under too and we pick them all up but when we stand up at the table again Paige's puzzle has gone. Amber and Lucia have it at the other side of the table and they're breaking it up.

Paige just looks and looks but she doesn't say anything so I say, 'Hey, that's Paige's puzzle, you have to give it back.'

Lucia says, 'It's not. It belongs to preschool so anyone can do it.'

I say, 'But Paige had it first!' and I lean over the table and grab it but Lucia pushes my hand away and says, 'Get off!' and Amber says, 'You don't snatch. It's not nice!' and I say, 'But you snatched it off Paige!' and Amber says, 'Paige wasn't playing with it so that means it's our turn now. You have to share.'

My cheeks sting and my breathing feels hot and spiky and I

make my most scary, tiger-fierce face and I shout, 'Give it back NOW!' and I grab the puzzle again and Lucia pinches my hand hard and it *hurts* and I'm crying and crying and then Lauren's right there saying, 'Girls, girls, what's going on here?' and me and Amber and Lucia all talk at the same time and I don't know what *they're* saying but I say, 'Amber and Lucia took Paige's puzzle when we went to pick up the pieces on the floor and I told them to give it back and Lucia *pinched* me!'

Lauren holds both her hands up and says, 'One at a time, girls,' and she says, 'Lucia, why did you pinch Jesika?'

Lucia says, 'She snatched!'

Lauren says, 'OK, but it's not nice to pinch. You should say, "Stop it, I don't like it when you do that." Can you try saying that?'

Lucia says it and then Lauren asks her to say sorry for pinching and she does and then Lauren looks at me and her eyes are sad and she says, 'Did you forget to ask for your turn nicely?'

I say, 'But it was our go!'

Lauren says, 'I know you wanted a turn, Jesika, but remember what we say? "Please can I have a turn when you're finished?" Can you try saying that?'

My heart spikes hot and my cheeks sting and I say again, 'But it was our go!' cos I don't think Lauren heard me the first time.

Amber picks up a piece of the jigsaw and she's putting it in the wrong way and Lauren leans over and helps her to turn it the right way round and then she says, 'Why don't you have a turn with one of these other puzzles while you're waiting. I'm sure Amber and Lucia will be finished with this one in a minute. Won't you, girls?'

Amber smiles and says, 'Yes, Lauren,' and then she stands up and leans over the table and sweeps all the pieces we picked up off the floor over to her side with her arm.

Lauren smiles big at all of us and says, 'There you go, girls,' and then she helps Amber to put another piece of the jigsaw in.

Paige tugs at my hand and whispers, 'Let's run and hide from those two meany girls,' and we both think of the same place to hide cos we both run all the way to the door and right outside and squeeze into the hidey-hole underneath the slide.

I say, 'That wasn't fair.'

Paige says, 'They won't find us here.'

I say, 'No, we're invibisle when we're in here. Only you can see me and only I can see you.'

Paige claps her hands and says, 'Yeah!' Then she leans forward and whispers in my ear, 'I missed you.'

I whisper back, 'I missed you too.'

Paige wraps her arms around me and she's squeezing me tight and tight like she's not never going to let me go.

Lorna's yellow sofa is bouncy under my bottom. I can't sit still! My heart is thumping fast and hard like it's about to burst like a balloon right inside me and then Lorna hands me her phone and I hold it in front of my mouth like Lorna did and I say, 'Hello, Mummy!' and there's a voice coming out of the phone and it says, 'Hello, Jesika, have you had a nice time at preschool?'

Lorna said it was Mummy talking on the phone but this voice doesn't sound much like Mummy and I say, 'Mummy? Is that you?'

The voice laughs and says, 'Who else would it be, poppet?' and then I know it's Mummy cos only Mummy laughs like that and only Mummy calls me 'poppet' and a giggle pops right out of my mouth and I shout, 'MUMMY!' and it feels like my heart really has just burst inside me and it's like fireworks and chocolate all at the same time.

Mummy says, 'So did you have fun at preschool today?' and I

nod my head and I pick up the card that Kali and Paige helped me to make after snack-time and I wave it at the phone and I say, 'Look, I made you and Toby a get-well-soon card!'

Mummy says, 'Oh, that's lovely, Jesika. I'll be able to see that properly when I come home.'

I say, 'Are you coming home today?'

Mummy says, 'Not today, poppet, but maybe tomorrow. The doctor thinks I might be well enough by tomorrow.'

I say, 'And Toby too?'

Mummy says, 'Maybe Toby too. We'll have to wait and see tomorrow. Fingers crossed!'

I try to cross my fingers like Mummy showed me another time but it's tricky fiddly and when I try to use my other hand to help make my fingers stay crossed the phone slips out of my hand and bounces on the carpet. Lorna bends down to pick it up and she's laughing at the phone and she says, 'She's trying to cross her fingers, bless her.' And then she says, 'Yes, yes, she's fine. Honestly, please don't worry. I know you'd do the same for me.'

Lorna passes the phone back to me and says, 'Your Mummy wants to say bye, Jesika.' I stop trying to cross my fingers and take the phone and I hear Mummy's strange not-Mummy voice saying, 'I'll talk to you tomorrow, Jesika. Be good for Lorna.'

I say, 'I will, Mummy. I love you, Mummy,' and Mummy whispers, 'I love you too,' and she whispers, 'Bye-bye, poppet,' and I whisper back, 'Bye-bye, Mummy,' though I don't know why we're whispering.

I know why Mummy and Lorna like being friends. It's cos they both like singing and dancing. I'm holding the living room door open a little crack so I can see right through into the kitchen and I can see Lorna standing at the cooker and she's stirring something and singing loud as loud and bopping her head and wiggling her bottom and bouncing up and down and sometimes stuff in the pan bounces right out cos her stirring is a bit too wiggly. Mummy does that sometimes.

Paige says, 'I can't hear the telly, Jesika!' So I shut the door again and Lorna's music goes quiet and that remembers me about Nina and the New Rons and the invibisle sound waves and I think maybe sound waves can't go through doors. Maybe they just crash against the door like a real water wave would do.

It's Postman Pat on the telly but it's not Postman Pat on CBeebies, it's Postman Pat on a deeveedee and that's a hard, shiny circle that you have to hold just by the edges and not touch and you slide it into the side of the telly and then it plays on the telly. I didn't know you could make your telly play what you want! I'm going to tell Mummy to look and see if we've got a deeveedee hole in our telly.

Paige has lots and lots of deeveedees so she can watch them whenever she wants. She's also got lots and lots of Postman Pat toys too and she's laid them all out on the carpet in front of the telly so we can play with them and watch the telly at the same time.

Lorna's music gets loud again and me and Paige look over to the door and Lorna's popping her head around the door and she says, 'Five minutes, girls, then I want you to wash your hands, please.'

Paige says, 'Can we have a telly-tea tonight, Mummy?' She squeezes her hands together and says, 'Please, please, please, pleeaaaassse!'

Lorna laughs and says, 'Oh, I suppose so, but only if you go and wash your hands now!' She walks over and picks up the telly remote and presses a button and everything Postman Pat is doing stops and he stands very still on the screen, just like we do when Tamanna calls out at preschool, 'Macaroni cheese, everybody freeze!'

I say, 'How did you do that?' But Lorna has whizzed back out of the room and Paige is dragging me by my hand and saying, 'Come on, we have to wash our hands *quickly*!'

I've *never* watched telly at the same time as eating my tea afore! Lorna tucks kitchen paper into our tops and it's tickly and we each have a tray for our food and it's got a squashy bottom so that it's not hard on our legs and Lorna gives us both juice in a carton with a straw to suck cos she says we can't spill them easily and we keep watching Postman Pat while we eat our tea that's pasta and cheese sauce and it's yummy.

Lorna's not eating pasta and cheese. She's whizzing in and out of the room so fast, like she's in a big hurry, picking things up and putting things down, and one time she says quiet as quiet, 'Car keys, car keys, car keys.'

Then she comes in and she's wearing a blue apron over her clothes and Paige says, 'Why are you wearing that, Mummy?' and when I look at Paige, her face is all screwed up and cross. Lorna stops rushing about and puts her hands on her hips and blows out a breath and says, 'You know why I'm wearing it, Paige.'

I say, 'I don't know why you're wearing it.'

Lorna comes over and sits on the edge of the small table and presses the button on the remote and Postman Pat freezes again right in the middle of driving up a big, big hill and she says, 'Do you remember me saying, Jesika, that I have to work sometimes and when I'm working Uncle Ryan will come and look after you both?'

Clatter! Crash!

Lorna leaps to her feet and shouts, 'Paige!' and I jump so much my juice carton falls over on my tray. Paige's tray is on the floor and her pasta and cheese sauce is spilled all over the carpet. Lorna runs out of the door and comes back straight away with a cloth and starts wiping up the cheesy mess and she looks at Paige and says, 'Pick up your things right now, Paige.'

Paige doesn't move cept for her arms that she crosses right around herself and her face that she makes even more crosser.

Lorna says, 'Paige, your friend is here to stay. Let's not do this now,' and her voice is soft and kind but her eyes look a bit scary, like she might turn into a monster, and I don't like it.

Paige gets off the sofa and picks up her tray and her bowl and her juice carton and then Lorna goes out of the room with the messy cloth and Paige says, 'I don't want you to go to work.'

Lorna stops at the door and leans her head against it like she's tired and she says, 'I have to go to work, Paige, otherwise how would I pay for this house you live in and the food you eat and the toys you play with?'

Paige stands up and stamps over to Lorna at the door and her arms are still crossed and her face is still all screwed up but now her lip is curled over like Toby's does when he's about to cry and she says, 'I don't *want* Uncle Ryan to put me to bed. I want *you* to put me to bed!'

Lorna says, 'Please, Paige, not today. Please don't upset Jesika. You know I can't. And anyway, you like Uncle Ryan doing bedtime.'

Paige stamps her foot again and her lip curls over even more. 'I don't!'

Lorna makes her lip curl over too and then she laughs and says, 'Of course you do,' and then she wiggles her hand through Paige's hair and says, 'And you know I'll be back before you wake up in the morning.'

She walks out of the door and goes into the kitchen and I can hear the splashing of water and I think she must be squeezing out the messy cloth in the sink. If Lorna worked in an office upstairs like Jane and Duncan, she wouldn't have to go to work and Paige wouldn't get cross. Maybe I should tell her cos maybe she doesn't know you can work in an office upstairs.

The splashy noise stops and she comes back with a pan and a

spoon and she says, 'If I give you more pasta, Paige, will you eat it this time instead of decorating the floor with it?' and she's smiling like it's a joke but I don't think Paige thinks it's funny cos she still looks so so cross and she says, 'Don't want it!' in a rude voice.

Lorna lifts her shoulders up and down and says, 'Suit yourself. I'll tell Uncle Ryan where it is in case you change your mind.' Then she turns to me and says, 'Would you like any more, Jesika?' and I do cos it's really yummy and I'm almost finished and I nod my head lots of times and Lorna walks over and her spoon goes SPLAT in my bowl and my bowl is all full up again with cheesy pasta. Yum!

I scoop a bit up on my fork but my bowl suddenly flies into the air and Paige has grabbed it and she shouts, '*I want more pasta!*' and I reach for my bowl and shout, 'Hey! That's mine! Give it back!' and lots of things all happen so so fast. My tray and my juice carton fall on the floor and the pasta falls off my fork and onto the floor and my foot squishes it and Lorna bangs the pasta pan down on the little table and she pulls my bowl of pasta out of Paige's hands but she pulls too hard and it flies out of her hand and lands upside down on the carpet and then Lorna is pulling Paige's arm and she shouts, 'That was *naughty*, Paige!' and Paige shouts, 'I don't want you! I want Daddy!' and Lorna shouts, 'I can't *give* you Daddy! Don't you think I would if I could!' and Paige leans her head down to Lorna's arm and Lorna lets go of her and shouts, 'Ow!' and she reaches forwards and hits Paige on the back of her legs and shouts, 'You DO NOT bite, Paige! I won't have that!' and Paige is crying and holding her leg and saying, 'Ow! Ow! Ow!' and Lorna pushes her hands against her mouth and she crouches down and she says, 'I'm sorry, Paige, I'm sorry. I'm so sorry. I didn't mean it.'

Paige bited Lorna and Lorna *hitted* Paige!

You're not allowed to bite or hit people and Lorna told Paige that but Paige also has to tell Lorna. Maybe I should whisper it in Paige's ear cos I think sometimes Paige doesn't know about telling people cos she didn't tell Amber and Lucia today about the puzzle and I had to do it for her. But if I go and whisper in Paige's ear, Lorna might see the pasta that's squished on the floor under my foot and then she'll get so cross with me too for making a mess and I might bite her and she might hit me too. I don't whisper in Paige's ear. I stand so still and I press my foot hard down on the pasta so nobody can see it at all.

There's a noise outside the living room, like a little crash and a bang, and then a voice calls, 'Hello! Anyone home?' and Lorna's cuddling Paige and I don't think they've heard. Then there's a zipping sound and a rustling sound and someone comes through the door and it's Ryan and he stops right in the doorway and jumps backwards like he's very surprised, but I know he's joking really, and he says, 'What's been happening in here?'

Now Lorna does notice him and turns her head round and says, 'Not now, Ryan,' and Ryan stops smiling and walks into the kitchen and when he comes back he's got a cloth and he picks up the bowl and clears up all the mess on the floor and I'm too scared to move cos my foot is still hiding the squished pasta. Ryan looks at me and he says, 'Are you OK, Jesika?' And he looks at me and looks at me and then takes my hand and pulls me gently and I don't want to move but I can't stop my foot moving off the squished pasta.

I look at Ryan and he looks at me and he looks down at the pasta and he looks at me again and he doesn't look cross at all and he puts his finger to his lips and quickly clears the pasta up off the floor and he whispers, 'See, all gone. Nothing to worry about.' And then he smiles and winks at me and says, 'Our secret.' And I smile my biggest smile back cos I'm so pleased that Ryan cleaned up the squished pasta afore Lorna saw it.

Lorna stops cuddling Paige and she stands up and she says, 'Right, I have to go now or I really am going to be late. Ryan, do bathtime, yeah? I didn't get a chance last night.'

Lorna walks to the door and Paige flings herself at Lorna's leg and holds on tight as tight and she's crying, 'Don't go, Mummy! Don't go! Don't go!'

Lorna bends down and pushes Paige off her leg and kisses her and says, 'I have to go. I'll be back in the morning. I love you, darling,' and her voice is like Mummy's 'Listen to me' voice, not Mummy's 'I love you' voice.

Ryan rubs Lorna's shoulder and says, 'Go on, she'll be fine in a minute,' then he pulls Paige away from Lorna and holds her tight and he's whispering something in her ear and Lorna says, 'Thank you, Ryan,' and runs away fast like she's being chased and there's noises outside the room and then a banging sound and everything is quiet cept for Paige sniffing.

After a few more sniffs, Paige pushes Ryan away and picks up the telly remote and points it at the telly and suddenly Postman Pat's van that's been frozen on the road for ages is whizzing up and down the hills again. Paige flops down on the floor next to her Postman Pat toys but she doesn't play with them, she just stares at the telly and keeps flicking the door of Postman Pat's helicopter open and shut and open and shut and open and shut.

Ryan looks at me and blows out a big breath and says, 'Well!' Then he says, 'You can sit down, Jesika!' and he laughs and I sit back down on the sofa and he's looking at me and I'm looking at him and he comes and sits next to me and taps his curled-up hand soft on my head like he's knocking on a door and says, 'What are you thinking about in there, Jesika?' and I'm thinking about Paige biting and Lorna hitting and I think maybe they don't like each other very much cept afterwards they cuddled for ages and Paige wanted Lorna to stay so I don't think that's quite right and it's all jumbled up in my head and I don't know which bit to say to Ryan first.

Ryan says, 'I know something to cheer you up,' and then he has his phone in his hand and even though there's lots of noise coming from Postman Pat on the telly I know exactly what the sound is coming from Ryan's phone, and my heart does a huge big jump in the air and I lean over his arm and I can see Toby on his hopsipal bed holding a blue toy and saying, 'MummaMumma-Mumma,' and he says it again and then the video stops and I say, 'Again! Again!' just like Toby does and Ryan starts it again and I cuddle closer to Ryan so I can see better and when the video ends I say, 'Again! Again!' and I keep saying this every time the video finishes so I get to watch it lots and lots of times til Ryan says it's time to stop so I can get ready for bathtime. But it's OK cos Ryan says I can watch it any time I want. I just have to ask.

18

MY BOTTOM SLIPS and slides backwards and forwards in the bath til little waves tickle right over my belly button and up towards my boobies. Mummy says that one day my tiny boobies will be big like hers but Toby's will always be tiny cos he's a boy and boys don't have big boobies. Mummy will be very surprised if she sees the water tickling right up to my boobies. That's cos Paige's bath doesn't have a crack in it like ours does so Ryan made the water much more deeper.

I slide my bottom backwards and forwards again but a bit too fast and the water splashes right up on the side.

Ryan calls out, 'Are you OK in there, Jesika?'

I shout back, 'Yes! Where are you and Paige?'

Ryan says, 'We'll be right there. Paige is sooo slow taking her clothes off!'

I swish round in the water and I shout, 'Come on, Paige!' cos it's a bit boring being in the bath all by myself, but Paige doesn't say anything back. She must be really busy taking the rest of her clothes off.

The door bumps against the bath and Ryan's there and he lifts Paige into the bath and I say, 'Yeah! Paige!' and I hand her one of the boats floating in the water and I say, 'Let's pretend these are pirate ships and we're looking for a treasure island!'

Paige stares at me but she doesn't take the boat and she's not smiling and she's not even moving.

Ryan says, 'That sounds like a good game, Paige.'

I push the sponge into the middle of the bath and I say, 'Hey, pretend this sponge is the treasure island and . . .'

Paige picks up her boat –

'. . . we're racing to see who gets to the treasure . . .'

– and she lifts it up in the air –

'. . . first.'

SPLASH!

Paige sunk the island! Ryan laughs and I laugh but Paige's face is mean and my laugh stops working and I don't think Paige sunk the island to make us laugh, I think she did it to be mean. That's not nice.

Ryan picks the sponge out of the bath and squeezes it and rubs soap all over it and then he washes Paige's front and back and over her shoulders and Paige is so still, like she's a statue, not like Toby when he wriggles about every time Mummy tries to clean him.

When Ryan says, 'Stand up, Paige,' she stands up and she doesn't try to jump or splash, she just stands so so still til she's covered in frothy soap, and Ryan even washes all the bits Mummy says you're apposed to wash yourself and Paige doesn't even grab the sponge off Ryan to do it herself.

Ryan says, 'Sit down, Paige,' and she sits down and he rinses all the soap off again and then he says, 'Scoot over, Jesika, and I'll wash you too,' but I already washed myself when I was waiting for Paige and I smile big and say, 'I've already done it! I did it afore Paige got in the bath!'

Ryan says, 'Are you sure you washed everywhere?'

I point to all the places I washed and I say, 'Here and here and here and here and here and here!'

Ryan says, 'Aha! You missed your back!' and I laugh and say, 'That's cos I can't reach my back, silly!'

So Ryan puts more soap on the sponge and he reaches over to my back and—

'NO!'

Paige hits the sponge out of Ryan's hand into the water and she shouts, 'NO!' again and then she hits the water with both her hands making lots and lots of splashes and she shouts, 'NO! NO! NO! NO! NO!' and water is exploding everywhere and I'm wiping and wiping it out of my eyes and, oh! Ryan's lifted Paige out of the bath and she's all wrapped up in a towel and Ryan is cuddling her on his knee and whispering something in her ear and then he stands her on her feet and he says, 'Time to get out, Jesika,' and he lifts me out onto the mat too and he wraps me in another towel and he says, 'Just wait there a second, Jesika, while I get Paige's pyjamas on and then I'll come back and get you dried,' and he picks Paige up and carries her out of the bathroom.

Water slides down my legs and little drips plop from my arms onto my toes. Paige and Ryan are taking for ages. I can hear Ryan's voice but I don't know what he's saying. I can't hear Paige at all.

It's shivery-cold waiting. I want to get back into the warm bath, cept I might not be allowed. I could dry myself and get dressed instead. I know how to get dried and I can put my pyjamas on cos they're in my bag that's on the floor just outside the bathroom.

When Ryan comes out of Paige's bedroom, I'm pulling my pyjama bottoms on and I jump up and down to pull them up and I say, 'I'm ready!'

Ryan says, 'Oh!' and he looks so surprised and I giggle and giggle and then he says, 'Teeth-brushing next,' and he goes back to the bedroom to get Paige and then we all do teeth-brushing at the sink and I show Paige and Ryan my special new crocodile toothbrush with the clever head and Ryan says, 'Wow! That's really cool,' but Paige doesn't even look at it. I think she's cross but I don't know why.

Paige's bed is clever. Underneath it there's another bed that slides out onto the floor and that's what I'm sleeping on but not right now cos right now Ryan's sat on it leaning against Paige's bed and he's reading a story about lots of different animals in the jungle. Paige is hiding under her covers and I think she might be going to sleep cos when I make all the animal noises for Ryan's story she doesn't say anything and I know she likes making animal noises, especially a tiger ROAR!

At the end of the story, Ryan says, 'Time to go to sleep now.'

I say, 'Can I see Toby's video again?'

Ryan laughs and says, 'Again?' but he gets out his phone and he presses the buttons that make the video play and I get to watch it three more times afore Ryan puts it away and tells me it really is bedtime now. He reaches his hand over to Paige's bed and he pats her covers with his hand and says, 'Night-night, Paige,' but she doesn't speak or move so she must be asleep. Then Ryan tucks my covers all round me and strokes them flat over my legs and he leans over me and his lips tickle my forehead and he says, 'Night-night, Jesika, it's nice having you stay here with Paige.'

I say, 'Is Mummy coming to get me tomorrow?'

Ryan stands up and walks to the door and says, 'We'll have to wait for tomorrow to find out.'

I always have to wait for tomorrow to find things out and then when tomorrow happens I have to wait for the next tomorrow. I hope tomorrow's tomorrow is the one that tells me when Mummy's coming home.

'No! NO!'

Eyes open. Night-orange dark.

'NO!'

Crying, loud. Someone's hurt.

A line of light on the carpet.

A shape zooming across the room.

A monster?

Hide! Under the covers! Heart thump-thump-thump.

Bed bouncing down and up, down and up.

Monster feet!

Lie still. Don't *move*.

Someone's still crying.

'Shhh, Paige, shhh, shhh, it's OK. Shhh, you'll wake Jesika. Just a bad dream, that's all. A bad dream. Mummy's got you now. Shhh.'

I know that voice.

Not a monster?

I push my covers up a tiny bit so I'm peeping through a teeny-tiny hole. Someone's sitting on Paige's bed, someone with long, long twisted hair like Rapunzel.

Lorna.

Lorna's got a big bundle in her arms and she's rocking and rocking and saying, 'Shhh, shhh,' then the bundle moves and I can see it's actually Paige and Paige is crying and sniffing and she says, 'Jesika hurted me. She *hurted* me.'

My heart thumps even more fast and hard. I didn't hurt Paige!

Lorna rocks her some more and says, 'Shhhh, shhhh, it's just a bad dream. I've got you.'

Paige says, 'It still hurts.'

Lorna says, 'What hurts, darling?'

Paige says, 'My tummy hurts.'

Lorna says, 'Do you need to go to the toilet?'

I don't know what Paige says but I think it must be yes cos now Lorna is carrying Paige out of bed and I bounce down and up, down and up on my bed when Lorna steps across it and then she carries Paige out of the bedroom and the light disappears and now it's just me in the bedroom and it's dark as dark.

I pull the covers back a bit more and I'm looking around Paige's room and as I look and look the dark is painted with night-orange again. It looks so different to the daytime. It's not like a princess bedroom any more, it's like an underground cave and the princess curtains are like cobwebs hanging down over Paige's bed where bats might hide. Or maybe huge, hairy spiders with tickly legs. Or monsters. I don't like monsters and I don't like Paige's bedroom in the night-orange, not by myself.

I push back the covers and creep on tippy-toes to Paige's bedroom door and open it a little bit and light zooms in a line across the carpet to Paige's bed. It's not hurty light. It's far away light and when I look out of the bedroom door I can see it's floated up from the bottom of the stairs.

Paige says, 'It hurts, it hurts,' and her voice is coming from the bathroom but I can't see her cos the door's not proply open, only a little bit.

Lorna says, 'I know, darling, but you've still got to try and wee.'

I creep forward a bit more cos I want to know what's hurting. The floor under my foot makes a loud creak and I freeze like a statue and my heart thump-thump-thumps and I think Lorna will come running out of the bathroom and be cross cos I'm not in my bed and I want to run back to my bed and hide but my legs are stuck. Then I hear Paige crying again and Lorna doesn't come out of the bathroom. I think she's too busy cuddling Paige.

She says, 'Still hurting? It must be another infection. Poor Paige. You keep getting them at the moment. We'll go to the doctor in the morning.'

I know what a fecshun is cos Toby gets fecshuns all the time. Maybe I should tell Lorna that sometimes the doctor can't make fecshuns better and she might have to take Paige to the hopsipal if she stops breathing proply like Toby.

There's a whooshing sound and I know that's the sound of the toilet flushing. Lorna and Paige are coming back! I run back to bed and hide. Under the covers, my breath is hot on my face. I listen and listen and listen for the sound of Lorna and Paige's footsteps and I think I can hear them coming but I'm not sure.

And then I feel my bed go down and up and down and up again and I know Lorna's there tucking Paige back in bed.

Paige says, 'Don't go, Mummy,' and Lorna says, 'Shut your eyes, darling. You'll be back asleep before you know it.'

Paige says, 'I want you to sleep on the bed beside me.'

Lorna says, 'I can't, sweetie. Jesika's on that bed tonight.'

'Can I have my music on?'

'Not tonight, darling, we might wake Jesika.'

I think I should tell Lorna I'm already awake but I don't know if I'm apposed to be so I don't say anything.

Lorna says, 'I'll stay right here until you're asleep,' and then everything is quiet as quiet and in the quiet I can hear three people breathing, me and Paige and Lorna, and I can hear the swish-ROAR-swish of veekles whizzing by but they sound far, far away, not like at home where Mummy says she thinks one day they're going to drive straight through the window. I keep telling Mummy that's silly cos our home is too high up for the cars and buses and lorries to reach us.

The bed goes down and up and down and up again and the door swishes shut and the light disappears. Now I can only hear me and Paige breathing and I think Paige must be asleep now cos Lorna's left the room and I wonder when I'm going to go back to sleep cos I don't feel sleepy at all.

Paige says, 'Mummy?' and her voice is wobbly-quiet. She's not asleep. I sit up and reach out my hand and I find Paige's hand and I hold it and she grips it hard and hard and I think she must be scared of her bedroom in the dark too and I say, 'Don't be scared, Paige, I'm right here,' cos that's what Mummy says to me when I'm scared of monsters.

Paige doesn't say anything for a while. We just hold hands in the night-orange listening to our breathing and the cars far away. Then Paige says like a whisper, 'I want a cuddle.'

AMANDA BERRIMAN

I can't let go of her hand cos she's holding it too tight so I stand up and I wriggle into bed next to her and we snuggle up so our noses are almost touching, and even though it's dark I can see right into Paige's eyes cos the night-orange is making them shiny. We lie like that for a while just breathing and blinking and breathing and blinking and I'm feeling wrapped up and snuggly and warm . . .

Paige says, 'You hurted me when I was sleeping,' but she doesn't sound cross and I don't think she is cross cos she's still cuddling me. It sounds like she's just saying it. I think about Lorna saying it was a bad dream and I say, 'Paige, I didn't actually hurt you, it was just a bad dream, wasn't it?'

Paige doesn't say anything and she breathes in and out and in and out and it's like she's gone to sleep, cept her eyes are still shining with the night-orange.

Then she says, 'Uncle Ryan hurted me.'

I say, 'Was that in your dream too?'

Paige breathes in and out and in and out, fast and fast, and then she says, 'He hurted me outside the bathroom.'

I say, 'How?'

Paige says, 'He maked my tummy hurt. He does this,' and Paige pokes me in my belly with her finger and I say, 'Oh!' cos I didn't know she was going to do that and Paige says, 'He always does it and I don't like it.' Paige grips my hand and presses herself against me but she's not being squashy and cuddly and nice, she's being hard and shivery and spiky.

I say, 'You have to say STOP IT in your Big Voice. That's what Kali and Mummy said you have to do and Mummy also said if your Big Voice doesn't work it's OK to hit and bite, but you have to use your Big Voice first.'

Paige says, 'I don't want to,' and she squeezes her eyes shut.

I say, 'But if you do it, he'll stop hurting you, won't he?'

Paige says, 'I don't *want* to,' and then she says something so quiet I can't hear.

I say, 'What did you say, Paige?'

Paige says, 'He'll be so cross,' and she breathes in and out and in and out, and she says, 'I won't be his special-good-girl and he won't give me the secret treats and then you'll be his special-good-girl instead,' and she snatches her hand away and opens her eyes and her face is mean and she says, 'And you're not *ever* being his special-good-girl. Not *ever*. Cos I'll never speak to you ever *ever* again.'

My eyes sting and I blink and blink. Why is Paige being mean? I don't even want to be Ryan's special-good-girl cos Paige is apposed to be his special-good-girl but he hurts her and that's not nice.

Paige says, 'Say it. Say not *ever*.'

I say, 'Not ever, ever.'

Paige closes her eyes again and reaches out for my hand and squeezes it tight and she breathes in and out and in and out and I'm thinking and thinking about Ryan hurting Paige and I didn't know he was a not-nice person who hurted people and I think about Paige not telling him cos he might be cross and I think about what I would do if Ryan was hurting me and I didn't want to tell him and I have a good idea. Paige can tell Lorna and then Lorna can tell Ryan to stop it. Ryan won't get cross with Lorna cos she's a grown-up.

I say, 'Paige?'

Paige's eyes stay closed and she's breathing slow. I squeeze her hand but she doesn't squeeze it back. I think this time she really is asleep.

I whisper, 'Paige, are you asleep?' but she doesn't answer me so I close my eyes too.

I'll tell Paige my good idea when it's morning.

19

MUMMY'S NOT IN BED.

No.

This isn't me and Mummy's bed.

Mummy's in hopsipal.

And Toby too.

Duncan and Jane's house.

But pink. Not yellow.

Did my bed move to a different room?

Princess curtains.

Not Duncan and Jane's! Paige's house and Paige's bed!

How did I get in Paige's bed? And where's Paige?

Someone moves on the other side of Paige's princess curtain.

I say, 'Paige? Is that you?'

'Ah, the beautiful princess awakes.'

It's a man's voice.

Duncan?

I sit up and rub my eyes. Silly Jesika, I'm not in Duncan's house, I'm in Paige's house and that's Ryan.

He pulls back the curtain and he's smiling and I say, 'Where's Paige?'

Ryan says, 'Lorna's just popped her to the doctors. She's got a poorly tummy. They won't be long. Do you want some breakfast?'

I nod.

Paige had a poorly belly in the night. I remember. That's how I got into her bed! Cos Ryan was mean and hurted Paige.

Ryan says, 'Come and get dressed, then.'

I shake my head.

Ryan smiles and says, 'Why not?'

I can't tell him it's cos he's mean, cos Paige said that would make him be cross. But he's still looking at me, smiling, and I don't know why not.

Ryan says, 'Look what I've done with your clothes,' and he steps back and it looks like there's a person on the floor but it's not really, it's clothes all laid out on the floor to look like a person. That's clever! But the pants aren't mine and the skirt's not mine either. I don't have any pants with pink flowers on and I don't have a yellow skirt. I slide out of bed and pick them up and say, 'These aren't my clothes!'

Ryan laughs and says, 'No, they're Paige's. Lorna said you needed to borrow some clean things from Paige.' Then he says, 'I bet you can't put all your clothes on before I count to twenty.'

I laugh and say, 'Duncan said that and I beated him!'

Ryan says, 'One, two, three, four, five,' very fast afore I can even take my pyjamas off and I giggle and say, 'Not that fast, Ryan!'

Then Ryan counts slow like a snail and that's much better but after I've taken off my pyjamas I can't find the flower pants and it's cos Ryan's holding them above his head, laughing cos I can't reach them, and I laugh too and try and jump to get them and I say, 'That's cheating, Ryan,' and then he gives them back to me and I'm thinking about Ryan being mean and I think maybe he hurted Paige by accident cos he's not really mean. He's smiley and laughy and funny. I think if Paige just tells Ryan that he hurted her, he'll be very sorry and he'll kiss it better.

Ryan's forgotted he's apposed to be counting. He needs to say eleven but he's just watching me get dressed and he's stopped counting. I'm going to win this easy!

Ryan makes me toast with butter and jam for breakfast and he lets me eat it in the living room so I can watch telly and eat and he doesn't put CBeebies on, he lets me choose one of Paige's deeveedees and I choose Peppa Pig.

I say, 'Mummy doesn't let me watch telly and eat!' Ryan smiles and winks and says, 'Our secret.' So now I have a chips secret and a squashed-pasta secret and a breakfast secret and a trampoline secret that I'm not apposed to tell anyone but I think I'll tell Mummy cos then she might let me eat and watch telly at the same time and if I tell her about the chips she might buy some for tea. I don't think she really knows how yummy they are.

Peppa Pig has a little brother called George and she helps him and plays with him and that's just like me and Toby. I swallow the toast in my mouth and say, 'Are Mummy and Toby coming to get me today?'

Ryan picks up his phone and says, 'Let's find out.' He tap-tap-taps the phone with both his thumbs. I think he's sending messages like Mummy did. Ryan's phone makes a funny bell sound and I say, 'Is Mummy phoning you?'

Ryan says, 'Just a message.' He stares at his phone, smiles and then says, 'Your Mum doesn't know yet.'

I say, 'Oh.' Then I say, 'Can I see Toby's video again?'

Ryan's mouth opens wide and his eyebrows go right up into his hair and he says, 'Again!' and I know he's just joking and I giggle and he looks at me and he pushes his mouth to the side like Mummy does when she's not sure about something and she's deciding what to do and I press my hands together and say, 'Please, can I?' and Ryan picks up the telly remote and makes Peppa and her friends freeze like statues.

He pats the sofa next to him like he's saying, 'Come and sit here, Jesika.' So I go and sit next to him but he puts his phone down and then he holds his two pointing fingers up and wiggles them and says, 'I'll let you watch Toby's video if you let me tickle you,' and I giggle cos when Mummy tickles me I can never stop laughing ever! Ryan wiggles his fingers closer and I giggle and giggle and Ryan laughs and says, 'I've not even started yet!' and then suddenly his pointy fingers are tickling me on my belly and my sides and up and down my legs and on my knees and I've fallen right back on the sofa and Ryan's leaning over and I'm wriggling away cos it's so so tickly.

I roll off the sofa and bump onto the carpet and I crawl away fast and the carpet is scratchy on my knees and Ryan says, 'I'm coming to get you,' in a pretend scary voice and I scream and giggle and crawl even more fast but Ryan catches me and I twist away and I'm lying on my back and he tickles me all over again and then his hands tickle under my T-shirt, all over my belly and under my armpits, and it's even more ticklier on my skin and I can't even giggle now cos my mouth has run out of breathing and I need to tell him to stop so I can breathe proply but it's too tickly and now he's tickling all up and down my legs again and, 'Ow!'

Ryan stops tickling and I sit up and say, 'You scratched me. That hurt!' and I lift up my skirt and there's a tiny, red scratch at the top of my leg near my pants. Ryan makes his mouth all stretchy and he says, 'Oops, sorry, Jesika! I didn't mean to,' and he's smiling and not cross and it remembers me about him hurting Paige by accident and I say, 'You have to say sorry to Paige too.'

Ryan laughs and says, 'But Paige isn't here.'

I say, 'I know, but she said you keep hurting her and you don't say sorry, and you have to say sorry and you have to not hurt her.'

Ryan stops smiling. He says, 'What did you say?'

I say, 'You have to say—' Ryan stands up quick and I stop talking.

He's at the door.

Now he's back sitting on the sofa.

Now he's standed up again and his hands are moving, moving in his hair and around his neck and over his face, and his eyes look like he's so scared, like there's a monster under the bed.

Now he's sitting down again. He presses his hands on my shoulders and his eyes are scary-wide and he says, 'Who else have you said that to?'

I don't know what he means. My belly whizzes round and my heart thumps. I don't like it. I want Mummy. Ryan grips my shoulders more hard and he says, 'Who else did you say that to?' and his fingers are poking into me and I say, 'Ow! Ow! That hurts!'

He lets go and covers his face with his hands and then wipes his hands away and he's smiling again and he says, 'Sorry.' He breathes. 'Sorry, Jesika, I shouldn't have done that. I am silly. I just need you to answer a question for me. Can you do that?' He keeps smiling and smiling and smiles are apposed to make the scary go away but it's not making the scary go away inside me cos what if Ryan gets cross again? Paige was right about not telling him.

Ryan says, 'Jesika? Can you?' He leans towards me and I can feel his breath tickling my cheek and it's hot and it smells like toast.

I want Mummy.

There's a crash and a bang outside the room. I know that sound!

Quick! Get up! Run!

'Mummy!'

Not Mummy.

NOT MUMMY!

I WANT MUMMY!

Arms tight round me.

A hand stroking my hair.

A voice says, 'Breathe, Jesika. Just breathe.'

My face is squashed against something soft like a cushion and the voice says, 'Like this, Jesika,' and it's Lorna's voice and I can hear her doing big breaths in and out and in and out and my face is squashed into her jumper and it's soft and it smells like flowers and my face moves up and down every time she breathes and it makes me breathe too and then I'm crying and she says, 'Poor Jesika. Did you think I was your Mummy?'

I nod my head and Lorna's jumper tickles my nose.

She says, 'Poor Jesika,' again and she doesn't feel like Mummy and she doesn't smell like Mummy and she doesn't sound like Mummy but she cuddles just like Mummy and I think when she's not being cross she's a kind Mummy and her cuddle is making the scary go away, just like my Mummy's cuddles do.

Lorna lets go of me and I can see again and she's kneeling on the carpet and she's looking at something above my head and she says, 'Do you think I should just say?' I turn round to see who she's talking to and Ryan's standing right ahind me. He looks at me and his face still looks scary and I don't want to see so I cuddle back into Lorna's jumper.

Ryan says, 'She doesn't know what's happening with . . . yet.'

Lorna strokes her hand down my hair and says, 'Yeah, you're probably right.' Then she laughs and says, 'Don't look so worried, Ryan. It's not your fault she's upset.'

Ryan says, 'I thought you were popping to the shops? And where's Paige?'

Lorna says, 'She's in the car. I've only come back for my purse – I think I've left it upstairs. At least I hope so, because I can't find it!' She undoes her cuddle and stands up and says, 'And I thought I'd take Jesika with me now, seeing as there's a chance . . . you know. Can you help her put her shoes and coat on while I go and look for my purse?'

Then Lorna runs up the stairs and Ryan's in front of me lifting down my coat from the high-up peg and I look at my feet cos I don't want to see his scary face and he holds my coat out for me and I turn round and push my arms in. He leans right over me to zip it up, just like Mummy does, and he says quiet in my ear, 'Jesika, that thing you said about me hurting Paige, you mustn't ever say it *ever* again.'

He turns me round to face him and he lifts my chin with his finger so I have to look at him and he says, 'Do you understand?'

I nod my head cos I know what it means to ever never say something ever again, like when I said the naughty words that the man downstairs said and Mummy got so so cross, and I say, 'Is it a naughty thing to say?'

Ryan nods his head and says, 'Yes, it's *very* naughty. If you said it to your Mummy or Lorna or any other grown-up they would be very angry and sad. You would be in a *lot* of trouble. Do you understand?'

I nod my head again cos I know what a lot of trouble is. It means that you get told off and sometimes you don't get to watch telly or you have to go to bed afore it's bedtime. But I don't know why it's a naughty thing to tell Ryan that he hurted Paige and he has to say sorry, cos that's not bad words, and I didn't shout or scream or say, 'I hate you.'

Lorna comes back down the stairs and she says, 'Found it! Phew!' and Ryan stares right into my eyes and says, 'OK, Jesika?' and Lorna says, 'All ready?' and holds out her hand for me and then she laughs and says, 'Shoes?' and then Ryan laughs and smacks his hand on his head and says, 'What am I like?' and Lorna laughs too and kneels down and helps me put my shoes on. But why is Ryan laughing? Isn't he cross?

Lorna stands back up and holds my hand again and says, 'Thanks for your help this morning, Ryan, you're such a life-saver!'

Ryan says, 'Don't mention it.'

Lorna opens the door and Ryan says, 'Jesika?' and I look back and he says, 'You can watch Toby's video later, as long as you're not *naughty* with Lorna,' and he smiles and winks.

Lorna laughs and says, 'Of course she won't be naughty. Will you, Jesika?'

Ryan laughs too, but when Lorna turns round to the door he stops smiling and he's not laughing, and he puts his finger to his lips and holds his phone up and points to it. I think he's saying that if I say the naughty thing again I'll be in lots of trouble and I won't get to watch Toby's video, and I want to see Toby again. I miss him.

Lorna pulls me out of the door after her. We walk down the path and there's Paige sitting in the back of a white car. I didn't know Lorna and Paige had a car. Paige lifts her hand and presses it against the window. I have to tell Paige what Ryan said cos she was right about not saying to Ryan and I better not tell her my idea about telling Lorna cos then she might get in lots and lots of trouble for saying the naughty thing. But I still don't know why it's naughty. Maybe if I tell Mummy that I know a naughty thing but I don't know why it's naughty, she'll say it's OK to tell it so she can tell me why it's naughty? I don't think Mummy will shout if I do that. I wish Mummy was here right now so I could ask her.

20

WE HAVE TO walk to the shops cos Lorna forgotted that she's only got one car seat. Paige stamps her feet on the pavement and says, 'I don't *want* to walk. My legs are too *tired*,' and she sits down and won't move at all til Lorna says she can have some sweeties if she walks all the way and doesn't whinge. I can do that. Me and Mummy and Toby always walk places and it's easy. Will I get sweeties too?

We walk along the road and then another road and another and I need to tell Paige about Ryan but Paige is on the other side of Lorna and she's not listening and all she keeps saying is her legs are tired and she doesn't want to walk and all Lorna keeps saying is, 'You won't get those sweeties if you keep moaning. Come on, it's really not that far.'

I want to stop holding Lorna's hand cos she's holding it tight and sore but when I pull my hand out she grabs it again and says, 'You must keep holding my hand, Jesika,' and her voice is snappy like a crocodile.

Then we walk around the side of a big car park and we're walking towards a building and I think I know this place. I look at the red bricks and the white around the windows and I've seen it afore but it doesn't look quite right. We walk down the side of the red-brick building and it gets squashy atween two walls and then it's a tunnel with a roof over our heads and when we come out of the tunnel we're at a busy, noisy street and I *do* know this place! This is *my* place! Mine and Mummy's and Toby's and I haven't been here for a long-a-long time!

I can see the red heart shop and the big food shop on the other side of the road and then Lorna's hand tugs me and my feet have to keep walking but I'm looking ahind me cos I know if I stretch my neck back even more I might see Ade's rainbow shop or Nandini's washing machine shop and past that is my house. I really want to see that.

But now I can't see anything cos Lorna's pushed open the door of another shop and we go inside and I know this shop too. This is where Mummy gets medicine when me or Toby or Mummy is feeling poorly and I know what the red brick building is now. It's where we go to see the doctor and it has a path for buggies that goes up to glass doors and when I'm with Mummy I'm allowed to run along next to the path on the pavement and then run up the stairs that go to the same glass doors and see if I can beat Mummy and Toby to the top and I always do cos I can run fast like a cheetah.

I pull Lorna's hand and say, 'I go to this shop too and the doctors with the buggy path.'

Lorna smiles and says, 'Do you?'

I say, 'Yes, and I know all the other shops too. I know the red heart shop and the washing machine shop and the big food shop and Ade's rainbow shop.'

But Lorna's talking to the man who gives her the medicine and I don't think she heard me so I tell Paige but Paige is just leaning her head on Lorna's leg and she's not listening either.

Outside the medicine shop, me and Paige have to hold Lorna's hands again and we cross the busy road at the green man and start walking up towards Ade's rainbow shop and I'm so excited cos we might actually be going to see Ade and I can tell him I've been sleeping in different beds for ages and he might have a treat for me and Paige cos Paige is my friend.

But we don't go to Ade's rainbow shop, we go into the big food shop, and Lorna gets a basket and she gets me and Paige to help her find things like milk and bread and then she picks out some apples and bananas and I say, 'You can get them at Ade's rainbow shop, Lorna,' cos maybe she doesn't know.

Lorna says, 'Can you?'

And I tell her all about Ade's shop and the colours and the things he gives us to taste and the special bags he gives Mummy and all of that but Lorna doesn't put the apples and bananas back and then we go and pay and I don't think she was really listening to me telling her at all.

Outside the big food shop, Lorna gets out her phone and she tells me and Paige to stand against the wall out of the way. I squash up with Paige and say, 'Have you ever been to Ade's rainbow shop?' But Paige doesn't say. Sometimes I think Paige can't remember her words and that's why she doesn't say things cos other times she has lots to say, like in the dark last night when she said lots of things. That remembers me!

I put my mouth right up to Paige's ear and I whisper, 'You were right about not telling Ryan.'

Paige turns her head away.

I put my mouth back at Paige's ear and I whisper again, 'Did you hear what I said?'

Lorna says, 'What are you two whispering about?' and she's smiling and I think I can't tell her what I'm saying cos Ryan said not to, and if I do say it Lorna won't be smiling cos she'll be cross and I'll be in lots and lots of trouble so I say, 'Nothing! It's just a secret for me and Paige.' And Lorna laughs and says, 'I hope it's a good secret?'

I say, 'Yes, it is,' cos it's good I'm telling Paige something so she doesn't get in trouble as well.

Lorna's phone makes a noise and Lorna looks at it and then she smiles and she says, 'I know a good secret too.' And her smile is big and big but she won't tell me or Paige what it is cept she says it's a good secret for me and then Paige gets cross and stamps her feet and says, 'I want a good secret too!'

I put my mouth to Paige's ear again and whisper, 'I've got a good secret for you,' but Paige pushes me away again and shouts, 'No! I don't want your secret!' and she pushes me again and, ow! My head bangs on the wall and it *hurts*!

Lorna says, *'Paige!'* and she pulls Paige away and she's talking to her fast and cross and my head hurts and hurts and I want Mummy to cuddle it better but Mummy's not there and then Lorna's there with Paige and Paige says, 'Sorry, Jesika,' and Lorna says, 'No more whispering secrets, Jesika. Paige doesn't like it, OK?' and her voice is spiky and cross and I think that means it was naughty to whisper to Paige. I'll have to tell Paige about Ryan later when Lorna's not listening and I don't have to whisper.

Lorna says, 'Time for a drink and a snack while we wait,' and Paige says, 'Yeah, yeah!' and Lorna says, 'Come on, then,' and we walk away from the big food shop and we're walking to Ade's rainbow shop and I can see the outside fruit getting more near and more near cept we don't get there cos we stop at a shop just afore Ade's and I remember this shop. It's the one with the tables and chairs and people sit at the tables and have something to eat and drink.

Paige jumps up and down and says, 'The cafe! The cafe!' and it remembers me that Mummy went to a cafe with Ryan and Ryan got me a yummy gingerbread man and maybe they went to this cafe and I jump up and down too and say, 'The cafe! The cafe!' cos it's so exciting cos I've never been in a cafe afore.

Lorna lets go of my hand and she's pushing the door open and then I hear, 'Jesika!' and I look round and Ade is standing next to

227

the outside fruit and he's smiling so big and waving and he's not leaning on any stick today so it must be a not-hurty day.

Lorna says, 'Come on, Jesika,' and I turn and she's holding the door open and I have to go but I smile and wave first.

Inside the cafe it's warm and it smells like the baking shop and we sit at a table and we drink hot chocolate and eat star biscuits that have sprinkles on them and Lorna has a giant*normous* piece of chocolate cake and she cuts a bit for me and Paige and it's so yummy and then Lorna says, 'Who was that man, Jesika?' and her face is frowny.

I say, 'What man?'

Lorna says, 'The one who called your name and waved at you.'

I smile big and I say, 'That's Ade!' and I laugh cos Lorna's being silly cos everyone knows Ade in the rainbow shop, don't they? And I say, 'Can we go and see him after this?'

Lorna frowns more and shakes her head and says, 'No, no, I don't think so.'

I say, 'Why not?'

Lorna says, 'Because I don't know if your Mummy would let you go and talk to him.'

I say, 'I talk to Ade all the time with Mummy. We go to his shop and we buy big bags with fruit and vegetables in them and sometimes he puts surprises in the bag and he gave Mummy a book to read one day too. Mummy says he's our friend now.'

Lorna says, 'Is he?'

I say, 'Yes, and Nandini and Emma in the washing machine shop. Can we go and see them as well?'

Lorna says, 'I don't know any of these people, Jesika. I think it would be better if your Mummy takes you to see them when she's back.'

Lorna smiles big like she's said something good, but it's not good cos I want to tell Ade and Nandini and Emma where I've been cos I've not seen them for a long-a-long time and they might not know I've been sleeping in different beds. I wish Mummy was back now.

We stay in the cafe for ages and Lorna has another drink and the man wiping all the tables gives me and Paige some pictures to colour in but Paige keeps snatching the pencils from me and then she scribbles on my sheet and I scribble on hers and Lorna is cross with both of us even though Paige did it first and it's not fair.

Lorna's phone rings and she's talking and smiling and when she's finished talking she drinks the rest of her drink fast and stands up and says, 'Time to go!'

We have to put our coats back on fast cos Lorna says there's not much time but she doesn't say why and she hurries us out of the door and we rush past Ade's rainbow shop and the shop with all the buckets and boxes outside and the hair cutting shop and then we stop right next to the bus stop and there's a bus there and people are getting on and off and Lorna says, 'Let's wait here for a moment.'

I say, 'What are we waiting for?'

Lorna smiles big and says, 'You'll see.'

ROARRR!

What was that noise? My heart thumps and thumps. It sounded like a-hundred-a-thousand lions all roaring at the same time! Then the bus starts moving and I laugh cos it was just the bus and then the bus has gone and I'm looking straight across the road at my house and I know what we were waiting for now. We were waiting to see my house.

I say, 'My house!'

A car whizzes past playing thump-da-thump music and Lorna says, 'What did you say, Jesika?'

I point over the road and say, 'My house! We came to see my house,' and I'm smiling and smiling but Lorna's not.

She says, 'You mean the flats over there with the black door?'

I nod my head and I keep looking at my house and I press my hand against my chest cos it feels funny, like it's hungry, but you don't feel hungry up where your heart is, you feel it in your belly where your food goes.

I say, 'Can we go inside and look?'

Lorna says, 'No, we'll just wait here.'

I say, 'Why are we waiting here?'

Lorna says, 'You'll see in a minute.'

I say, 'I really want to go and look inside. Can we?' I look at Lorna and her face is all twisted like she's tasted something horrible.

She says, 'Your poor Mum,' and shakes her head.

I say, 'What's wrong with Mummy?' and now my belly feels funny too and I don't like it and I don't know why Lorna looks so sad. I want Mummy.

Another bus stops at the bus stop and I can't see the house any more.

Lorna says, 'Nothing's wrong with your Mummy. Nothing at all,' and I'm looking at her face and she's smiling big and big. And then she points ahind me and I turn and look and there's a lady walking away from the bus and she's holding . . .

MUMMY! TOBY!

I run forward and crash into Mummy's legs and I'm holding and holding tight as tight and then Mummy's bending and I have to let go and she puts Toby down and her arm is around me hugging and hugging but Toby's pulling at Mummy's jumper and her hair and crying and yelling, 'Up, up, up, UP!' and Mummy has to let go of me and stand up with Toby hanging around her neck and I try to cuddle Mummy again but her legs are not as cuddly as the rest of her but this is still the best day *ever*!

Mummy says, 'Thank you,' lots and lots of times to Lorna and then Lorna gives Mummy a shopping bag and she says, 'I got you some milk and bread and a few bits and pieces just to help out today,' and Mummy says, 'Thank you,' a lot more times and she hooks the bag on her arm that's carrying Toby and Lorna says, 'Do you need help carrying things up to the flat?' and Mummy says, 'No, no, we'll be fine, thanks,' and then Lorna and Paige have to go.

But I don't think we are fine cos when we get across the road Toby keeps wriggling and crying and Mummy's bags keep slipping off her arms and she keeps blowing out big breaths and it takes for ages to get to our house cos Mummy has to keep stopping.

We stand in front of the big black door and I see the bit where the paint is scratched off and the bit at the bottom of the door that's all bashed and I reach out my fingers and I feel the cold, bumpy metal on the doorknob and Mummy pushes the door open and it's dark and smelly inside like a bear cave and Mummy says, 'Shh,' but I already remembered we have to be quiet, but not cos there's a bear in the cave, cos it's not really a cave and there's not any bears here, it's cos there's a shouty man ahind one of the doors. But Toby's not remembered cos he's still wriggling and crying and if he's not quiet soon the shouty man might come out.

Mummy stands at the bottom of the stairs, breathing and breathing, and I say, 'Why aren't we going up?'

Mummy says, 'Just catching my breath first.'

I say, 'How do you catch your breath?' And I put my hands out in front of my mouth and breathe on them and I look but I can't see if I've catched it cos you can't see breath, cept when it's shivery-cold.

Afore Mummy can tell me how to do it, the big, black door bangs open and a man bashes past us and runs up the stairs and then the shopping bag is on the floor and I can see the bread and the milk and two apples roll out and Mummy makes a moaning sound and drops her head down and she just stands and looks at the bag on the floor with everything spilled out of it and it's going dark again cos the big door is closing but then the dark stops and it goes light again and I hear *jingle-jingle-jingle* and I jump round and shout, 'NANDINI!' and I'm smiling and smiling and smiling cos Nandini is right there and she's picking up all the spilled things and she says, 'I thought I saw you go past. You were going to text me for a lift home!' and Mummy says, 'They let me go earlier than I thought. You've already taken loads of time away from the shop,' and Nandini says, 'We've been over that one, Tina. It's never any trouble,' and she picks up the shopping bag and she takes Mummy's other bags and she tries to take Toby too but he wraps his arms tight as tight around Mummy's neck and shouts, 'GO 'WAY!' and pushes his face into Mummy's chest and I think Nandini will be cross cos he shouted but she laughs and strokes his head and we all go up the stairs together.

Mummy and Toby are slow and slow but I want to keep going fast cos I can't wait to be back in our house, so I pull and pull on Nandini's hand and she says, 'Slow down, Jesika, there's no rush.'

I say, 'I want to play with my toys. I've not played with them for ages!'

Mummy says, 'You've only been away for two and a half days!'

I say, 'Well, that's a long-a-long time and Baby Annabelle might have forgotted me!'

We go up and up and round and round and up and up and when we're nearly up to our house I let go of Nandini's hand and run up the last stairs and Mummy shouts, 'Jesika, wait!'

I whizz round the corner and there's our front door and I shout, 'Come on, Mummy! Come on, Toby!'

Nandini gets there first. Mummy and Toby take for ages to catch up and when they get to the door Mummy's huffing and puffing and she says, 'Don't run away from me, Jesika. You know you're supposed to stay near.' And my feet are bouncing and bouncing and I say, 'Sorry, Mummy, can we go in now?' and Mummy puts

Toby down and leans over and pushes the key into the lock and twists it and pushes the door hard with her shoulder and the door zooms open and Mummy almost falls over and she says, 'Oh!'

Nandini says, 'Sorry, I should have said, Leon fixed your door.'

Mummy stands in the doorway and says, 'But . . . how?'

Nandini says, 'When you gave me your keys to check if you'd left your lights on. I couldn't get the door to shut after and Emma was at work so I asked Leon to help.' Nandini lifts her shoulders up and down. 'It didn't take him long.'

Mummy says, 'But I can't . . . how am I going to pay him?'

Nandini says, 'Tina, he doesn't want paying. He was happy to help.'

Mummy says, 'But . . .' then Toby pulls at Mummy's trousers and shouts, 'Up! UP!' and Mummy picks him up and walks through the door and now I can run inside too and I run round the living room and there's Baby Annabelle in the pram and my colouring book is on the little table with my bag of pens and the building blocks are in the box in the corner and everything looks exactly right like it's apposed to be. I run into the bedroom and there's our bed and the stripy bars on Toby's cot and I run back out and into the bathroom and I lean over the bath and check the crack is still there and it is and then I run out of the bathroom and into the kitchen and it's all the same in there too, cept Nandini's in there putting things inside our fridge and Nandini's not ever been in our kitchen afore.

I run back into the living room and Toby's hugging Mummy's leg tight and his face is hided in her trousers and Mummy's still got the door open and Next-Door Lady is there and Mummy says, 'Thank you. We're all fine now.'

I run over and I say, 'Mummy and Toby had to sleep at the hopsipal and I had to sleep in two different beds and we've been away for . . .' I look at Mummy. 'Was it two years?'

Mummy smiles and Next-Door Lady laughs and laughs and I can see all her rotten teeth and she says, 'They are funny. My little boy – just the same.'

I stare at Next-Door Lady. I didn't know she has a little boy.

I say, 'Where is your little boy?'

Mummy says, 'Jesika!' so I think I wasn't apposed to ask that but Next-Door Lady opens her mouth wide and laughs just like a witch and when she's finished laughing she says, 'Time flies, boys grow up. They forget all about their poor old Mums.'

I think that's so strange and I say, 'I won't grow up and forget *my* Mummy.'

Next-Door Lady laughs and pats me on the head and says, 'I'm sure you won't.' And she laughs even more and then waves her hand and walks back to her house.

I say, 'She's nice, but I think she should go to the dentist.'

Mummy says, 'Don't you ever say that to her!' but she's smiling big so I smile too and then Mummy says, 'I don't even know her name.'

I say, 'You can ask her next time you see her.'

Mummy smiles and says, 'Yes, I can.'

I say, 'Cos if we know her name, that means we can make friends with her and it's nice making friends, isn't it?'

Mummy shuts the door and she doesn't even have to bang it. It goes click and it's shut.

I say, 'Leon did good fixing on the door,' and Mummy smiles and smiles.

Nandini comes out of the kitchen and she's holding two mugs that are steamy hot and she puts one of them on the little table and she says, 'I've put a couple of sugars in yours, Tina. You look like you need it.'

Mummy says, 'Thanks, Nandini,' and she picks Toby up and sits down on the sofa and cuddles him and Nandini sits down on the chair and I run over and sit next to Mummy and Toby. Mummy reaches over and strokes my hair and Toby's eyes are doing slow blinking and I think he'll be asleep soon. I cuddle up to them and I can hear the busy-ness outside of cars and lorries and people and a door bangs and the thump-da-thump-da-thump music is playing and inside me I'm all warm.

I say, 'I like being here again.'

Someone shouts in another room and another door goes BANG!

Toby lifts his head and looks at me and pushes me hard and says, 'Go 'way!'

I smile and say, 'Don't be silly, Toby, we're doing cuddles.'

He pushes me again and shouts, 'NO! GO 'WAY!' and his face is cross and mean and my eyes sting and I blink and blink and I look at Mummy cos she needs to tell Toby to stop being mean and then we can all cuddle again but she says, 'He's very tired, Jesika, and he doesn't really understand what's been happening the last few days,' and she cuddles Toby close but I can't cuddle too cos Toby keeps pushing his hand at me. He blinks his eyes slow, slow and then closes them.

Nandini puts her mug down and says, 'Tina, let me take Jesika downstairs for a bit. She can help me for a couple of hours and you and Toby can both have a good sleep.'

Mummy frowns and closes her eyes.

Nandini says, 'Tina? Trust me, let me help.'

Mummy says quiet as quiet, 'Leave the door open and trust will come to you.'

Nandini says, 'What's that?'

Mummy opens her eyes and smiles a tiny smile and says, 'Life lessons with Magda.'

Nandini leans forward and puts her hand on Mummy's knee and says, 'It's hard to trust when you've been through tough times, when someone undermines your trust, and then losing someone so important and, on top of all that, not having your Mum and Dad around to support you. You've really been through it.'

I look at Mummy and frown and say, 'Do you have a Mummy and a Daddy?' cos I don't think I know about them.

Mummy says, 'My Mummy and Daddy died a long, long time ago, remember? Long before you were born.'

I know who Mummy means now and I say, 'Are they the ones that had a crash in a car?' and that's a sad thing cos they died like Bab-bab and I didn't even get to ever see them.

Mummy says, 'Yes, poppet,' and then she turns her head to Nandini and says, 'Magda was more support to me than my parents ever were. I miss her so much. My parents drank and shouted and played me off against each other . . .' Mummy looks at me, and then at Nandini. 'Anyway, it's all in the past.'

Nandini says, 'These things stay with you.'

Mummy squeezes her lips tight, then she says, 'Yes.'

Nandini says, quiet as quiet, 'And you still miss them.'

Mummy squashes her lips up small and small and shuts her eyes tight and then she whispers, 'Every day,' and then her mouth is open and she says, 'Oh, oh, oh, oh,' and her shoulders are shaking up and down and Nandini kneels in front of her and holds her in a great big hug and Mummy's crying and she's crying and crying and crying cos it's sad when people go away and never come back.

There isn't space for me to cuddle Mummy so I fetch Baby Annabelle from her pram cos she needs a cuddle too cos she missed me lots and lots when I wasn't sleeping here. I go ahind the sofa and I whisper in her ear all about the ambulance and the hopsipal and Duncan and Jane and Paige and Lorna and Ryan and when I'm finished Mummy's not crying any more, she's just sniffing lots and lots.

Nandini says, 'You really do need to rest, Tina.'

Mummy says, 'Jesika? Where are you?' and I come back round to the front of the sofa and Mummy says, 'Jesika, do you mind going to help Nandini, just while me and Toby get some rest?'

I do mind. I want to stay here and play with all my toys and cuddle Mummy and Toby but I can't make the words in my mouth and Mummy says, 'It would be really helpful, poppet.' And I do want to be helpful but I can also be helpful here, at home, with Mummy and Toby. I'm always helpful.

Nandini stands up and holds out her hand to me and her bracelets jingle and she says, 'Come on, Boss, you can help me keep everyone in order downstairs.' And Mummy says, 'Go on, poppet. I can play with you later when I don't feel so tired.'

I put Baby Annabelle down and stand up and walk over and hold Nandini's hand and Nandini says, 'Just text if you need anything.'

Mummy whispers, 'Thanks,' and then we're at the door and Nandini is opening it and I'm looking over my shoulder at Mummy and Toby cuddling on the sofa and even though Toby's eyes are shut I can hear his voice is shouting GO'WAYGO'WAYGO'WAY inside my head and the Big Hurty squeezes and squashes and I blink and blink and blink and then we're outside on the landing and the door's shut.

Mummy doesn't want me to stay and be helpful.

Mummy only wants to cuddle Toby.

21

NANDINI'S HAND IS smooth and warm and her bracelets jingle against my arm each time we step down and sometimes she squeezes my hand but not one, two, three for 'I love you' cos she doesn't know the secret code, and the Big Hurty is squeezing and squashing so hard.

Nandini stops at the bottom of the stairs and she crouches down and now she's holding both my hands and she says, 'Are you OK, Boss? You've hardly said a word on the way down,' and I'm thinking that maybe Toby shouted at me cos he's forgotted who I am and maybe he's always going to shout GO 'WAY at me now and then Mummy will have to tell me to go away too cos she only wants to cuddle Toby and I'll have to find a new house to live in and a new Mummy and I don't want to and Nandini is watching me and her eyes are kind and her face is crinkly and I say, 'Toby shouted at me,' and my lips are all wobbly and my voice sounds funny.

Nandini says, 'He didn't mean it, Jesika. He's just tired and grumpy and needs a good sleep.'

I nod my head and my eyes are stingy and I blink and blink and Nandini says, 'Come here, Boss,' and she lifts me up and then I'm sitting on her knee on the bottom step and she's cuddling me and she smells like lemons and biscuits and she says, 'You are being such a helpful girl coming with me. Your Mummy and Toby can have a really good sleep and I get your help with all that washing I have to do. We're all so lucky that you like helping people so much.'

I do like helping. I am a helpful girl.

Nandini says, 'What does Toby really like to play with?'

I think and I say, 'He likes the bricks and he likes building things and then knocking them down.'

Nandini says, 'I think if you play with the bricks when you get home later, Toby might come and join in. Is that a good idea?'

That is a good idea. My mouth feels smiley and wobbly and the Big Hurty still squeezes but only a little bit.

Nandini stands up and holds my hand again and she says, 'Let's go, Boss, there's work to do,' and we walk to the big front door and Nandini opens it and all the busy-rushy sounds zoom into my ears and Nandini says something else but I can't hear the words proply.

There's two men on the seats inside the washing machine shop. One's a man I don't know and the other I can't see proply cos he's holding up a big paper in front of his face but I can see his shiny head over the top and it's Leon and Nandini says, 'Thanks for that, Leon,' and he folds the paper up and nods at Nandini and he says, 'No probs. Everything OK?' and Nandini says, 'OK, considering.'

I say, 'You did good fixing on our door. Mummy doesn't even have to bang it now,' and Leon smiles and rubs his head and says, 'My pleasure,' and then Nandini says, 'Jesika's come to help me out for a couple of hours.'

Leon says, 'Don't let her work you too hard,' and then he winks and unfolds his paper again.

It's not hard work at all but Nandini says I'm being so helpful. All I have to do is sit at the table in the kitchen and draw lots and lots of pictures and eat lots of yummy jam sandwiches and tell

Nandini every time I hear a machine beeping in the other room cos that means we have to pull all the clothes out, and if they are wet they go in a drier and if they are dry they go somewhere else. Nandini pushes an iron onto clothes to make them flat and her bracelets *jingle-jingle-jingle* and the iron makes noisy steam and I think the noises go right in her ears and stop her hearing things cos every time I shout, 'BEEPING!' she looks so surprised like she didn't hear the beep too.

After a long-a-long time, when there's no jam sandwiches left and I've drawn pictures for everyone, there's a different beeping noise and I shout, 'BEEPING!' but Nandini doesn't go to the machines in the other room. She's holding her phone and looking at it and she smiles and she says, 'Time to go home, Jesika,' and I jump off my chair and I say, 'I can go home now?' and Nandini laughs and she walks over to the table and helps me to tidy the pens back into the bag and I give her the picture of me helping with the washing machines and she says, 'Oh, that's lovely, Jesika,' and she stands it up ahind the kettle so it can't fall down and she says, 'I'll stick that on the wall later,' and then I give her another one that's got Leon doing fixing on our door with his hammer and I say, 'Can I give this to Leon?' and Nandini puts it back on the table and says, 'He's gone home, but I can keep it safe for him,' and then I give her one more with lots of rainbows and an ambulance and I say, 'This one's for Emma,' and Nandini says, 'Oh, she'll like that.'

I say, 'The rainbows are cos everyone likes rainbows and the ambulance is cos I saw her in an ambulance the other day in the middle of the night.'

Nandini smiles and says, 'That's right, you did! And that's how we found out your Mummy and Toby were in hospital.'

I smile and smile and say, 'I know. My Mummy told me. And she said you and Emma and Ade and Leon are our friends now,' and I think Nandini likes this cos she's smiley all the way back home.

Mummy and me are having a race to see who can build the biggest tower with the bricks. Mine's more bigger than Mummy's cos Toby is resting on Mummy's knee and that means she can't build fast like me. I put one more brick on but everything wobbles and then my tower falls down and I shout, 'KABOOM!' and Mummy laughs and Toby reaches out to Mummy's tower and takes two bricks out of the middle and Mummy's tower falls over too and I look at Toby and he's smiling at me! Toby's smiling! Quick as quick I build my tower again and this time I knock it over on purpose and shout, 'KABOOM!' again and Toby does a tiny giggle and I say, 'Do you want to knock my tower over this time, Toby?' but Toby shouts, 'GO 'WAY!' and presses his face into Mummy's jumper so I can't see him now.

Mummy says, 'Keep building them, Jesika, he'll join in when he's ready,' so me and Mummy start building new towers and I'm going to make this one more higher than ever, afore I knock it down, and I'm making a pattern that goes green, yellow, blue, red, green, yellow, blue . . .

Bang! Bang! Bang!

The red brick jumps out of my hand and bounces on the carpet and Mummy's mouth makes an 'Oh!' but she's not getting up to answer the door.

BANG! BANG! BANG!

I say, 'Mummy, why . . . ?'

'SHHHH!' Mummy's eyes are scary-wide.

I think it's a baddie at the door.

Toby bangs his two bricks together and says, 'Bangbangbang!'

Mummy grabs his hands to stop him banging them again. Toby's face squashes together like he always does just afore he cries loud and loud and I don't think Mummy wants Toby to do that so I make a silly face quick but he presses his face into Mummy's jumper again.

SNAP!

What was that?

Mummy lifts Toby off her knee and Toby rolls onto his back and bangs the two bricks together *bang-bang-bang, bang-bang-bang*. Mummy stands up and walks slow to the door. She bends down and picks something up. Oh! It's a letter. It was the postman snapping the letterhole, cept he usually comes when it's breakfast time. Mummy rips the letter open and looks at it and then she's shaking her head and her mouth and her eyes go wide and she pulls the door open and she runs out and she shouts, 'You can't do that! We haven't done anything wrong!'

A different voice is speaking. It's grumbly like a bear but quiet so I can't hear the words. Is it the postman? What has he done?

Mummy shouts, 'That wasn't us! I complained to *you* about those things!'

The grumbly bear voice says something else. I slide off my chair and tiptoe to the door so I can see the postman but all I can see is Mummy standing at the top of the stairs and she shouts, 'How am I going to find somewhere else in fourteen days? Where do you expect us to go? I've got two small kids!'

The grumbly bear says, 'I don't deal with troublemakers.'

I know that voice! That's not a grumbly bear and it's not the postman. It's the Money Man!

Mummy shouts, 'You BASTARD!' and her voice fills up all the space around me and I didn't know her voice could be that loud.

I hear STOMP, STOMP, STOMP on the stairs and the Money Man's head pops up above the railing and his face is mean and Mummy steps backwards and he says, 'I want you out by ten a.m. on the twenty-first. I've someone else moving in, so if you give me any trouble I'll have the bailiffs round to remove you.'

Mummy whispers, 'You can't do that.'

The Money Man points to Mummy and says, 'That bit of paper says I can, darling,' and he smiles but it's not a nice smile and then he turns and stomps back down the stairs.

Mummy stands still like a statue. The letter is on the floor next to her foot. I pick it up and I hold it out and I say, 'You dropped your letter, Mummy.'

Mummy turns round and takes the letter and says, 'Oh, Jesika!' and she holds my hand and pulls me back into our house and she bangs the door shut even though it doesn't need to be banged any more and then she sits on the sofa and she doesn't say anything, not even when Toby knocks my tower over and says, 'Aboo!'

I say, 'Are you OK, Mummy?' Mummy nods her head and does some big breaths in and out and then she shakes her head and she says, 'That stupid woman told me to complain, so I did, right away, that afternoon. I got it all down in writing like she said. Made it official.' Mummy breathes and breathes. 'And now we don't have anywhere to live.'

I say, 'What do you mean, Mummy?'

Mummy shakes the letter in her hand and says, 'This letter says we have to leave our flat in two weeks. TWO WEEKS!' She stands up then sits down again then rubs her hands through her hair. 'How am I going to find us somewhere new? It was hard enough finding this place.'

Mummy's face is scrunched up like she's worried, but I think she's forgotted that you can live in other people's houses when you can't live in your own house and I say, 'We can ask Duncan and Jane if we can live in their house. It's got lots of bedrooms and it's got a garden and there's a trampoline and a bird house.'

Mummy looks at me surprised and then she cuddles me hard and says, 'I wish you were in charge of the world, Jesika.'

There's a buzzing sound and Mummy stops cuddling and she picks her phone up from the table and she stands up and puts it to her ear and says, 'Hiya, yes, yes, we're all fine. Well, sort of.' And then she walks into the kitchen and I go back to the bricks and build another tower and I can hear Mummy saying about the letter and finding a new house to live in. Maybe it'll be a house like in the Tilly books, or maybe a huge one like Duncan and Jane's or it might be one like Paige's with flowers on the wall. I hear Mummy say, 'There just aren't enough houses!' and I think maybe that means someone needs to build some more houses and that remembers me about the story of the three pigs who all go and build houses and maybe what we should do is find a nice man with some bricks and ask him if we can have some and we can build ourselves a new house like the pigs did. But as long as it's bricks and not straw or sticks cos they aren't any good for houses.

Toby says, 'Aboo!' and knocks my tower over and giggles.

And it has to be proper house bricks and we have to stick them together with glue or Toby or anybody might just come and knock it all down.

I push some bricks to Toby and say, 'You build a tower, Toby?'

Toby picks a brick up and then he throws it down and he shouts, 'No! GO 'WAY!' and he rolls over onto his belly and hides his face. Has he forgotted that he likes building towers?

When Mummy comes back through, she's smiling and smiling and I say, 'You look happy, Mummy,' and Mummy smiles even more bigger and says, 'Relieved, Jesika, but yes, that is a kind of happy. Ryan's said if we can't find another house straight away, we can stay at his flat.'

I say, 'Do you mean live with Ryan?' My belly squeezes. I don't want to live with Ryan. I don't like his scary face.

Mummy says, 'No, not with him. That would be a bit . . . weird.'

I say, 'Does that mean horrible?'

Mummy laughs and says, 'No, it means strange. I know he's nice and his flat is much better than this one, but it would be strange to share it with him. He's very kindly said he'll stay with Lorna and Paige until we find somewhere else.'

I say, 'So it's just me and you and Toby going to live in his flat?'

Mummy says, 'Yes.'

I say, 'And Ryan isn't living there too.'

Mummy says, 'No, he's going to live with Lorna and Paige.'

I say, 'Good,' and my belly stops squeezing. But then I think maybe it's not good cos maybe Paige doesn't like Ryan too. And it's remembered me that I've not asked Mummy about the naughty thing.

I say, 'Mummy, why is it naughty to tell someone to stop hurting someone?'

Mummy's holding her phone up to her ear again and she says, 'Mmm? What was that, Jesika?' and then she says, 'Hold on, ask me again in a minute, poppet.' And then she walks back into the kitchen and she's not saying anything so I shout, 'Mummy?' And Mummy says, 'Shh, Jesika, I'm trying to listen.'

Toby's got his eyes closed and he's breathing slow and slow like he's sleeping. Is he pretending? That's one of Toby's games. He says, 'Do bed, Des-des,' and that means getting his covers and his Zebra and covering him up like a real bed and he pretends to sleep and I pretend to read him bedtime stories. Maybe he wants me to play that game today. I get down on the floor and put my face close to his and I say, 'Do bed, Toby?' but he doesn't answer me. He just breathes and breathes. I think he really is asleep.

I have a good idea! I run into the bedroom and pull his covers out of his cot and over the stripy bars and go back into the living room and tuck the covers over him. Then I get Zebra and tuck him aside Toby. Then I get Baby Annabelle too cos I think she wants to cuddle Toby so he feels better. Then I go to the bookshelf and I pick out my fayvrit Tilly book, and when I come back, Toby's squeezing Zebra and Baby Annabelle in a cuddle so maybe he's not quite asleep. I turn the pages of the book and I say what's happening in all the pictures but I can't really tell the story like Mummy does cos I don't know what all the words say but I don't think Toby minds and he doesn't tell me to go away.

I close the book at the end and Toby rolls over and opens his eyes and closes them and says, 'Foh, fee, foh, fy, wonsa, wonsa fish a-ly,' and his voice is singy and that's cos we always do a song after the story. He sings it again, 'Foh, fee, foh, fy, wonsa, wonsa fish a-ly,' and I giggle and I say, 'That's not a song, Toby!' and then he sings it again and he's still got his eyes closed but he's pointing at his fingers and I was wrong cos it is a song and I know which one! And I lie down on my belly next to Toby and I say, 'It goes like this, Toby,' and I point at his fingers and I sing, 'One, two, three-four-five, once I caught a fish alive,' and then I stop cos I can't remember what comes next.

Toby smiles and says, 'Foh, fee, foh, fy,' and his voice is just a whisper now and then he's just breathing and breathing and I say, 'Let's sing it again, Toby,' but he doesn't sing with me this time and then Mummy comes back into the room and she blows a big breath out of her mouth and then she sees me and Toby on the floor and she smiles and says, 'Aw, did Toby ask for a bed?'

I shake my head and I say, 'I just thinked it was a good idea cos he's sleeping.'

Mummy sits down on the floor next to me and strokes Toby's head and he doesn't move at all and his mouth is open a little bit and he's breathing slow and slow.

I say, 'Is it good that he's sleeping?' cos sometimes it makes Mummy cross and sometimes it doesn't.

Mummy smiles and says, 'Yes, it's good. Every time he's sleeping he's getting a little bit better.'

Mummy cuddles me tight and says, 'So, what was it you were asking me, Jesika?'

I say, 'What do you mean?' cos I wasn't asking Mummy, I was singing with Toby.

Mummy says, 'Before. You asked me something when I was on the phone.'

I think hard and hard but I don't think I asked Mummy a question, did I?

Mummy smiles and says, 'Never mind. If it's important it'll come back to you.'

I pick up the Tilly story and I say, 'Can you read it to me?' and she does and when she's finished I remember I do have something important to ask Mummy.

I say, 'Mummy, do you know the rest of the fish alive song?'

22

IT'S MY TURN to cuddle with Mummy on the sofa cos Toby's asleep and that means he can't push me and tell me to go away. He's on the sofa too next to Mummy cos Mummy said it was more comfy than the floor and she moved him there and he didn't even wake. I want him to be asleep for ages so I can cuddle Mummy for a long-a-long time.

Bang! Bang! Bang!

I look at the door and Mummy is looking at the door too and she's not answering it. Is it the Money Man again?

I whisper, 'Is it—'

Mummy says, 'Shh!' and puts her finger to her lips.

Bang! Bang! Bang!

Toby wakes up and cries and Mummy lifts him onto her knee and now we can't cuddle.

I want the Money Man to go away and leave us alone.

SNAP!

The letterhole.

'Tina? It's Ryan.'

Mummy huffs out a big breath and stands up, still holding Toby, and says, 'It's OK. It's Ryan,' and she smiles.

I don't smile. I was cuddling Mummy. And I forgotted to ask Mummy about the naughty thing. Will Ryan tell Mummy I said it? Will Mummy be cross with me? I have to tell Mummy I don't know why it's naughty and then she might not shout and she might explain it to me.

Mummy opens the door and says, 'Come in,' and Ryan is there smiling and he holds up a bag and says, 'I bring chips!' and I can smell them and I look at Mummy cos I don't know if we're allowed chips and she doesn't know I had chips the other day but she's smiling and she says, 'You're a star, Ryan,' and she shuts the door, click, and I say, 'Leon fixed the door,' and Ryan looks surprised and Mummy says, 'It was a bit tricky to close before.'

Ryan puts the chips bag on the little table and he's holding two other bags, and one of the bags is mine! How did he get that?

I run over and say, 'That's *mine*!'

Mummy says, 'Jesika!' and I remember that Ryan has a mean face and I hide ahind Mummy cos I don't want to see it but Ryan laughs and Mummy laughs.

Ryan says, 'I didn't steal it, Jesika. I've brought back all the stuff you left at Lorna's.'

Mummy says, 'Silly sausage,' and I peep round Mummy's back and Ryan's still smiling and he's holding out my bag for me so I take it and Para-Ted's paw is sticking out and I'd forgotted about him! I pull him out and I run over and hide him in the pram with Baby Annabelle and then I run and hide the bag in the bedroom just in case Ryan tries to steal it again and I run back out and Mummy's put Toby down and she's holding the chips bag and Toby's shouting, 'Up! Up! UP!'

Mummy says, 'Do you want a brew?'

Ryan says, 'Let me do it. You should be resting.'

Mummy says, 'No, it's fine. I'll only be a minute,' and she turns and tries to walk to the kitchen but Toby runs over and wraps his arms around her leg so she can't move. She tries to lift him off and she says, 'Come on, poppet. Stay here with Ryan while I make the tea.' But Toby won't let go and when Ryan crouches down to talk to him Toby shouts, 'GO 'WAY!' and hides his head ahind Mummy's leg and cries.

Mummy says, 'He's not quite himself yet.'

I say, 'He says "go away" to everyone, cept Mummy.'

Ryan puts his hand into the other bag he's still holding and he says, 'I know what'll do the trick,' and he pulls out something and I can't see what it is cos he turns round and crouches down and I can only see his back.

I look at Mummy and say, 'What is it?' and Mummy lifts her shoulders up and down like she doesn't know either but she's smiling so I think it's going to be something nice.

HOOT! HOOT! Chuffa-chuffa-chuffa . . .

What was that?

HOOT! HOOT! Chuffa-chuffa-chuffa . . .

Toby lets go of Mummy's legs and he claps his hands and he says, 'Thom-Thom!' And he's right cos atween Ryan's legs there's a Thomas train chuffing across the carpet.

Mummy says, 'You didn't buy that, did you, Ryan?'

Ryan stands up and turns round and Ryan's smiling at Mummy and Mummy's smiling at Ryan and he lifts his shoulders up and down and he says, 'It's not new. I just spotted it in the charity shop on the way over.'

I look at Toby crawling after the Thomas train across the carpet. Did Ryan bring something for me too?

Ryan puts his hand back into the bag and he says, 'I bet you're wondering if I brought you something, Jesika.' And that's just what I thinked! How did he know that?

Mummy says, 'Oh, Ryan, you didn't need to.'

Ryan puts the bag ahind his back and I can hear the bag crunching and crackling and then he says, 'I know how much you like playing pirates and how much you like dressing up, so . . .' He smiles a very big smile. The bag floats to the ground ahind his back then he brings one hand round and he's holding a pirate hat and a pirate eye-patch and then he brings his other hand round and he's holding a pirate sword. I can dress up as a fierce girl pirate!

Mummy says, 'That's so thoughtful of you. Thank you,' and she presses her hand to her mouth and then she turns away and she walks to the kitchen with the chips bag and she says, 'I'll just make the tea,' and Toby doesn't even follow her this time cos he's too busy playing with the Thomas train.

Ryan holds the hat and the eye-patch and the sword out to me and I reach out to take them and I'm smiling and smiling but when I pull them Ryan doesn't let go. He crouches down and he's not smiling now and he says, 'I just need to know that you've been a good girl, Jesika.'

My heart thumps. I have been good. I haven't said the naughty thing. But I still don't know why it's naughty.

He says, 'Have you, Jesika?'

I nod.

Ryan keeps looking at something ahind me. I turn and look but it's only Toby crawling after his Thomas. I can't see Mummy. I can only hear the kettle whooshing in the kitchen.

Ryan puts his mouth close to my ear and his breath is hot and he says, 'And you haven't said the naughty thing to anyone?'

I shake my head. I haven't said it cos I keep forgetting to ask Mummy.

Ryan says, 'Because I can keep bringing you toys. But I'll only do that if you don't *ever* say it to *anyone*. Do you understand?'

I nod cos I know that means I can't tell it to anyone, not even Mummy.

And then I shake my head, cos . . .

Ryan says, 'Why are you shaking your head?'

I shake my head again. I can *not* say it to Paige and I can *not* say it to Lorna, but I have to say it to Mummy cos she has to tell me why it's naughty and then I won't have to say it again ever.

Ryan says, 'Not *ever* to *anyone*, Jesika. Do you understand?' A drop of water is running down the side of his head. Did he get wet in the rain? He lets go of the pirate costume and all the bits drop to the floor and he grabs my hands and squeezes hard and it hurts but I can't say cos his eyes are zapping and he's made his teeth scary like a wolf. My belly whizzes round and round and my heart thumps and thumps and I need to tell him to stop cos I don't like it but he pulls me close and he presses my hands against his jumper and it's soft and he whispers, 'Because if you tell your Mummy, she'll be so angry and maybe she'll have to send you away to live with someone else again. Is that what you want?' and his hot breath puffs in my nose and I don't like the smell and I don't want to breathe it but I can't stop my nose breathing and my belly feels scary like monsters under the bed and Mummy and Toby in hopsipal and I don't want to live with someone else again and I want Ryan to stop squeezing and hurting and scaring.

I say, 'No,' but my voice is squeaky and he doesn't stop squeezing and I need to use my Big Voice and say the words Kali says you have to say but I can't remember them and I say, 'No,' again but my voice is still tiny and shaky and I try to look ahind me to see Mummy but he tugs my arms back and I say, 'No,' again and my voice is a bit bigger and I say, 'No. No. No!'

NO-NO-NO-NO-*Let-go*-LET-GO-BITE!

I'm on my bottom on the floor and Ryan is rubbing his hand and his mouth is a big 'Oh!' and someone's picking me up and cuddling me and it's Mummy and she says, 'What was that all about?'

I push my face into Mummy's jumper.

Ryan says, 'I'm sorry, she didn't want to put the costume on and I was persuading her to give it a go. I didn't mean to upset her.'

That's not right! I push my face harder into Mummy. She pushes me back a little til she can see my face and she says, 'Jesika? What happened?'

I push my face back into Mummy's jumper.

Ryan says, 'It's been a tough few days for you all. Maybe I should just . . .'

Mummy says, 'No. Don't go,' and she blows out a fast breath and I think she sounds cross and then she pushes me back so she can look at me and I don't want to look and I stare at her knees and she says, 'Jesika, was it like Stella and Jane? Did you bite Ryan because you felt scared?' and her voice isn't cross and I look at her face and it isn't cross too and I nod.

Ryan says, 'I didn't mean to scare you, Jesika.'

Mummy says, 'Why were you scared?'

Ryan says, 'This is all my fault. I made a pirate face and it must have been too scary. Lorna tells me off all the time for making faces that are too scary. I'm so sorry, Jesika.'

I don't know what Ryan means. He didn't make a scary pirate face. He made a mean face and he hurted my hand and he wouldn't let go cos of the naughty thing.

Mummy says, 'Oh, Jesika. You have to tell people to stop if you don't like something. Remember? You only bite if they won't stop and nothing else is working. OK?' And she cuddles me again and my mouth is close to Mummy's ear and I say, 'He didn't stop. He got so so cross.' And he told me I would have to live with someone else, but I don't want to tell Mummy that cos I'm thinking about Mummy and Toby cuddling and Toby telling me to go away and maybe Mummy will think it's a good idea.

Mummy says, 'Poppet, he was only pretending. It was just a game.'

But it wasn't a game, and he wasn't pretending. I press my mouth right up against Mummy's ear and I say, 'It's cos I said the naughty thing.'

Mummy pushes me away again and her face is frowny this time and she says, 'You said the naughty thing?'

Ryan says, 'Oh, this is all my fault too. Tina, this is about something that happened at Lorna's house and I feel like a complete idiot about it and I've probably handled it all wrong.'

Mummy's still frowning and she says, 'Oh?'

Ryan rubs his hand on the back of his neck and says, 'The other day, Paige got hurt when we were playing a rough and tumble game, she banged her head, and Paige . . . well, as you know, she doesn't handle things very well at the moment and she gets very angry when something goes wrong, even when it's an accident. She told Jesika I hurt her on purpose and I didn't say sorry, so Jesika told me I had to stop hurting Paige and I had to say sorry and I told her it was all sorted out but she kept saying it and . . . I didn't get cross but I did get a bit impatient with her and she got upset and then I felt like a complete idiot because she was only trying to help Paige, weren't you, Jesika?'

Ryan looks at me and his face isn't mean at all now and he's right cos I was trying to help Paige and he did hurt Paige and he didn't say sorry. But it was her belly he hurt, not her head. Why is he saying it wrong?

Mummy says, 'Is that what happened, Jesika?'

I say, 'He hurted Paige's belly, not her head.'

Ryan says, 'No, she banged her head on the door frame.'

I frown and shake my head and I say, 'You poked her and hurted her belly.'

Ryan rubs a hand across his face and he looks at Mummy and holds out his hands and says, 'We were playing the tickle monster game, maybe a bit rough, and she fell over and hurt her head.'

That's not right! I say, 'You hurted her *belly*.' I look at Mummy and I say, 'Belly and tummy are the same thing, aren't they?' Cos Paige says tummy but that means belly.

Mummy says, 'Yes, they are, but Jesika,' and she blows out a breath, 'it was an accident. It doesn't really matter if it was her belly or her head. Ryan knows he hurt Paige and he's said sorry.'

My chest feels hot and spiky and my foot stamps and I say, 'But—'

Mummy says, 'Enough, Jesika!' And her voice is snappy like a crocodile and I don't want Mummy to be cross. She says, 'Ryan's here to help. He brought you presents. He's our friend!' Then she strokes my hair and she says, 'Come on, poppet, let's eat these chips before they get cold,' and she kisses my head and stands up and walks into the kitchen.

Ryan looks at me and shakes his head and his eyes are sad and he bends down close to my ear and he says, 'I told you not to say it, didn't I? I said you'd be in trouble,' and then he goes into the kitchen too and I can hear Ryan and Mummy talking and laughing in quiet voices.

My breathing hurts and hurts.

My head and my legs and my arms and everything feels wobbly.

HOOT! HOOT! Chuffa-chuffa-chuffa . . .

Oh! I turn round fast and my foot slips and something cracks and Toby screams and then he cries and cries and Mummy rushes out of the kitchen and says, 'Jesika!' and I look down and Toby's train is on its side and the funnel is broken off and I think it's cos I standed on it by accident and Mummy's crouching down and Ryan comes over and crouches down too and Toby's crying and crying and I didn't mean to break it and Mummy's face is so cross and she says, 'That was so naughty, Jesika! What do you say to Toby?'

My mouth opens and closes. I didn't mean to break it. It was an accident!

Ryan says, 'It's OK, it's not actually broken. Look, this bit just slots back in here,' and he fixes it as quick as quick.

Mummy looks at me hard and says, 'If you feel cross, you can shout and stamp your feet but you may *not* break your brother's toys. Understand?'

But I wasn't cross and I didn't mean to and it's not even broken now. It's not fair!

Ryan gives Toby the train and I say, 'See, Toby, it's not even broken.'

Toby hits me hard on my leg and shouts, 'GO 'WAY!' and Ryan looks at me and he smiles like it's a funny thing and Mummy lifts Toby up for a cuddle and she says, 'Poor Toby, it's OK now, it's fixed, look!' and nobody is looking at me and nobody is telling Toby off even though he hitted me and it hurt and Mummy thinks I'm naughty and she might tell me to live in a different place and inside my head she's shouting, 'FIND YOURSELF A NEW MUMMY!' And I don't want to. I want to stay with *my* Mummy.

I run fast as fast into the bedroom and slam the door and get into bed under the covers. Mummy can't make me live somewhere else if I don't ever never get out of bed ever again!

I breathe and breathe and my breath is loud in my ears.

The bedroom door opens.

Mummy says, 'Jesika, don't be silly. Come and eat your chips.'

My face gets hot and hot with all my breathing.

Mummy says, 'Come on, poppet, you can't go to bed without any tea.'

It's hot cos I'm trapped in a cave and there's a dragon guarding the way out and breathing fire at me. I swish my pirate sword at the dragon and roar, 'GO AWAY!'

Mummy says, 'Jesika, Ryan brought the chips specially for you. You told him you loved the chips he got you for lunch yesterday.'

The covers tickle my nose and the dragon disappears. Why did Ryan tell Mummy about the chips? *I* was going to tell Mummy. He told me it was a secret not to tell. I don't like Ryan, I don't like chips and I'm not getting out of bed til Ryan's gone away for ever and ever and Mummy promises I can always live with her.

I hear Mummy blowing out a breath and then I hear the bedroom door swishing shut.

I hear Ryan say something and Mummy say something and Toby giggling.

I pull back the covers and slide out of bed and creep over to the door and push Mummy's dressing gown out of the way so I can peep through the hole in the door. Toby is in his high chair and I can see Ryan's back and Mummy's next to Toby and everyone's eating chips cept me, and Toby's giggling and Mummy's smiling and everyone's happy, cept me.

I creep back to bed.

Eyes open.

Dark and noisy.

Music and veekles and shouting.

Something's pressing hard on my belly.

Need a wee.

Really need a wee.

I roll over and dangle my legs til I feel the scratch of the carpet on my feet. I creep past Toby's cot. I can see his lumpy shape and I put my ear close to the stripy bars and he's breathing and breathing, slow and slow. I whisper, 'I love you, Toby,' and then the hard thing presses on my belly again and it remembers me I really have to go.

The living room is all in night-orange. Where's Mummy? Why isn't she here?

I say, 'Mummy?' cos maybe she's hiding ahind the sofa, but she doesn't jump out. And she's not in the kitchen and the bathroom is dark.

Where is she?

My belly does scary jumps.

I *really* need to go.

It's too dark in the bathroom.

Where's Mummy?

I run back into the bedroom and up the other side of the bed that's Mummy's side and a giggle pops out of my mouth. Silly Jesika. Mummy's hilly bump is right there under the covers. I shake her shoulder and I can see Mummy's eyes shining and she says, 'Jesika? What's the matter?'

I say, 'I need a wee.'

Mummy's shiny eyes disappear again and she says, 'Go on then, poppet.'

I shake Mummy's shoulder again and put my mouth close to her ear and I say, 'It's dark in the bathroom. There might be monsters.'

Mummy opens her eyes and sits up and the covers fall down and she says, 'Come on, then.'

In the bathroom, I sit on the toilet and Mummy sits on the side of the bath and it remembers me about the night when Lorna took Paige for a wee in the dark. Did she sit on the side of the bath too? Paige didn't like weeing cos it hurted her.

I say, 'Did Toby's wee hurt when he had his chesty fecshun?'

Mummy says, 'No, why would his wee hurt?'

I say, 'Cos Paige said her wee hurted and Lorna said it was a fecshun and she had to go to the doctors.'

Mummy says, 'That's a different kind of infection.'

I say, 'I think it's the same cos Lorna says Paige is always getting them and you said Toby always gets his too.'

Mummy says, 'No, it's not the same.'

I say, 'What makes it?'

Mummy says, 'What makes what?'

I say, 'The fecshun that Paige got.'

Mummy says, 'Oh, all sorts of reasons. Poor Paige. Urine infections aren't nice.'

I say, 'She was crying.'

Mummy says, 'I bet she was. Have you finished, poppet?' and she yawns a big, big yawn and if the light was on I bet I could see right to the back of her mouth where the dangly bits are.

We creep back through the night-orange and I see something I didn't see afore. It's Toby's Thomas train on the table and next to it is my pirate costume. I stop and my belly whizzes round fast.

Ryan.

Mummy says, 'Come on, poppet, let's get back to bed.'

I forgotted about Ryan being here. And I forgotted about going to bed and not having my chips and Mummy being cross. She's not cross now. Is she?

I look down. I've got my pyjamas on.

I say, 'I didn't put my pyjamas on.'

Mummy laughs and says, 'No, I changed you into them when I came to bed and you didn't even wake up.'

She holds out her hand and I take it and it's warm and soft and we go back into the bedroom and I'm thinking about the chips and Ryan and everyone being cross and my belly's still whizzing and then it growls and I say, 'I'm hungry.'

Mummy tucks me up and slides into bed on the other side and she says, 'It's a bit late for that now.' She wriggles about and pulls the covers up high and then I wriggle too and squash up against her and I say, 'I like being in the bed with you again.'

Mummy says, 'Me too. Night-night, Jesika.'

My belly growls. I say, 'I can't get to sleep. I'm hungry.'

Mummy says, 'You haven't tried yet.'

I say, 'What time is it?'

Mummy says, 'Half past nine.'

I say, 'Is that past my bedtime?'

Mummy says, 'Yes.'

I say, 'Is it past your bedtime?'

Mummy says, 'No, but I need the sleep. So let's go to sleep.'

I say, 'I'm hungry.'

Mummy says, 'You can have a big breakfast in the morning.' And then she says, 'Maybe next time you'll eat your chips.'

I say, 'Everyone was cross and I didn't like it.'

Mummy blows out a breath and wraps her arms around me in a cuddle and she says, 'No one was cross, really. We all just need time to settle back to normal.'

I think about this and I want to ask Mummy if I can stay with her but it's scary cos she might say no, so I say, 'Will Toby stop shouting at me?'

Mummy squeezes her arms and says, 'Of course he will.'

I say, 'And can I go to preschool again?'

Mummy says, 'Yes, but you'll have to wait until Monday because it's the weekend tomorrow. But if the weather's dry, how about we see if Paige can come with Lorna or Ryan for a play at the park? That'll be nice, won't it?'

I say, 'Not Ryan.'

Mummy says, 'Why not Ryan?'

I say, 'I don't like Ryan. He's not nice.'

Mummy says, 'Why do you think he's not nice?' She pushes up in the bed and leans over me so I can see her face in the dark and it's frowny and she says, 'Is it because he made a scary face at you?'

I nod my head and then I shake my head cos it's lots of things and I don't know which one to tell Mummy cos she got cross when I told her afore and Ryan said it's cos I said the naughty thing.

Mummy blows out a breath and her face stops frowning and

she strokes my cheek with her hand and says, 'Poppet, I know you two had a little clash but he didn't mean to upset you. He's our friend and he's been so helpful. Give him another chance, OK?'

I say, 'What's a chance?'

Mummy says, 'It means you don't decide you don't like someone because of one thing that you don't like. You wait and see, because they might actually be nice and that one thing might have been a mistake.'

Ryan hurted me and he hurted Paige and it was on her belly, not on her head, and he wasn't playing tickle monster cos Paige said he hurted her outside the bathroom and I was inside the bathroom and tickle monster is a noisy game and I didn't hear him playing tickle monster. That's one, two, three . . . lots of mistakes! But I don't say it cos Mummy might be cross and if she's cross she might want me to live with someone else.

Mummy kisses my head and says, 'Back to sleep now, or you'll be so tired in the morning.' She undoes her arms around me and wriggles about a bit more and I think her eyes are closed cos I can't see them shining and her breathing goes slow and slow and slow.

I close my eyes but I don't go to sleep.

Ryan's inside my head. He's mean and scary and he says everything wrong.

I don't like him.

23

MUMMY'S BENDING OVER Toby's buggy and she's coughing and coughing. Each time she coughs my belly squeezes hard. She stops and stands up straight and she breathes big and slow and wipes her hands across her eyes and she sees me looking and she says, 'What's wrong, poppet?'

I say, 'Have you got another chesty fecshun?'

Mummy strokes my hair and says, 'No, it's the same one, but I'm much, much better. Coughs just take a long time to go away. Did you hear me and Toby coughing in the night too?'

I shake my head. I didn't hear anything in the night. I was asleep.

Mummy says, 'At least it's not raining now and we can get outside for a bit. Fresh air helps.'

That remembers me about waiting at our house for a long-a-long time for the rain to stop and seeing the big rainbow in the sky. I look up but the rainbow isn't there now. The sky is blue and hurty-bright. My nose tickles . . .

Atchoo!

Atchoo!

Atchoo!

Mummy says, 'Sun-sneeze!' She laughs and then coughs but only two times.

I say, 'Why does the sun make us sneeze?'

Mummy says, 'I have absolutely no idea.'

There's a noise like a faraway car beeper in the sky and I look up again and . . . oh! There's lots of wobbly dots in the sky and they're making a shape like an arrow and they're moving fast across the sky. Birds!

Mummy says, 'Keep walking, Jesika.'

I say, 'Look up there, Mummy,' and I'm pointing at the birds. Mummy says, 'Oh, yes, the geese. Well spotted!'

The birds are flying across a fluffy white cloud and they are teeny-tiny and making lots of car beeping noises. I say, 'They're not geese! They're too small!'

Mummy says, 'They're a long way away so they look smaller than they are, but they are geese. Can you hear that honking sound?'

I say, 'Like the car beeper?'

Mummy says, 'Yes. That's the sound geese make.'

We wait for the green man and then we cross over the road. I can't see the birds now.

I say, 'Why do they fly like an arrow?'

Mummy says, 'The bird at the front is showing the rest of them where to go.'

'Where are they going?'

'To their summer home.'

'Their summer home?'

'The geese fly south to warmer winter homes when it gets too cold here and then they fly back north to cooler summer homes when it gets too hot there.'

'So they have to keep moving houses?' I wrinkle up my face. I heard Mummy talking in the phone when me and Toby were eating breakfast and she said moving houses is hard work.

Mummy says, 'Yes, but they don't mind. They do it to stay alive.'

'Is that why we have to move to a different house?'

Mummy blows out a breath and says, 'Not exactly.'

'Why do we have to move to Ryan's house?'

'It's complicated.'

'What does complicated mean?'

'It means it's difficult to explain.'

We walk through the park gates and I let go of the buggy cos I only have to hold it along the roads and I say, 'Why is it difficult to explain?'

Mummy says, 'Because it is. See if you can spot Paige.'

I look and look but there's lots of people and I can't see her and every time I look Mummy says, 'Come back, Jesika,' and 'Wait, Jesika,' and 'Slow down, Jesika,' but I'm not going fast, I'm just skipping and that's not fast like running. It's cos Mummy's walking too slow.

Now I can see the playground and I think we must've beated Paige and Lorna cos I still can't see them and then Mummy says, 'I can see a pirate!' and I look at the pirate ship and there's Paige looking through the round looking-out hole and I run and run all the way to Paige on the pirate ship and there's a shark chasing me and it almost bites my leg off but I jump on the pirate ship just in time and I run up to Paige and I say, 'Pretend everything that's not on the ship is the sea and there's lots and lots of sharks and if you go into the sea they chase you and you have to not be catched or they eat you up!'

Paige turns away from me and she doesn't say anything.

I say, 'Paige, did you hear me?'

Paige looks over her shoulder and says, 'I don't want to play,' and then she climbs down the hatch to the hidey-hole that goes to the bottom tunnel. I climb down too. Paige is crouched in the corner and her face is sad. I crawl over and say, 'What's the matter, Paige?'

Paige says, 'My tummy hurts.'

My eyes go wide and wide and I say, 'Did Ryan poke you again?'

Paige holds her hand up like STOP and says, 'I'm not telling you.'

I say, 'Why not?'

Paige doesn't say, she just crawls out through the bottom tunnel. I crawl after her. She runs to the slide and climbs up and slides down and I run to catch her at the bottom of the slide but she jumps off the bottom and runs to the roundabout and I think she's going to jump on it but there's lots of children spinning fast so she just runs all the way round it and back to the pirate ship and up the ramp and I chase after her and she's climbing up the little ladder to where the steering wheel is so I climb up too and I shout, 'Why aren't you telling me, Paige?' and Paige turns round afore I can climb off the ladder and she stands right at the top so I can't go up and she says, 'Uncle Ryan says it's none of your business! I'm his special-good-girl and NOT YOU!'

I say, 'But he's not apposed to hurt you. That's not nice.'

Paige says, 'I'M NOT TALKING TO YOU! GO AWAY!'

I wobble on the step. Why is she being mean? My cheeks are spiky-hot. I say, 'But you're my best friend, Paige.'

Paige says, 'I'm not your friend.' Her eyes go small like black lines. 'You made Uncle Ryan be sad and cross and he didn't give me sweeties and it's all *your* fault. He said so.'

Why is it my fault?

Is it cos I said the naughty thing?

Did Ryan tell Paige I said it?

Did he tell Lorna too?

Is everyone cross?

I jump off the ladder and I run off the ship and everything feels wobbly and I'm crying and crying and I want Mummy but I can't find her and then Lorna's there and she says, 'What's the matter, Jesika? Have you hurt yourself?' and then Mummy's there too and she says, 'Point to where it hurts, poppet,' and it hurts all over me and I don't know where to point and Mummy cuddles me and cuddles me til I'm not crying and she says, 'Did you hurt yourself?' and I shake my head and I want to tell Mummy that I didn't mean to say the naughty thing and I don't like everyone being cross but I don't want Mummy to be cross again cos she might tell me to live somewhere else and I don't want to, so I say, 'Paige said she's not my friend,' and my lips wobble and then I'm crying again and Lorna says, 'Oh, she doesn't mean it, Jesika. I'll go and have a chat with her.'

Mummy cuddles me again and I stop crying and I say, 'Every-one tells me to go away,' and then I'm crying again and Mummy says, 'Oh, poppet, not everyone. Toby won't be so grumpy when he's feeling well again. And Paige is a bit unwell too, remember, with her infection. It's not your fault.'

But it is my fault. It's cos I said the naughty thing.

Toby shouts, 'Mu-mu-mu-mu!' and I look round and he's on the swing and he's not swinging, he's shouting and his face is all crumpled up like he's about to cry.

Mummy says, 'Oops, better go and rescue Toby!' and then she stands up and holds out her hand and says, 'Come on, he likes you pushing him.'

We go to the swings and Mummy pushes Toby first and he's giggling and giggling and then I push but he stops giggling and shouts, 'NO! Mu-mu oosh,' and my eyes sting and sting and Mummy whispers in my ear, 'Tickle his feet,' and that's a good idea cos he really likes that so Mummy pushes and every time he comes near me his face is frowny and then I tickle his feet and he giggles and he keeps doing it, frowning and giggling and frown-ing and giggling, and me and Mummy can't stop laughing.

Lorna brings Paige over and Paige is looking at her feet and Lorna says, 'What do you say, Paige?' and Paige says, 'Sorry,

Jesika,' but then when Mummy and Lorna start talking, Paige sticks her tongue out at me so I don't think she really is sorry.

Mummy says it's lunchtime and she lifts Toby out of the swing. Lorna has a big blanket and she spreads it out on the grass next to the bench and it's for me and Toby and Paige to sit on but Toby wants to sit with Mummy and Paige wants to sit with Lorna so Mummy and Lorna come and sit on the blanket too and it's a bit squashy.

There's lots and lots of boxes on the blanket with teeny sausages and pizza and tomatoes and cucumber and carrots and pieces of cheese and grapes and apple slices and even crisps that look like teddy bears and there's juice cartons for everyone too. Lorna says we can help ourselves to anything and we don't have to ask first. We eat and eat and eat and it's all YUMMY!

Lorna says, 'I've left Ryan moving all those boxes out of the spare room into the attic. His mate says he can borrow the van on Tuesday and he'll move his stuff to ours in the morning and move your stuff while Jesika's at preschool in the afternoon.'

I don't want to leave our house and I don't want to move to Ryan's house. I don't like Ryan.

Mummy says, 'I feel so relieved to be leaving that flat. I don't know how I'm ever going to repay you both.'

Lorna says, 'It's what friends do, isn't it?'

Mummy says, 'Lorna . . .' then she looks down at her knees and presses her lips together and then she says, 'I've never told you what it meant to me to have a place to escape to when my parents were going at each other. I know we never really talked about it, but you must have known that your house was like my safe place.'

I say, 'We have a Safe Place at preschool and that's where you choose the Feelings Dollies.'

Lorna says, 'You don't need to—' but Mummy holds her hand up and says, 'No, let me say this. You really helped me before and after they died – but when I moved away and met Alex and got pregnant with Jesika, I just let things drift, cut myself off from my old life, and so I wasn't there for you when David died. After everything you did for me, I should have been and I wasn't. I don't deserve all this help you keep giving me.'

Lorna says, 'We both lost touch, not just you.'

I say, 'Mummy, what are you and Lorna talking about?'

Lorna says, 'Look, Tina, when David died, a whole bunch of people rallied round and helped to sort out the funeral, the legal stuff, me. I wouldn't have managed without their help. And now I can help someone else. I can make space for Ryan in our house so you can leave that awful flat. It's easy. And later, when you're sorted, you can help someone else. It's not about paying it back, it's about paying it forward. Do you see?'

Mummy smiles all wobbly.

I say, 'I don't want to move to Ryan's house,' and Paige says, 'I don't WANT Uncle Ryan at our house.'

Lorna and Mummy both blow out a breath and Lorna says, 'We've talked about this, Paige,' and Mummy says, 'It's complicated, Jesika,' and Paige shouts, 'NO! NO! NO!' and then Lorna reaches into her bag and says, 'Ah, look what I've got here! Who's finished and ready for a treat?' and she holds out a packet and it's chocolate cake rolls like we had at preschool one time and they are even more YUMMIER!

I say, 'ME!' and so does Toby. Paige makes a frowny face and I think that means she doesn't want one but she takes one when Lorna holds it out.

Mummy says, 'I should have brought the treat, considering all you're doing.'

Lorna says, 'You're the invalid. Just sit back and enjoy!'

Mummy shakes her head but she's smiling too and she says, 'Ade's making our tea tonight, too!'

I say, 'Are we having tea at Ade's rainbow shop?'

Mummy says, 'No, that's not where Ade lives. He just works there. He's cooking something in Nandini and Emma's oven and—'

I say, 'We're having tea at Nandini and Emma's!' I stand up and dance about, singing, 'Yeah, yeah, yeah!' and Mummy says, 'No, Jesika . . .' and then, 'Careful!' but it's too late cos I feel something squish under my foot and then Paige is standing up and crying and shouting and I look down and Paige's chocolate cake roll is stuck to my shoe and I say, 'I'm sorry, I'm sorry!' and Lorna says, 'It's OK, Paige. Look, I've got some more,' but Paige shouts, 'Jesika squashed it on PURPOSE!'

Lorna says, 'No, she didn't, Paige, it was just an accident.'

Paige shouts, 'WAS NOT!'

Mummy pulls the chocolate cake roll off my foot and she squeezes my hand and she kisses my cheek but Paige is still shouting and crying and she is so cross and my eyes sting and sting and then Lorna smiles and says, 'I know! Why don't we all go back to our house for a play? I bet Uncle Ryan's finished moving those boxes now.'

Paige stamps and stamps her foot and shouts, 'NO! NO! NO!' and she pushes her hand at me and shouts, 'YOU'RE NOT COMING TO MY HOUSE EVER EVER EVER!' and she stamps over and sits on the bench with her head down and her arms wrapped round herself.

Lorna says, 'Paige . . .' and she closes her eyes and presses her hand to her head and Mummy cuddles me tight with one arm and whispers, 'She doesn't mean it, poppet. Remember she's not feeling well,' and then Lorna opens her eyes and looks at Mummy and says, 'This isn't really working today. I think we'd better just head home by ourselves and let Paige rest this afternoon.'

Mummy puts her other hand on Lorna's arm and says, 'It's fine, don't worry,' and then Mummy and Lorna get up and pack all the picnic stuff away and Lorna keeps saying, 'I'm sorry,' and Mummy says, 'I understand,' and 'Don't worry,' and 'Honestly, it's fine,' and then they have a cuddle and Lorna wipes her eyes and Lorna says quiet as quiet, 'All these urine infections – the doctor said it's probably stress, losing her Dad, and then moving away soon after. I feel like a failure,' and Mummy puts both hands on her shoulders and says, 'You're not a failure. These things take time. It will get easier.'

I say, 'What will get easier?' and Mummy and Lorna look at me all surprised and Lorna wipes her eyes and they both laugh but I don't know why.

Lorna says, 'Thanks, Tina. Text you later, OK?' and then she goes to the bench and takes Paige's hand and they walk away and Mummy tells me to say bye-bye to Paige but there's a big hurty lump in my neck cos I heard Lorna tell Paige to say goodbye and she didn't even wave her hand at me. Mummy keeps saying Paige doesn't mean it and it's cos she's not feeling well and she'll feel better soon. But she won't feel better soon cos Ryan keeps hurting her and I want to tell Mummy but I can't tell Mummy or anyone cos it makes people cross.

24

IT'S A LONG-A-LONG walk home up the steep hill and Toby falls
asleep so Mummy leaves me with Nandini outside the washing
machine shop cos Nandini tells Mummy she has to have a sleep
too. Mummy says she'll try to if she can keep Toby asleep all the
way up the stairs. Sometimes he stays asleep and sometimes all
the bumping wakes him up.

Nandini takes me inside and through and through to the kitchen and I think I'm going to help her with the washing machines
again but she has a different job today. I have to play with a boy
and his name is Dharesh and he's four just like me and his
Mummy is Nandini's sister and she's at the washing machine
shop too but she's too busy to play with Dharesh cos she's talking
to Nandini and feeding his baby sister with her boobies, like
Mummy used to do with Toby.

Dharesh is zooming cars around on the kitchen floor, cept not
where Nandini's standing at her iron board cos Nandini says he's
not allowed cos the iron is hot and dangerous. I sit on a chair and
watch. I don't want to play. I'm thinking about Mummy saying
you have to wait and see if someone made a mistake and they
might actually be nice. I don't think Ryan is actually nice but if I
tell Mummy she'll be cross again and I don't want to live somewhere else.

Nandini slaps the iron forwards and backwards jingling her

bracelets and she says, 'You can play too, Jesika. Dharesh has lots of cars. Give her one of your cars, Dharesh.'

Dharesh picks up a sparkly red car and gives it to me.

His Mummy laughs and says, 'Gosh, the special one. You are honoured, Jesika.'

I don't know what she means and I don't know if I'm apposed to say something so I just hold the car in my hand and watch the floor where Dharesh is zooming the cars around. The cars go super-speedy on the floor and sometimes they crash into the table legs and flip right over and it does look really fun.

Dharesh looks up at me and says, 'Do you know how to play car crashes?' and I know this game cos me and Toby play it all the time and I nod and he says, 'Let's play it!' and Nandini says, 'Go on, Jesika, get stuck in,' so I get down on the floor and we whizz our cars together and it is a fun game and it's even more fun cos on Nandini's kitchen floor the cars zoom together so fast and when they crash they spin and spin far, far away from each other. We do it lots and lots of times and Dharesh shouts crashing noises and we giggle and giggle and I think Toby will like to play this after he's had his sleep.

Dharesh's Mummy stops feeding the baby and she puts the baby in the pram and then she pushes it into the room with the sofa cos the baby needs quiet to sleep and Nandini says, 'Maybe that game's too noisy now. Why don't you both go into the yard and play with the football for a little while?'

I say, 'Where's the yard?'

Nandini says, 'Out here,' and she opens the door that goes out-side and me and Dharesh go through it and we're standing on bumpy stones and I can hear the sounds of veekles and people but I can't see anything cept the tall buildings cos there's a high brick wall all the way round and a big wooden gate that's brown and scratchy and has a big lock on it like a treasure chest.

Dharesh kicks the football against one of the walls and he shouts, 'SCORE!' and then runs around in a big circle with his hands above his head. He says the wall is the goal and we both take turns kicking the ball at it and scoring lots of goals and shouting and running around with our hands above our heads and then we just run about kicking the football anywhere and it bounces all over the place and we have to keep chasing it.

After ages, Dharesh says, 'Let's go back inside,' and we run into the kitchen and, oh! Mummy is there and she's holding Toby and she sees me and blows me a kiss and she's talking to Dharesh's Mummy and Dharesh's Mummy is pushing the pram forwards and backwards and forwards and backwards and she says, 'Five minutes, then we have to go, Dharesh,' and Dharesh grabs my hand and says, 'We have to hide!' and he pulls me to the door that goes through to the sofa room and I've never been in there afore but then Dharesh's hand is pulled out of mine and Dharesh swings up into the air and he's yelling and giggling and I look round and Emma's holding Dharesh high up in the air and she says, 'There's no escape!' and she keeps putting Dharesh down so his feet touch the ground and then swinging him up high afore he can run away and it's very funny.

Then it really is time for Dharesh to go and everyone's saying goodbye and Dharesh's Mummy says, 'Nice to meet you, Tina,' and Mummy says, 'You too, Sabia,' and everyone's smiling and I am too cos now I know what Dharesh's Mummy is called.

It's quiet after Dharesh and his Mummy and baby sister have gone. Nandini and Emma and Mummy sit at the table drinking tea and Toby is snuggled up on Mummy's knee. I'm on the floor whizzing a car around cos Dharesh forgotted to take one away with him and Nandini said I can play with it til it's time to go home. I don't know when it's time to go home but it's not yet. We have to wait til Nandini's oven beeps cos our tea that Ade maked is cooking in there but I don't know when he put it in cos I didn't see him and I don't know what it is cos Nandini says it's a surprise but I think it's going to be yummy cos it's making the kitchen smell warm and cheesy and bakey and I can't even smell all the washing machine smells now.

Nandini says, 'It would be lovely if Dharesh and Jesika end up at the same school. When do you find out?'

Mummy says, 'A couple of weeks, I think?'

I say, 'Is Dharesh coming to my preschool?'

Mummy says, 'He goes to your preschool now!'

I say, 'No, he doesn't.' Cos I know all the children at preschool and I've never played with Dharesh afore today.

Mummy laughs and says, 'He goes before lunch and you go after lunch.'

I say, 'Oh,' cos I didn't know preschool did afore lunch too. Then I say, 'Can I go to preschool afore lunch and play with Dharesh?'

Mummy says, 'I'm afraid not, poppet,' and Nandini says, 'But you can play with Dharesh here another time. You had fun today, Boss, didn't you?'

And I smile and nod and whizz Dharesh's car fast under the table. It was lots of fun.

Nandini says, 'How about the house-move? Is it all sorted? Do you need any help?'

I look up and Mummy's smiling big and big and she says, 'Tuesday. It's going to be such a relief. Ryan's borrowing a van off a mate.'

I bang the car on the floor and I say, 'I don't *want* to live at Ryan's house.'

Mummy says, 'Jesika . . .'

I frown at Mummy and say, 'And Paige doesn't want Ryan to live at her house too!'

Mummy blows out a breath.

Emma says, 'What's wrong with Ryan?'

I say, 'He's not nice.'

Emma says, 'Why is he not nice?'

Mummy says, 'He gave Jesika a bit of a fright, not deliberately but—'

I say, 'It *was* deliberate!' cos deliberate means on purpose.

Mummy says, 'Jesika, do you remember we talked about people making mistakes and giving them a chance to not make mistakes again?'

I say, 'But he keeps—' and then I stop cos if I say he keeps hurting Paige, that's the naughty thing and Mummy will be so so cross.

Mummy says, 'He keeps what, Jesika?' and her voice is snappy and she pushes her fingers into her hair and she looks cross and I've not even said the naughty thing.

I say, 'I've forgotted,' and I pick up the car again and whizz it along the floor.

The oven beeps and Nandini lifts a blue pot out of the oven and it's time to go and Mummy says, 'Do you think I should be worried?' and she's frowning and looking at the pot that Nandini's put on the cooker and I don't know why Mummy is worried cos it smells yummy.

Nandini says, 'It might just be a phase. There's been a lot of upheaval and uncertainty, for both of them.'

Mummy says, 'I don't think she really forgot what she was going to say.'

I say, 'Who forgot, Mummy?'

Nandini laughs and says, 'You've got sharp ears, Boss,' and I touch my ears but they're not sharp, they're soft and bendy and I giggle and tell Nandini she's silly.

Emma says, 'You know her best. Trust your gut. Ask her again later when there are no distractions.'

I say, 'Who are you asking, Mummy?' and Mummy says, 'I wish you would listen this well when I'm asking you to put your shoes on!' and everyone laughs and then it's time to go home and Emma comes with us to help carry the blue pot all the way up the stairs and my belly keeps growling like it's saying hurry up, hurry up, hurry up, and then at last we're eating Ade's tea and it's cheesy pasta and big chunks of bacon and Mummy says it's mackerony cheese and it's the most yummy tea ever!

I say, 'Mummy, can you make this?'

Mummy says, 'Maybe one day when we have an oven that works.'

I say, 'Will our new house have an oven that works?'

Mummy says, 'We don't have a new house yet, poppet.'

I say, 'But will it?'

Mummy says, 'Maybe. We'll see,' and then she lifts Toby out of his high chair and takes our empty plates into the kitchen to wash. Toby follows and pulls at Mummy's trousers and says, 'Up, up, up!' and Mummy says, 'Jesika, see if you can get Toby playing something while I wash these dishes,' and I say, 'What do you want to play, Toby?' and Toby says, 'Go 'way!'

I have a think about what games Toby likes and that remembers me about playing with Dharesh and I thought at Nandini's that Toby would like the car game so I run to the toy box and I get two cars and I sit on the scratchy carpet just outside the kitchen where Toby can see me and I crash them together. Toby looks and smiles. I hold the cars out to Toby so he can have a turn but he turns and hides his face in Mummy's trousers. I crash them again, but they don't crash fast like on Nandini's kitchen floor. I rub my hand on the scratchy carpet. It tickles my hand. I lean over and rub the kitchen floor. It's smooth and cold. Maybe cars can't go fast when they're being tickled. I crawl into the kitchen and push one of the cars across the kitchen floor. It skids and spins super fast!

Mummy says, 'Not in here, Jesika. You'll get right under my feet.'

I say, 'But the cars go fast in here!'

Mummy says, 'Yes, and they'll also get broken when I acciden- tally stand on them because you're pushing them under my feet.'

But I'm not pushing them under Mummy's feet. I'm pushing them around her feet. I open my mouth to tell Mummy but she says, 'Somewhere else, Jesika,' afore I can say it.

I think and then I pick the cars up and say to Toby, 'Come on, Toby, I've got a good idea!' and I run into the bathroom cos the bathroom carpet isn't scratchy and tickly, but the cars don't go fast. I rub my hand on the bathroom carpet. It's smooth but it's not cold. Maybe cars need smooth and cold. But only the kitchen floor is smooth and cold.

I know!

I pick up one of the cars and balance it on the edge of the bath and then push it and it zooms down into the bath and skids and spins fast as fast. I lean over the edge and pick it up and then I balance one car at each end and then push one and hop to the other end and push the other and they both zoom down into the bath and they flip and spin and CRASH! It works!

'Me! Des-des, me!'

I spin round and Toby is leaning over the bath trying to reach the cars but his arms are too little so I pick them out and he takes one and I take one and we put our cars at different ends of the bath and I say, 'Three, two, one, GO!' and we push the cars into the bath and they spin and skid and flip and CRASH!

Toby giggles and giggles and says, 'Again, Des-des!' and so we do it again and again and again and again and we're both giggling and giggling til Mummy comes into the bathroom and says, 'What are you two doing in here?' and I think she's going to be so cross cos we're not apposed to crash cars in the bath but then she's laughing too and then Mummy goes and gets another car and now we're crashing three cars in the bath and it's so much fun!

After, when Toby's in bed and me and Mummy are sitting on the sofa and Mummy's brushing all the tugs out of my hair, Mummy says, 'You were brilliant with Toby today. He's so lucky to have a big sister like you,' and I smile and smile and inside me everything is warm like sunshine and Mummy says, 'I told you he'd stop being grumpy soon, didn't I?' And Mummy did tell me. And Toby didn't tell me to go away, not even when I gave him a kiss and a cuddle and a stroke at bedtime.

Mummy keeps brushing and it's not tuggy now, it's tickly-shivery.

Mummy says, 'So, you know, it'll be the same with Paige. I'm sure she'll be feeling better at preschool on Monday and then maybe you can play something with her that she really likes and you'll be best friends again in no time.'

The warm sunshine inside me goes away and my belly squeezes. Mummy's wrong.

I want to tell Mummy about Ryan hurting Paige's belly again.

Mummy says, 'What do you think is Paige's favourite game?'

I don't want Mummy to shout and tell me to get a new Mummy.

Mummy says, 'What about hide and seek? Lorna says she loves that.'

Paige says you have to have sweeties to play hide and seek but Ryan didn't give her sweeties today and it's cos I said the naughty thing.

Mummy says, 'And you like playing it too, don't you?'

What if I take some sweeties to give to Paige? Maybe she won't be cross with me then?

I say, 'Can I have some sweeties?'

Mummy laughs and she stops brushing so she can cough and cough and then she says, 'No! It's almost bedtime!'

I say, 'But I need them for preschool to play hide and seek with Paige.'

Mummy says, 'Why do you need sweeties for hide and seek?'

I say, 'Cos that's how Paige plays it and Ryan didn't give her sweeties today cos he's sad and cross.'

Mummy brushes my hair again and she says, 'What do you mean?'

I say, 'Ryan's sad and cross and so he didn't give Paige sweeties and it's my fault.'

Mummy says, 'That's silly, Jesika. Why would that be your fault?'

I don't want to say. I don't want Mummy to be cross.

Mummy says, 'Jesika . . .' She stops brushing and she breathes in and out and then she says, 'Jesika, there's something you're not telling me, and I'd really like you to tell me what it is.'

My belly whizzes round. I whisper, 'I don't want to.'

Mummy says, 'But you know you can tell me anything, don't you? You've always told me anything.'

I turn round and push my face into Mummy's jumper and breathe and breathe and breathe.

Mummy presses her mouth on my head and then says, 'Tell me, what's the scariest thing of all?'

I sit up again and look at Mummy. I know those words, but they're not Mummy's words. Mummy's eyes are shiny and she blinks and blinks and her mouth is making a funny shape and she holds my chin in her hand and she says, 'That's what Bab-bab always said, wasn't it? She always said if you say the scariest thing of all, it scares it away and then nothing else is so scary.'

I know what the scariest thing of all is.

Ahind Mummy, Bab-bab blinks her eyes, one-two-three, and I reach out my hand, and then she's gone.

I whisper, 'I don't want to live with someone else. I want to live with you. I don't want to go away again.'

Mummy cuddles me tight and says, 'Oh, Jesika. You're not going away again. I'm back and Toby's back and we're all together now. Always together, OK?'

But it's not OK, cos that's not what I meaned. I meaned cos Paige's belly hurts and she won't be better and be my friend cos Ryan keeps hurting her and I have to tell Mummy to tell him to stop so Paige can be my friend again but I can't tell Mummy cos it's a naughty thing to say and if I say the naughty thing Mummy will be so cross and she'll tell me to live with someone else cos Ryan said so.

I say, 'But if I be naughty . . .' and my lips wobble and I don't know what to say next cos there's so many words to say.

Mummy puts her hands on my shoulders and rubs her thumbs round and round and she says, 'Jesika,' and her voice is telling me to look and I do and her eyes are telling me to listen and she says, 'If you're naughty, I'll tell you and we'll talk about it. I won't send you away. Even when I'm cross, you know I still love you always and your home is still always with me and Toby. Understand?'

I don't understand. Is it like when Ryan said he hurted Paige's head when he actually hurted her belly? Are grown-ups allowed to say things that are not true? Mummy blinks one-two-three and my eyes sting and sting and it's all hurty inside and Mummy strokes her hands down my arms and holds my hands and she says, 'Why would you ever think that I would let you go somewhere else? You're *my* beautiful girl,' and she looks at me and her eyes blink again, but more slow, one – two – three.

I say, 'That's what Ryan said.'

Mummy smiles and frowns all at the same time and says, 'Ryan said you're his beautiful girl?' and I didn't know Mummy's voice could be spiky and smiley at the same time.

I say, 'No, he said I would go away. Was he saying something not true? Like when he said he hurted Paige's head and not her belly?'

Mummy says, 'No, poppet, he did actually hurt her head, not her belly.'

I say, 'But Paige's belly hurts and it's always hurting cos—' I stop. I almost said the naughty thing!

Mummy says, 'Yes, because of the urine infections.' And then Mummy sits up straight and turns to me and squeezes my hands and smiles and says, 'Jesika, when did Ryan say you had to go away?'

I say, 'When he bringed the pirate costume.'

Mummy says, 'And what did he actually say?'

My heart thumps and thumps cos this is the scary thing again and I don't like it. Mummy strokes her thumbs round and round on my hands and says, 'Just say the scariest thing, Jesika, and then it won't be scary, remember?'

I look down at my hands and I watch Mummy's thumbs going round and round and round and I say, 'He said if I told you the naughty thing, you would be cross and you would tell me to live with someone else.'

Mummy's thumbs stop stroking.

I look up. She's still smiling.

She says, 'Do you think it might have been a joke that you didn't understand?'

I say, 'No, cos his face was scary and he said it mean and he hurted me.'

Mummy breathes in and out and her lips wobble and she presses them together. Is she cross? She smiles and squeezes my hands. No, not cross.

She says, 'There, see? You've told me the scariest thing of all and nothing bad has happened.' And then she says, 'I think now you should tell me what this naughty thing is.'

I don't want to. That's scary too.

Mummy says, 'I promise I won't shout and I promise I won't be cross and I *promise* you're not going to live anywhere else.'

And it's still scary but Mummy promised so it's OK to say it, isn't it? She won't shout or be cross or make me live somewhere else. She promised. I can tell Mummy. Can't I?

Mummy says, 'You can tell me anything, Jesika.'

I can tell Mummy anything.

I say, 'Ryan keeps poking Paige's belly all the time and she doesn't like it cos it hurts and she told me and I told Ryan to stop and say sorry and he got so cross and he hurted me and told me it was a naughty thing to say and I wasn't to say it to anyone not ever cos you'd all be cross and I'd be in big trouble and then another time I thought that I could ask you why it was naughty and he got cross and hurted me again and he said you would tell me to live with someone else if I ever ever said it.'

Mummy's hands are squeezing tight-tight-tight and her eyes go small and I can't see her lips and her face is scary.

I've said the naughty thing.

She's going to shout.

I say, 'Sorry, sorry, sorry!' and I'm crying and crying and trying to cuddle Mummy cos I don't want to live with someone else but she's pushing me away and her face is tiger-fierce and she says, 'No, NO, NO! Don't you *dare* say sorry! Don't you DARE!' and she's so so cross and then she cuddles me so so tight and she doesn't say anything for a long-a-long time, just breathes fast and fast and fast.

After for ages, when her breathing is slow and she's not squashing me so much, she lets go and she sits back and she holds my hands and she smiles but it's wobbly and her eyes aren't smiley, they're red and sore like she's rubbed them too hard. My belly squeezes and hurts cos I said the naughty thing and Mummy promised she wouldn't be cross but she was cos it must be such a naughty thing.

Mummy says, 'I promised not to shout and then I did,' and her voice is shaky and she stops and breathes and then she says, 'But I'm not angry with you, darling. You did the right thing to tell me that. It was *not* naughty. It was not naughty at all.'

I don't understand.

Mummy breathes and breathes and says, 'That's all I'm saying for now. You're not in any trouble, OK?'

I nod and Mummy strokes her hand down my face, gentle and soft.

Mummy says, 'Tell me about the sweeties.'

I say, 'What sweeties?'

Mummy says, 'You said that Paige didn't get her sweeties today because Ryan was cross. Does he give her sweeties every day?'

I say, 'I think only when they play hide and seek,' cos that's what Paige said.

Mummy says, 'You mean Paige has to find the sweeties?'

I say, 'No, Paige says you hide and then you get found and be a special-good-girl and then you get sweeties.'

Mummy breathes in fast.

I say, 'Do you think that means you have to do really good hiding?'

Mummy says, 'Yes. Yes, I'm sure that's what it means.'

I say, 'So maybe Paige didn't do good hiding today and that's why she didn't get her sweeties?'

Mummy says, 'Yes, yes, maybe that's why.'

She stands up quick and runs into the bathroom, and she doesn't come back for ages so I run after her and she's bending over the sink and splashing water on her face.

I say, 'What are you doing, Mummy?'

Mummy stands up and dries her face on the towel and says, 'I needed to clean my face. Come on, poppet,' and she holds out her hand and we go and snuggle on the sofa again.

Mummy says, 'Did you get sweeties when you played hide and seek with Ryan?'

I say, 'No, and anyway Paige says I'm not allowed to be Ryan's special-good-girl cos that's only her and not me.'

Mummy breathes in big and blows out slow.

She says, 'Do you remember what I told you and Toby about private pants?'

I giggle cos Mummy said pants. Mummy smiles but then her smile goes away again and she says, 'Jesika, I need you to think very carefully. Can you point to where your private parts are?'

I point to my bottom and say, 'Private pants,' and I make a farty noise and giggle but Mummy doesn't laugh.

Mummy says, 'Has anyone ever . . .' She stops and closes her eyes and then opens them again and smiles and says, 'Has anyone ever touched you where your pants are?'

I giggle and I say, 'No!' cos that's silly and then I remember hiding with Paige under the slide at preschool the other day and I say, 'Paige did this,' and I push my hand in and out of Mummy's legs quick and I say, 'But only on my trousers and not on my pants. And then she holded my hand and did this,' and I pull Mummy's hand to my belly and pull my pyjama bottoms down a little bit but Mummy pulls her hand away and says, 'I get the idea, Jesika.'

I say, 'And then Tamanna told us to stop hiding. And you're not apposed to touch other people's pants, are you?'

Mummy says, 'No, you're not.'

I say, 'Do you think Paige doesn't know that?'

Mummy blows out a long, long breath and then says, 'I think there's a lot Paige doesn't know.'

I say, 'What doesn't she know?'

Mummy says, 'It's too complicated to explain tonight, poppet. I've got a lot of thinking to do first. I promise I'll explain it another day.'

Mummy wipes both her hands down her face and she looks sad. I squeeze up close and I say, 'I love you, Mummy.'

She says, 'I love you, too.'

In the bedroom, Mummy tucks me in and I say, 'Are you coming to bed now, Mummy?' and Mummy says, 'Not yet, darling, but soon,' and she cuddles me and kisses me and she says, 'You were so brave telling me all your scary things tonight, Jesika. I'm so proud of you. I hope it doesn't feel scary any more.'

It doesn't feel scary. It feels something else. I think about Kali and the Feelings Dollies at preschool and I say, 'Mummy, I feel sad.'

Mummy says, 'Why do you feel sad?'

I say, 'Cos Paige isn't my friend and cos Ryan hurted her.'

Mummy says, 'I'm going to try and fix that, poppet. I promise.'

And then she whispers the moon words in my ear and she whispers, 'I love you,' and everything is warm and soft and all the bedtime noises, like the cars and the people and the music, aren't so loud tonight cos I can hear Toby breathing slow and slow and my eyes are sleepy and I whisper, 'I love you too.'

25

ME AND TOBY and Mummy have been awake for ages and we've had breakfast and brushed our teeth and I'm looking out the window and all the shutters on the shops are still down.

I say, 'Is it Sunday?' cos that's the day when all the shops are shut, cept for Nandini's washing machine shop that's always open.

Mummy says, 'Jesika, don't touch the window.'

I say, 'I'm not touching it, I'm looking,' cos I know the window's dangerous and I'm not allowed to touch.

Mummy says, 'Come over and play here anyway, where I can see you.'

I come back over to the little table where my colouring book is and I pick up the brown pencil and finish colouring the horse in the field and I say, 'But is it Sunday?'

Mummy says, 'Yes.'

I say, 'When is it preschool?'

Mummy says, 'Monday.'

I say, 'When is Monday?'

Mummy says, 'It's when it was the last ten times you asked me,' and I think Mummy sounds sad and I look where she's lying on the sofa and her eyes are closed and I say, 'Are you sad, Mummy?'

Mummy blows out a breath and she says, 'Just lots to think about, poppet.'

I say, 'Like when preschool is?'

Mummy's mouth makes a teeny-tiny smile and she says, 'Yes, like when preschool is.'

I say, 'Is it yesterday?'

Mummy's smile goes bigger and she says, 'You mean tomorrow?'

I say, 'Is that when preschool is?'

Mummy says, 'It's one more sleep, Jesika. One more sleep and then it's preschool. That's tomorrow.'

One more sleep! One more sleep! I've not been to preschool for *ages*!

I jump up and dance around the table singing, 'Yeah, yeah, yeah, yeah,' and Toby claps his hands and giggles.

I say, 'What are we doing today?' and I know it won't be the park cos outside it's rainy.

Mummy says, 'You and Toby are going to play really nicely together and I'm going to lie here and do lots of thinking.'

Mummy lies on the sofa for a long-a-long time. Me and Toby play cars in the bath and we play towers and Toby walks Baby Annabelle and Zebra and Para-Ted around in the pram and I pretend I'm a tiger roaring and I keep jumping out from ahind bushes and trees and Toby giggles and giggles and I think he's forgotted all about telling me to go away cos he must like all the games we're playing today.

Mummy gets up to make lunch and she brings two plates through with sandwiches and crisps and apple slices and she puts them on the little table not the big table and I say, 'Why are you putting them there, Mummy?' but Mummy's gone back into the kitchen and then she comes back with two drinks, one for me and one for Toby, and she turns the telly on and puts it on CBeebies and she says, 'You two have been so good playing together this morning. You can watch some telly while you eat your lunch,' and then she lies back down on the sofa and closes her eyes again.

I say, 'We can watch telly *and* eat our lunch?' cos Mummy never lets us do that and I think maybe she's made a mistake and she meaned we could watch telly *after* we've eaten our lunch.

Mummy says, 'That's what I said.'

I say, 'We can watch telly *and* eat our lunch?'

Mummy says, 'Yes! You can watch telly and eat your lunch.'

She does mean it. This is the best day *ever*!

When me and Toby are finished eating, I think Mummy will tell us that telly time is finished but she doesn't so we keep watching and watching and watching and I didn't know you could watch so much telly all at once!

Tap-tap-tap.

Is someone knocking on the door? I don't think it's the Money Man cos he bangs loud.

Tap-tap-tap.

I push Mummy's arm and say, 'Mummy, is someone knocking on the door?'

Mummy's eyes open and her arm goes hard.

The letterbox flaps open and then, 'Tina? Are you in there?'

I shout, 'Emma!' and dance over to the door and I can see a bit of Emma's face smiling in the letterhole and she says, 'Hey, Jesika, are you OK?'

I say, 'We're watching lots of telly!'

Emma says, 'Is your Mummy there, Jesika?'

I look round and Mummy's still lying on the sofa and her eyes are closed again and I say, 'Yes, she's over there,' and I point.

Emma says, 'I can't see her. What's she doing?'

I say, 'She's lying on the sofa.'

Emma says, 'Is she asleep?'

I say, 'No, she's just got her eyes closed.'

Emma says, 'Is she . . . ?' and then Mummy says, 'I'm fine,

Emma,' and I look round again and Mummy's eyes are open but she's still lying down.

Emma says, 'You've not been answering any texts today, Tina. We were worried.'

Mummy sits up and rubs her hands on her face and says, 'Nothing to be worried about. I'm tired, that's all.'

I say, 'And Mummy's been doing lots of thinking. That's why we have to play quietly and watch telly.'

Emma says, 'Tina? Has something happened?'

Mummy presses her hands to her face and shakes her head.

Emma says, 'Tina?'

I say, 'She's shaking her head.'

Emma says, 'Tina, open the door,' and her voice is saying Do It Now, and Mummy gets up slow as slow and she walks to the door and her feet swish-swish-swish on the carpet and she opens the door and Emma says, 'Leon should bill that landlord of yours for doing his job for him,' and Mummy says, 'Yeah, well, not much point now,' and she walks back over to the sofa and sits down and she's bent over looking at the floor.

Emma says, 'Is that what this is about?'

Mummy nods her head and then shakes her head and she says, 'I've done a really stupid thing. Actually, I've done two really stupid things and . . .' and then she's breathing in fast and fast and fast and I think she can't breathe. Mummy can't breathe! And Emma is kneeling in front of her and I'm trying to push past her and I'm shouting, 'Mummy! Mummy! Mummy!'

Emma says, 'Jesika, stop!' and her hand is on my chest, strong and hard, and she keeps it there and her other hand is on Mummy's shoulder and she says, 'Breathe. Like this, Tina,' and she's breathing in big and blowing out slow and she does it lots and lots of times and Mummy's breathing gets more slow and more slow til it's the same as Emma's and she whispers, 'Sorry, I'm fine now, sorry.'

Emma says, 'You're not fine,' and she drops her hand from my chest and she says, 'Jesika, put your shoes on,' and I say, 'Is Mummy going back to hopsipal?' and my heart is thumping and thumping and the Big Hurty is pushing and squeezing inside me and I don't want Mummy to go away again. I want her to stay here.

Emma says, 'No one's going to hospital. You're all coming downstairs because your Mum needs a cup of tea and a chat with some friends,' and then Emma is telling Mummy what to do and she's telling Toby what to do and she's telling me what to do and we all do it all straight away cos Emma's voice says Do It Now, and Toby even lets Emma carry him down the stairs cos she says, 'Stop fussing. Your Mummy's too tired to carry you.'

It's busy inside the washing machine shop and we have to squeeze past a lot of people to go through and through to the kitchen. When we get there, Nandini says, 'Here they are!' and she jumps up and pulls a chair out for Mummy to sit on and Ade's sitting at the table too on the other side and he smiles big so I can see all his teeth and his whole face is happy and he says, 'Hey, Jesika!' and he holds his hand up and I run over and give him the biggest high five ever cos I've not seen him for ages and *ages* cept when I was with Lorna and Lorna didn't let me talk to him.

Emma puts Toby down and he runs over to Ade too and points to his ear and says, 'In deh, in deh,' and Ade says, 'Are you show-ing me your ear?' and Toby points faster and says, 'In *deh*, in *deh*!' and Ade laughs and says, 'I know you want something, Toby, but you got me stumped,' and I laugh cos I know exactly what Toby wants and I say, 'He wants a magic strawberry in his ear, Ade,' and Toby pulls on Ade's trousers like he's trying to climb up and Ade says, 'You want up?' and he bends down a bit and stops and makes a hurty face and says, 'Nope, not happening,' but it doesn't matter cos Toby puts his foot on the wooden bar atween the chair legs and then pulls on Ade's trousers and wriggles his belly til he's all the way on and turns round and sits on Ade's knee and slaps his hands on the table with a big smile on his face.

Mummy says, 'How did you get up there?' and Toby says, 'Me up!' and smiles and claps his hands and no one knows how he got on Ade's knee cept me.

Toby turns to Ade again and points to his ear and says, 'In deh, in deh,' and Ade laughs and says, 'My magic only works in the shop,' and Toby frowns like he doesn't understand and I say, 'No magic here, Toby,' and he frowns more and I think he might shout and then Ade laughs big and it makes his hair bounce and Toby grabs Ade's springy hair in his hand and pulls and lets go and it bounces back up and Ade says, 'Ping!' and Toby giggles and he pulls another handful and Ade says, 'Ping!' and Toby giggles and giggles and he keeps doing it again and again and I think he's forgotted about the magic now.

Emma gives all the grown-ups a cup of tea and gives me and Toby a drink of juice and she puts a plate on the table that's full up with biscuits that have chocolate on them. My mouth fills up with water. Am I allowed one?

I say, 'What are the biscuits for, Emma?'

Emma says, 'Eating,' and she sits down on one of the chairs.

Does that mean I can have one?

I look at the plate and I look at Mummy and I look at the plate and I look at Mummy and Mummy's looking at Nandini and Mummy says, 'I told him he could stuff his rent and stuff his flat because we'd be gone by Thursday.'

Nandini says, 'Can you tell him you've changed your mind?'

Mummy shakes her head fast and says, 'Already tried. He told me he took that as my notice and he's got a new tenant moving in on Friday.'

Ade says, 'Can he do that?'

Nandini says, 'He makes up his own rules,' and she takes a biscuit and nibbles round the edges. Can I have one?

Emma says, 'He can't make up his own rules. Phone the housing people tomorrow. Get them on your side. Whatever he says, you've got a piece of paper saying you have two weeks.'

Ade points his finger at Emma and says, 'She has a point.'

I look at Emma but she's not got anything pointy and I say, 'Who has a point?'

Nandini says, 'OK, that's a plan to start with.'

Mummy says, 'I'm fighting to stay in the dump. Who would have believed it?' and she smiles a wobbly smile.

Nandini says, 'And if it doesn't work, surely whatever it is that Lorna's angry about can be sorted before Thursday? She wouldn't want to see you without a home, would she?'

I say, 'Why is Lorna angry, Mummy?'

Mummy looks at me and looks at Nandini and she says, 'Oh, just . . . it's grown-up stuff, poppet,' and she looks at Emma and she says, 'You said to trust my gut, and I did and we had that chat with no distractions, and I think . . . I don't *know*, but I think . . . hang on, I'll show you,' and she presses her fingers on her phone and slides it to Nandini and she says, 'I phoned first but it didn't go well. She hung up. Then we had this conversation by text . . .' She points at the phone.

Why is Mummy's face sad? I say, 'What's on your phone, Mummy?'

Mummy smiles and the sad goes away and she says, 'Nothing for you to worry about, poppet,' and she pushes the plate of chocolate biscuits towards me and says, 'Go on, have one,' and I say, 'Can I have two?' and Mummy says, 'Go on, then,' and I say, 'Can I have three?' and Mummy laughs and says, 'No!'

I take two and then I give two to Toby cos he's reaching for them but his arms can't stretch that far and he holds one in each hand and bites one and the other and I do the same and we're both giggling cos we're eating two biscuits at the same time . . .

'Bloody *hell*!'

Nandini's eyes are scary-wide and her mouth is a big open circle. She says, 'Sorry, sorry, not in front of . . . but, Tina! They looked after . . . *he* looked after . . . are you *sure?*' and she passes the phone to Emma.

Mummy stares at her hands and says, 'No, I'm not sure, I've gone back and forth on it all night. I know something's not right and I know he threatened . . .' Mummy stops and her mouth is wobbly and she says, 'He threatened . . .' and her voice is all squeaky and she blows out a breath fast and her mouth stops being wobbly and she says, 'Whatever's going on, I really thought Lorna should at least have the conversation with her, and make sure, you know?' and I say, 'What is Lorna doing?' and Nandini says, 'Do you think he . . . ?' And she nods her head sideways and Mummy says, 'No. No, I asked and . . . no. I am sure about that.'

Emma stands up and passes the phone to Ade and she walks over to the sink and I can't see her face and Toby is trying to grab the phone off Ade and Ade holds it out a long way from himself so Toby can't reach it and I say, 'Let me see! I want to see!' and Mummy says, 'It's grown-up stuff, Jesika. Really boring,' but I still want to see so I squeeze under Ade's arm and look and I can see lots of numbers and words and I say, 'Is it a story?' but Ade doesn't answer. He shakes his head and air whistles out of his mouth and the lumpy bit on his neck wobbles up and down and up and down and I say, 'Ade, what does the story say?'

Ade says, 'It's a story about a brave girl and brave lady who chase away a baddie.'

I say, 'Is the baddie a monster?'

Nandini shakes her head and says, 'That's one word you could use.'

Mummy says, 'But I'm not sure . . .'

Ade says, 'Tina, if you even suspect . . . There's another person in this. You have to tell someone else.'

I say, 'Tell someone what?'

Emma turns round quick and says, 'This is ridiculous. We can't have this conversation in code.'

She walks into the sofa room and comes back and she's holding out some flat boxes in her hand and they have pictures on them and I know some of those pictures and there's . . .

'Thom-thom!'

Toby claps his hands and grabs the box and Emma says, 'Thomas OK for you too, Jesika?'

I say, 'What's it for?'

Emma says, 'To watch on TV.'

I say, 'More telly time?' cos we've already had lots and lots and I look at Mummy and she smiles and nods and says, 'Just today, Jesika. Don't get used to it,' and then Emma takes me and Toby through to the sofa room and she puts the deeveedee on the telly and me and Toby sit on the sofa and watch Thomas and Toby shouts all the names of the engines and I don't think he's really listening to the story but I'm trying to and I say, 'Shhh, Toby, I'm listening,' and I have to keep saying it all through the first story and then in the second story Toby doesn't shout at all and that's cos he's lied down on the sofa and gone to sleep.

Oh. He's gone to sleep. Will Mummy mind?

I skip through the door to tell Mummy but no one sees me cos they're all talking and talking and then Mummy says, '. . . he told her it was naughty to say it and she believed him,' and Nandini says, 'Well, she would. She's only a child!'

Ryan's inside my head and he's cross and scary. I don't want to look at him.

I say, 'Why is it naughty to say it, Mummy?' cos I still don't know.

Mummy and Nandini and Emma and Ade all look at me and Mummy says, 'Oh!' and Emma says, 'We have a ninja amongst us,' and I don't know what that means but everyone's smiling.

Mummy holds her arms out and I go to her and she lifts me up onto her knee and she says, 'Is Toby OK?' and I say, 'He's asleep. Is that perfect?' and Mummy laughs and says, 'Today, that is perfect,' and I say, 'Good,' and I say, 'Why is it naughty to say it, Mummy?'

Mummy says, 'It isn't naughty to say it. Ryan lied to you. *He's* naughty, not you.'

'And he lied to me?'

'Yes.'

'Does that mean he told me something that's not true?'

'Yes.'

I say, 'What did he tell me that's not true?' cos Ryan told me lots of things.

Mummy says, 'He told you that it was naughty to tell another grown-up about Paige being hurt. It's never naughty to tell another grown-up if you're worried about something. No one should ever make you keep things secret.'

I think about this and I think about the chips secret that Ryan already told Mummy and the squished pasta secret and the breakfast secret and I think about Lorna saying some secrets are good secrets and I say, 'Are secrets good or bad?'

Mummy blows out a breath and says, 'Some secrets are good – like a surprise for someone's birthday – but there are also bad secrets.'

I tell Mummy about the other secrets and I say, 'Are they bad secrets?'

Mummy says, 'They're not really secrets at all. You didn't need to keep them a secret.'

I don't understand cos Ryan said they were secrets.

Mummy says, 'Maybe if someone tells you to keep a secret,

and you're not sure if it's good or bad, you could tell me. I can be your secret-checker, and if it's a good one I'll help you keep it. Do you think that's a good idea?'

I nod and then I say, 'Cos I can tell you anything, Mummy.'

Mummy says, 'Yes, you can,' and her voice is squeaky like a mouse and she turns her head away from me and Nandini puts her hand on top of Mummy's hand.

Ade says, 'That's where you put your trust, Tina. You can't know everything about everyone. You build trust with your family so they are never afraid to say when something is wrong.'

Mummy says, 'I know,' and her voice is still squeaky and her face is still turned away and she says, 'But I still wish I'd never met him. Even if he didn't . . . I can't forgive him for what he said to Jesika.'

Mummy means Ryan cos he's bad and he tells lies.

I say, 'I don't want to see Ryan again. I don't like him.'

Mummy says, 'I can't say you won't see him, Jesika, but I can promise you that I won't let him come anywhere near you or Toby ever again.'

I cuddle Mummy tight and I can feel her heart thump-thump-thumping on my cheek.

Nandini's cheeks are shiny and she wipes them with her hand and Emma stands up and cuddles Nandini from ahind and whispers something in her ear and Nandini says, 'I know, but that little girl is still . . .' and she stops and Emma squeezes harder and whispers something else.

I say, 'What about Paige?'

Mummy says, 'What do you mean?'

I say, 'Can you not let Ryan come near Paige as well? Cos I think she doesn't like him too.'

Mummy kisses my head and says, 'That's not up to me, Jesika darling. Lorna has to decide that.'

Emma says, 'And if she won't?' She lets go of Nandini and she stands up tall and she looks scary cos she isn't smiling. She says, 'Tina, you can't leave it with Lorna, not if she's going to ignore it.'

Mummy blows out a breath. 'But it might not be happening.'

I say, 'Ignore what?'

Mummy says, 'And who do I tell?'

Emma says, 'Social services.'

Mummy says, 'But how . . . ?'

Nandini says, 'Or she could tell one of their teachers at preschool. That might be less scary and they'll know how to handle it.'

Preschool?

I say, 'It's one more sleep afore I go to preschool yesterday,' and Mummy presses her cheek on my head and cuddles me tight and tight and she says, 'Do you think? Yes. Maybe. I need to think some more.'

Ade says, 'You have to trust yourself too, Tina.'

Nandini says, 'And we're here for you any time, any day.'

Mummy blows out a breath and cuddles me even more tight.

26

AFTER WE GET up and have breakfast, Mummy lets me and Toby watch telly for ages cos she has to stand in the kitchen and talk to lots of people on her phone and then after that it's a rushy-busy morning. We rush to the washing machine shop first but Nandini says we don't have to stay with our washing cos she can sort it out and then we rush to Ade's for fruit and vegetables and Ade does a magic strawberry for me and Toby and then we rush to the big food shop and we rush to the doctors cos they have to listen to Toby's chest and Mummy's chest and the doctor says it's all sounding much better and she wants to check it up again on another day and she says Mummy and Toby might cough for a bit longer but it will stop soon if they have all of the medicine and I tell Toby to listen to the doctor cos he keeps spitting his medicine on his chin and then we rush to the bank and Mummy talks to a man and then a lady and then we go all the way home again and Mummy says it's lunchtime and we have to eat quick as quick cos we're going to preschool early and I'm so excited cos I love, love, love preschool and I can't wait to tell Paige about the car bath game cos I bet she'd like to play that too.

Lots of grown-ups and children are coming out of preschool when we get there but they look different and I don't know them and my heart thumps and thumps and I say, 'Who are all those different people? Is preschool finished?' and Mummy says, 'No, that's all the children who go in the morning,' and, oh! There's Dharesh! Mummy's right! He does go to my preschool! Dharesh's Mummy sees us and waves and Mummy stops and chats and I say to Dharesh, 'I played car crashes in the bath!'

Dharesh says, 'I baked a biscuit and I got to decorate it all by myself,' and he holds out a bag in his hand and there's a biscuit and it's got white icing and sparkly dots all over it.

I say, 'I want to do that!'

Then Dharesh's Mummy is hugging Mummy and she says, 'Call me later if you want a brew and a chat,' and Mummy says, 'Thanks, Sabia,' and then Mummy says it's time to go in.

Inside, Mummy tells me and Toby to play in the preschool room and Tamanna and Lauren are sitting at one of the tables eating their lunch and there's no one else cos we're the first ones here and Mummy's gone into a different room that's not a playing room with Stella and Kali. I show Toby all my fayvrit things like the house corner and the Feelings Dollies but not the hidey-hole under the slide cos Tamanna says we have to stay inside for now.

After a long-a-long time, Mummy and Kali come into the pre-school room and Mummy says, 'Jesika, can you come here for a minute?' and I run over and she says, 'Stella and Kali want to ask you some questions about Ryan and Paige. Is that OK?'

I say, 'Are you coming too?'

Mummy shakes her head and says, 'I'm going to stay here with Toby.'

My belly whizzes round fast and fast. I don't want to say about Ryan and Paige to Stella cos she gets cross about things.

Mummy says, 'It's OK, poppet. Remember how you can tell me anything? That's the same with Stella and Kali because I'm saying it's OK,' and she blinks her eyes one-two-three.

I say, 'But why can't you come too?'

Mummy says, 'Because Stella and Kali want to hear your words, not what I remember you saying, and that'll be easier if I'm not in the room.'

I frown, cos I don't know what Mummy means.

Mummy says, 'It's only for a few minutes, poppet.'

And Kali crouches down and says, 'What toy would you like to bring with you?'

I say, 'Can I bring Baby Annabelle?'

Mummy says, 'She's under the buggy.'

We all go through to the peg room and Mummy gives me Baby Annabelle and then Kali takes me into a different room that's got chairs and a little table and a sink and cupboards and a kettle and pictures on the wall.

Stella's sitting next to a window and she's got a book on her knees and a pen in her hand and she smiles and says, 'Sit wherever you like, Jesika,' and her voice isn't squeaky like normal and my belly squeezes and squashes. I don't know where to sit but I don't want to sit next to Stella in case she gets cross so I pick a chair far away and then Kali sits down next to me and she turns herself round so she's facing me and now I can't see Stella and I can only see Kali's face and Kali won't be cross.

Kali asks me to tell her about Ryan and Paige and I say about him hurting Paige and hurting me and being so cross and scary and saying about the naughty thing that Mummy said was a lie and when I'm finished Kali says, 'Jesika, have you ever seen Ryan hurt Paige?'

I say, 'No, cos the bathroom door was shut.'

Kali says, 'Ryan and Paige were in the bathroom?'

I say, 'No, I was in the bath and Ryan hurted Paige afore she got in the bath but I didn't see cos the door was shut.'

Kali says, 'How do you know he hurt her?'

I say, 'Paige told me.'

Kali asks me to tell her about what Paige said and I do and then she says, 'Thank you, Jesika. You've been very helpful.'

I say, 'Will you tell Ryan to not hurt Paige? Cos then I can be Paige's friend again.'

Kali says, 'You're a good friend, Jesika,' and she stands up and says, 'Let's get you back to your Mummy,' and she holds out her hand and I don't know if she's going to tell Ryan or not.

Kali takes me out of the room and back into the preschool room and Mummy picks up Toby and we all go to the peg room and there's some grown-ups and children I know that go to my preschool like Amber and Big Toby and I see Paige and Lorna and I shout, 'Paige! Paige!' and Lorna drops Paige's coat and bag on the floor and she rushes up to Mummy and she looks so so cross and she says, 'Have you been talking about us? Have you told her? You have, haven't you? You've *told* her! How *could* you?' And she turns to Kali and she says, 'It's *lies*, it's vicious, vicious *lies* made up by a damaged and twisted little girl.' And I look at Paige and she's standing at the door not moving and I want to go and talk to her but Mummy's grabbed my hand and she's squeezing it tight and Kali says, 'Lorna, come and talk to me. We'll go somewhere quiet while Paige plays.'

Lorna says, 'She's not playing with *her!*' and she spins round and rushes back to Paige and she picks up Paige's coat and bag and she shouts, 'And there's *nothing* to talk about!' and she grabs Paige's hand and pulls her to the door but there's lots of other children and Mummies and Daddies coming in and she has to wait and Mummy steps forwards and says, 'Lorna, *please.*'

Lorna turns and stares at Mummy and her face is scary and I don't like it.

Mummy says, 'Ask her. Please, *please* just ask her.'

Lorna shouts, 'You make me *sick*,' and she pushes past Azim and his Mummy and drags Paige out of the door and disappears.

The peg room is quiet after she goes and everyone's looking at Mummy, and Big Toby says, 'Why did that lady shout, Daddy?' and I look at Mummy and she's crying. Mummy's crying! Kali rubs her hand on Mummy's back and Stella comes into the peg room and she's telling everyone in her squeaky-happy voice to hang up coats and bags and go into preschool quickly and stop staring, Amber, and time to say goodbye to Daddy, Lucia, and she hurries and rushes everyone away til it's just me and Mummy holding Toby, and Kali and Stella.

Kali's talking to Mummy and Mummy's wiping her eyes and Toby's wriggling and wriggling til Mummy puts him down and he runs over to his buggy and picks up Zebra and he bumps down on his bottom and plays with Zebra on the floor.

Stella bends down to me and holds my hand and says, 'Come on, Jesika, let's get you inside too. Mummy's having a chat with Kali and she'll be just fine,' but she won't be fine cos she's still crying and I don't know why Stella's being all squeaky-happy when Mummy's crying and I don't want to go, I want to stay with Mummy and I hold tight and tight to Mummy's hand and press my face against Mummy's arm and Stella tugs my other hand and says, 'Come on, Jesika, we'll show your Mummy how grown up you are,' and she tugs again.

Mummy says, 'Let Jesika make her own decisions, please,' and her voice is snappy like a crocodile and Stella stands up fast and her mouth is smiling but her eyes are zapping and Mummy cuddles me tight and Kali says, 'It's all right, Stella, I'll bring her in when she's ready,' and Stella sniffs and then walks away into preschool.

Mummy crouches down and she's not crying now and she says, 'Jesika, it's time to go in, OK? I'll be back for you very soon.'

I whisper in Mummy's ear, 'I don't want to go.'

Mummy says, 'You don't have to, but you really wanted to this morning, didn't you?'

I whisper, 'But Paige isn't going and I won't have anyone to play with.'

Kali crouches down too and she says, 'We're making biscuits today and there's some new scooters to try in the outside area. Do you think you might like that?'

I press my face up to Mummy's and she cuddles me tight and she says, 'That sounds like fun, doesn't it?'

I say, 'Dharesh put icing and sparkly bits on his biscuit.'

Kali says, 'You can do that too.'

I say, 'Can I do it now?' and Mummy smiles and Kali says, 'You certainly can,' and I say, 'And can I try the scooters after?' and Kali says, 'Yes, of course you can,' and she holds out her hand and I hold it and she doesn't tug and I let go of Mummy's hand and Kali stands up and Mummy kisses me and says, 'Have fun, poppet. I can't wait to see your biscuit,' and I go into pre-school with Kali.

I don't get to make one biscuit, I get to make THREE biscuits cos Kali says I can make a biscuit for Mummy to cheer her up and then she says I should make one for me and Toby too cos then everyone will have one, and after I get a turn on the scooters with Azim and Amber and we play races and Amber does super-fast zooming cos she says she's got her own scooter and I try to do it fast too but it's tricky and Tamanna says I have to keep practising but then it's Lucia's turn and Tamanna says I can practise tomorrow.

I do painting and jigsaws and trains and water play with the bubbles but I don't go in the house cos when I go to the door I think about Paige and I feel sad cos she's not here and Lorna's angry and I don't know why.

Mummy's waiting in the peg room with Toby at home-time and she smiles and smiles when I show her my three biscuits that I maked. Cos it's sunny and not rainy, we go to the park on the way home and Mummy says we can eat our biscuits and they are yummy and then me and Toby play for ages on the playground til Mummy says it's getting too cold and we have to go home.

The wind is bitey on my nose and my cheeks and Mummy says we need to hurry quick cos it's not good weather for Toby's cough and I think it's not good weather for my fingers too cos the wind is biting them right through my gloves and they hurt. I tell Mummy and Mummy says we'll be home soon and in the warm, but when we get home, Mummy is cross cos the pilot in the boiler has gone again and that means our house is shivery-cold and all our breathing is coming out of our mouths like smoke.

I say, 'Where did the pilot go?'

But I don't think Mummy's listening is switched on cos she's only talking to the boiler in a cross voice and not talking to me.

I go back into the living room and I look out of the window. I can see Ade way, way down. He's moving all the fruit and vege-tables back into the shop cos it's almost time to pull the shutter down and go home. I know cos the shutter is already halfway down so people know they can't shop there now. I keep waving and waving at him but he doesn't see me and I shout, 'Ade! Ade!' but he doesn't hear me.

Mummy shouts from the kitchen, 'Keep away from that win-dow, Jesika!'

I say, 'I *know*, Mummy.' I'm not even touching it. I know I'm not allowed.

It's a bit dark outside. Not night-time dark but the dark just afore night when the street lights come on and make the night-orange. They go pink first and if you look and look and look they change to orange. But I never see them change. It just happens without me seeing even though I'm looking. I think it's magic and so does Mummy.

CRASH!

I run into the kitchen and Toby runs in ahind me. I say, 'What was that crash, Mummy?'

Mummy's leaning her head on the boiler and her eyes are closed. She opens them and says, 'Just me hitting the boiler.'

I say, 'Does that make the pilot come back?'

Mummy blows out a breath and says, 'Unfortunately, no. But I feel better.'

I say, 'Do you mean it makes your cough go away?' and Mummy laughs and pulls her phone out of her pocket and then she goes into the living room and she's looking on the table and in the drawer and under the buggy and in her bag and I say, 'What are you looking for, Mummy?'

Mummy says, 'My phone charger. You know, the thing I plug my phone into sometimes. Have you seen it?'

I say, 'Maybe it's in the bedroom,' and Mummy goes to look in there but she doesn't find it and she doesn't find it in the bathroom or the kitchen and she's getting more and more cross and then she comes back into the living room and she says, 'Right,' and she bends down and picks up Toby and says, 'Come on, we'll pop downstairs and see if Emma or Nandini have a charger I can borrow, and maybe they know how to get the boiler going again too.'

We all put our shoes and coats on and go out the door and I hold Toby's hand while Mummy shuts the door and twists the key and then she picks Toby up and we walk to the top of the stairs and Mummy stops and turns fast and says, 'Back to the flat, NOW!' and I hear a voice shouting, 'Tina! Wait!' and Mummy runs to our door and she's twisting the key and opening the door and the voice is still shouting Mummy's name and I know that voice, and I don't like that voice and my heart is thumping and thumping and we go through the door and Mummy pushes the door shut but a foot squashes into the gap and Mummy's pushing and pushing but she can't close the door and I can hear Ryan huffing and puffing and he says, 'I just want to talk, Tina! I need you to understand!' and Mummy pushes and pushes and she turns her face to me and she says, 'Jesika, pick up Thomas and get Toby to chase you into the bedroom. Like a game, OK? And you shut the door and stay there until I say so, OK?' But I don't think it is a game cos Mummy's voice is saying, 'Do it RIGHT NOW,' like she'll get cross and shouty if I don't.

I run to the table where Thomas is and pick him up and my legs are wobbly and I can see my breath puffing out of my mouth fast and fast and I say to Toby, 'Look what I've got, Toby!' and my voice is wobbly too and Toby reaches out his hands and says, 'Thom-thom!' and I think he's going to cry so I smile and waggle the train in my hand and say, 'Chase me, Toby!' and Toby gets up and he runs after me and when we're both in the bedroom I put Thomas on the floor and shut the door. Toby presses the button and Thomas chuff-chuffs across the carpet and Toby crawls after him. I kneel at the door and push the dressing gown to the side so I can peep through and the door to our house is open.

Ryan is in our house.

He says, 'I can't help who I am, Tina. I didn't choose to be this person,' and Mummy's stepping backwards away from him and she says, 'I want you to leave, Ryan.'

I want Ryan to go away too.

Ryan says, 'I didn't mean it to happen. I swear I didn't. And I promise I never touched Jesika.'

He touched me lots of times like when he played tickle monster and when he hurted my hand. Does Mummy know he's telling lies again?

Mummy says, 'I don't want to talk to you.'

Ryan holds out his hands and his mouth is making a funny shape, all big and stretchy, and he says, 'Why did you have to tell Lorna?' He steps forward and Mummy steps back. 'Why didn't you talk to me first? If you'd told me to go and get help, I would have listened to you but now everything is ruined. Why didn't you talk to me first?'

Mummy says, 'Please, Ryan, please just go.'

Ryan's not listening to Mummy. He steps forward again and Mummy steps back til she's next to the little table. She needs to use her Big Voice. Use your Big Voice, Mummy!

Ryan says, 'I need help, Tina. I need someone to help me. I need you to talk to Lorna, to explain to her that it's not my fault.'

Mummy says, 'Not your *fault*? Fucking *hell*, Ryan! GET OUT!' She pushes Ryan. 'GET OUT!' Push. 'GET OUT!' Push. 'GET OUT!'

Oh! Ryan's gripping Mummy's shoulders and his face is red and he's shouting and . . .

Pull-door-open-run-run-RUN!

'STOP IT! LEAVE MY MUMMY ALONE!'

Mummy twists away from Ryan.

'JESIKA, STAY BACK!'

He tries to grab her again.

Oh!

Mummy's falling, falling . . .

THUMP!

Oh, the table! Mummy's head! Oh!

Mummy's not crying.

'Mummy?'

Not moving.

Ryan, eyes scary-wide . . .

Mummy's face squashed on the floor. Can't see her eyes.

'Mummy! Mummy!'

Not moving. Not speaking.

Ryan bends down, reaches out a hand. He smells like toothpaste.

Why can't Mummy speak?

Ryan stands up, steps backwards, turns, runs through the open door. Where's he going?

'Mummy?'

He bangs the door shut.

'MUMMY!'

I shake Mummy's shoulder.

A sound comes out of her mouth, like a cow. Is she pretending?

Mummy moos again and moves her head. I can see her face now.

Eyes closed. There's something dark on her forehead, like black paint, and it's sliding down the side of her face.

I bend over and touch it with my finger. It's wet and when I hold my finger up, my finger isn't black, it's red. Mummy's bleeding on her head.

I don't think Mummy's pretending to be a cow.

I think Mummy might die cos Paige's Daddy died when he bleeded from his head.

This is a mergency.

Is that why Ryan ran away? Did he go to get help?

I listen and listen but I can't hear footsteps running to our house. I can only hear the music and the doors and the shouting and the busy-ness outside.

Mummy's head is still bleeding.

Ryan's not coming back.

I know what to do.

Mummy's voice speaks inside my head and says, 'Slide it like this to unlock, press green, then 9-9-9.'

But where's Mummy's phone?

There! On the little table.

I slide it like Mummy said but the screen stays black. It's apposed to light up. I slide it again, and again. It's not working. Why isn't it working?

I say, 'Mummy, why is your phone not working?' but Mummy's still mooing.

HOOT! HOOT! Chuffa-chuffa-chuffa.

I stand up and I can see Toby crawling after his Thomas train and I say, 'Toby, take Thomas back into the bedroom NOW!' and I say it like Mummy does when she's feeling cross and Toby stops and looks at me and then he picks up Thomas and he runs back into the bedroom with him and that's good cos I think if Toby sees the bleeding on Mummy's head he'll be scared and he'll cry.

I'm scared.

It's a mergency but Mummy's phone doesn't work.

I have to think a different answer.

Who else can help us?

Nandini and Emma! But they're a long way down the stairs and I'm not apposed to go down the stairs by myself.

But it is a mergency.

But I can't open the outside door cos it's too big and heavy.

Next-Door Lady!

Mummy said she was kind and she's just next door. That's not going down the stairs and I don't have to open the outside door.

I run to our front door and I tug on the handle but the door won't open and there's a sticky-out button high up on the door that Mummy always touches to open the door but I can't reach it even stretching and I don't know how it works and Next-Door Lady can't help if I can't open the door.

Ade! He might be still outside his shop and I can wave and wave my hands and he might see me this time.

I run to the window. Outside is busy with cars and lorries and buses and it's proply dark now and I look for Ade at the rainbow shop and he's there! He's leaning on one stick and pulling the shutter all the way down and I wave and wave both my hands but he's not looking and I shout, 'Help! Ade! Help!' but he doesn't look. Maybe he can't see me. I climb up on the rainy-hater and it wobbles and then I get my knee on the windysill and I can feel the cold air rushing through the crack at the side of the window but I don't touch it cos it's broken and I'm not allowed.

I wave and wave and I shout, 'Help! Ade! Help!' again and he doesn't look and I bang my hands on the window and it shakes and rattles and makes lots of noise but he doesn't look and the shutter's all the way down and he's standing up and he's walking away and he's not heard me at all. Why can't he hear me?

Oh! I know! Nina and the New Rons said sometimes the invibisle waves bash against things and make sounds small. I think my sound is bashing on the window. I have to open the window! Quick! Afore Ade disappears!

I lift the handle on the window and push hard and all the busyness noises rush loud into the room and the wind blows my hair all over my face and I can see Ade and I lean forward on the handle and use the most Biggest Ever Big Voice and shout, 'ADE, ADE, ADE, ADE!' and he stops and turns and looks right up at me!

CRACK!

The window snaps forward, hanging, wobbling, hand slips, knee slips, belly whooshes and . . .

belly-squeezing-tight-can't-breathe-falling-back-back-back-BUMP!

'Jesika! You nearly . . . Jesika!'

We're both on the floor and Mummy is crying and hugging and I'm squashed and I can't breathe and then Mummy lets go and shouts, 'TOBY! WHERE'S TOBY!' and she goes up on her knees and she's looking all around and her eyes are scary-wide and her face is bloody and there's a horrible hole on Mummy's forehead and it's leaking blood and that's not what heads are apposed to look like and my heart thumps and thumps and she grabs my shoulders and shakes me and shouts, 'WHERE'S TOBY!'

HOOT! HOOT! Chuffa-chuffa-chuffa . . .

Toby runs out of the bedroom ahind Thomas and shouts, 'BOO!'

Mummy does a hiccup, and then another and another and she crawls over to Toby and lifts him up and she's not hiccupping, she's laughing and laughing but there's also crying coming out of her eyes and it's mixing with the blood on her face so it looks like her crying is red and she brings Toby to where I am on the floor and she takes my hand and she pulls me in front of the sofa and it's not so windy there and then we're all hugging and laughing and crying all at the same time.

Then Mummy says, 'What were you *thinking*, Jesika? How many times have I told you not to touch that window?'

I'm looking at Mummy's still bleeding head and I'm trying not to look at the horrible hole and I say, 'Your phone wasn't working and . . . and . . . it was a *mergency*!'

Mummy says, 'Oh, Jesika,' and she says, 'The battery was dead, remember? I couldn't find my charger. But I'm glad you didn't phone anyone.'

I say, 'Why?'

Mummy hugs me tight and says, 'I've only just come out of hospital. I'm not going back again!'

I say, 'But what about your head? Someone needs to fix the hole,' cos even though Mummy is talking and being not dead, Paige's Daddy is dead cos his head was bleeding, and I don't want that to happen to Mummy.

Mummy says, 'Heads always bleed a lot. It'll be fine in a minute.' And she reaches her hand up to her head and touches it and sucks breath into her mouth and then smiles and says, 'It's fine. Can you help me, though? Can you run and get the toilet paper from the bathroom?'

I get up and run into the bathroom and take the toilet paper off the holder and I run back. It's blowy standing up. The window is still open, stuck to a metal stick and wobbling in the wind.

I give the toilet paper to Mummy and I say, 'Ade's coming to help so he can check your head is OK and we can ask him to fix the window so it's not so cold and blowy. Do you think he knows how to fix windows?'

Mummy says, 'I don't think Ade's coming to help, poppet.'

I say, 'He is! I shouted and shouted at him from the window.'

I sit down next to Mummy and she pulls off some paper and touches it to her head and she says, 'I don't think he would have heard you from up here, darling. I'm afraid it's just us right now until my head stops bleeding.'

The paper on Mummy's head turns red. What if Mummy's head keeps bleeding til she dies?

I say, 'Ade *is* coming to help.'

Mummy says, 'Darling, Ade wouldn't manage to get up our stairs.'

I say, 'Then he'll tell Nandini and Emma and they'll come and help cos they're our friends.'

Mummy shakes her head and says, 'Another bit, please,' and holds out her hand for some more toilet paper and I say, 'They *are* our friends and they're coming to help!' and Mummy says, 'I know, Jesika, but they don't know we're in trouble and my phone's dead. We're on our own for now.'

Mummy's wrong, cos Ade is getting us help. He is.

But he needs to hurry afore Mummy does too much bleeding.

27

THE PILE OF red toilet paper on the floor is getting more bigger like a mountain and Mummy says, 'And another bit, Jesika,' and I hold out another bit and she touches my cheek first and I say, 'Why do you keep touching my cheek, Mummy,' and Mummy says, 'You fell,' and I say, 'No, Mummy, you catched me,' but Mummy shakes her head and says, 'I don't remember catching you,' and then she shakes her head again and says, 'Another bit, Jesika,' but I've not got another bit cos the roll is empty and I have to run back into the bathroom and get a new roll and it's tricky-fiddly to get it started cos the paper's stuck down and Mummy has to help me with the hand that's not pushing the paper on her head and that means she's not cuddling Toby and he gets shouty and it all takes for ages afore Mummy's got it started.

Mummy takes the new bit and swaps it quick with the red one and all I see is messy blood and not the horrible hole and she drops the red one on the floor with all the other red ones and presses the white one to her head. It turns red, like magic, but it's not really magic, it's blood and I don't know how much more blood Mummy's got afore it's all runned out.

Where's Ade?

I get up again cos I think maybe I can sneak a look out of the window while Mummy's not looking and see if I can see Ade coming to help but Mummy says, 'Don't go near that window,

Jesika,' and I don't know how she knew I was going there cos she's still got her hand pressed over her eyes. I look at the door cos that's where Ade will come in and he might be coming in right now. But I don't know how to open the door. What if Ade can't open it too?

Mummy says, 'I don't know how I'm going to fix this one,' and her voice is wobbly and quiet.

I say, 'It's OK, Mummy, Ade's coming to help.' He might bash the door open with his sticks!

Mummy takes her hand away from her eyes and says, 'Jesika, he's not. I'm sorry, poppet, I know you want to—'

BANG! BANG! BANG!

SNAP!

'Tina! Open the door!' And it's Emma's Bossy Lady voice coming through the letterhole.

Mummy's mouth opens wide and then she moves and stops and holds her head and says, 'Can't move.' And then she says, 'Keys, Jesika. On the table. Push them through the letterbox.'

I run to the table and pick up Mummy's keys and push them into the hole and they tug out of my hands and something jingles and Emma shouts, 'Move back!' and I do and the door opens fast and Emma and Nandini rush through.

I *said* Ade would get them, didn't I?

Mummy's mouth makes another big 'Oh!' and Nandini and Emma rush over and they're kneeling down next to us and Emma's talking to Mummy and Nandini's asking me what happened and we're all talking loud at the same time and Toby opens his mouth wide and cries and cries.

Emma says, 'Enough!' And her voice is loud and scary and everyone goes quiet, even Toby.

Emma points to the bedroom and says, 'Nandini, take Toby in

there.' I get up to go too but Emma says, 'No, Jesika, you stay here for a minute. Tina, I need to see how deep the wound is.'

Mummy says, 'I am NOT going back to hospital, Emma. It's not happening. You can't make me,' and Emma better listen to Mummy cos she's doing her scary voice that means someone is in trouble.

But Emma makes her face tiger-fierce and she says, 'It's a head injury. You'll do as you're told.'

I stare at Emma. Now Mummy's going to shout.

But Mummy gasps in a breath and says, 'I can't leave them again. I can't. I almost lost Jesika,' and she presses her lips tight til they disappear.

Emma's tiger face goes away and she says, 'You may not have to. Just let me look, OK?' and Mummy nods her head.

Emma reaches for a bag like Mummy's green plaster bag but more bigger and she pulls out something stretchy, like a balloon, and she pulls the stretchy balloons over her hands and they're gloves. I've never seen stretchy gloves afore.

She says, 'OK? Let's have a look.'

Mummy nods her head and peels away the red tissue and now I can see the horrible hole and it's still leaking blood and I don't want to look at it but I can't make my eyes not look. Emma reaches out her hand and touches Mummy's head just where the hole is and Mummy sucks in a great big breath and there's blood running down Mummy's face again. Emma pulls something else out of the plaster bag and she rips it open and inside there's a white squashy cloth and she gives it to Mummy and tells her to press it on the hole and it's like the tissue but it doesn't turn red right away.

Emma says, 'Might need stitches.'

Mummy says, 'I'm not going to hospital.'

Emma says, 'Steri-strips might do it but . . .' She looks at me and says, 'Jesika, what happened after your Mummy hit her head?'

I say, 'Ryan ran away and Mummy lied on the ground and didn't move.'

Emma's holding a little torch and she shines it into Mummy's eyes and asks Mummy to follow the light with her eyes and Mummy's eyes go side to side.

Emma looks at me again and says, 'Was she awake on the ground?'

I say, 'Yes, cos it's not bedtime.'

Emma says, 'I mean, was she saying things or making noises?'

I shake my head and say, 'She didn't talk for ages and then I shaked her shoulder and she made a sound like a cow.'

Emma smiles and says, 'OK,' and Mummy says, 'I wasn't unconscious. I could hear Jesika calling me, and Ryan . . . Ryan put his hand on me and then I heard him running out the door. I couldn't speak or move because of the pain, not until I heard Jesika opening the window and then . . .' Mummy starts crying. 'I keep seeing her falling. I keep seeing it. I didn't catch her and she fell and . . . I can't stop seeing it!'

Emma says, 'It's shock. Don't torture yourself. Jesika's safe. She's right here, see?'

I say, 'Ryan shaked Mummy and she fell over and he ran away and he didn't get help. That's cos he's not our friend.'

Mummy says, 'Jesika,' and she reaches out her hand to me and I hold it and she squeezes one, two, three and I say, 'Is he coming back?' and Mummy says, 'I don't know,' and her voice is wobbly and whispery and she looks at Emma and my belly is twisting and squeezing and I don't want him to come back. I don't like him. He's scary.

Emma puts her hand on Mummy's shoulder and says, 'Tina, you're safe. You're all safe.'

The front door swings wide and a voice says, 'Hello?' and me and Mummy and Emma all look round and someone wobbles into the room. *Oh!*

I jump up and shout, 'Ade!'

He's smiling and smiling and so am I and I turn to Mummy and I say, 'I *told* you Ade was coming!'

I look back at Ade but now he's not smiling and he says, 'Tina! What happened?' and then his knees start bending and he says, 'Uh-oh, need a chair.'

Emma jumps up quick and pulls over one of the chairs from the table and she gets it ahind Ade's bottom just as he sits down on it. She says, 'Mm-hmm,' and lifts her eyebrows right up.

Ade says, '*Man!* You got a lot of stairs, Jesika,' and he sticks his tongue out at Emma. That's rude! But Emma doesn't get cross.

She says, 'Don't whinge to me about the pain.'

Ade smiles big and says, 'I wouldn't dare!' He winks at me and then he leans forward to Mummy and says, 'I saw Sarah on the stairs. She's gone to fetch Leon. He might be able to do something with that window.'

I know Leon. He's Shiny-Head Man and he fixed our door but I don't know who Sarah is. Mummy just nods.

Emma says, 'Let's get you fixed, Tina.' And she turns to me and says, 'Jesika, go and play with Nandini and Toby now.'

I say, 'Can I watch?' cos I want to see how she fixes Mummy.

Emma says, 'No. Go and play,' and Mummy says, 'Emma needs to concentrate, poppet. It's only for a minute.'

I run into the bedroom. Nandini is sitting on the bed but I can't see Toby anywhere.

I say, 'Where's Toby?'

And then the covers on the bed wriggle and Toby's head pops out of the end and he says, 'BOO!' and Nandini presses both her hands on her chest and all her bracelets jingle and she says, 'Oh! What a fright!'

Toby giggles and I giggle and then I jump under the covers

and I play peekaboo too and we do it for ages and ages til Toby says, 'Toby sleep,' and he puts his head on Mummy's pillow.

Nandini says, 'Poor love, I think he's ready for bed.'

I say, 'Is it bedtime?'

Nandini says, 'I don't know. What time do you go to bed?'

I say, 'I'll ask Mummy,' and I run out of the bedroom.

Oh! Leon is standing at the broken window and he's twisting a screwdriver and, oh! Emma's putting long white stickers on Mummy's head and the horrible hole isn't there now and Ade waves at me and then Next-Door Lady comes out of our kitchen and she's carrying two mugs and I didn't know she was here too! Everyone's in our house today!

I run over to Mummy and I want to ask about Leon and the stickers and the hole and Next-Door Lady but it's all jumbled in my head and so instead I say, 'Mummy, is it bedtime?'

Mummy's head moves and Emma says, 'Keep still. Almost done.'

Mummy says, 'Not yet, poppet.'

I run back into the bedroom and I say, 'Not yet, that's what Mummy says,' but Toby's already asleep on Mummy's side of the bed and I say, 'We have to wake him up,' but Nandini says, 'No, leave him to sleep. Little darling.'

I run back out of the bedroom and Emma is packing things into her green bag and Mummy is getting up and Next-Door Lady is pulling out a chair for Mummy to sit on and Ade is still sitting on a different chair and Leon is still fixing the window.

I run over to Mummy and I say, 'Toby's asleep on your side of the bed!'

Mummy says, 'It's OK, Jesika. I've got bigger problems to worry about right now.'

I say, 'What problems?'

But Mummy doesn't say cos Next-Door Lady puts a cup of tea down on the table in front of Mummy and Mummy wraps her hands around it and says, 'Thanks, Sarah,' and I say, 'How do you know Next-Door Lady's name?' and Mummy says, 'I asked her.'

I smile and lean into Mummy's side and I say, 'I told you to do that.'

Mummy puts her arm around me and squeezes and says, 'I know you did.'

Next-Door Lady Sarah smiles too so I can see all her rotten teeth and it remembers me that Mummy said not to tell her about going to a dentist and I whisper in Mummy's ear, 'Is it a good secret to not say about the dentist?'

Mummy says, 'Jesika!' and she sounds cross but Next-Door Lady Sarah laughs and laughs and then Mummy's laughing too and she keeps trying to speak but then she's laughing again and I don't know what the joke is.

Then Mummy breathes in big and big and makes her laughs go away and she says, 'Sarah, grab a chair and a brew for yourself,' but then Next-Door Lady Sarah says, 'I've done my bit. Time to go,' and she does go, right out the front door.

Mummy bites her lip and she says, 'Did we upset her?'

Ade says, 'No, Sarah never sticks around for long. She can't cope with too much company.'

Nandini comes through from the bedroom and pulls the door closed and says, 'Fast asleep, Tina. I even managed to change his nappy, put his babygrow on and put him in his cot and he didn't even stir. Reminded me of when Dharesh was little.'

Mummy says, 'Thanks, Nandini, and thank you everyone. We're so lucky.'

Emma comes out of the kitchen and she says, 'I've got to dash or I'll be late. Tina, I've tried to get the boiler going again but I can't work out the controls. It's nothing like ours.'

Leon says, 'I'll take a look in a sec when I've fixed this.'

Mummy says, 'Leon, I don't know if I've got enough to pay for all this.'

Leon says, 'I'll send Darren the bill. It's a disgrace renting out a place in this state, and to a single mum with wee bairns. The man's an unethical shitebag.'

I say, 'What's a nunny thickle shitebag?'

Emma bends down to Nandini and makes a snorting sound and Ade puts his hand up to his mouth.

Leon says, 'It's someone more interested in money than safety,' and Mummy says, 'And not a word I want you repeating!' and her eyes are wide and her voice is loud but she's smiling so I don't think she's actually cross.

Leon stands back from the window and says, 'Right, that'll stay put for now but you can't open it. Forget asking Darren to fix it, I'd report it straight to the housing people in the morning if I was you and get them to inspect this place. Fucking disgrace,' and he walks away into the kitchen.

I say, 'What's a—'

Mummy says, 'NOT a word I want you saying, Jesika!' and then she smiles and then covers her smile up with her hand and makes her eyes go cross but I can still see her smile peeping out of the corner of her hand so I think she's just pretending.

Emma says, 'Tina, I've got to go, but Nandini's staying.'

Mummy turns to Emma and says, 'She doesn't need . . .'

Emma makes cross eyes and says, 'You'd rather be in hospital?'

I look at Mummy and my belly squeezes. Is she going to hopsipal?

Mummy looks at me and says, 'I'm not going to hospital, Jesika.'

Emma says, 'As long as Nandini stays.'

Nandini lifts her hands and her bracelets jingle and she says, 'I'm not going anywhere. I've got my orders.'

I think it's going to be squashy in our bed tonight if there's Mummy and me and Nandini, but afore I can ask, Emma says bye to everyone and then Ade says he should go too and Emma says she can help him down the stairs and then everyone's hugging and kissing and me and Ade do a high five and then they're gone.

I say, 'Where did Emma and Ade go?'

Nandini says, 'Ade's gone home to sleep and Emma's gone to drive ambulances.'

Me and Mummy and Toby went in an ambulance at night-time but it wasn't Emma driving it, it was the Green Man and the Green Lady. My belly squeezes hard. I didn't like Mummy and Toby going away and leaving me.

I say, 'If Mummy goes to hopsipal, will Emma drive Mummy's ambulance?'

Mummy says, 'I'm not going to hospital, Jesika. I'm staying right here, OK?'

Leon comes out of the kitchen and says, 'Tina, there's a smell of gas in the kitchen.'

Mummy says, 'Yeah, that's normal. Darren says it's because I don't open the window enough but . . .'

Leon scratches his cheek and says, 'Is it always that strong?'

Mummy says, 'I don't know. I've got used to it.'

Leon says, 'Did Darren give you a copy of the gas safety certificate?'

Mummy says, 'He showed me something about gas safety when we moved in but he said he had to keep it for his records.'

Leon says, 'I'll take that as a "no".' He breathes. 'It's a legal requirement, for fuck's sake!'

That's another bad word! I think Mummy has to tell Leon to stop saying bad words. But she isn't cross, her face is wrinkled up and she says, 'Is there a problem?'

Leon scratches his head and it makes a scrape-scrape-scrape sound and he says, 'Tina, I'm not an expert, but I know that when the pilot light goes out, gas leaks out until the cut-out thing shuts it off. If there's anything wrong with the boiler, and that one through there's a relic and we're talking about Darren here so that's a high probability, the gas might not shut off properly and it can build up and . . .' He looks at me.

Mummy says, 'And what?'

Leon looks at Mummy and looks at me again and he squashes his face up like something is hurting and he turns away from me and says something quiet as quiet and I think he doesn't want me to hear and I go to Mummy and hug her arm and he's saying, 'some kind of spark and . . .' He sees me and stops talking again, then he flicks his hands open in the air.

Mummy says, 'Oh!' and Nandini stands up, slapping her hand against her chest, and says, 'Oh my God, Tina! You can't stay here!'

Mummy's mouth and eyes are wide and wide and I say, 'Mummy, what is it?' and she says, 'But . . . I don't . . .'

Leon pulls a phone out of his pocket and taps it with his fingers and he says, 'I'm calling my plumber mate. You and the bairns should go somewhere else until she's looked at it.'

Mummy says, 'But where? I don't . . .'

I say, 'Mummy, what's Leon saying?'

But Mummy doesn't tell me and Nandini says, 'Come on. We've got a travel cot that Dharesh used to use. You and Jesika can go in our bed and I'll go on the sofa. Emma's on nights until Thursday so she can sleep in the bed during the day. Just grab some clothes and let's get out of here. Leave it to Leon.'

Leon's talking on the phone and Mummy runs into the bedroom and Nandini says, 'Jesika, shoes and coat on so you're all ready to go when your Mummy comes back,' and then everything is rushy and loud and I don't know why we have to go and sleep in Nandini's bed but Mummy gives Toby to Nandini and her door keys to Leon and she's picking up washing bags stuffed with our clothes and Nandini's cuddling Toby, asleep in her arms, and Mummy says, 'What if we can't come back? Where will we go?' and Nandini says, 'They can't leave you homeless, Tina. They'll sort you with something,' and we're rushing out the door and I look back at our house and our sofa and our table and our toys and I can see Baby Annabelle and Para-Ted and Zebra on the floor and Mummy said what if we don't come back and I can't leave them there and I wriggle under Mummy's arm and she shouts, 'Jesika! Come back here!' and I whizz over to the sofa and pick up Baby Annabelle and Para-Ted and Zebra and I cuddle them tight and tight and Leon points at the door and says, 'Get out of here!' but he's smiling and I wave at him and he waves at me and he goes back into the kitchen and I run back to Mummy and she holds my hand and we walk down and down and down the stairs and out the big, front door into the busy-ness. A lorry roars in my ears and we walk fast and fast down the steps to the street and run and run to the washing machine shop and Nandini pushes the door open and . . .

WHUMFF! BOOM!

28

I LIKED THE bumpy bus the first time I ever went on it, but I like it even more now cos we get to go upstairs every time. Sabia gave Mummy a sling for Toby and a sling is like a bag you put on your back and Toby goes inside it so his legs and arms dangle and he can fall asleep on Mummy's back if he gets tired. Sabia said Dharesh used to fall asleep in it too but I don't think she's right cos Dharesh is too big to go in the sling.

Today there's space on the front seats and I go in first and then Toby and then Mummy and we all squash up and I can see everything all around us like the shops and the roads and the gardens and the planes in the sky and the tall towers far away.

Mummy says, 'What did you do at preschool this morning? Did you play with Dharesh?'

I say, 'Yes, we played on the scooters cept Dharesh fell over and his knee bleeded.'

Mummy says, 'Oh, poor Dharesh.'

'And I drawed a picture of Leon. Kali sticked it into my special book.'

Mummy puts her arm around me and squeezes me tight.

I say, 'Leon died.'

Mummy says, 'Yes, he did.'

'And he was helping us.'

'Yes, he was.'

'No one lives in our house any more. Not in any of the houses.'

'That's right. Everyone had to go and live somewhere else.'

'That's cos our boiler exploded and maked a big hole in the front of the house.'

'That's right.'

I think about the last time I ever saw Leon and inside my head I can see him waving at me and walking into our kitchen and I say, 'And I didn't know light switches could make boilers explode.'

Mummy says, 'We don't know that's definitely what happened, poppet. And remember, it was the boiler that was dangerous, not the light switch. You don't need to worry about light switches.'

I say, 'The boiler was dangerous cos Darren didn't fix it proply.'

Mummy says, 'He didn't check it was safe.'

'And the policeman put him in prison.'

'He's been arrested but he's not in prison at the moment. It takes a while to decide if someone has to go to prison.'

'He should go to prison cos he made Leon die and some of the people in our house went to hopsipal.'

'Yes, they did.'

'But they didn't die.'

'No, they didn't.'

I say, 'And Sarah wasn't even in the house, she was in the shop, but she had to go to hopsipal too.'

Mummy says, 'Yes, but she wasn't hurt, she was scared and sad about not having a home to live in and that made her poorly.'

I say, 'Will she get better?'

Mummy says, 'I hope so.'

'We didn't go to hopsipal.'

'No, we were incredibly lucky.'

'And now we live far away in the new house but it's just for a mergency.'

Mummy says, 'Sort of. It's temporary, for now.'

'And I go to morning preschool now and we have lunch at Nandini's every day.'

Mummy says, 'Yes, sort of. It just made a lot of things easier. Remember, it's only until they find us a new place to live.'

'Will we go back to our other house?'

'No, that's not going to happen.'

'Will we live in a different house?'

'I hope so.'

I say, 'What's the different house like?' and I'm thinking about all the different houses I know, like Nandini and Emma's, Lorna and Paige's, Duncan and Jane's . . . Maybe the house will have a garden and a trampoline.

Mummy says, 'I don't know the answer to that yet, darling.'

'Does it have a green door?'

'I don't know.'

'Does it have lots of windows?'

'I can't answer that, poppet.'

'Does it have a garden and a trampoline and a—'

'Jesika, I don't know. I won't know until they tell me that there is a house for us and we go and look at it.'

'But does it have a roof?'

Mummy laughs and says, 'Yes, I think that's one thing I can say for certain. If they find us a house, it will definitely have a roof!'

I think about our house that we're never going back to. It's got a roof too but there's a big hole in the wall, cept you can't see it now cos it's all covered up with a giant*normous* sheet that Mummy says is made of plastic and it crackles and snaps when it's windy and there's people ahind the plastic doing fixing to mend the big hole.

I think about the scary bang and I say, 'I was scared when our house went bang.'

Mummy says, 'I was too.'

I say, 'It's sad that Leon died.'

Mummy says, 'Yes. Yes, it is. It's very sad.'

We sit on the bumpy bus for a long-a-long time and then I see the yellow house that means we're almost back and I say, 'Press the button, Mummy!' and Mummy reaches over and presses the button that's red and says S-T-O-P, and I know those letters cos I've been learning them at preschool and Mummy says they go together to say STOP.

Mummy puts Toby back in his sling and she stands up and lifts him onto her back and I stand up too and the bus does stop and it makes me wobble and we walk down the windy stairs and Mummy says, 'Hold the rail, Jesika,' and we step off the bus and Mummy holds my hand tight cos there's so many people rushing about and we walk and walk for ages til we get to our street that's got the little wall all along it. I jump up on the little wall and Mummy holds my hand so I don't fall off and I can see our brown door getting more and more nearer and there's a lady sitting on the wall just afore our door and that means I have to jump down.

The lady turns round and Mummy says, 'Oh!' and I say, 'Oh!' too cos I know that lady! It's Lorna! But I can't see Paige. Lorna stands up and she pushes her hands into her pockets and now we're standing right in front of her and I say, 'Where's Paige?' cos I've not seen Paige for ages.

Lorna looks at me and says, 'She's with her Granny,' and then she says, 'Hi, Tina. How are you doing?'

Mummy says, 'How did you find us?'

Lorna looks down at her feet and back up and she says, 'I . . . I saw a piece of paper in the preschool office. I was waiting there for Stella and I saw . . . I'm sorry, I shouldn't have looked, but I really wanted to see you and I didn't think you'd answer a text.'

Mummy says, 'Well, here we are.'

Lorna looks at Mummy and Mummy looks at Lorna and I don't know why they're not speaking, then Toby shouts, 'Down! Down!' and Lorna says, 'Can I come in for a chat?'

Mummy lifts her shoulders up and down and walks past Lorna to our brown door and opens it with her key and we all go inside and Mummy gets her other key to open the next door that's only our room.

I run inside in front of Mummy and take my coat and shoes off and I put my shoes under the table and I hang my coat on the back of the chair. Mummy's sitting on the bed so she can undo the clips on the sling and Toby falls back onto the bed giggling like he always does when Mummy makes him fall out of his sling. Lorna stands in the doorway not smiling, like she's sad, maybe cos she misses Paige, and she's looking all around our room at the bed and Toby's new cot that has bendy sides not stripy bars and the sink and the cupboard and the wardrobe and the table and the two chairs.

I say, 'This is our new house but we're only living here for a small time cos we're going to find a different house.'

Mummy stands up from the bed and says, 'Do you want a tea, or a coffee?'

Lorna says, 'I . . . uh . . . tea, please.'

Mummy walks over to the table and pulls one of the chairs out til it touches the wardrobe and says, 'Have a seat. Sorry, it's a bit of a squash.'

Lorna pushes our door shut and walks over to the chair and sits down. Toby bounces and bounces on the bed and giggles and giggles and Lorna smiles too so maybe she's not all sad.

Mummy's not smiling and she says, 'No, Toby! You're not start- ing that again!' She gets her phone out and presses it with her fingers and says, 'Toby play Pop?' and Toby grabs the phone from Mummy and shouts, 'Me Pop! Me Pop!' and then he lays down on his tummy and stops being bouncy cos you can't be bouncy and play the Pop game.

I say, 'Can I have a turn after Toby?' and I go and lay next to Toby to see what he's doing but he pushes me away and says, 'No! Me Pop!' and Mummy says, 'Jesika, you know he doesn't like that. Do some colouring or something and you can have a turn soon.'

I bounce off the bed and go and sit on the other chair at the table cos that's where all my colouring pens and paper is and I've got a picture of a castle and a princess that I've not finished. Mummy squeezes past me so she can go to the sink and put water in the kettle.

Lorna's still looking all round her and says, 'I know this is probably a stupid question, but where's the bathroom?'

I jump off my seat and I say, 'Do you need a wee? I know where you have to go.'

Lorna says, 'No, no, it's OK, I just wondered . . .'

Mummy says, 'It's upstairs.'

I say, 'There's *two* toilets. One by itself and one that's got a bath and a shower and a sink and we have to remember to take the keys with us cos one time Mummy shut our door here and she forgotted the keys and we couldn't get back in and Mummy had to phone a lady and the lady had to unlock the door and she wasn't very nice, was she, Mummy?'

Mummy says, 'No, not very.'

Lorna's mouth is open. She closes it and then opens it and then she says, 'You share a bathroom? How many . . . ?'

Mummy squeezes back past with the kettle and puts it on the windysill and pushes the plug back in. She says, 'Five families, including us.'

Lorna says, 'But, Tina, that's . . .'

Mummy says, 'It's temporary. We're fine.'

I say, 'We're going to live in a different house after this one.'

I colour the flag on the castle in rainbow stripes and that's the last bit of the picture. Maybe our new house will be like a castle? But that's silly cos only princesses live in castles and I'm not a real princess, I'm only a princess when I do dressing up pretend.

I open my picture book that Ade got me for drawing my own pictures and I think about what sort of house me and Mummy and Toby might live in but I can't decide how many doors and windows it's apposed to have.

Mummy gives Lorna a steamy cup and sits down on the bed opposite with another cup in her hands.

Lorna says, 'You stopped coming to preschool.'

Mummy says, 'They swapped Jesika to the morning session because the buses didn't work out for the afternoon. Kali said it was important to keep up familiar routines so I'm trying to keep everything the same for the moment, until we know where we're going to be living.'

Lorna nods her head and says, 'Everyone was talking about the explosion, and then you weren't there . . . and Stella wouldn't tell me anything because even in a situation like this, that bloody woman can't let up, but then Kali said you were all safe and she offered to pass a message on and I thought about it, but I wanted to apologize to your face.'

I say, 'Leon died.'

Mummy says, 'Yes, he did, Jesika, but let's not talk about that again right now. What are you drawing?'

I put the brown pen down and pick up the green one and I say, 'I'm drawing me and you and Toby and our new house,' cept I still don't know how many doors and windows to draw so I think I'll just draw a great big roof over the top of our heads cos Mummy says every house has to have a roof.

Lorna says, 'Tina, I know I said . . . horrible things. I'm sorry, I really am, and I'm glad you're safe. Can you forgive me for what I said?'

Mummy doesn't say anything and it's quiet and quiet and then Lorna says, 'Please?'

I look at Mummy and she's staring at her cup, then she blows out a breath and looks up at Lorna and says, 'There's nothing to forgive.'

Lorna scrunches her hands tight and presses them against her mouth and then she slides her hands along her legs and says, 'Tina, I'm living a nightmare.'

Nightmares are scary.

Mummy puts her cup on the floor, leans forward and holds Lorna's hands and says, 'I know. I'm so sorry.'

Lorna says, 'I just couldn't . . . I just couldn't believe it, you know?'

I say, 'What couldn't you believe?' but Lorna's only looking at Mummy and Mummy's only looking at Lorna and they both have scrunched-up sad faces.

I don't want Mummy to be sad. I'm going to draw my fayvrit garden next to me and Mummy and Toby under the roof. I'll draw the horse and the apple tree and the swing and the pond but I won't put tadpoles in it this time cos Mummy mixes up tadpoles and moles and she really doesn't like moles at all. I'll draw a bouncy trampoline instead. Mummy won't be sad when she sees my picture.

Lorna says, 'It still doesn't make sense, doesn't feel real. It's like when David died and it was so sudden and shocking, and I still feel like I'm walking around inside a bubble a lot of the time. But this . . . it's even worse because . . . because he's my *brother* and . . . and . . .'

Suddenly Mummy slides off the bed and she's kneeling down on the floor in front of Lorna and she's squeezing Lorna tight and tight and Lorna's squeaking like a mouse and Mummy says, 'It's OK, it's OK, it's OK,' lots and lots of times.

Lorna stops squeaking and she sniffs and sniffs and Mummy sits back on the bed but she's still holding Lorna's hand and she says, 'What's happening? Did you tell the police?'

Lorna nods and says, 'He's admitted it and he's been charged.'

Mummy says, 'That must be a relief.'

I colour the trampoline in green, like the one me and Liam bounced on, and I say, 'Are the police putting Ryan in jail?' cos I think that's who Mummy and Lorna are talking about and I heard Nandini tell Emma that she hoped Ryan would rot in jail for ever and I think that's why Lorna's sad cos Ryan's apposed to be kind cos he's Paige's Uncle but he isn't kind, he's mean and he hurted Paige.

Lorna looks at me and looks away again and Mummy says, 'Finish your drawing, Jesika, and I promise I'll talk to you about Ryan later, OK?' and then she says to Lorna, 'Is there anything I can do to help?'

Lorna shakes her head and says, 'I should never have moved back here. It was stupid to move so quickly after . . . after . . .' She stops and breathes in and out and in and out. 'We're moving in with my mother-in-law for a while. At some point, when I've got my head straight, I'll sell the house up here but Diane says there's no hurry to sort anything and we can stay with her as long as we need to.'

Mummy says, 'When are you going?'

Lorna says, 'Saturday.'

I say, 'Is Paige going with you?'

Lorna nods her head.

I say, 'Can we come and play?'

Lorna smiles all wobbly and she says, 'It's a long way to travel, Jesika, but maybe you can visit, one day.'

Mummy and Lorna talk more about the place that's a long way away. Is it far away like Poland? I finish the leaves on the tree and pick up my red pen to colour the red apples.

Lorna stands up and says, 'I have to get back before Paige misses me too much. Thanks for listening, Tina.'

Mummy and Lorna go to the door and Lorna says, 'I don't blame you. I need you to know that. You did the right thing, and I do want to stay in touch. Just give me some time to get settled, OK?' and then Mummy and Lorna hug tight and tight.

I colour in the last apple and slide off my chair and take the picture over to Mummy and I say, 'Look, Mummy!'

Mummy and Lorna let go of each other and Lorna says, 'That's a lovely picture, Jesika.'

Mummy says, 'Is that me and you and Toby?' and I nod and Mummy says, 'We're all very smiley.'

I say, 'That's cos we like our new house.'

Mummy says, 'Where's the house?'

I point to the roof and I say, 'There, silly!'

Mummy says, 'Oh, is that a roof on top of our heads? I thought it was an umbrella!'

I laugh and say, 'No, silly!'

Mummy says, 'But where's the rest of the house?'

I say, 'We don't know what it looks like yet.'

Mummy laughs and says, 'But you've decided what the garden will be?' and she points to the garden and says, 'A horse and a swing and an apple tree and . . . is that a pond?'

I say, 'Yes, but there's no tadpoles.'

Mummy says, 'No tadpoles, OK.'

I say, 'And no moles too,' cos maybe Mummy might think there's moles even though there's no tadpoles.

Mummy laughs and says, 'Mould, Jesika. I keep telling you it's mould I don't like. A home without mould would be lovely.'

That's what I said, didn't I?

Lorna says, 'I better go. You look after your Mummy, Jesika. I'll be in touch, Tina,' and she opens the door and goes quick and quick and me and Mummy only just get time to wave afore the big outside door bangs shut.

Mummy pushes our door shut and she lifts me up and sits me on her knee on the bed and we do a squeezy cuddle and my face is pressed into Mummy's jumper and her smell is in my nose and I breathe and breathe and breathe.

BANG! BANG! BANG!

What was that?

BANG! BANG! BANG!

Toby shouts, 'Doh! Doh!'

Mummy lets go of me and we both look round at the window where Toby is pointing. Lorna's standing there. Her mouth is moving like she's saying something and then she points to the side.

Mummy frowns and jumps up from the bed, swinging me down to the floor, and says, 'She must have forgotten something.'

She opens the door and says, 'Hold it open, Jesika, don't let it shut,' and she runs to the big outside door and opens it.

Lorna rushes in and stands in the hallway and says, 'Live at my house!'

Mummy says, 'What? I don't . . .'

Lorna says, 'It's perfect! Diane said not to rush into selling the house. She said why not think about renting it until I know what I want to do. You could rent it!'

Mummy says, 'But . . .'

Lorna says, 'It's near the park, and preschool, and school when Jesika starts in September, and near your friends and it's got a garden and I wouldn't have to charge much rent because the mortgage is tiny and . . . and there's no mould anywhere in that house, I can promise you. Please let me do this for you,' and she's smiling and smiling and then Mummy's smiling and laughing and then she's crying too and I didn't know you could laugh and smile and cry all at the same time and I let go of the door cos I want to give Mummy a cuddle and Mummy shouts, 'Jesika! Door!' and she leaps towards it and catches it afore it closes and then Lorna says she has to go and she'll phone Mummy later and me and Mummy go back into our room and Toby's bouncing on the bed but Mummy doesn't tell him not to, she kneels on the bed and holds his hands and bounces him higher and higher and higher and Toby's mouth is wide, wide open and his giggling is so funny, me and Mummy laugh and laugh too.

29

IT'S MORNING AND we're on the bumpy bus going to preschool and there's the lady getting on with the squashy purple hat that's got white flowers on and she always smiles and waves and chats and today she sits next to us and she says, 'Any news on the new house yet?'

I say, 'No, it's taking for *ages*!'

Mummy laughs and says, 'It's only been a week since Lorna came to see us. There's lots to organize, Jesika,' then puts her hand over her mouth and moves Toby on her knee so she can lean over to the lady and says something and I can't hear what it is and the lady's eyes go wide and smiley and Mummy smiles big too and then the lady nods and puts her finger to her lips, like for a secret.

I say, 'Did you tell that lady a secret, Mummy?'

Mummy and the lady laugh and Mummy says, 'I might have done.'

I say, 'Is it a good secret?'

Mummy says, 'Definitely.'

I say, 'What is it?'

The lady says, 'You'll have to wait and see.'

I blow out a big breath and say, 'Mummy *always* says that!'

When we get off the bus, the lady waves and says, 'You all take care of yourselves,' and she blows kisses and she never does that usually.

I hold Mummy's hand and we walk along the road to

preschool but then Mummy turns down the wrong street and I say, 'This isn't the way to preschool, Mummy.'

Mummy smiles and says, 'I know.'

I tug Mummy's hand and point and say, 'But we have to go that way to get to preschool. Why are we going this way?'

Mummy says, 'We're doing something more special than preschool this morning.'

I say, 'What is it?'

Mummy smiles again and says, 'You'll see.'

I say, 'But I want to go to preschool.'

Mummy says, 'I promise you'll like this even more than preschool.'

And we keep walking and walking and then we turn a corner and I know where we are now, I know this street and I know that house with the green door and I say, 'That's Paige's house where we're going to go and live soon!' And Mummy doesn't say yes or no but her smile is big and big.

We walk up Paige's path and Mummy lets go of my hand and she's looking inside her bag and I think she's forgotted that she has to ring the doorbell so Lorna knows we're here and then Mummy takes her hand out of her bag and she has a key in her hand and I say, 'Why have you got a key, Mummy?'

And Mummy says, 'Because today, this is our new house.'

I say, 'Are Lorna and Paige here?'

Mummy says, 'No. They've moved to their new house now.'

I say, 'And we're moving to this one today? Is that the special thing?' and Mummy says, 'Yes,' and I jump up and down and say, 'Yeah, yeah, yeah,' and Toby giggles and Mummy's right cos this is the bestest thing ever, even better than preschool.

Mummy's pushing the key in the door and it's taking for ages and I say, 'Is it stuck, Mummy?' and Mummy laughs and says, 'I can't stop my hand shaking,' and then she says, 'There, it's in.'

She turns the key and pushes the door and we all go into Paige's house and I stop and look cos I can see the flowers on the walls but everything else doesn't look like the inside of Paige's house. Toby shouts, 'Up! Up!' and Mummy picks him up and he grabs all Mummy's hair and pulls hard so she says, 'Ow! Toby, not my hair!'

I run into the front room and it looks not the same too. The yellow sofas are there and the chairs but the table and the telly and all of Paige's toys are gone and the room is much more bigger than it was afore and I run back out to Mummy and I tell her all the things that are missing and I say, 'And someone's made the room go bigger.'

Mummy laughs and says, 'That's because Lorna and Paige have taken some things to their new house. They've left the things they don't need for us to use and soon Ade and Emma will be here with the van that's got all our other things in it.'

I say, 'But you said all our other things got broken in our old house when the boiler exploded.'

Mummy says, 'Yes, those things did, but lots of people have helped out and given us new things that they don't need any more.'

I say, 'I'm going to look upstairs. Can I, Mummy?' and Mummy says, 'Go on,' and then she says, 'Ow!' cos Toby's still pulling her hair, and I run to the stairs and I stop and I say, 'Mummy, did Lorna not need her flowers?' cos there's a huge pot of flowers at the bottom of the stairs, all wrapped up in bendy plastic, but Lorna likes flowers and all her other flowers are gone.

Mummy puts Toby down and reaches her hand inside the flowers and pulls out a letter and I say, 'What's that, Mummy?'

Mummy opens the letter and reads it and she crouches down and pulls me and Toby into a squeezy hug and then she lets go and I can see the words on the letter and I point to a word and I say, 'That's my name!' and Mummy says, 'Yes, it is,' and I say,

'What do the other words say?' and Mummy points to each word and says, 'To Tina, Jesika and Toby, with love from Lorna and Paige. Welcome to your new . . .'

And Mummy's voice wobbles and stops and she leaves her finger on the last word and I know what that word says now.

It says, 'Home.'

Acknowledgements

IN OCTOBER 2003, years after I had last written anything creative, I wrote a story opening to use in a lesson with my primary-school class. It sparked an idea, which sparked a novel. Not this novel, but it was a beginning that eventually brought me here. In getting to this place where I am now, so many people have helped me in so many ways. I hope I remember you all!

Thank you:

Maureen Crandles, for the puppets and their stories of night-time adventures when school was shut. John McColl, Ian Jordan, Harry Quinn and Pippa Donald for inspiring my love of language and teaching me how to use it properly. Pippa, this one is especially for you, for giving me the tools and the courage to explore my voice. I stopped 'pigletting' in the end and just got on with it; wish you were here to see it.

Emily, Helen, Hannah, Anne, Michelle and Marj, for being the best of friends through all the ups and downs of school and remaining friends a long time after, and Catrin, for unwavering friendship and support, and so many laughs! To Rachel, for friendship, motivation and getting me out on my bike – a place where ideas are inspired and problems are solved. And to Vicky, Sam, Julia and Marianne – I've survived a decade of parenting (and so have the boys!), thanks to you, sharing highs and lows along the way; I couldn't have written as much as I did without all your help and encouragement.

To those who were on the Arvon course at the Hurst in April 2006, especially Linda Newbery, for your belief that I could do it (it took me a bit longer than predicted!), and Nick Manns, for teaching me that there's plenty of time to be nice when you're not writing, and that the scariest things of all are those you can't see.

To Kryss, who became a valued critiquing partner post-Arvon. I learned so much from that experience. And to Penny Holroyde, who had the patience to read several drafts of my first novel over several years, teaching me loads about writing in the process.

A huge shout-out to all my lovely Word Cloud friends – thoughtful, generous, astute, and always encouraging – with a special mention for AlanP and his writing competitions, which pushed me to write all sorts of stuff I might never otherwise have, and to Squidge, Whisks, Daedalus and Tenacity for friendship, encouragement, inspiration and feedback over many years.

Through the Cloud, I am also so very fortunate to have met John Taylor, Rachael Dunlop and Debi Alper. Thank-you isn't enough. John and Rachael, I love everything you write and I'm already camped out at the front of the queue for when you both get published. And Debi, my mentor, I wouldn't be the writer I am today without you. You are a truly wonderful, generous and talented human being.

To Harry Bingham and all at the Writers' Workshop who have advised and encouraged me for the last twelve years, especially Nikki and Laura, and all those responsible for the fantastic York Festival of Writing, Julie Cohen and Andrew Wille for epiphany-inspiring workshops, and Debi Alper and Emma Darwin for their online self-edit course – the most influential and productive writing course I've ever done. Lightbulbs a-plenty!

To Stories for Homes (https://storiesforhomes.wordpress.com) and Claire King's The Night Rainbow for appearing in my life at the right time and place to trigger the idea that brought Jesika to life. To Shelter (www.shelter.org.uk), the charity that Stories for Homes supports, for doing such important work advising and helping the 150 families that are made homeless every day, the 120,000 children who were living in temporary or unsuitable accommodation last Christmas, and all the other people affected by homelessness or bad housing. Jesika is my invention, but she represents many, many real-life children in similar or worse conditions. And to the NSPCC (www.nspcc.org.uk) for all the work they do in protecting children – 'Private Pants' is their campaign and I urge all parents to look it up and talk PANTS with their children.

To everyone who answered my endless questions, big and small, but especially Tors and Bill Busby for the photos and detailed medical/ambulance-related explanations and Tim McArdle (UKFostering) for explaining the realities of fostering. Any mistakes are my own.

To my agent, Jo Unwin, for being all-round brilliant, lovely, kind and inspiring, to Shelley Harris for introducing us, to Isabel Adomakoh Young for your insightful editing comments, and to Tor Udall for your kindness and for helping me to own The Fear when I was feeling overwhelmed.

To my editor, Susanna Wadeson, and to Lizzy Goudsmit, Kate Samano and everyone else at Transworld, for truly understanding and loving Jesika as much as I do. It has been so much fun working with you all.

And thank you to my family who have all cheered me on, especially Doug, Elspeth, Sam and Gary, and to Kate for allowing me to bore you with my stories when you needed something to read.

To Ros and Bill Berriman, for welcoming me unconditionally into your family, for your love and support, and for Martin. Words cannot express how much you are both missed.

ACKNOWLEDGEMENTS

To Mum, for filling the house with books and our heads with stories, for not minding too much when you caught us reading under the covers with torches after bedtime, for opening our minds, inspiring our ambitions, and for your financial resourcefulness, which meant we always had a safe roof over our heads, even through the tough times.

To Lucy, for over a decade of companionship on walks when the writing wasn't flowing. Missing you so much. To our boys, Sam and Peter, for all the love, laughs and adventures. And to Martin, for always being there. You knew I could and you knew I would. Thanks for the push.

Amanda Berriman was born in Germany and grew up in Edinburgh, reading books, playing music, writing stories and climbing hills. She works as a primary school teacher and lives on the edge of the Peak District with her husband, two children and dogs.